Sam Llewellyn

Illustrated by David Roberts

PUFFIN

PUFFIN BOOKS

Published by the Penguin Group
Penguin Books Ltd, 80 Strand, London WC2R 0RL, England
Penguin Group (USA), Inc., 375 Hudson Street, New York, New York 10014, USA
Penguin Books Australia Ltd, 250 Camberwell Road, Camberwell, Victoria 3124, Australia
Penguin Books Canada Ltd, 10 Alcorn Avenue, Toronto, Ontario, Canada M4V 3B2
Penguin Books India (P) Ltd, 11 Community Centre, Panchsheel Park, New Delhi – 110 017, India
Penguin Books (NZ) Ltd, Cnr Rosedale and Airborne Roads, Albany, Auckland, New Zealand
Penguin Books (South Africa) (Pty) Ltd, 24 Sturdee Avenue, Rosebank 2196, South Africa

Penguin Books Ltd, Registered Offices: 80 Strand, London WC2R 0RL, England

www.penguin.com

First published 2004
6

Text copyright © Sam Llewellyn, 2004
Illustrations copyright © David Roberts, 2004

Set in Monotype Baskerville
Typeset by Rowland Phototypesetting Ltd, Bury St Edmunds, Suffolk

Made and printed in England by Clays Ltd, St Ives plc

British Library Cataloguing in Publication Data
A CIP catalogue record for this book is available from the British Library

ISBN 0–141–31691–8

Disclaimer: No resemblance is intended between characters
or uniforms in this book and those of individual nannies or their
agencies, alive, dead or only sleeping.

www.samllewellyn.com

LITTLE DARLINGS

This is the story of how Cassian, Primrose, Daisy,
a nanny, several burglars and the bum of a very
expensive bear escape captivity in the Darling
family home and embark upon a great quest for
freedom. In an ocean liner. Full of burglars. Where
they meet the delicious and beautiful lady Captain.
And discover a very important secret . . .

Books by Sam Llewellyn

Who was Admiral Nelson?

Pig in the Middle
The Magic Boathouse
The Polecat Café

*For dear Auriol, Fan, Connie
and nannies everywhere*

Dramatis Personae

Little Darlings
Meet the family. And some other people.

Daisy Darling
Age: $12\frac{1}{2}$
Likes: clothes, sticky situations
Dislikes: nannies, idiots

Cassian Darling
Age: Roughly $11\frac{5}{16}$
Likes: machinery, explosions
Dislikes: pink things, flowers, washing

Primrose Darling
Age: Just 10
Likes: cooking, sometimes with little-known poisons
Looks: pinkish, and absolutely sweet
Actually: very dangerous

Papa Darling
Occupation: international business executive
Skills: deploying effective management strategies in the
domestic sphere
I beg your pardon? Sorry. Bossing people around

Mrs Darling II
Age: Has been 26 for the last 20 years
Likes: lovely things, e.g. jewellery and Caribbean holidays
Dislikes: dirty, smelly, messy things, e.g. children

The Captain
Age: ageless
Occupation: ship's captain
Appcarance: effortless glamour
Top secret fact: you don't think I'm going to tell you, do you? Read the book!

Nanny Pete
Occupation: nanny, burglar
Hobbies: Violence, being kind to children
Drives: a big black Jag

Nosey Clanger
Occupation: pygmy burglar
Hobby: interfering
Appearance: tiny, tattooed, toofless

In the splendid front hall of Number One, Avenue Marshal Posh, Nanny Dodgson unbuttoned the starched cuffs of her uniform blouse and rolled up her sleeves.

From the first landing of the great oval staircase came the whine of a hairdryer. Signor Tesiwesi, Mrs Darling's award-winning hairdresser, was tonging away at Mrs Darling's sticky blonde beehive. As usual, Papa and Mrs Darling were going Out to Dinner.

From a huge doorway off the marble-floored hall came the bark and grunt of Papa Darling, President and Chairman of Darling Gigantic, plc, giving instructions for the building of another office block on another nature reserve.

From upstairs on the nursery floor, where the little Darlings were held captive, came a deep, deep silence.

Nanny Dodgson finished her sleeve-rolling with the neat tuck she had learned at the Royal and Ancient Academy of Nannies. Her chin was square. Her eyes gleamed calmly beneath the brim of her brown bowler hat. But under the snow-white starch of her apron a flock of butterflies swooped and trembled. It was quiet. It was too quiet. Nanny Dodgson did not like it. She did not like it at all.

But this was what she had been trained for.

Taking a deep breath, she placed one shining brogue on the first of the stairs and started to climb, muttering under her breath comforting words: *'Children should be seen and not heard, the Devil finds work for idle hands, mind your Ps and Qs, Patience is a virtue, virtue is a grace, Grace is a little girl who wouldn't wash her —'*

'Nanny,' said a thin, refined voice. Nanny Dodgson realized that her Good Thoughts had got her as far as the first landing. She stood smiling nicely, hands folded, waiting for orders. 'Yes, Mrs Darling?'

'We'll be out tonight,' trilled Mrs Darling, Signor Tesiwesi tunnelling away in her hair. 'Will you be all right with the children?'

'Sottinly, madam, lovely little people.'

Mrs Darling's lipsticky smile froze a little. It was such a trial, when one was simply rushed off one's feet with dinner parties, and of course poor Colin had to do business at all hours and sometimes in the Bahamas. People really had no idea of the *stress* involved in bringing up children, particularly someone else's . . .

Which reminded her of something she had been meaning to ask for days. 'Nanny,' she said, 'how old would you say they are now?'

'Who, madam?'

'The children.'

'Daisy the eldest –'

'I always did say she was the eldest,' said Mrs Darling, nodding. She prided herself on being in touch.

'*Porca miseria*, keepa still da head,' hissed Signor Tesiwesi.

'– is twelve and a half on Tuesday, naughty lumpkin,' said Nanny Dodgson. 'Cassian is eleven and a quarter on Wednesday next, the wee caution.'

'We'll be at Lady Mortdarthur's,' said Mrs Darling. 'They've been in Mustique, you know.'

'Cassian is the mechanical type,' said Nanny Dodgson, sniffing. 'And Primrose is ten, lovaduckles ickle. Her birthday was two weeks ago. You were at the Teagardens' –'

'No, the de Barpas',' said Mrs Darling. 'Such flowers! And tell me, are the children at home?'

'Yes, madam.'

'How lovely. Oh, I must dash.'

'Not before is feenish the head,' said Signor Tesiwesi.

Nanny Dodgson trudged on towards the silence upstairs.

If she had not been a nanny, she could have sworn that she smelt smoke.

But nannies never swear.

Three children sat in front of the nursery fire. The mantelpiece was made of Italian marble. The coal in the fireplace came from the finest seam in the country. The fork on which they were toasting a neatly trussed city pigeon was made of gold and platinum.

The walls were covered with pictures of sweet children by Renoir, and teeny dolls' clothes in gilt frames, each with a label: Yves Saint Laurent, Hardy Amies, Balenciaga. Among these sweet works of art were polished mahogany shields bearing the heads of nursery mice, trapped by Cassian after complaints from Daisy, and stuffed by Primrose. Among the little shields was a bigger shield, bearing a round-ish, brownish object, made of threadbare plush. The brass plate under it read, 'THE ROYAL EDWARD – PART'. Under the plate, a bad child (there was no other kind in the nursery) had carved in neat capital letters: 'BEAR'S BUM'. And indeed, dear reader, a bear's bum it was; the bum of the rarest, most priceless, most squabbled-over bear in the world.

But we are getting ahead of ourselves. One thing at a time. Are you sitting comfortably?

Well.

High on the nursery wall, a tiny bell tinkled.

'Here she comes,' said Daisy. Daisy had freckles,

thoughtful eyes of acid green, and splendid blood-red fingernails, which she was drying in the heat of the fire.

'Come on, Nanny, make my day,' said Primrose out of the side of her mouth. Primrose had straight blonde hair, an Alice band, and mild blue eyes which were squinting at the faintly sizzling pigeon. Primrose was a keen and skilful cook.

'Engaging circuits one and two,' said Cassian, a stocky boy with black hair that grew low over an oil-stained forehead. It made him look as if he was frowning with concentration, which in fact he usually was. 'Ready? Three, two, one. Go.'

How very shocking! thought Nanny Dodgson, when she saw the toy car on the landing. She had been in the Darling household eighteen days precisely, and she was not yet having the effect she could have wished for. The parents were all a nanny could desire, of course – no interference there. A papa who was a busy man whose time was not his own. A mummy who was, well, not the actual mummy. More like the papa's secretary, who had spent more time with the papa than the mummy, until the mummy had been sent away and the secretary mummy had come instead. And, of course, the Mrs Secretary mummy knew what was best for the children, namely a nanny, strict but fair.

Ooh yes, thought Nanny Dodgson, with the pea-sized brain in the 30-cm-thick skull under the reinforced brown bowler. This was just about a perfect billet. No interference here.

Though the children were difficult, no question. For instance, thought Nanny, the toy car on the top stair. What nicely brought up child would leave a toy lying about after Nanny had told it to put its things away? Really, it was too much!

Nanny stooped to pick up the car, wheezing slightly. She was a stout, busty, solid woman, an excellent shape for a nanny, but not so good for climbing stairs.

Perhaps that is why she did not see the wires that ran from the toy car, under the Turkey carpet and through a hole hidden by the elaborate carving on the nursery door.

Nanny's fingers closed on the car. Two hundred and forty volts of electricity shot through her body. Her brown bowler whizzed off her head and lodged in the ceiling. Her iron-grey hair stood clean on end, and she fizzed like a bottle of Papa Darling's

Bollinger, which is, of course, a kind of champagne, astonishingly fizzy and amazingly expensive.

The car dropped from her smoking fingers. She put out her hand for the nursery door-handle. Then, remembering what had happened last time she had touched something made of metal in this house, she changed her mind. Crying, 'I am coming in, wicked children!' she charged the door with her shoulder.

Reader, you may say that nannies do not charge doors like rugby forwards. Reader, you are wrong, and on this fateful evening Daisy knew better than you. 'Now,' she murmured, blowing on a blood-red nail.

Cassian opened the door. 'Good evening, Nana,' chorused the children politely.

And in came Nanny Dodgson, sideways, at forty miles an hour. She bounced off the back of the nursery sofa, was flung sharp right, and hurtled towards the door of the nursery bathroom, which Primrose opened for her.

Nanny Dodgson now seemed to be skating. She had one thought, and it was this. She could definitely smell burning. Then the time for thinking was over, because the world had turned yellow.

Yellow?

The Darling children stood in the bathroom doorway. They nodded with quiet satisfaction as Nanny Dodgson's thick brown brogues shot her across the well-soaped floor towards the bath. They shook hands gravely as she tripped and crashed into the tub, throwing up a mighty sheet of custard.

Custard?

The Darling children knew what they liked, and it was not custard, particularly when burnt. It had been one of the first things they had told Nanny Dodgson. So for the next fortnight, Nanny Dodgson had fed them burnt custard for breakfast, lunch, tea and supper, not letting them leave the table till they had eaten it All Up.

'Do you think she'll drown?' said Daisy, who was interested in consequences.

'We'll see,' said Cassian, using a phrase much employed by Darling nannies (there had been eighteen of them, so far).

'She'll boil before she drowns,' said Primrose, who had been responsible for lighting the small fire of logs smouldering underneath the bath. 'Oops! Scatter!'

For Nanny Dodgson was rising in the bath, swathed in a daffodil veil of custard. She made a bubbling noise, in which was dimly audible a drizzle of nanny talk: 'Never in all my born days . . . your poor parents . . . it will never do . . . go to bed without your suppers.' The custard mountain stepped out of the bath and blobbed yellowly out of the door.

'Phase three,' said Cassian, taking up the slack on a small winch.

Nanny Dodgson squelched towards the top of the stairs. She was seeing red, mixed with yellow.

What she was not seeing were trip-wires.

Her brogue caught Cassian's ingenious contrivance. She plummeted down the stairs like a custard Catherine wheel.

Mrs Darling put the finishing touches to her forehead polish, fluffed up the tulle flounces of her bodice, and blew herself a sticky scarlet kiss in the huge gilt mirror. Lady Mortdarthur would be green about her hair. Signor Tesiwesi had done such a divine job –

But what was all this noise?

She stepped out on to the landing. Sixteen stone of Dodgson knocked her flat. Tangled together, Mrs Darling and Nanny descended to the hall like a bulk delivery of custard. They lay under the chandelier, moaning.

Papa Darling stepped out of his study. 'Are we in a total preparedness situation, my dear?' he said.

'My dress!' cried Mrs Darling. 'My jewels! My hair!'

'My impression is that your appearance is highly acceptable,' said Papa Darling, brushing feebly at a splash of custard. He looked at his watch and frowned. 'We are in a negative punctuality situation.'

'Brute!' cried Mrs Darling.

Papa Darling helped her up. He knew he had said the wrong thing, and he was going to take it out on someone. He turned his eye on Nanny Dodgson, moaning, electrocuted, custard-soaked, concussed. 'You,' he said. 'You are to be outwardly redeployed as part of an *ad hoc* child-care staff downsizing.'

'Pardon?' bubbled Nanny Dodgson.

'You're fired.'

'Nooo!' cried Mrs Darling. 'You don't know what you're doing! You didn't hear what the agency said last time. She's our last hope. They'll never –'

'Hush, little one,' said Papa Darling, using the exact masterful tone he had used to summon Mrs Darling from the typing pool that marvellous morning they had first met. 'Outsourcing is a major part of my skill profile, as you are aware. Using these skills I shall find another childcare operative. Out of my house, wicked Nanny Dodgson! Now, this instant!'

Daisy was watching from high up at the nursery window as Nanny Dodgson reeled out of the front door. 'Steady,' she said. 'Steady. Bombs away.' Cassian released the extra-heavy loaf of bread Primrose had baked specially. They watched it fall, 15 metres straight down, on to the centre of the custard-splattered bowler hat. They watched the nanny knees buckle. They watched the nanny uniform sprawl in the gutter. They turned away from the window, dusting their hands.

Five minutes later, ambulance sirens filled the street. The children picked up their books of hard sums and waited good as gold for the feet on the stairs.

'When will they ever *learn*?' sighed Daisy.

'Come on,' said Papa Darling. 'We're going to be late.'

'But you don't understand!' moaned Mrs Darling. 'Those nanny agencies won't – they warned me last time . . .'

'Incorrect, my dove,' said Papa Darling, who believed everything could be fixed, as long as it was him trying to fix it, using money. 'You go and redeploy your personal grooming. I shall initiate a resolution to our personnel problem.'

'But –'

'Shoo, little woman!' cried Papa Darling. And Mrs Darling shooed, shaking her head and muttering darkly. She did not like being called little woman, or told to shoo. When she had been Papa Darling's secretary, she had run his life. Who did he think he was? Well, let him find out for himself, and then she could have a little bit of a gloat. They would be late for Lady Mortdarthur's party, but that would allow her to make a grand entrance. It was the perfect night to wear her sapphires.

Papa Darling dialled.

'Nenny Acedemy,' said a woman's voice, very prim.

'Good evening,' said Papa Darling. 'I am seeking to appoint a child-care assistance operative, experience crucial, ability to grow in post essential, no timewasters.' A picture of his children rose before his mind, dimly, because he had not met them recently. 'Anyone you've got. Ten minutes would be about right. Number One, Avenue Marshal Posh, it's the biggest house in the town, gold Roller in the driveway, you can't miss it.'

'So,' said the voice, which now sounded like a prim glacier. 'Am I speaking to Mr Darling?'

'You are engaged in an ongoing dialogue with

that selfsame person. But you can call me Colin.'

'Ai have no desire to call you anything whatever, Mr Darling. Ai have to inform you that Nanny Dodgson has just been brought back here in a state of collapse and when she leaves hospital will need complete reprogramming. Like, I may say, her seventeen predecessors in your employ.'

'Listen,' said Papa Darling. 'The remuneration package will be highly attractive. We are talking double wages, tell a lie, triple. Plus bonus, free access to wine cellar and choc locker, latest model Honda Aerodeck –'

But the Nanny Academy had hung up.

'Tch!' said Papa Darling. 'Poor communication skills. Well, plenty of fish in the sea.' Peering at the Yellow Pages, he dialled the next number.

And the next.

And the one after that, and the one after that.

Acme Nursery Staff said that unfortunately all their nannies had suddenly gone down with a mystery virus. Babychums Unlimited, on hearing his name, started suddenly to pretend they were an answering machine. Child-care Specialists hung up on him. And Never Mind Nannies seemed to have got the same virus as Acme Nursery Staff.

Papa Darling pulled at his lower lip. His years of management experience had not prepared him for this. He dialled Expert Nursery Logistics. ENL gave him the chill, too. He said to the usual prim voice on the far end, 'I am having some difficulty in interpreting this negative response situation.'

'I beg your pardon?'

'Why can't I get a bleeding nanny for my nippers, 'scuse my French?'

There was a sharp nanny sniff. 'I could not say,' answered the voice.

'All right,' said Papa Darling. 'Are we on some sort of blacklist?'

Silence. Then the voice, slimy as a society eel. 'Put it like this, Mr, er, Darling. You are indeed on a Nanny Network list and, as you have correctly surmised, it is by no means a white list. Good evening to you.' *Click*, went the telephone, and *hum*, went the dialling tone.

'Coo-ee,' said the suspiciously sweet voice of Papa's little woman on the stairs. 'Solved my little problem, have you? Are you read-ee, Papa?'

Daisy was scowling at the fire. Cassian was in the corner, welding teeth on to a mousetrap. Primrose was at her Doll's Kitchen Wee Stove, shaking dark-brown powder into a cake mixture from a jar labelled OPIUM.

'I wonder what the next one'll be like,' said Daisy, gloomily.

'Whoever she is we'll be ready for her,' said Primrose, stirring with both her little white hands.

'Amazing they can find 'em, really,' said Cassian, pushing up his welder's mask. 'I mean, I wouldn't look after us, would you?'

'Certainly not,' said Daisy, horrified. 'They'll get someone, though. They'll have to. Can you imagine them not going out every night? Can you imagine actually *talking* to them?'

There was a silence.

Nobody could.

Papa Darling had not got hugely, insanely, bloatedly rich by giving up easily. His new wife's voice, sweet, cracked and tough as overcooked toffee, reminded him that in the matter of finding a replacement nanny, he faced humiliation. Panic fluttered in his breast. *Me?* he thought, Chief Executive Officer of Darling Gigantic, a major player in the expanding nature-reserve concreting field, get done over by an old crow in brogues and wool stockings? No way, José. Do me a favour.

But what was he going to do? He could ring up Miss Excellent, his devoted, hideous, handpicked new secretary, and insist that she came in and baby-sat. Then he had a vision of Miss Excellent's patient face horizontal, the rest of her trussed to the rotisserie in the stainless steel kitchen, with Cassian bypassing the safety switches, Daisy sharpening a carving knife, and Primrose making pencil notes in a book on sauces for meat. Little scallywags, he thought, almost (but not quite) fondly. Plus, good secretaries were hard to find and harder to keep.

At this point his eye fell on an advertisement so huge that he had not even noticed it before. It covered an entire Yellow Page at the beginning of the Childcare section. 'AAA Aardvark Child-minding and Security,' it read. 'We Understand the Problems of the Wealthy. Keen Rates. Unaffiliated. Forget the Rest, Hire the Best. Royal Refrinces available . . .'

But Papa Darling had stopped reading at the word 'unaffiliated'. Unaffiliated meant, if he had read it right, that AAA Aardvark was not connected to the Nanny Network. No Nanny Network, no blacklist.

He was already dialling.

The telephone on the other end rang for a long time. Finally, a man's voice said, 'Yeah?'

'Is this AAA Aardvark?'

'What if it is?' said the voice, and sniffed, long and bubbly.

This was not a tone that Papa Darling expected from nanny agencies, no matter how unaffiliated. But they were already two minutes late for dinner. So he said, 'I have a nanny requirement.'

'Pardon?'

'I . . . we . . . need a nanny.'

'When?'

'In the short to medium term.'

'Come again?'

'Ten minutes, max.'

The voice sucked its teeth. 'Dunno,' it said. 'I mean, we've got Nanny Big Georgina out at the Queen of Tonga's, lovely little saucepans –'

'What?'

'Saucepan lids. Kids. Plus we've got Nanny Doberman out at Hoxton with Mad Dave the Artist, nasty little ankle-biters, but we have hopes the rabies injections may take this time. Maybe we could fit you in Tuesday.'

'An interesting point of view,' said Papa Darling. 'And if we modify it a little, I feel sure that we can arrive at a meaningful consensus –'

'Huh?' said the voice.

'Listen, sunshine,' said Papa Darling, low and dangerous. 'Me and my lady wife are going out to dinner with the kind of people you can only dream about meeting, and we want one of your little people round here yesterday, or somewhat sooner. Are you with me?'

Something happened to the voice. 'Oo,' it said, with a note like the coo of a London pigeon. 'Out to dinner, sir, or should I say my lord? You should have said earlier. Triple A Aardvark will of course have great pleasure in putting on our, ahem, emergency special service in the person of Nanny Pete, which is to say Miss Petronella Fryer. And what address would that be at, your highness?'

Papa Darling found himself suddenly liking this unconventional but respectful person. 'Number One, Avenue Marshal Posh,' he said.

There was a pause, into which Papa Darling read admiration. The voice turned to even more syrup.

'Is that right?' it said. 'Very nice, if I may make so bold as to remark. Nanny Fryer will be round as soon as she has popped her stun gun in her ditty bag, to coin a phrase, heh, heh.'

'Make it so,' said smug Papa Darling, and put down the phone. Funny, they normally asked for money.

'Well?' said Mrs Secretary Darling, not toffee any more, but broken glass. 'You haven't found anybody, and bang goes dinner. I told you, nannies, they're like gold dust. Men, you just don't underst –'

'Darling,' said Papa Darling. He was going to make a remark about his life being enhanced by her luxury personal adornment strategy, but she was glittering so powerfully he thought he might have some kind of epileptic fit. This was one of those times when only plain language would do. 'Blow me down,' he said, shading his eyes with his hand. 'You are looking proper radiant, my love. I always did say that sapphires go lovely with diamonds, and the cabochon rubies are just the finishing touch. Nanny Fryer will be round in five.'

The children sat on the nursery windowsill, banging their heels against the brickwork and scowling into the dark void of Avenue Marshal Posh – strictly against the rules, of course, but there was no nanny to tell them what the rules actually were. A black saloon came round the corner on two wheels and stopped at the kerb with a screech of brakes.

'Funny car,' said Daisy.

'Jaguar,' said Cassian. 'Mark 2, split windscreen. Classic bank robbers' getaway vehicle. Needs new piston rings.'

The doors of the Jaguar burst open. A figure stumbled out into the road and stood hunched against the breeze. It was wearing a brown bowler hat. From up here, everyone looked stocky. Not as stocky as that, though.

'Looks nervous,' said Cassian, focusing his night glasses.

'Should hope so too,' said Primrose.

The nanny pulled something out of her bag, something that glinted in the light from the Darlings' huge French windows. She raised it to her mouth and jerked her head back. 'Whisky,' said Cassian. 'Old Sporran.'

'Poor benighted woman,' sighed Daisy. 'Here she comes.'

The nanny had wiped her mouth with the back of her hand, squared her broad shoulders, and marched up the marble front steps. Far below in the house, the doorbell rang.

'They're off!' cried Primrose.

Sure enough, the front door was opening, and Mrs Secretary Darling, a vision in gold lurex, was gliding towards the Rolls. Behind her came Papa Darling, looking, as usual, at his watch.

'Nana!' they cried sweetly, scooping up a cushion each and hauling open the nursery door.

The Darling children had a well-established routine for greeting new nannies.

What happened was this.

The banisters of the splendid oval staircase made a gleaming helix of mahogany all the way from the nursery floor to the hall. 'Saddle up!' cried Daisy, who had seen *The Charge of the Light Brigade*, a film approved of by nannies.

The children slapped their cushions on the polished mahogany.

'By numbers, mount, walk, trot. One!'

Cassian was One. He broke into a run, pushing his cushion along the rail. When he reached the top stair he leaped on to it, so he was sitting astride the banister, facing downwards, accelerating down the wooden slope, while behind him Daisy yelled, 'Two!' and Primrose climbed aboard, and 'Three!' and climbed on herself. Then they were all hurtling downwards, faster and faster, yelling, 'CHAAARGE!'

Cassian had calculated terminal velocity at 31.03 miles per hour. Whatever it was, nannies found it most upsetting. Nanny Danvers had scuttled hastily out of the door without even putting down her suitcase. Nanny Dredd had pretended not to have noticed anything was amiss, got Cassian's boots slap in the centre line, and been removed to the Nanny Sanatorium in two separate ambulances. Normally, nannies with good reflexes dived under the heavy marble and gilt hall table. Their prestige never really recovered.

This one was different.

With the usual great cry of 'BANZAI!' a solid battering-ram of children whizzed off the bottom of the banisters and shot feet first towards where the new nanny should have been standing in her brogues, saying, 'Prune,' and smiling at the same time, as only nannies can.

But there was no nanny. Instead, Cassian noticed

an abnormal pile of cushions that someone had put to break his impact. Then he and his sisters landed with a *whump*.

As Cassian sorted out his legs from those of the girls, he could hear them talking. 'Interesting,' Daisy was saying, in the tone of voice that meant she was working out what made someone tick. 'Very interesting.'

Primrose was readjusting her Alice band and smiling sweetly. 'From now on,' she muttered, 'No more Mr Nice Guy.'

But Cassian was watching the nanny.

She was short, and wider than any nanny he had ever seen. She was standing just inside the door of the dining room. One of the sideboard drawers was open. The nanny had a jeweller's glass screwed into her eye, and was squinting at a handful of cutlery. Feeling Cassian watching her, she looked up. 'Hello,' she said. 'And who are you?'

'Mind your own business,' said Cassian, anxious to get on the right footing after the failure of the Charge.

'What do you think you're doing?' said Primrose.

'Jus' looking around,' said the nanny. 'Scouting

out the lie of the land, like. Very nice class of spoon here, if I may make so bold as to pass comment.'

'You may not,' said Daisy. The children gave her the Silent Stare. The nanny eased her tight starched collar and looked slightly flustered. Daisy said, 'What are you called?'

'Nanny First-class Petronella Fryer,' said the nanny. 'But you can call me Pete.'

'It is time for our nice supper, Nanny Fryer,' said Daisy, still freezing.

'Oh, ah,' said Nanny Fryer. 'What d'you fancy, then?'

There was a stunned silence. Nannies did not ask you, they told you. Daisy dug the others with her elbows. It was probably a trick. They would ask for chicken, chips, strawberries and cream, and the nanny would give them lumpy porridge and burnt custard anyway.

'We don't know,' said Daisy, simpering horribly. 'We're shy, you see.'

Nanny Fryer had been gaping round the hall at the statues and chandeliers, whistling a little tune. Now she took her chin between her thumb and forefinger. There was a distinct rasp of stubble, which was odd, because most nannies didn't shave, not even ones like Nanny Clamp, who needed to. 'Tellyawhat,' said the nanny, pulling out a mobile phone. 'We can do Indian, Chinese or pizza.'

More silence, genuinely baffled this time. Finally, Daisy said, 'We've never had Indian.'

'Nor Chinese either,' said Cassian.

'What's pizza?' said Primrose.

The nanny drew down eyebrows huge even by nanny standards. She went to the drinks tray and poured herself a stiff whisky. She picked up the telephone, dialled Khan's, Lee Ho Fook's and Antonio's, and talked to each of them for five minutes. When she had finished, she turned with a kindly twinkle in her eye and said, 'Kids, tonight is the first night of the rest of your lives. The future starts here.'

The children sat stunned. They had been ready to massacre this nanny, as usual. But somehow they could not think of anything to say.

Except something they had never ever said in all their lives.

'Yes, Nanny,' they said.

3

It was some evening.

The food took a bit of getting used to, for children whose normal diet was Irish stew and burnt rice pudding. But it was good stuff, packed with many flavours, particularly the pineapple, peppermint and tuna-fish pizza. And it was even better when you ate it in the big drawing room, sitting on bearskins (Papa Darling shot a lot of bears, mostly from helicopters) round the fire, spitting chicken bones and olive pips into the flames of the Kosiglo Massive Inferno gas-log hearth.

Daisy asked Nanny Pete a lot of questions. Unlike most nannies, who were of the opinion that curiosity killed the cat, Nanny Pete actually answered. Though on the whole the answers were quite hard to understand. From what she said, it sounded as if Nanny Pete had looked after a lot of horses and playing-cards as well as children. Daisy could not quite work out how it all fitted together. Besides which, Cassian kept interrupting to find out how the card games worked, and Primrose kept on butting in to ask whether everybody thought the red stuff on the tandoori chicken was ketchup or varnish or a mixture of the two. Still, they got on famously. And Daisy had the distinct impression that Nanny Pete was just as curious about the little Darlings as the little Darlings were about Nanny Pete. Which for a nanny was odd, going on totally weird.

Still, there was not much time to think about weirdness. First, Nanny Pete gave a small but seamanlike exhibition of hornpipe dancing. Then she outlined the rules of poker – the children caught on fast, and Nanny declared the game closed after she had lost £11.50, and said she saw great futures ahead for them. Then they all did more hornpipe dancing. All in all, the big drawing room, with its black marble floor and hugely expensive paintings of fat ladies with no clothes on, had never witnessed such a scene. When the dancing was finished, everyone chatted and laughed. Nanny Pete leaned back in a gold brocade armchair with a silver tankard of Papa Darling's Rare Old Port, and lit a Capstan Full Strength. She pointed to the piano. 'Gissa tune, someone.'

'Can't,' said Daisy. 'And anyway, it's out of tune.'

'Out of tune?'

'Ever since Mummy left. Real Mummy. Ages ago. We don't remember. She used to play it. 'Stand by Me' was her favourite tune, Papa said once. They used to sing it together. Then Mummy went away and Papa started up with Secretary Mummy and now Papa won't let anyone touch the piano.'

'Shame, choice joanna like that,' said Nanny Pete. 'Well, kids, what time do you like to garden up the apples?'

'Uh?'

'Garden hoe. Go. Apples and pears. Stairs. The wooden hill to Bedfordshire. To bye byes.'

'Oh, sometime about midnight,' said Cassian.

'If not later,' said Daisy hastily.

'When we feel like it, really,' said Primrose. This nanny seemed to be a lot better than the others, but there was no sense letting your guard down. The Darlings had had nannies for long enough to have learned that kindliness was the same as weakness.

Nanny Pete drained her port, belched and pitched her cigarette butt into the Kosiglo. 'Tough,' she said. 'New regime. It's off you go. Now.'

'Oh, Nana,' whined the children like one child. Daisy caught Cassian's eye. Cassian nudged Primrose. They all went and clung to Nanny Pete, saying, 'Nana,' and 'Pleeease,' and 'You promised.' Nanny Pete actually blushed, as if she were not used to this sort of treatment. Daisy went 'Gidgygidgygidgy,' and tickled her ribs.

'Hee, hee, hee,' went Nanny Pete, poor unsuspecting creature.

For Daisy had given the signal. And while Primrose and Cassian tickled Nanny, Daisy's skilled hands went through the pockets of her uniform. It was a routine they always used with a nanny who showed any sign of weakness.

Nanny Pete heaved herself up, shedding little Darlings like a mountain shedding stones. 'Oi!' she cried. 'Off!'

And off they scampered up the stairs, shrieking with childish glee.

'Nanny will be up in ten!' cried the voice from below.

The nursery door closed. 'Right,' said Cassian, wiping the gooby look from his face. 'Leave it to me. Ready in five.'

'Check,' said Primrose.

'Check what?' said Daisy. 'Oh, no. Not the Junior Car Thief Kit again.'

But Cassian was already busy. He opened an Action Man box in the corner of the nursery. Inside the box was not a plastic idiot in camo trousers, but a key-copier Cassian had assembled from meccano and parts of a kitchen blender Cook thought she had thrown away. Into the machine he clamped the key Daisy had stolen from Nanny's pockets – the key, if he was not mistaken, of the truly excellent Jaguar in which Nanny Pete had arrived.

Most nanny cars he had stolen had been small and feeble, appallingly tidy and painted beige. Cassian really fancied a go in a Jag.

He made two copies of the key. As he was putting the machine away, heavy brogues crunched on the stairs. 'Coming!' hissed Daisy. She and Primrose were already in their beds in the night nursery. Cassian leaped into his pyjamas without touching the sides, and hurled himself into bed.

'All right!' cried Nanny Pete. 'Into your pits, the lot of you!'

'We already are, Nana dear,' said Daisy. 'Aren't we, children? And we've brushed our teeth.'

'And our hair, 100 times,' said Primrose.

'And our shoes,' said Cassian, sickeningly. The children lay there good as gold, with the sheets pulled up tight under their little chins.

'Kiss us goodnight, Nana!' said Daisy.

Nanny Pete said something under her breath. It sounded like, 'Ugh.' She took a deep breath, and kissed Daisy. Then she kissed Primrose. Then she went to kiss Cassian. But Cassian said, 'Yuk,' and pushed her away. As he did so, he secretly dropped the car key back in her pocket.

'Shy boy!' said Nanny Pete, sounding strangely relieved.

'Tell us a story, Nanny Pete!' cried Primrose.

'Don't know any,' said Nanny Pete.

'Sing a song, then!'

'Ah,' said Nanny Pete. 'Yur. Mi-mi-mi-mi-mi-mi-

mi-miiii. Ahem.' In a strangely gruff voice, she began to sing:

> *Restez endormis, mes enfants,*
> *défense de s'égarer la nuit,*
> *car des millions de voleurs immondes*
> *se trouvent blottis au fond de vos lits**

It went on like this for some time.

'What does that mean?' said Primrose.

'It's French,' said Nanny Pete. 'Read the footnote later.'

'It was lovely,' said Daisy, who was not used to bedtime songs.

But Nanny Pete was gone.

They heard her stump into the day nursery. They heard the slight clatter as she put up the gold-plated fireguard. They heard running water and clanking as she washed up the pigeon fork in the nursery sink. Then there was more shuffling, a sharp exclamation, and the scrape of a chair.

'What's she doing?' said Primrose.

* Stay in your beds little Darlings
  don't wander about in the night
  for millions of 'orrible villains
  is waiting to give you a fright

'Straightening pictures,' said Daisy.

Nannies loved things to be in straight lines. Things were normal again. The children lay there for a moment, happy and reassured, until the nanny brogues had receded downstairs.

Then Cassian was up, followed by Primrose, then Daisy.

The pictures in the nursery were very straight, the fireguard gleaming, all traces of pigeon grease gone from the grate. Cassian and Primrose naturally did not waste time admiring all this spick and span-ness. They beetled towards the door, jaws set, narrow-eyed and determined, like you had to be when you were off to twock a Jag.

'Wait,' said Daisy.

Her brother and sister turned. She was frowning at the wall, one beautifully manicured fingernail on her pretty chin. 'Something's wrong,' she said.

Primrose said, 'It always looks bad when they do that to the pictures.'

'No,' said Daisy. 'It's the Bear's Bum.'

'Uh?'

'It's gone.' She waved an elegant hand at a bare space on the wall. 'Used to be there,' she said. 'Is there no longer.'

'Probably cleaning it,' said Primrose. 'Dusty ol' thing.'

'They're always cleaning things,' said Cassian.

Still, Daisy thought it was odd. Nobody knew what the Bear's Bum was for, really. It had a reputation for being expensive, goodness knew why. There were a lot of things on the walls at Number One, Avenue Marshal Posh simply because they were expensive. After a while, you gave up asking, because some nanny would tell you Curiosity Killed the Cat, and even if you got an answer you could be pretty certain it would be too boring to understand. There was something else about the Bear's Bum, though. It had arrived very soon after Real Mummy had disappeared . . .

Did I not tell you? Sorry.

The first Mrs Darling had been a kind person – everything a mother should have been, in fact, except that the nannies locked her out of the nursery. One day, without saying anything to anyone, she had gone. Soon after she had gone, the Bear's Bum had arrived.

And from about the time of the arrival of the Bear's Bum (it was hard to remember, exactly; they had been so young) the little Darlings had been brought up by nannies. Their upper lips were stiff, their shoes brushed and shining. If they Made a Fuss, they Went to Bed Without their Suppers.

So they became nicely brought up children. They were Seen and not Heard, they Minded their Manners, and they were Upstairs in the Nursery. Silent, polite, and invisible, they took a terrible revenge on all nannies.

Now, they crept silently downstairs. Clanking noises came from the dining room as they crept across the hall. Noiselessly, they opened the front door. Keeping in the shadow of some enormously expensive bushes, they crept up to the car.

It was a beautiful thing, gleaming black in the street lamps, giving off a faint, sharp reek of burned castor oil. 'Race tuned!' said Cassian.

'As if you knew what that meant,' said Daisy.

'It's just a car,' said Primrose. 'And it smells.'

'You wait,' said Cassian, and he put one of the duplicate keys in the door. The locks opened with a deep, heavy clunk. 'Custom,' said Cassian. 'Hop in, girls.'

This was the bit the girls hated, because Cassian

might be a brilliant mechanic but he was an awful driver, and besides, he was not really tall enough to reach the pedals.

'I'm feeling sick,' said Primrose.

'Sicken chicken,' said Cassian, shutting the doors so they were three abreast across the front, and leaning forward to put the key in the ignition.

'Well, I'm going back to bed,' said Daisy, 'and poo to your silly old Jag – oh hell.'

The front door had opened. Nanny Pete was standing on the doorstep. She looked a little unsteady. Perhaps it was the whisky and port. Or perhaps it was because of the enormous sack she carried over her shoulder.

'Wha . . . ?' said Cassian.

'Down,' said Daisy, quicker thinking. And all three of them leaped into the back and squeezed down behind the front seats.

'Hold your breath,' hissed Daisy.

Keys rattled outside. A voice, muffled by steel and glass, hummed a tune.

The boot opened.

There followed a great clanking and grunting, as if someone were trying to jam a very big thing into a very small space. Cassian know what was happening. 'The Jaguar Mark 2, while in almost every respect the ideal vehicle, suffers from a boot space more suited to the casual weekender than the serious touring motorist,' he whispered, quoting from one of the huge pile of car magazines in his room. 'The back-seat space, however –'

Someone swore. The back door opened. Something that felt like a metal landslide buried the children. Daisy felt an elbow in her ribs.

'What?' she hissed.

'There's somefing in my mouf,' said Primrose. 'Ptoo. It's all fmelly and horrid and dufty. I fink –'

She stopped, because the driver's door had opened. Someone heavy plumped on to the driver's seat. The starter coughed. The engine roared. Tyres squealed as the Jag shot away from the kerb in a perfect getaway, Nanny Pete's brown bowler hat low over the steering wheel.

'What's happening?' said Cassian, under the thunder of the V6 engine.

'It's like this,' whispered Daisy, who had been working things out. 'That nanny isn't a nanny. She pretended to be a nanny to get into the house and she's pinched everything and she thinks we're all safely tucked up in bed. But instead, thanks to your stupid car thing, Cassian, we are on our way to a whatever-you-call-it of burglars.'

There was a long, thoughtful silence, except for the mighty roar of the engine. Primrose finally managed to get whatever it was out of her mouth. Her fingers felt plush, and a mahogany shield with a label on it. It was the Bear's Bum. 'A den of burglars,' she said.

'Stolen goods,' said Cassian.

'Secretary Mummy and Papa will be horrified,' said Daisy.

Another pause. Then, all together in the silence under the huge sack of silver, they whispered, 'Fantastic!'

But Cassian's mind was only partly on what he was saying.

As they had shot out of the drive, he had managed to peer out of the window and had seen something most peculiar.

A large, pale vehicle had drawn up under the trees up the road. It had looked like an enormous van. A white van, with rusty wheel arches. As the Jag had shot down the road, the sides of the van had dropped, turning into ramps. Down the ramps had rolled big machines. They had looked like a digger, a dumper and a dozer, and they had turned in between the twin gate lodges of Number One, Avenue Marshal Posh. Nanny Pete had glanced round. Cassian had seen her bare her teeth, and say, 'Heh, heh!'

Then the Jag had turned a corner, and it had all been hidden.

It was odd. Very odd.

Lady Mortdarthur's had been a bit of all right,
definitely. Mr Darling had worked out that he was
richer than anyone else in that roomful of very rich
people. This was always nice. And Lady Alfonsine
de Luxe, on seeing Mrs Darling's subtle blend of
gold lurex, diamonds, rubies and sapphires, had put
on dark glasses. That was always nice, too.

'Oo, Papa, if only tonight would never stop!' cried
Mrs Darling in the car afterwards.

'It can be conveniently transformed into an

ongoing situation,' said Mr Darling, whipping out his mobile. When he had finished talking, he blew into the speaking-tube and roared, 'Chauffeur!'

'Aye, aye, sir,' said the chauffeur, dabbing his spitty ear with a handkerchief.

'Airport!' barked Mr Darling. 'First-class Caribbean departures!'

'Caribbean?' said Mrs Darling.

'Antigua for breakfast,' said Mr Darling. 'Sun, sand, a beach-concreting initiative. We deserve it.'

'Oo, yes. And I can buy whatever I need . . .' Mrs Darling sank into a pink dream of shopping. Then she said, 'But what about the children?'

'The nanny will take care of them. Nice woman.' Mr Darling preened himself. 'I am, as you know, not inexperienced in the human resources sphere. Highly skilled judge of character.'

'Yes, dear,' said Mrs Darling. But she still sounded unsure.

'And I tell you what,' said Mr Darling. 'When we get to Antigua, we'll send them a picture postcard.'

Mrs Darling beamed. Never let it be said she did not care for her husband's kids, whatever their names were. 'Oo, you are clever,' she said, snuggling up against him. 'Papa Darling, you are the bestest Papa in the whole wide world!'

It is not at all easy to see where you are going when you are face down under a wheelbarrow-load of precious metals and a Bear's Bum in the rear footwell of a Mark 2 Jaguar. On the whole, the best you can do is listen.

The sounds were confusing. There was the engine, of course, a great throaty roar. Then there was something that sounded like a town, with honking horns and a railway bridge, and a lot of stopping and starting, probably at traffic lights. After that there were a lot of corners, and voices shouting in foreign languages. Finally there was a bump and a rumble, as if the wheels were travelling over cobbles, and the Jaguar came to a halt.

The driver's door opened and shut. Nanny Pete's footsteps crunched away into the distance. Cassian found that by wriggling his shoulders, he could make a little space under the avalanche of silver and gold. He forced his head between the door and the Homebuilders' Federation Challenge Cup awarded to Papa Darling for the massacre of three endangered species. Finally, he could see out.

'Golly,' he said, and fell into an astonished silence.

'What is it?' said Daisy, pinching his leg.

But her brother was too astounded to speak.

The Jaguar was parked on a cobbled quay. A full moon shone from a cloudless sky. It glittered on the waters of a broad, inky creek, lined with buildings deadly grey under the cold kiss of its light. Nothing moved on the surface of the creek, except the wavelets, always shifting, always the same.

Nanny Pete was walking down a set of rusty railway lines towards a high wall. The wall was part of an enormous building, covered with turrets and little spires. It might have been the chancy shadows of the moonlight. But it seemed to Cassian that there had once been writing up there, enormous writing, on the broad band of masonry that divided a row of smashed and sagging oriel windows (like blisters, he thought) from a rank of buttresses (like the roots of some awful spooky stone tree, he thought.)

Nanny Pete arrived at a gigantic double door, studded with nails.

'What is it?' hissed Daisy, pinching Cassian again.

Cassian described the scene.

Daisy said, 'I'm not sure about this.'

'I am,' said Primrose.

'That is because you are too young to know any better.'

'Ooooo!' said Primrose and Cassian, both together. 'Listen to Nana!'

Daisy felt a hot blush of shame mount her cheeks. They were right, of course. As the eldest, one sometimes forgot oneself, and had what almost amounted to nanny thoughts. 'I do beg your pardon,' she said.

'Think nothing of it,' said Cassian.

'One understands perfectly,' said Primrose.

'The point is this,' said Cassian. 'There is nowhere to hide. If we run away now she will drive after us and catch us.'

Daisy made the tutting sound that elder sisters have made ever since their younger brothers suggested that sabre-toothed tiger skins would make really nice rugs for the cave floor. 'And if we don't and she takes us through that door?'

'We'll be in the den,' said Cassian.

'Loot,' said Primrose. 'Piles of it.'

'And the Bear's Bum is here.'

'That is indeed slightly mysterious.'

'I suppose it is.'

There was a silence, as their thoughts gently circled the bum, and its appearance back in the fog of extreme youth, and its attempted disappearance tonight.

'Hmm,' said Daisy, after a longish pause. 'So we follow the bum?'

'Might as well,' said Primrose.

'Sh!' said Cassian.

Nanny Pete had turned a vast key in one of the doors. She was trundling it open. The arch opened, a gaping mouth of darkness. She started back to the car.

Cassian gasped and turned a silver ice-bucket over his head so he would not have to look. In the moonlight, he had seen a terrible thing.

Nanny Pete had taken off her bowler hat.

Nannies always had nice brown hair, which they brushed tidily and did up in nets so it looked like horse dung.

But Nanny Pete's head shone pale as an egg under the moon.

Nanny Pete was bald.

The driver's door slammed. The engine roared. Nanny Pete drove through the doors, pulled them to, and locked them. The Jag moved forward. The horn blatted, dit, dit, dit, dah. There was a winding, grinding noise that filled the car.

'This is getting a bit terrifying,' said Daisy, muffled under the silverware.

'More than a bit,' hissed Primrose.

'Just about completely,' whispered Cassian.

'Interesting, though,' murmured Daisy.

'Makes a change,' hissed Primrose.

'You bet your sweet bottom,' whispered Cassian.

'Cassian!' hissed his sisters.

'Beg your pardon,' whispered Cassian. 'Overexcited.'

'Us too,' hissed Primrose and Daisy.

There was a great and very interesting sound of grinding machinery. 'What now?' said Cassian, aloud.

Daisy came to a decision. 'Heave!' she said. The three children heaved, and surfaced in a glittering swamp of precious metal.

'Oi!' said Nanny Pete, turning round so fast they heard her neck click. There was something tattooed on the crown of her skull. An eagle, now Daisy came to look at it.

'You're a man!' cried Primrose.

'Course I am,' said Nanny Pete, who had a dazed look. 'And who are you?'

'The Darling children, Nana,' they said, all together.

'Stone me,' said Nanny Pete. 'So you are.'

They began to babble sweetly; obviously, childishness was the only solution here. 'Don't you remember? You came to our house and dodged the Charge and bought us weird food and put us to bed and sang us a song . . .'

'And swiped the spoons,' said Cassian, coolly.

'And the Bear's Bum,' said Daisy.

Until that moment, Nanny Pete had been leaning back in the driver's seat, cleaning his fingernails with a flick knife. Now he clicked the knife shut with a horribly practised jerk of the wrist and slid it smoothly up the starched cuff of his nanny blouse. 'What about the Bear's Bum?' he said.

This might be a man with an eagle tattooed on his shaved head. But it was also a person dressed in a nanny uniform, and therefore a Legitimate Target. 'Bear's bum?' they said, using the old 'Mention It, Get it Mentioned Back, and Deny All Knowledge' technique, which had put Nanny De'Ath into a lunatic asylum after two weeks.

Nanny Pete shook his head, as if puzzled. 'I did ought to take you straight home,' he said. 'Only it's not as easy as that.'

'Anyway,' said Daisy, 'you've brought us, and now we'd like to stay a little.'

'I should cocoa,' said Nanny Pete, grimly. 'I mean, that would be very nice.'

'Oh thank you, Nana!' chorused the Darling children, excitedly.

'Less of the Nana,' said Pete.

The children nodded. Each knew that this should all be rather worrying, but each was busy with private thoughts. Primrose was wondering if getting a tattoo on your head hurt a lot, because sometimes she felt she had had enough of Alice bands and mild pink complexions. Cassian was admiring the gigantic crane that was lowering a cargo net from far over-head, and wondering what sort of building it was that they were parked next to. As usual, Daisy was thinking about the Situation, and devising ways to get answers to some of the thousands of questions in her mind. 'You're probably wondering what to do with us,' she said.

'Too right,' said Nanny Pete.

'You'll have to be nice to us, of course,' said Daisy.

'You're not in your mansion now,' said. could knock you on the head and roll you into 'oggin, no worries.'

''Oggin?' said Daisy.

''Oggin,' said Nanny Pete, 'is what us seagoing folk call the sea.'

'Oh no you could not,' said Daisy, though actually she was not feeling 100 per cent confident. They were in a strange car, behind studded doors, and the cargo net was very close.

Tch, she told herself. Look on the bright side. They were on their own. There was no nanny, unless you counted Pete, which she did not, and no parents. It was a state of affairs they had been longing for for years.

'So what,' said Pete, 'is stopping me drowning you, then?'

'Oh, really,' said Daisy, with an impatient click of the tongue. 'You're a burglar, not a murderer. What about your professional pride?'

'Good point,' said Pete. 'But maybe I'm a murderer too. Multi-tasking, like.'

'Never,' said Daisy, though her mouth was frankly rather dry.

''Scuse me a minute,' said Pete. The cargo net was

51

children saw there were two men
... ts sides. One of them was only a
... oth had shaved heads and tattoos.
... to secure the net around the car. 'Make
... d up she goes.'

... ges?' said the metre-high man, who had no
teeth, as he peered through the window of the Jag.

'Hostages,' replied Pete, chuckling horribly. Daisy
thought the horribleness sounded forced.

'He's fibbing,' said Daisy. 'We're guests. Honoured ones. Take her up, boys.'

'Oi!' said Pete, and Daisy had a very strong feeling
that she was right, and that beneath that tattooed
exterior lurked a geezer of purest diamond.

The net was secure round the Jag, and the ground
was already sinking away from them.

'Listen,' hissed Pete. 'This wasn't my idea. All
I want is a nice quiet life. I'll take you home, right?'

'We don't want to go home,' said Primrose. 'If
you take us back, we'll grass you up. Stitch you up
like a kipper.'

There was a silence, except for the grinding of
the crane. Daisy tried to concentrate on what would
happen at the top. There were, however, distractions.

The wall up which they were being lifted was

perhaps 30 metres high. Now they were up here, they could see that they were passing rows of round brass portholes. There were lights on in some of them. Through one, Primrose saw an enormous cast-iron kitchen stretching away to vanishing point. Through another, Cassian saw polished brass generators. 'Ooh!' cried Daisy, as they passed a ballroom.

'It's a ship,' said Cassian.

It certainly was a ship; an absolutely enormous ship. They rose past decks, galleries, lifeboats. They caught a glimpse of great round funnels towering among wreaths of steam. Far below, shrunk to a ribbon with distance, was the quay. Glancing across at Pete, Daisy saw that a sort of soupy grin had pasted itself to his face. The burglar was proud of the ship, it seemed. Daisy decided to win him over. 'This is the most amazing thing I have ever seen,' she said.

'It is, innit?' said Pete, blushing slightly. 'SS *Kleptomanic*. We are alongside in the private docks of the Transglobal Steamship Company. Once the pride of the fleet. Now the property of AAA Aardvark Childminding and Security.'

'So how did you get hold of the ship?'

'We nicked it. Sort of.'

'What do you mean, sort of?'

Pete blushed. 'Just nicked it.'

'But it's still here.'

'Yeah,' said Pete. 'Story of our life.'

'Brilliant,' said Daisy, rather sarcastically.

'No need to be like that,' said Pete, wounded. 'We're getting better all the time. I'll explain when we get there.'

A face appeared at the window. 'He'f right, you know,' said the very small person with no teeth clinging to the cargo net. 'Practiff makef perfect. Fcufe me. Couldn't help overhearing. Nosey Clanger, at your ferviff. Coming in to land any minute.'

And indeed the net with the Jag was now swinging over shuffleboard courts and a swimming pool full of what looked like coal, towards a green deck with a white J painted on it.

And landing.

Five men with wheelbarrows appeared. They emptied the back seat of the car of silver and gold, and carried the Bear's Bum away with strange reverence. There was only enough gold and silver to fill three and a half barrows. 'Is that all?' said Nosey. He sounded disappointed.

'Certainly is,' said Nanny Pete, defensively.

'Oh. Great. Only . . .'

'Yeah?'

'Well it'f not much, if it? I mean there muft of been Turkish carpetf, a ftereo, couple of tellief, free peef fweet and vat. And what about the fafe?'

Pete was scowling horribly. 'Listen,' he said. 'I am there in a brown bowler hat in a strange house. I do my best. I got the Bear's Bum.'

'You got vat?' said Nosey. 'Unbleeble. Waf it –'

'Shhh,' said Pete, jerking his head at his passengers. 'So anyway when I get in I reckon I've got approx three hours to get it done because of, one, the parents coming back and two, nice as I was those kids are not easy, you will find out for yourself. Spirited, you could call them. And three, there was that white van following me all night – '

'White van?'

'Yes.'

'*Bad* white van?'

'Yep.'

'And what do you mean, kidf?' said Nosey.

'The kids in the car.'

'Oh,' said Nosey, who perhaps was not too bright. 'Fo not the fame kids wot has just runned off and gone down that there hatch into the bowlf of the ship.'

Pete turned round. It had been a long, long evening. He saw the car and the deck, empty, a hatch open. 'Bowels,' he said.

'Pardon?'

'Not bowls. Bowels. As in innards. We'll never find 'em now.'

'No time,' said Nosey. 'Captain wantf to fee you.'

'Never rains but it pours,' said Nanny Pete.

5

'They'll never find us now,' said Cassian.

Neither of his sisters answered. They did not approve of people stating the obvious. They kept climbing down the vertical ladder of greasy iron. It descended into a darkness that smelled of oil. From far below came weird clankings and rumblings, and once what sounded like a voice howling. It was not an encouraging noise. Neither Primrose nor Daisy wished to find out what was making it. So they were most delighted when Cassian stepped off the ladder at a sort of landing. He switched on his pocket flashlight, clamped it between his teeth, and began to turn the locking-wheel on a huge metal door. Pulling the door open a crack, he peeped out.

'Well?' hissed Daisy.

'All clear,' hissed Cassian back.

The girls followed him through the door.

They were in a long corridor that stretched away as far as the eye could see in both directions. Underfoot was a soft, wine-red carpet with yellow piping at the edges. The walls were made of mahogany. From the ceiling hung cut-glass chandeliers. 'Quite charming,' said Primrose.

'Highly select. But where are we?' said Daisy.

Cassian, a keen student of shipbuilding, said, 'Probably the first-class accommodation deck.' He pointed down the left-hand wall, in which were set many doors. 'Suites, I should think,' he said.

'Marvellous,' said Daisy. She grasped a brass doorknob and shoved open the door. 'Well I must say that this is really perfectly acceptable.'

She was right.

The Darlings were standing in an enormous stateroom, with gold-mounted sofas, a walnut dining-table with six Chippendale chairs, and a grandfather clock. 'Commence exploration procedure. Report back in five,' said Daisy out of the corner of her mouth, shooting the large brass bolts on the door.

Five minutes later, the children were gathered, flushed and happy, on the sofa. 'Bathroom,' said Primrose. 'Fizz bath, swirl bath, power shower, needle shower, wash basin, ivory toothbrushes provided. Hot water switched on.'

'Check,' said Daisy. 'Cassian?'

'Three bedrooms,' said Cassian. 'Four-poster bunks, brocade bedspreads, reading lamps, voice-tubes and room-service menus.'

'How delightful,' said Daisy. 'And I have discovered a map.'

The map was a large object, framed. It showed all the decks of the ship. Three of the decks were marked, 'FOR THE ATTENTION OF OUR HONOURED PASSENGERS'. These showed the first-class cabins, ballroom and dining accommodation. Another two decks were marked, 'FOR THE ATTENTION OF PASSENGERS'. These were the second-class and third-class cabins, small, windowless, and close to the propeller shaft and the crew lavatories. And another six decks, marked,

'BENEATH THE ATTENTION OF PAS-
SENGERS', showed the locations of the engine
rooms, the kitchens, the laundries, livestock units,
freezers, skate-sharpening workshops, bridge, and
all the other facilities (it said on the map) installed on
the *Kleptomanic* to give her passengers the Atlantic
Crossing of a Lifetime – Luxurious, Efficient, Speedy
(six days!).

'Engine rooms first,' said Cassian.

'Kitchens next,' said Primrose.

'But what,' said Daisy, 'if they catch us?'

'Judging by Nanny Pete,' said Primrose, 'they
could not catch a cold.'

'Not if they used both hands,' said Cassian.

'Well, time to freshen up, and off we go,' said
Daisy.

She took a needle shower and a power-blast
bath. Primrose jumped into the whirlpool, and swam
against the spin for a few minutes. Cassian wetted his
hand and patted his hair a bit flatter. Refreshed, they
set off.

This time, they noticed things.

The empty corridor outside the cabin had been
empty for some time, judging by the puffs of dust
their feet raised as they walked along it. The hair

Cassian had left across the iron emergency door was unbroken; they had not been followed. The shaft was still dark and oily. The worrying clankings and churnings still rose from the darkness below, but the howling had stopped. 'Must we?' said Daisy.

'I have got to do what I have got to do,' said Cassian nobly. 'You don't have to.'

'All for one, and one for all!' said Primrose.

Down they went; down, down, into the heart of darkness, blackness illimitable. The noise of grinding and churning grew louder. 'I say!' said Cassian. 'How thrilling!'

'Mmm,' said his sisters. Daisy would have quite liked to take Cassian's hand, and she suspected the same was true of Primrose. But you cannot hold hands on a vertical ladder, and besides, the nanny training (brave little men! whether you were boys or girls) stood in their way.

'We're here,' said Cassian's voice from the darkness below. They stood on a metal deck. They saw the torch beam play on a steel door. They saw the wheel turn, the door open, light stream in, a ruddy light that flickered. They walked out of the shaft.

They were in a huge hall, with things like pillars rising from the middle of its floor. The light came from a grate in the bottom of one of the pillars, inside which an enormous fire was burning. Two men with shovels were digging coal from a great mound on the floor and hurling it into the fire. High in the shadows great beams and levers turned, slow and smooth.

'Fantastic,' breathed Cassian.

'Ahem,' said Daisy, in a strange, high voice.

For standing watching them were two giants. Both of them were two metres tall, and carried huge, dripping oil cans. Both of them were as wide as houses. The one on the right was probably the bigger of the two. There was a handle on the back of his head, though Daisy could not imagine anyone strong enough to lift him.

Cassian smiled, the smile of someone completely at home. 'Ah,' he said. 'The engine room.'

'Actually, it's the stoke-hold,' said the man without the handle.

'Thank you. And you are?'

'George,' said the man without the handle. 'And this is Giant Luggage.'

'Hur, hur,' said the man with the handle.

'Where's the Chief?'

'There,' said George, pointing to a glassed-in

control room on the far side of the floor. 'He won't see you, though.'

'We'll see,' said Cassian, briskly. 'Carry on oiling, men.'

George gave him a sort of half-salute. Giant Luggage said 'Hur, hur.' They lumbered off into the shadows.

'Well done,' said Primrose.

'Most effective,' said Daisy.

'Huh?' said Cassian, and his sisters realized that they might as well have told a fish how clever it was to be such a good swimmer. 'Let's see the Chief.'

The closer they went to the control room, the odder it seemed. It was basically a room attached to the side of the stoke-hold, with glass walls. But the glass walls had been painted black from the inside. Only a pair of clear patches remained. As they drew closer, they saw that the clear patches had eyes behind them – brown eyes, red-rimmed, rolling horribly. Above the clank and boom of machinery and the hiss of steam came a strange, worrying noise: the sound of dozens of clocks, chiming.

There was a door in the wall of the Chief's shack. Beside it was a doorbell. Beside the bell was a label that read, 'RING AND DIE.'

'Perhaps we'll leave it,' said Daisy.

But Cassian was approaching the bell, not with his thumb, but with a little gadget he had taken from his pocket. He touched the brass bell-push. There was a crackle and a flash that for a second lit up the lofty vault of the stoke-hold, with its gantries and walkways and slow-turning cams. 'Goodness me,' said Cassian, reading a dial on the gadget. 'Ten thousand volts. How very impressive.'

'Just as well you didn't put your thumb on it,' said Primrose.

'Do me a favour,' said Cassian.

'Sorry.'

The door opened as far as its three chains would allow. A face appeared in the crack. It had a long chin and blubbery red lips, with eyes to match. 'You're alive,' it said.

'Of course,' said Cassian. 'We would like some information, if you please –'

'Go away!' howled the Chief, mopping his eyes with a filthy handkerchief.

'Perhaps we should come back when you are feeling better,' said Daisy.

'Noooobody loves me!' howled the Chief.

'Frankly,' said Daisy, 'I am not surprised.'

64

'Yowooooo!' howled the Chief. The door slammed shut. There was the sound of dozens of bolts sliding home.

'That's the Chief, then,' said Cassian.

'No manners,' said Daisy. But she said it slowly.

For her mind was not on that figure whose face had hung tear-stained in the door-crack. She was thinking about what she had glimpsed past him, in that weird black-walled room. The walls had been covered in clocks: cuckoo clocks, grandfather clocks, ships' chronometers. In the middle of the clocks, was an elaborate glass case, its top rising in a sort of pyramid to a gilt crown, the crown itself surmounted by the gilt figure of an eagle, but an eagle with four necks and four heads. And in the case, staring out at the world with mournful eyes of amber glass, the head of a teddy bear. Only Daisy could have seen it, absorbed it in a lightning flash of her huge mind . . .

'Did you see that bear's head?' said Primrose. 'Bit odd, I thought.'

'Chief engineers are often slightly eccentric,' said Cassian.

'Everybody knows that,' said Daisy. 'Come this way.'

'Where are we going?' said Primrose.

'Wait and see,' said Daisy, folding her lips. She had no idea, of course. But she had been brought up by nannies, and nannies are never, ever wrong.

First, there was a deck full of machines that Cassian said were generators. 'Up, up,' cried Daisy, thrusting open a door. Beyond the door were corridors and more corridors; the smell of cooking, which was tempting, and the sound of voices yelling, which was not. Actually, all three Darlings were beginning to feel extremely tired, and absolutely starving. 'It is way past our bedtime,' said Daisy.

Then, somehow, they were standing by a railing, looking down. Far below was the gleam of polished wood, and something like a stage. Daisy said, in a breathless sort of voice, 'The ballroom! How lovely!' The sound of a piano floated up from below, a jazzy, bluesy tune, happy and sad at the same time. The playing stopped. The figure of a woman in a red velvet ball-gown floated across the ballroom floor, and was gone.

The little Darlings stood with their chins on the railing, watching the emptiness below. They were away from home, without Nanny, Papa or Secretary

Mummy. It was way past their bedtime. They should have felt as empty as the ballroom.

But when you have been brought up by nannies, you learn that having each other is enough. There was only one kind of emptiness they were feeling.

'I'm starving,' said Primrose.

'Where are those kitchens?' said Cassian.

'They'll be down there, so the waiters can bring delicious food to the ladies in the lovely dresses in between dances with charming men in tail coats,' said Daisy.

'Swoony trollop,' said Cassian, and started marching downstairs.

The ballroom was fearsomely dusty, except for the grand piano on the stage, which gleamed, as if polished frequently. In the back regions beside a bar was a cupboard in the wall, with two buttons next to it. One of the buttons read, 'KITCHEN'.

'It's a dumb waiter,' said Cassian. 'Hop in.' Primrose hopped.

'No,' said Daisy.

Voices sounded at the other end of the ballroom. They were gruff and over-excited. 'Thisaway!' they cried. 'Look! Tracks!'

'It's probably not us they're looking for,' said

Daisy. 'They didn't seem to mind us in the stoke-hold.'

'D'you want to find out?' said Cassian, leaping into the dumb waiter.

Daisy pointed her toes and swung her legs elegantly in after him. Cassian stuck his frowning black head out and pressed the 'KITCHEN' button. Down they went into the dark, Daisy clutching Primrose's hand; though Primrose seemed quite calm, which probably had something to do with being close to a kitchen.

The lift came to a halt. Through its open front, they were looking between endless rows of black cast-iron stoves. Between the stoves was a bottom the size of an elephant's, dressed in gigantic black-and-white checked chef's trousers. Above the bottom was a white jacket, filled with fat the way a sausage skin is filled with sausage. On top of all this was a tiny head with ears like fungi, on which was balanced a tall, thin chef's hat. One of the arms seemed to be throwing a ladle at somebody. 'They're not HERE!' a voice was yelling, in a sort of thick squeak. 'I haven't SEEN any children! I've looked EVERYWHERE! Now get out of my KITCHEN –'

'Galley,' said a timid voice.

'– SHUT UP, SHUT UP, because I've worked my fingers to the BONE and now I'm off to BED!'

'They're looking for us, all right,' said Daisy.

The chef picked up a roast chicken and waddled off, gnawing. The lights went out. Cassian tiptoed out of the dumb waiter and turned them on again.

'Steak and kidney pies,' said Primrose, lifting a pot lid and sniffing. 'Baked beans. Warm white bread. Chips. Get some plates.'

There was then a long silence, broken only by the clash of knives and forks. Nannies did not hold with pies, chips, beans, or any bread except brown yuk that tasted like cardboard. This was a fantastic treat. And it was hard to think that anyone who could eat food this delicious could really be dangerous.

Daisy finished her second plateful. 'Tired,' she said.

'Back to the cabin,' said Cassian.

'Suite,' said Daisy.

'Thank you, dear,' said Cassian.

Primrose merely yawned.

They washed up, procured some bread and eggs for breakfast, climbed back into the dumb waiter and pressed a button that read 'CABINS'. As they went past the ballroom, the lift filled with piano music. There was a brief glimpse of a figure in a red velvet dress on the stage; then the darkness again, then a corridor lined with doors, lit by small yellow lights stretching away as far as the eye could see. Daisy scowled at the map, and took them up shafts and round corners and into the empty land, where the wine-red carpets were frosted grey with dust. Here they found their suite, and slept like logs.

Next morning, early, Primrose cooked an excellent breakfast of fried bread and stolen eggs over a small fire Cassian made from a couple of chairs in the stateroom grate. It felt quite homelike, once you got used to it. After breakfast, they had fizz baths and explosion spa showers, and got dressed. Daisy was wearing a pensive frown. She said, 'We've got to do something.'

'About what?'

'Secretary Mummy and Papa.'

'What about them?'

'Somebody ought to see if they're all right.'

Her brother and sister shrugged. 'If you want.'

'So,' said Daisy. 'We'd better find out who runs the place round here.'

'The Captain,' said Cassian.

'There won't be a captain on a messed-up ship like this,' said Primrose.

'Bet there will,' said Cassian.

'But will he be a person of goodwill?' said Daisy.

There was a silence. Everyone saw what she meant.

'We could have a look round,' said Daisy.

'Case the joint,' said Primrose.

'See how it all works,' said Cassian.

'And Secretary Mummy won't even notice we're not there,' said Daisy.

'Nor will Papa,' said Primrose.

There was a silence as this gloomy truth sank in. 'Well,' said Daisy eventually. 'We can't sit here moping all day. Off we go.'

Off they went.

They started in the engine room again. The giant with the handle on his head raised a paw and said, 'Hur, hur,' with an expression on his face that might have been a grin. This was encouraging. The Chief Engineer's eyes were still whirling in his spyholes, in time to a weird tintinnabulation of clocks. This was not encouraging. The girls removed Cassian from the fascinating generator rooms by threats of violence, and marched down the trail of delicious smells that led to the kitchens. This time they did not use the dumb waiter, but walked over the deep carpets of an empty dining saloon with long mahogany tables laid with gleaming silver and bright glasses. There was a serving door, with round portholes. From behind the door came shouting and the clank of pans. Primrose made a beeline for it.

'Wait,' said Cassian. 'Where are you going?'

'Aren't you hungry?' said Primrose.

'Well, yes, of course,' said Cassian.

'But there are burglars after us,' said Daisy. 'It is not wise.'

'Wise, schmise,' said Primrose, out of the side of her sweet pink mouth. 'A chef loves a compliment.' She marched forwards, shoved open the doors, and stepped into the kitchen.

The ceiling was low, the heat intense. Cast-iron stoves stretched into the distance. Scurrying figures came and went behind rolling banks of steam. Primrose marched straight into the nearest steam bank, became hazy, and vanished. Daisy and Cassian were beginning to follow when a huge voice boomed out of the fog. 'WHAT,' it roared, 'ARE YOU DOING IN MY KEETCHEN?'

The fog rolled away. Primrose was standing with her thin white hands on her pink gingham hips, her head thrown back, looking into a vast, lard-white face. On top of the face was a chef's hat the size of a pillowcase. Below the face was a white coat and a pair of enormous check trousers, both filled to bursting. In the middle of the face were two little black eyes, a button nose, and a rosebud mouth, from which the voice was booming.

'Relax, Chef,' said Primrose. 'My brother and sister and I wished to say that not finding you here last night, we took a little dinner –'

'THREE PIE!' roared Chef. 'Eight slice bread! Six thousand and twelve bean! Also egg, bacon, tomato –'

'We would have asked, of course,' said Primrose, bending the truth with great casualness. 'But there was no one here. And of course we –'

'FOOD THIEFS!' bellowed Chef.

'But now we have owned up. And apologized. It is,' said Primrose, 'a fair cop, Chef.'

'Ah.' The chef looked nonplussed.

'And we wanted in addition and on top,' said Primrose, 'to present our compliments. You do an exquisitely baked bean. Also a very light touch with suet. I know my brother and sister agree. Not so, Daisy? Cassian?'

Daisy and Cassian said, firmly, as they had been taught by their nannies. 'Yes,' and 'Aye,' and 'Excellent.' And watched in astonishment as this mountainous chef shifted his feet and looked at the floor and simpered and actually blushed.

'Well,' said Chef, in a new, smaller voice. 'Maybe you hungry, eh? We have here, let me see, leetle fillet shtcak with onion smother and kartoffel dauphinoise, any good to you?'

'Sure is,' said Primrose, slapping him on the back. Minions arrived with heaped-up plates. The children fell on the delicious viands at a table in the corner while the chef, cooking all the while in huge iron pans, chatted amiably about Great Sausages he had known. Having topped off a mighty elevenses with apple dumplings and Horlicks buried under Alps of whipped cream, the children made an appointment for lunch and prepared to resume their explorations.

At this point a voice in the mists said, 'Ahem.'

A figure stepped into a patch of clear air.

The uniform was gone. Instead, there was a striped jersey, blue trousers and army boots. But the face, large-chinned and heavy-browed, was unquestionably that of Pete, alias Nanny Petronella Fryer.

'You and me,' said Nanny Pete, 'have a duty to perform. We are off to see the Captain.'

'Gulp,' said Daisy.

Two more burglars strolled out of the steam, their big hands hooked into their wide leather belts. They fell in behind, cutting off all possibility of escape.

'If you would be so good as to sleepy me?' said Pete.

'I beg your pardon?'

'Sleepy Hollow, follow.'

'Ah.'

They climbed stairs and went down corridors and side decks, miles of them. After ten minutes, they were on the green landing-strip where the Jag was parked. In front of it was a building like a castle made of steel, with an elaborate door painted navy blue and decorated with gold anchors. In the middle, a design in gilt ropework and butterflies read, 'CAPTAIN'.

Pete opened the door and walked in. The children followed him. 'Sit down,' said Pete. Daisy sat down. The nanny burglar's face was closed. Daisy began to think that perhaps it would have been better not to have stowed away in the Jaguar.

Too late now. 'Chin up,' she said.

'Obviously,' said Cassian.

'Natch,' said Primrose, adjusting her Alice band.

They began to look around them.

They were in a long room, with windows all down the opposite side to the door. There was a steering wheel in the middle, with a compass in front of it. The compass was made of brass. There was a pink frill round it. There were matching frills on the engine room telegraphs beside it, and a huge vase of pink roses on the chart table. Beyond the windows, the gigantic offices of the Transglobal Steamship Company frowned over the pointed bows of the ship.

Cassian was scowling darkly. He had never been on a ship's bridge before, but he was pretty sure that normal bridges would not be this frilly.

Suddenly, a red telephone started ringing. Nanny Pete started towards it. But before he was halfway, Daisy had picked it up. 'Hellay?' said a voice on the other end. 'Hellay?'

Daisy said, 'Hello.' Nanny Pete had stopped in mid-stride. Agonized suspense furrowed his brow.

'Is this AAA Aardvark Child-minding and Security?' said the voice, which sounded like a horse gargling with cut-glass.

'At your service, madam,' said Daisy, sliding smoothly into nanny mode.

'I need someone immediately,' said the voice. 'Honestly I'm at my wits' end.'

'What have they done this time?' said Daisy, soothingly.

'Dropped a ball,' said the voice. 'A tennis ball. On the carpet. And who's going to pick it up, I'd like to know?'

'Who am I speaking to?'

'Lady Orthodonta Strimlingham,' said the voice, now sounding like a horse close to tears. 'All the servants have gone and now Nanny and there's this ball, just . . . lying here.'

'Give me your number,' said Daisy. 'We'll call you right back.'

'Oh thank you, thank you!' said the voice. 'But do hurry!'

Daisy hung up, and scribbled the number on a pad of scented pink paper tied with a ribbon to the steering wheel. Nanny Pete was staring at her, shaking his head in astonishment. 'Respect,' he said. 'Nice one.'

'Oh, I don't know,' said Daisy, pleased despite herself.

'What now?' said Cassian. His mind was full of mighty cylinders, colossal steering gear, titanic generators, bunkers filled with mountains of coal and lakes of sticky black oil. He hated all these frills.

'Well, quite,' said a voice from the other end of the bridge. 'What, indeed?'

All three children spun round. Nanny Pete knuckled his forehead respectfully. In a doorway stood a tall woman with black hair and dark glasses. She was wearing a crimson velvet dressing-gown. Daisy noticed that her toenails were beautifully painted.

'We are Daisy, Cassian and Primrose,' said Daisy, politely. 'And who, may I ask, are you?'

The woman gazed upon them for a worryingly long time. 'I'm the Captain,' she said.

'You can't be,' said Cassian, horrified.

'Of course she can,' said both his sisters together.

The lady yawned. She was very tall, and her scent was like a spring garden, and her make-up was impeccable. 'But what are you doing on my ship?'

'We stowed away with Nanny Pete here,' said Daisy. Nanny Pete blushed tomato red, and looked at his boots. 'We quite like it here. But we think we ought to tell our parents. They fret if they're on their own, you know. Well, Papa might, anyway.'

The Captain pulled down her dark glasses and studied Daisy with great interest. 'You think so?'

'Probably not, actually,' said Daisy, gloomily. It was sometimes possible to have fantasies about being loved and wanted, but they never seemed to last. She took refuge in efficiency. 'Oh, by the way. There was a telephone call.' Conscientiously, Daisy told the Captain about Lady Strimlingham and the ball horror.

'Excellent.' The Captain picked up the phone and dialled. There was a distant yammering. 'An operative will be with you directly, my lady,' she cooed, and hung up. 'Pete, duty nanny to the Jag deck.'

'Aye, aye,' said Pete.

'Now then, children,' said the Captain. 'Your parents. I honestly think you'd better go straight back to them.'

'Last thing we want,' said Cassian. 'We like it here.'

'And of course Nanny Pete stole a whole lot of stuff,' said Daisy sweetly. 'And we might tell someone.'

'Plus the food at home is absolutely awful,' said Primrose.

'Was,' said the Captain.

'I beg your pardon?'

'You saw a white van,' said the Captain.

'How did you know?' said Cassian.

'Psychic,' said the Captain, looking grim. 'When I said back to your parents, I meant back to your parents, not back home. I shouldn't think there's much of home left. But if you don't want to go, you don't want to go. So,' she said, beaming, as if the bright side of something had suddenly occurred to her. 'Welcome aboard. But you'll have to work your passage.'

'Work?' said Daisy.

'My spies tell me Primrose is an enthusiastic and skilful cook,' said the Captain.

'Does a bear go to the lavatory in the woods?' said Primrose, mildly.

'And that Cassian has . . . engineering talents.'

''Spose,' said Cassian.

'And that you yourself . . . Daisy, is it not? . . . have watched nannies in action.'

'Closely, and with great vigilance.'

'Too right,' said Pete.

'Well, then.' A small, unshaven nanny trotted on to the bridge. 'Ah, Fingers. Are you duty nanny?'

'Yes'm.' Fingers giggled, and bit off a chew of tobacco from an evil-looking black plug. 'Awright, kids?' He held out a bag. 'Gobstoppers,' he said. 'Go on, have two. 'Scuse me, gotta spit.' Fingers went outside.

The Captain pressed a button with a long red fingernail. 'Jag crew, prepare launch pad,' she said.

'Are you serious?' said Daisy.

The Captain looked hard at Daisy. 'Is there a problem?'

'Well,' said Daisy. 'It was just that he didn't seem, well, all that nannyish.'

The Captain seemed shocked. 'What was wrong?'

'Chewing tobacco,' said Daisy.

'Spitting,' said Primrose.

'Gobstoppers,' said Cassian.

'And some of the things Nanny Pete did were actually *kind*,' said Primrose. 'So we knew there was something odd going on straight away.'

'Though he was very good at not getting hurt,' said Daisy, in fairness. 'Exceptionally good, really.'

'Ah,' said the Captain, looking at Nanny Pete, who was shifting from foot to foot in the background.

'Pete, you may go.' She filed her nails as Pete made a sharp exit. 'Well, of course, our people have been trained in Wormwood Scrubs and Sing Sing, not the Nanny Academy.' She paused. 'So you're nanny experts, eh?'

'We've had eighteen,' said Primrose, with simple pride.

'Nineteen,' said Cassian.

'The last one didn't count.'

'And now,' said Daisy, 'I think we should ring up Papa and tell him that we are unavoidably detained in a safe place.'

'By all means,' said the Captain.

But there was only the answering machine. 'Mr and Mrs Darling are in the Caribbean,' it said. 'Please leave your invitation after the tone. Bing bong.'

'Hello,' said Daisy. 'We are away with our new nanny. See you some time.' She put down the receiver. 'You heard that?'

'Yup,' said her brother and sister. There was a gloomy silence. It is nice to be cared about by your parents, even if you hardly know them.

Outside the bridge, Nanny Fingers spat more tobacco juice, climbed into the Jag, waved to the

Darlings, and was swung over the side. They watched from the bridge as the black car beetled down the quay and out of the dock gate.

The Captain gave them a dazzling smile. 'Lunch, anyone?' she said, brightly. 'I'll get Chef to rustle something up.'

It was yet another amazing repast, consisting of tomato soup, shrimp-burgers, pancakes with maple syrup, and four kinds of juice, each more delicious than the last. The Darling children ate deeply, then leaned back in their chairs. 'Excellent,' said Daisy. Frankly, the notion of meeting this Captain of Burglars had been a daunting one. But she seemed to be turning out as nice as she was beautiful.

'I know it's not like being at home,' said the Captain, 'but in our simple way we try, we try.'

'Burnt porridge is what we get at home,' said Cassian.

'Well,' said Daisy. 'Back to the suite, I think.'

'One moment,' said the Captain. 'Daisy, would you do me a favour? A word, perhaps?' She walked to a bank of voice-pipes, blew into one of them, and said, 'Nanny Pete to bridge, chop, chop.'

The Captain led Daisy into a small boudoir

decorated with framed watercolours of famous crime scenes and a large bunch of freesias. 'Sit down,' she said. 'Drink?'

'Bit early for me,' said Daisy.

'Ah,' said the Captain. 'Quite. Now, dear . . . what were your brother and sister called again, by the way?'

'I'm Daisy,' said Daisy. 'And they're Primrose and Cassian.'

The Captain poured a small glass of clear liquid from a decanter, and downed it at a gulp. 'Yes,' she said, her beautiful features for a moment distant and pensive. 'Quite so, quite so. Well, the question is, er . . . Daisy, what are we to do with you? You cannot simply . . . be here.'

'Suppose you explain what "here" is,' said Daisy. 'Then perhaps we can come up with a plan.'

'Excellent idea,' said the Captain. She pulled a silken cord, and a curtain swished back from a whiteboard. 'We have as you know, er, pinched the SS *Kleptomanic* –'

'Which is still here,' said Daisy.

'Bear with me,' said the Captain, a pained smile flitting over her scarlet lips. 'On the *Kleptomanic* are 293 burglars, first-floor men, cat operatives, ram-raiders and allied trades. Some of the worst and most incompetent burglars, if I may for a moment blow our trumpet, that crime has ever seen. But a very nice type of burglar. Not the kind of burglar at home in the urban jungle. The kind of burglar at home in an older, more forgiving world. Who prefers jewellery and antique paintings to DVD recorders, whatever they are. The kind of burglars who wish to burgle their way to the quiet life. It is my plan one day to sail away with my burglars to that quiet life, or anyway, somewhere where their special talents will come in useful.'

'So why haven't you already gone?'

The Captain uncapped a felt-tip pen and wrote on the whiteboard the words, 'LACK OF FUNDS'. She began to write something else, changed her mind and put the top back on the pen.

'Funds?'

'Money.'

'Ah.' Daisy nodded politely.

'But do not worry your head about this,' said the Captain. 'What we aim to do on the *Kleptomanic* is improve skills and develop, ahem, other sources of income. And this is where you come in.'

'Me?'

'Yes, you,' said the Captain. 'Ah, Nanny Pete! Enter!'

And into the room sidled Nanny Pete, looking kindly, tough, and a little flustered. Behind him came Primrose and Cassian.

'Pete,' said the Captain. 'Daisy here is on the nanny project. And if it is all right with them, we'll attach Primrose to the galley, and Cassian to the engine room. Would that suit, do you think?'

'Down to the ground,' said Daisy. 'But what is it you want me to do?'

'Observe our nannies in action,' said the Captain. 'And having observed, make recommendations, and report to me. With your experience of the nanny world, your views will be of the greatest help. I am having rather a busy time, just now –'

'The Edward,' said Pete. 'White Van Dan.'

'I beg your pardon?' said Daisy.

'Nothing,' said the Captain firmly, frowning at Pete, who blushed to the roots of his tattoo.

'Dear me, you do look peaky. A junior aspirin, Pete, and off to bed with you!' said Daisy, folding her lips.

'Perfect!' cried the Captain, ushering her out of the door. 'Total nanny! Now run along and get a

uniform and Pete will introduce you to the key burglars and you can get settled in. Now, is everybody
sure they are happy?'

'Lots of machinery,' said Cassian gruffly. 'Nice.'

'And it's all sorely in need of a service!' cried the
Captain.

'Working by the side of Chef!' cried Primrose.
'Such a sweet person! Such an artist of the spoon
and saucepan!'

'Hmm,' said the Captain. 'So off you go. Excellent. Excellent!

In a huge walk-in wardrobe of nanny gear, Pete Fryer found Daisy a brown bowler hat, a greenish uniform that fitted pretty well, an apron, a pair of brogues and a notebook. She spent the rest of the day exploring. At suppertime, she saw Nanny Fingers being helped down the ship's main stairs on his way back from his nanny mission. There were scorch marks all over him. 'They tied him up and ironed him,' said Pete Fryer. 'Little perishers.'

'What did he expect?' said Daisy, sighing.

A couple of days passed in the purest enjoyment. Then a bell shrilled, and the tannoy said, 'Sub-nanny Daisy to bridge, in uniform.'

With a beating heart Daisy donned overall, apron, bowler and brogues, and put the notebook in her pocket. Pete Fryer knocked on the suite door. 'I'll see you up to the windy,' he said.

'I beg your pardon?'

'Windy ridge, bridge. Come on now.'

On the way up the stairs, Daisy took off her nail varnish, though Pete said there was no need. (Daisy made a note.) Nanny Huggins was duty nanny – a small, scrawny burglar, just about clean shaven, with a kind smile that showed a gold tooth. (Daisy made a note.) 'The Marchesa di Costaplenti. Interesting client. Would you mind going along as Sub-nanny and observer?' said the Captain, who today was wearing a sharply tailored suit with a pencil skirt.

'I should be delighted,' said Daisy.

The Jag swung down. Nanny Huggins drove at top speed out of the docks, through the Old Town, and into Happy Valley, where the big houses were. As the Jag shot past, a builder stopped digging a hole, straightened up, and made a rapid call on a mobile phone.

The Costaplenti house was huge and pink and more or less invisible from the road. Huggins stopped the Jag in a yellow fan of expensive gravel. (Daisy made a note.) Huggins jumped out, ran up the steps to the front door and walloped on the panels with her bowler hat. A butler opened up. 'Hello, big boy,' said Huggins. 'We're the new nannies.' (Daisy made a note.)

'I will inform her ladyship,' said the butler, looking down his nose. 'She has asked that you commence your duties immediately. She does not require to meet you. The servants' entrance is round the back, you can't miss it, just look for the dustbins. The nursery wing is adjacent.' A watery smile played on his lips. 'And may God have mercy on your souls.'

'Very nice,' said Huggins, rubbernecking as they marched round the back of the house. 'Solid gold door knocker, don't see many of them nowadays, incitement to crime really. Oh look, some poor child has left his sweet liddle teddy bear –' He bent down to pick up the charming animal, stretched out his hand –

'Nooooo!' cried Daisy, grabbing hold of the green elasticated belt and yanking Nanny Huggins back.

Huggins looked puzzled. 'But it's a dear little stuffed koala,' he said.

'Hah!' said Daisy scornfully. She cut a bamboo from a nearby clump and gave the koala a good jab. As soon as the stuffed Australian moved a fraction of a millimetre, a huge pair of steel jaws leaped out of the dead leaves and came together with a dreadful clang, cutting the bamboo clean in half.

'The old Killer Koala trick,' said Daisy, writing in her notebook. 'You were saying?'

A new, hard light glinted in Huggins's eye. 'Nothing,' he said.

Daisy picked up the koala shreds and walked through the cloud of flies over the dustbins scattered around the servants' entrance. Huggins came after her, trying to look as if he was not hanging back.

Rollo and Pandora di Costaplenti were dressed in matching green velvet suits, with buckle shoes. Their nursery wing was horribly tidy. 'Well!' cried Nanny Huggins, who had recovered her composure. 'What shall we do today?'

'Wanna go rollerblading,' said Rollo.

'Indoors,' said Pandora.

'Lovely idea!' cried Nanny Huggins. (Daisy wrote

in her book.) 'Wait here, Nanny Daise.' She sidled off into the house.

Daisy had to admit that Rollo and Pandora had excellent technique. Once they had got the roller blades on their little feet, they hauled ice-hockey sticks down from the walls and began to play at an exceptionally high level of violence. They smashed the chandelier, two of the windows, and all the Peter Rabbit crockery in the kitchenette. Then they started fighting. Daisy finished the note she was making in her book and stepped between them. An ice-hockey stick smote her on the head, but the hats worn by nannies are built by the same company that makes hats for motor-cycle racing. So she only staggered a little, took a deep breath, and cried, 'STOP IT!'

Actually, the word 'cried' does not even half describe the sound that came out of her mouth. It was so loud that it cracked one of the few unbroken windows in the children's wing. Rollo and Pandora stared at her, white-faced. 'Now then, children,' said Sub-nanny Daisy. 'Let's not be rough and naughty.'

Rollo's face took on an unpleasant twist. He opened his mouth to curse her.

Sub-nanny Daisy had been brought up by nannies, and knew exactly what to do. 'Into the bathroom!' she cried, gripping his ear with the Nanny Earlock and swinging him off his feet. 'Wash out his nasty mouth with soap and water, not that nice scented soap, no, this nasty yellow soap, rubadubadubadub!'

'Groo!' cried Rollo. 'Arghblblblbl!' His pasty face disappeared behind a cloud of bubbles.

'We'll be good!' shrieked Pandora. 'Weally, weally, weally good!'

'That's as may be,' said Sub-nanny Daisy, sniffing. 'Now off we go to bed with no supper.'

'Oh Nana!' bubbled Rollo.

'Unfair!' moaned Pandora.

'Quick march!' snapped Daisy. 'Go!'

Whimpering, they went.

Daisy tucked them up and read them a story. They fell asleep, good as gold. Daisy tiptoed out of the bedroom, shooting the bolts behind her. There was no sign of Nanny Huggins in the nursery wing. So Daisy pushed open the green baize door, and went into the house.

She found it pretty ordinary. The marble floors were normal marble floors, and the chandeliers glittered away very much as expected. The usual pictures of chilly ladies hung on the walls, and the carpets lapped over the ankles in an unsurprising manner. A few servants skulked here and there, not paying any attention to each other. The sound of breaking glass and sea shanties came from the butler's pantry. 'Ho, hum,' said Daisy to herself, and headed for the dining room.

And sure enough there was Nanny Huggins, up to his elbows in spoons.

Nanny Huggins jumped slightly, clanking his swagbag. 'Oh, it's you,' he said.

'It is indeed I,' said Daisy, smoothing her apron.

'So do me a favour,' said Huggins. 'Have a look round, and see if you can find . . .' he took a scrap of paper out of his pocket '. . . a portion of bear.'

'A bear?'

Huggins's lips moved soundlessly as he read. 'Yur,' he said. 'On a . . . diagonal . . .'

'Mahogany?'

'What I said, mahogany – er shield.'

'Very good,' said Daisy, and scooted off. Frowning.

There were long galleries, short galleries, saloons, coal, wine and root cellars, and a basement containing a cricket net and a medium-sized theatre. A small door in the side wall of the theatre said,

TROPHY ROOM. Daisy strode up to it, pushed it open and stopped dead. She nearly said, 'EEK!' But since she was in nanny uniform, she merely said, 'My goodness!'

She was staring at a tiger.

She counted to ten, then gave a little sigh. Of course it was only a stuffed tiger. All around it were other animals, bravely shot at extreme range by the Marchese di Costaplenti, stuffed and mounted on shields. There was an elephant's head. There was a pygmy shrew. And high on the wall was something that looked like an anteater's nose, made of worn, brownish plush. A brass plate underneath it read, 'LEFT LEG OF THE ROYAL EDWARD, LORP TOMBOLA, YEAR OF THE RAT'.

Ignoring the hundreds of glass eyes gazing beadily upon her from the walls, Daisy climbed on to a stool, unhooked the left leg and its shield, and returned to the dining room.

She and Nanny Huggins dragged the swagbags back to the nursery wing. The children were still as good as gold, or anyway their bedroom door was still bolted and there was no sign of a tunnel.

'How did you do it?' said Huggins.

Daisy told him.

'Poor little devils,' said Huggins.

'They'll be grateful later,' said Daisy. 'Now tell me, what do you know about the Royal Edward, the LORP and tombolas?'

'Wha?' said Huggins, jaw swinging.

'Very little, I see,' said Daisy. 'Are you going to stand there all day, or are we going to get out of here?'

'Sorry,' said Huggins.

A lugging of swagbags. A screech of Jaguar tyres, Huggins's brown bowler low over the wheel. Behind them, something huge and white coming into the road. A flop of ramps. A digger, a dozer, a dumper roaring into the Costaplenti drive. A huge cloud of dust rising in the still, blue air . . .

Then they were round the corner.

Daisy made a note, and put the book away.

Back at the ship, there was the Captain, wearing a tight black satin dress slit to the hip. 'Well?' she said.

'Got some loot,' said Huggins.

'And Sub-nanny Daisy?'

'Perfectly acceptable,' said Daisy.

'Nah,' said Nanny Huggins, head hanging. 'Captain, I cannot tell a lie. Was it not having been for

Sub-nanny – no! – Senior Nanny Daisy, I shudder to think what would have happened.' He did indeed shudder. Daisy knew he was thinking of the Killer Koala.

The Captain raised a perfect eyebrow.

'Too true, one fears,' said Daisy.

The Captain pressed a large pink button. 'Mug of cocoa,' she said. 'Then debrief.'

'Then what?' said Daisy, who had questions of her own.

'It is like this,' said the Captain. 'My dear burglars are . . . well, perhaps a little softhearted. In childhood, many of them were very close to their parents. There are things about life that only someone who has been brought up by nannies can explain. And explain someone must, before one of our boys gets hurt. Do you get my drift?'

'Of course,' said Daisy. 'You would like me to make a small speech.'

'Indeed.'

A klaxon was sounding in the bowels of the ship. A steward arrived with a mug of cocoa on a silver salver. Daisy drank, extending her little finger. Far in the distance was a muffled clanging and thundering, like the sound of big boots on iron ladders. A loudspeaker on the wall said, 'Five-minute call for Captain and Nanny Daisy.'

'Frightfully good cocoa,' said Daisy.

'Your sister made it,' said the Captain. 'She tells me the secret is to put the merest suspicion of whisky in it. Now drink up and come along, darling.' She led Daisy to an area of the ship she had not previously visited, down huge, lyre-shaped stairs to a round landing crusted with gold. 'In here,' she said. And suddenly they were in dusty corridors slung with cables, full of a sound like the sea breaking on rocks.

'We're on!' said the Captain. She swished on to a huge deck, surrounded by red velvet curtains. Daisy stood dazzled by lights.

It was a stage. Beyond the lights was a sea of burglars. Daisy stood in her nanny uniform, hands folded, trying not to look surprised. 'Ladies and gentlemen, cullies and nannies,' cried the Captain. 'I have the honour of presenting . . . Nanny Daisy!'

There was a roar of applause. Obviously Huggins had been spreading the word. Daisy kept her hands folded, and was annoyed to feel her cheeks go pink. The Captain swept aside, hand out, bowing. Daisy stepped up to the lectern.

'Ahem,' she said. 'These remarks will, I hope, be

of use to one and all. AAA Aardvark caters for a most exclusive type of parent, too rich to show affection to their children, too busy to remember their names. The children are remorseless and clever. One must be continually on guard against the little brutes, displaying no chink in the nanny armour. During the recent assignment, I took notes. I thought they might come in useful for those seeking hints on correct nanny deportment.' She opened her notebook. 'So here we go. On stopping the nannymobile outside the client's house, gravel was blasted everywhere, which was very nice but not nanny behaviour. Nanny Huggins has a nice smile but it shows teeth. The correct nanny is at all times saying, "Prune", and, "Prism", and never shows amusement, or,' Daisy, looked up, 'gold teeth.'

There was a murmur, with nervous grinning and a discreet xylophonic tooth tapping.

'Next,' said Daisy, 'we come to the Killer Koala. Never, never touch a toy until you have made a detailed check for cables, tripwires, laser beams and other trigger devices.'

'It was a sweet little teddy,' said Nanny Huggins from the audience.

'The sweeter the bait, the sharper the hook,' said

Daisy. 'How many fingers have you got?'

There was a short pause for counting. Then, 'Ten,' said Huggins,

'And how many would you have had if you had picked up that teddy?'

Silence.

'And as for rollerblading indoors,' said Daisy, 'well! Can anyone tell me one thing in its favour?'

'Great,' said a voice in the front row. 'Fun, like.'

'Fun!' said Daisy, in a voice that had a bad smell under its nose. 'Oh. I see. And how many things can you tell me against it?'

There was a puzzled silence. Finally, a voice in the dark said, 'Might bump your head?'

'Might – bump – your – head,' said Daisy, in a voice whose nose now had icicles on it. 'Well, it may interest you to know that nannies recognize four excellent reasons for not playing this rowdy and stupid game.'

'Four?' said a voice.

The Captain nodded, smiling brightly. 'That's what the nanny said.'

'One,' said Daisy, 'little ladies do not play rough games.'

The Captain smiled.

'Two,' said Daisy, 'little gentlemen are never rough with little ladies.'

The Captain beamed.

'Three,' said Daisy, 'roller skates, whether side by side or in line, are a modern horror. The only suitable place for skating is a private ice rink with a membership of the nicest type.'

'How very true!' cried the Captain.

'Four,' said Daisy, ' and worst. All games are bad if they are rough, that goes without saying. But the worst games of all are games that force young ladies to show their Ls.'

'Ls?' said a voice.

'Ahem!' said the Captain discreetly, from behind the red velvet curtain into whose shelter she had backed. 'I think Nanny Daisy is referring to . . . dread word . . . legs!'

'Aieeee!' shrieked Nanny Daisy, toppling sideways in a dead faint.

Cassian and Primrose jumped out of the audience and on to the stage and dragged their sister into the wings. Once out of sight of the audience, Daisy stood up. 'Was I all right?' she said.

'Bit over the top,' said Cassian. There were streaks of oil on his face.

'Why did you do it?' cried Primrose, who had flour in her hair. 'They hated it!'

'Because if they're going to dress up as nannies they'll have to behave like nannies,' said Daisy. 'Or they'll get caught. And hurt,' she said, shuddering at the memory of the Killer Koala.

There was a silence. 'How can they be so stupid?' said Primrose.

'Because they love children,' said the Captain's voice behind them. 'They think that bad parents are creeps who deserve anything they get. But they think that bad children are really sweet and kind and have just gone astray, and can be brought back to their senses with kindness. That's why Pete bought you takeaways and sang you bedtime songs.'

There was a pause as this shocking idea sank in.

'Weird!' said Cassian.

'Half-baked!' said Primrose.

'Naive!' said Daisy. 'Lesson one at the Nanny Academy teaches nannies that all children are evil, wicked, mean and nasty.'

'So evil, wicked, mean and nasty is what they get,' said Cassian.

'It would be unkind to disappoint them,' said Primrose.

'Actively rude,' said Daisy.

'Hostile, even,' said Cassian.

'I see,' said the Captain. 'Come up to the bridge.'

On the bridge, they sat on a chintz helmsman's suite. Daisy thought the Captain looked sad. 'Cheer up,' she said, brightly. 'We were all children once, you know. Things get better.'

The Captain filed a long red nail, shaking her head sadly. 'It's not that,' she said.

'So what is it?' said Cassian. He had spent all day re-grinding a condenser valve, just one of the fantastic things there were to do in the *Kleptomanic*'s engine room. The shadow on the Captain's lovely face was an astonishment to him. How could anyone be unhappy in this paradise of oil and steel?

'You don't want to know,' said the Captain.

'We certainly do,' said Primrose. She had spent all day perfecting a recipe for Action Buns, whose ingredients included treacle, gin, and essence of greyhound. She was as much in her element as a croissant in an oven.

Daisy said, 'You are hiding something from us For Our Own Good.' The Captain concentrated extra hard on her nail. 'But we can look after ourselves, thank you very much.'

'You are children,' said the Captain.

'What difference does that make?' said Daisy.

'We resent the imputation,' said Primrose.

'Scandalous,' said Cassian.

'And,' said Daisy, 'you can be quite sure that we know about the Royal Edward, and –' here she groped a little in her mind, seeking half-heard remarks and half-glimpsed traffic items '– white vans.'

Primrose was staring at her with her mild blue eyes. 'Royal Edward,' she said, in a faint, puzzled voice. 'Sure do.'

Cassian was scowling at her under oily brows. 'White vans?' he said, in tones whose bemusement only Daisy could hear. 'Absolutely.'

'And we want the full official story,' said Daisy.

The Captain sighed. 'It's a fair cop,' she said. 'What should I tell you?'

'Everything,' said Daisy. 'Why you dress up as nannies. The lot.'

'Starting from the top,' said Primrose.

'Omitting nothing,' said Cassian.

The Captain sighed again, and glanced at her jewelled Bulgari watch. 'Very well,' she said. 'I have a few moments. But afterwards, I am going to ask you some favours, and I wish you to agree with them. Understood?'

The Darlings nodded. The Captain flung her nail file across the bridge. It stuck in the steering wheel, quivering. 'All right,' she said, 'you asked for it. Are you sitting comfortably? Then I'll begin.'

8

'Well,' said the Captain. 'We are, as you have seen, a ship full of honest burglars, trying to scratch a living in this troublesome world. And it is not easy, let me tell you. Burglars with a vision –'

'Ahem,' said Daisy, sternly.

'Sorry,' said the Captain. 'Where was I?'

'Burglars, not visions,' said Daisy. 'Stick to the point.'

'Ah, yes. We have given up violence, mostly. But it is in our nature to nick stuff. We get into houses, and have it away with the spoons and other valuables. Disguised as nannies.' A curious look came into the Captain's eye – a little sideways, and almost shifty.

'Hardly sporting,' said Daisy.

'Less of that,' said the Captain. 'We nick from the rich, and give to the poor, which is us. And reflect. Only rich families have nannies. And only families who are creepy as well as rich would ever ring up a nanny agency they have never heard of and get a complete stranger round to look after their children while they go out to dinner.'

'Or to Antigua,' said Daisy, grimly.

'Or, as you say, to Antigua. But there is a problem.' The Captain sighed. 'In life one finds so many. My burglars are a trusting bunch of lads and lasses, kind to small children and animals. Most of them are all right at self-defence, and I flatter myself that we have among our number some pretty capable muggers. But they simply cannot believe the stupidity and cruelty of nannies, or the vicious cunning of children who have been brought up by them. They were shocked by your lecture, Daisy.'

'They needed to be,' said Daisy.

'Wet behind the ears,' said Primrose.

'Like babes unborn,' said Cassian.

'It is better to be a naive nanny than no nanny at all,' said the Captain. 'My burglars bring an evening of sweetness and light to children, while robbing their parents. Is that so very wrong?'

'Yes it is,' said Daisy. 'Because nannies without proper training are going to get hurt. Leaving this aside for the moment, what is all this stuff about teddy bears?'

A curious rigidity spread over the Captain's skilfully made-up features. 'Bears?' she said.

'One particular bear,' said Daisy. 'Known, unless I am greatly mistaken, as the Royal Edward.'

'Royal Edward?'

'Whose bum was stolen by Nanny Pete from our nursery. And whose left leg Nanny Huggins removed from the di Costaplenti residence this very day.'

'Ah,' said the Captain, and looked deeply shifty. 'Yes. That Royal Edward. Quite a prize.'

'In what way?'

'A classic. A great classic. The finest ever product of the legendary Bavarian bearsmith Gustav Barbauer, with plush head, agate eyes, and a voice box modelled on the larynx of the great Russian bass Chaliapin. Barbauer was bearsmith by appointment to the crowned heads of Europe during the Golden Age of bears, which is to say the early twentieth century, before the arrival of upstarts like Teddy Ruxpin and Pooh. Russian Archdukes fled into exile clutching their Gustavs. Queen Victoria was never without hers till the day she died. Edward VIII's only quarrel with Mrs Simpson was nothing to do with his abdication of the crown of England. It was about who got to kiss his Gustav and push its tummy so it said, "*Gute Nacht*, your royal highness". The only Gustav ever to come on the open market, known as the Royal Edward, arrived by dubious means after the abolition of the Icelandic monarchy. A revolutionary plot, by all accounts; the bear was stolen, sold for three shiploads of dried cod to an unscrupulous middleman, and turned up at a LORP tombola in Happy Valley –'

'Meaning what?' said Daisy.

'I beg your pardon? Oh. LORP is a self-help organization founded to help people come to terms with massive personal wealth. It stands for the League of Rich People. A tombola is a sort of lottery.'

'But why is the bear in bits?'

The Captain gave the Darlings a sad, beautiful smile. 'Because rich people are bad losers. There was a frightful battle when the winner was announced. When the dust settled, the Royal Edward had been torn into seven pieces, and the people with the bits had jumped out of the windows and sprinted into the night, or anyway as far as their limousines.'

'How extraordinarily silly,' said Daisy.

'Quite so,' said the Captain. 'But the only person sillier than the last rich person you met is the next rich person you meet, I always find. Anyway, I regard this as a great tragedy. And I have made it my mission in life to pinch back the bear bits, and return them to their rightful owner.'

'This Iceland bloke.'

'His Serene and Royal Highness the Crown Prince Beowulf of Iceland, Holder of the Order of the Codfish and Volcano First Class, M.Sc. (Marine Engineering) Reykjavik.'

'I see,' said all three children, though frankly, they did not. 'Easy as that, then. Nothing in it for you.'

'Well,' said the Captain.

'Well what?'

'This is indeed the most valuable bear in the world. Smoothby's the auctioneers would give their eye teeth to get hold of it. Possessing all its pieces would have its . . . rewards.'

'Ah,' said Daisy. 'And are you the only person trying to get hold of it?'

There was an embarrassed silence. 'Not exactly,' said the Captain, finally.

'Hence the white van,' said Daisy.

It worked a treat. The Captain's mouth fell open. 'What do you know about the white van?' she said.

'What you are going to tell us.'

The Captain shook her head wearily. 'All right,' she said. 'I can see you're not the sort of people one can hide things from. The fact of the matter is, they want the Edward too.'

'But who are they?'

'White Van Dan,' said the Captain. 'And Hilda the Builder. And the Firm.'

'Who?'

'It started a year ago. We were happy, then. We'd just started AAA Aardvark. The boys and girls loved the dressing up, and we were just knocking off knick-knacks, you know. Then all of a sudden we heard that after we had, ahem, finished at a premises someone would come along and tear out a side wall and move in with a JCB and not so much knock off knick-knacks as knacker the gaff. Not a brick left standing on brick,' said the Captain. 'Apparently they used to go round doing building work, and pinching the silver. Then they started to flatten the houses with some huge machines they built, and pick the swag out of the rubble, and get the contract to rebuild the houses, and very badly they do it too, because all their machinery's breaking down, and they don't know how to mend it so it works. Then just at the wrong moment they heard about the Edward and they started following us around, getting bits of it. Any minute now, people will be blaming us for their burglaries.'

Primrose said, 'You mean they knock down the house to get at the stuff inside?'

'Go and have a look at what's left of One, Avenue Marshal Posh.'

'No, thank you,' said Cassian. 'We much prefer it here.'

'Dear child,' said the Captain. 'Have a cigar. No? Ah, well. So anyway our name is mud.'

'And what about the police?' said Daisy.

'Who?'

'The filth,' said Cassian.

'The fuzz, the cuffies, the Old Bill,' said Primrose. 'The long arm of the law, the busies. The boys in blue.'

'Oh I see,' said the Captain. 'That lot couldn't find a boiled egg on a billiards table, do me a favour. But really business is terrible, you wouldn't believe.'

'Hmm,' said Daisy. 'Quite. How many bits of the Edward have they got?'

'One,' said the Captain. 'The right arm.'

'Well? You've got three, haven't you?'

'Couldn't you copy one?'

'No,' said the Captain. 'It wouldn't smell right.'

'Smell?'

'Experts are experts,' said the Captain, and assumed an expression of such distress that even Daisy could not bring herself to probe further.

'So you've got to get the arm back, and steal the rest of the bear.'

'Yes. Three more bits.'

'And you know who's got them?'

'We do.'

'And do the White Van Mob?'

'Not as far as I know. We think it works this way. Whenever the Jag goes out with the duty nanny, a builder spots them and passes the word –'

'Any builder?'

'They're all in it. Heard of the Freemasons? It's a

sort of secret society. Masons, builders, same difference. So out comes the white van, extra-large size,
a sort of mobile garage, really, with digger, dumper
and 'dozer. And down comes the house. They're
usually too late, of course; did you ever hear of
a builder arriving on time? And their van keeps
breaking down. But that doesn't stop 'em trying.'

'So how did they get the arm?' said Daisy.

'Nanny ex-navy. Charming chap, used to be a
pirate. Got followed to a job by the white van. Pure
coincidence. The builders pulled the arm from the
ruins by sheer unscrupulous sitework.'

Daisy stood up. 'Thank you, Captain,' she said.
'You have given us much to ponder.'

'*Il n'y a pas de quoi*,' said the Captain, with old-
world courtesy. 'Daisy, could we do some nanny tests
to make sure the chaps are up to scratch? In about
half an hour?'

'Willingly,' said Daisy. The Captain left.

There was a silence.

Naturally, it was Daisy who spoke first. 'That was
a load of cobblers,' she said.

'Codswallop,' said Primrose.

'Sheer 100 per cent disinformation,' said Cassian.

'Most of it, anyway,' said Daisy. 'We have here a

Captain of Burglars who is stealing the parts of a royal bear in order to reassemble it for the delight of an ex-crowned head of Europe. A pretty minor ex-crowned head, I may say, in no position to do her a favour. Well?'

'Tell it to the marines!' said Primrose.

'Pshaw!' said Cassian.

'And White Van Dan and the builders,' said Daisy. 'They may exist. But why would they want a bear?'

'Rubbish,' said Primrose.

'Bizarrely hard to credit,' said Cassian, scowling.

'And the bear's arm –'

'Which cannot be forged because of the wrong pong –'

'Bit strong!' said Cassian. 'I mean, what does it matter what it smells like?'

'Quite. And finally,' said Daisy, 'how does she know about this LORP tombola? I mean, unless she was there?'

'And her a career burglar,' said Primrose.

'Highly improbable,' said Cassian. He frowned, as far as it was possible to tell. 'And yet . . .'

'Yes?' said Daisy.

'Spit it out,' said Primrose.

'I know it sounds silly. But, you know, I sort of . . . trust her.'

Another silence, deeply shocked and rather embarrassed. Finally, Primrose said, 'Know what you mean.'

Daisy sniffed, and folded her lips. But she knew what Cassian meant, too. There was something about this Captain.

'And another thing,' said Cassian. 'The Chief Engineer's got a bear's head in his control room.'

More silence, devoted to the adjusting of ideas.

Finally Daisy stuck her chin in the air, expressing impatience. 'Can't be doing with all this humbug and thinking and so on,' she said. 'We watch and wait and speak when spoken to and be a bit seen and not at all heard.'

The other two nodded, soothed by this high-grade nanny talk.

'And when the time is ripe,' said Daisy, 'we pounce.'

'What on?' said Primrose.

'Stop asking stupid questions,' said Daisy. 'Now. Time for the nanny test. Gather your equipment, and let's save some lives.'

*

The tests were over by teatime. The Captain came in. 'You have done marvellously well,' she said. 'I am sure it must have been very taxing. Did any of them pass?'

'Two,' said Daisy. 'Plenty of doubtfuls and improvers. But only two certainties, which is to say Pete Fryer and Giant Luggage. Though Giant Luggage, well . . .'

'Quite,' said the Captain, raising her hands.

'The handle,' said Daisy. 'The size. The hat is not worn properly because of the handle. The size is large.'

'Beautifully put,' said the Captain.

Daisy folded her lips. 'I always do say you should call a spade a spade,' she said.

The Captain frowned. 'Daisy,' she said, 'a personal question. But . . . do you ever feel you might be *turning into* a nanny?'

'Heaven forbid!' cried Daisy.

'Yes,' said Primrose. 'We do. We can see it.'

'How dare you!' cried Daisy. 'You can both go to bed without your –'

'See?' said Cassian.

Daisy felt suddenly exhausted. She leaned against the Captain, who smoothed her hair. 'There, there,' said the Captain. 'These are powerful forces, and we tamper with them at our peril.'

At that moment there threaded among the late-afternoon sunbeams the silvery tinkle of the AAA Aardvark Nanny Line.

The Captain made a gesture. Daisy glided swiftly to the bridge. Pete Fryer was there, receiver to ear. 'Hold on a minute, ta, modom,' he said, and handed the telephone to Daisy.

'Kin ai hep yew?' said Daisy.

The person on the other end was sneezing. 'Sorry,' said a man's voice. 'Guitar string up my nose.'

'How painful,' said Daisy, with authentic nanny coldness. 'Hau kin ai hep yew?'

'Nanny needed,' said the voice. ''Ullo? Who am I talking to?'

'AAA Aardvark Childminding and Security,' said Daisy. 'Just like you were before.'

'Nice one,' said the voice. 'Listen, man, I can't find anyone. I was wondering if you could maybe get round here and, like, find someone?'

'Someone?'

'Like, the kids?'

'Are they lost?'

'Mislaid. Yeah, orright, lost.'

'The address?'

'Stratocaster Hall, Oncebitten Golf Club.'

'And the name?'

'Eric Thrashmettle. Prolly heard of me. Listen, I got to go out now. Key's under mat, right?'

'Thank you,' said Daisy, making a note. 'I shall just check.'

'Thrashmettle?' hissed the Captain, at her ear. 'Eric? They were at the bear tombola. Get the job.'

'Ai am happy to say,' said Daisy, 'that we will be there in fifteen minutes.'

'Who's that?'

'Still AAA Aardvark.'

'Oh. Yeah. Too much.' The telephone went down.

There was the usual palaver. Bells rang, booted feet thundered on steel staircases, and the Captain's voice on the tannoy said in a flat, metallic voice, 'Duty nanny to the Jag deck.' Actually, the levels of noise were unnecessary, now that the duty nannies were down to two. But (as the Captain pointed out) burglars love a bit of an emergency, or they would not have become burglars in the first place.

'What do you think?' said Daisy to her brother and sister as she charged up her stun gun in the suite.

'Weird,' said Cassian.

'Something stinks,' said Primrose.

'So we take a long, hard look,' said Daisy. 'And we report back.'

'Later,' said Primrose.

'Later.'

'Later.'

And there were Daisy and Nanny Pete, in the Jag, speeding towards Stratocaster Hall.

Cassian's heart got steadily lighter as the carpets ran out and the stairs turned to iron and he clomped ever deeper into the *Kleptomanic*'s innards; assuming, that is, that he had a heart. He himself was not sure. There was something in his chest that ticked away, and seemed at bad times to be made of lead, and at less bad times to be made of something lighter, aluminium maybe. Whether or not it was a heart he could not say, and did not, frankly, give a monkey's –

I beg your pardon. It is traditional to start new sections of a book in an arty fashion, setting the scene and giving the reader an idea of the mood of the person whose actions you are about to describe. The message here has got nothing to do with innards or ball-bearings. The fact was that as Cassian got closer to the engine rooms, he felt happier, because engines were his favourite thing.

Clear?

Good.

On we go.

Giant Luggage was on the stokehold floor. He was dressed in nanny gear, now much stained with coal dust, and shovelling coal into a boiler. Cassian had just about worked out which boilers ran which engines. He had also crawled around the engines themselves, which seemed to him to be in an excellent state of maintenance and repair. Cassian hated to see a machine lie idle. He said to Giant Luggage, 'Shall we turn her over?'

Giant Luggage said, 'Hur, hur,' which was just about all he ever said. There was a small scurry on the pile of coal, and Nosey Clanger appeared. 'Can't be done,' he said.

'But surely –'

'Fwitchgearf in the Chief'f control room,' said Nosey. 'E'f on ftrike.'

'Pay?' said Cassian. 'Conditions? What's his problem?'

'Unhappy man,' said Nosey. 'Ever finfe he loft hif –'

'AIEEE!' cried a great voice from the control room. The door flew open. The Chief Engineer stood there, eyes rolling wildly. He was dressed in a uniform covered in gold braid, with a spiked helmet on his head. He was sucking his thumb.

'Fee?' said Nosey.

'Not to touch nuffink,' shrieked the Chief, round his thumb. '*Nuffink.*'

Cassian had a brief but powerful urge to smack the Chief's bottom and send him to his room to eat dry bread and water. Then he realized that that was a bit of leakage from Daisy. Besides, the Chief was three times his size. So he decided to play the never-failing Interested Child card. 'Gosh,' he said. 'What a super uniform. I am really interested in triple expansion condensing steam engines. I have got a fantastic collection of Ships of the World bubblegum cards and my heart's desire is to see a Crombie and Wychbold 5.01 actually working.'

The Chief took his thumb out of his mouth and

allowed his mad brown eyes to rest on eager wee Cassian. 'Insect,' he said.

'No, really, actually,' said Cassian. 'If I am not mistaken this is the 5.01 with the modulating pitch-valve, and –'

'Silence!' cried the Chief loudly. 'NOBODY TOUCHES THE ENGINES BUT ME NOT EVEN WITH THEIR EYES AND IF YOU TALK TO ME ANY MORE I WILL HOLD MY BREATH TILL I AM DEAD AND THEN YOU WILL BE SORRY.'

'Ah,' said Cassian. This large person seemed to be malfunctioning in some way, but it was beyond his skill to work out how. If he had been a machine, it would have been different, of course. Well, perhaps Primrose could make one of her special mixtures to calm him down. Better still, Daisy could perhaps come and give him a good talking to.

But Primrose was in the kitchens, doing research on the ideal pizza. And Daisy was far away, doing her nanny duty . . .

Later, thought Cassian. Meanwhile, it would be just as well to familiarize himself with the machinery. There was probably some switch gear in the world that Cassian was unable to short-circuit, but he had not yet come across it. Research, was what was needed. Research and preparation.

Cheered, he clambered up an iron ladder and disappeared into the belly of the machine.

The Jag hurtled through the night. Neither of its bowler-hatted occupants noticed a man high on a scaffolding drinking tea and swinging his feet. The man stuffed his copy of the *Daily Nudes* into the pocket of his overalls, climbed into a van, and accelerated after the Jag. As he drove, he unhooked a microphone. 'Target in sight,' he said.

Silence.

'I said, "target in sight." '

'Who are you calling a git?' said a furious voice.

'Target. As in black Jag.'

'Why didn't you say so?' said the voice.

'I did.'

'Dint.'

'Did.'

'Shut up and follow them,' said the voice. 'Note their destination. We'll send a back-up team.'

'Oh, yeah, right,' said the man in the van, continuing the pursuit. Builders always said they were going to turn up, but they hardly ever did. He would believe it when he saw it.

Stratocaster Hall seemed to be somewhere in the suburbs. The buildings were thinning out, the headlights freezing owls and rabbits in their white cones. Daisy, in the passenger seat, sniffed disapprovingly.

'Nice carving,' said Pete.

'I beg your pardon?'

'Carving knife, wildlife,' said Pete Fryer, bowler brim low over the steering wheel.

'Wild animals are disorderly and wrong. A disgrace, in fact.'

'I quite like them, myself,' said Nanny Pete.

'Suitable animals for children are tortoises and guinea pigs,' said Daisy.

'Noted,' said Nanny Pete, sneaking a glance

at his young companion's resolute nanny profile.

'And by the way,' said Daisy, introducing a question the Captain had not chosen to touch on. 'What's wrong with the Chief Engineer?'

'Chief?' said Nanny Pete. 'Highly strung, like so many engineers. A man with a good heart, sorely wounded by life, haunted by a deep sense of personal betrayal.'

'What *are* you talking about?' said Daisy, full of nanny impatience.

'He had a loss,' said Pete. 'Feels it deeply, very deeply indeed. He thinks the world has done him a great wrong – here we are!'

He stamped his nanny brogue on the brake. The Jag went into a tearing skid, and shot between a pair of white marble pillars with statues on top. The lights glanced over a bronze plaque that said Oncebitten Private Estate and Golf Course – The Rich and Famous Only – No Hawkers No Circulars No Rubbish. A security guard bowed deeply. A long white road snaked through groves of astonishingly rare trees. Huge houses stood back from the road, buried in priceless shrubberies.

Behind the Jag, a small van shot through the gates, shouted, 'Builders!' to the security guard, gave him two fingers, and began to crawl after the distant red eyes of the nannies' rear lights.

'Rock and roll heaven,' said Nanny Pete. 'Plus the odd dictator. The very odd dictator, actually. Bloke called Ponque. Reckons it's his job to conquer the world, using poultry instead of soldiers. Oi, oi. Wozzis, then?'

A curious figure had slouched out of a driveway ahead. It had very long hair and a face the colour of lard. It was wearing a singlet, flared trousers, a belt with a huge Celtic buckle, snakeskin boots and dark glasses. Having come out of the driveway, it turned sharp right, walked into a tree and apologized. Then it marched out in front of the Jag.

Nanny Pete brogued the brakes. The Jag stopped, just touching the flares of the long-haired person's trousers. 'Goodness,' said Daisy. 'It's Death Eric.'

'Death who?' said Nanny Pete.

'Eric Thrashmettle,' said Daisy. 'Something of an idol of my brother Cassian, though of course I think he is too silly for words.' She rolled down the window. 'Mr Thrashmettle!' she cried, in a stern nanny voice. 'We have arrived to care for your children!'

'What children?' said Death Eric.

'Yours.'

'Oh,' said the rock-and-roll hero. 'Yeah. I've lost 'em.'

'We are terribly sorry to hear that.'

'Yeah,' said Death Eric. 'We was, like, watching TV and when the programme finished I was, like, where the bleep are they? and I was, like, I dunno, do I? So I ring the agency.'

'And here we are!' cried Daisy, brightly. 'So let us find your children, shall we, and put your mind at rest!'

'This way,' said the long-haired man, walking into a rhododendron.

'Take off your dark glasses, why don't you?' said Daisy.

'Wha?'

'Lose the shades,' said Nanny Pete.

'Oh.' Death Eric took off his glasses and stood blinking in the light of the street lamp. 'Yeah.'

'Now then.'

'Leave the wheels,' said Death Eric. 'C'mon.' He led them down the drive, and up to the front of a large, dark house. He turned the front door-handle. 'Locked out,' he said.

'Where are your keys?'

'Dunno.'

'Ahem,' said Nanny Pete discreetly. 'If I might be permitted?' He fumbled a moment with the lock. The door swung open. A burglar alarm began to shriek.

'Far out!' said Death Eric, tapping a snakeskin toe to the alarm's infectious rhythm.

Nanny Pete fumbled with the burglar alarm, which stopped. Death Eric nodded and grinned. 'OK,' he said. 'Find the kids, right? I'll be watching TV.' He plonked himself down in a huge chair in the hall and groped for the remote. Yatter, yatter, yatter, went the TV. Eric's jaw dropped. His eyes goggled. He became Elsewhere.

The nannies searched the house.

It was, in Daisy's view, an odd house for a rock star. There were a lot of military uniforms and photographs of guns and bombs. There were various golden trinkets and a few loose jewels, which Pete swept into his nanny case. But there seemed to be no nursery. And no children. And absolutely no limb of the Royal Edward. It was all (thought Daisy, tutting) most peculiar.

So downstairs they went. The TV was still blaring away in the hall, Death Eric slumped in the mighty lounger, his lips moving as he talked along with a *Teletubbies* repeat. Nanny Pete said, 'Blowed if I understand.'

'Me neither,' said Daisy, with a callous disregard for grammar. 'Is something wrong?'

For Nanny Pete was gazing at a picture on the wall.

It was a big picture, in a heavy gold frame. It was a picture of a man in military uniform crusted with gold. He was standing on a rock, saluting, an odd salute, right arm extended, three fingers in the air, halfway between the Nazis and the Scouts. In front of the rock was a large field. The field was full of chickens. They seemed to be listening to a speech the man was making.

'Poultry,' said Nanny Pete, pensively. There was a pause. Then he bellowed, 'Mister Thrashmettle?'

'Yur,' said Mr Thrashmettle, absently.

'Are you sure this is your house?'

'Wodjermean?' said Death Eric, not moving his eyes from the screen.

Briskly, Daisy hauled the mains lead out of the wall.

'Oi!' cried Death Eric, gazing around him wildly. Then, 'What are we doin' here?'

'You may well ask,' said Daisy.

'In the house of Erminegildo Ponque, the Odd Dictator,' said Nanny Pete. 'And Mr Thrashmettle lives –'

'I live next door!' said Death Eric. 'Wodjew playin' at?'

They tumbled on to the front steps. 'Over, like, here,' he said, and began crashing through the shrubbery.

Daisy frowned. Behind the sound of splintering rhododendrons there seemed to be a distant grind of very big engines.

Death Eric patted his pockets. 'No keys,' he said.

'They're under the mat,' said Daisy.

'Howdja know that?'

'You told me.'

But Eric's soupy mind was already far away. He opened the front door, walked across the marble-floored hall and into a room with a blood-red shag-pile carpet and a conversation pit, in which conversation would not have been audible, because of the TV, which was turned up all the way. 'They was in here!' bellowed Death Eric.

'Who?'

'The kids.'

'You mean the kids on the sofa over there?'

'Yeah.' Death Eric's face broke into a muddy grin of relief.

Daisy found the remote and turned off the TV. Both the children turned round and started screaming at her to turn it back on. 'SILENCE!' she cried.

Their little jaws dropped. Their little eyes widened. Nobody had ever talked to them like that before.

'Your poor papa lost you,' said Daisy. Far above in the house, she could hear bumping noises. That would be Pete Fryer, searching for bits of Royal Edward.

''Course he did,' said the elder of the two children, a fat little brute with cross eyes and a button nose. 'He forgot to look.'

'Look where?'

'To his left.'

'You were on the left?' said Death Eric. 'You normally like sit on the right.'

'Not this time,' said the boy, who seemed to be the elder of the two children. 'Silly old hippie.' He began to play an imaginary Fender, sticking out his tongue.

'Heir guitar,' said Death Eric, shaking his head

wearily. 'Comes of being brought up by roadies.'

'Where's their mother, for goodness' sake?'

'California,' said Death Eric. 'Or maybe Rome. Who can tell?'

'Dearie me,' said Daisy, briskly. The noises upstairs were continuing. And there was another noise; a large, mechanical noise, from outside. 'Well, children. Nanny will burn you some nice custard, and then it's off to bed with –'

The noise outside was so loud that she could not finish the sentence. And she did not get a chance to try again, because at that moment, the wall of the room bulged inwards and collapsed and someone drove a bulldozer into the conversation pit. It sat there, roaring and twitching.

'Wow,' said Death Eric.

'Dearie me!' said Daisy.

Nanny Pete's head appeared round the door. 'Scarper!' he cried.

Suddenly the room was full of dust and rubble and noise.

And builders: dozens of builders.

Daisy grabbed a child in each hand, and scarpered through the hole in the wall and into the night.

'This way!' cried Pete from the darkness ahead.

The night was full of engines, it seemed. Daisy started to ask the first of sixty questions. But she did not have the breath, and besides, it took all her strength to keep hold of the sticky little hands in hers. They were trying to get away, but she hung on for dear life. 'On!' cried Nanny Pete.

'Coming!' she cried, dragging her little charges through the roaring night.

'Aargh!' cried Death Eric, who seemed to be crashing around in the rhododendrons. There was the sound of a body hitting a tree, and his voice said, 'Sorry, man.' Behind them, there was a slipping roar, and a huge SPROINGG! 'Me guitar collection!' cried Eric. *Whap*, went another tree trunk. 'Sorry, man,' said Eric.

Then something was gleaming faintly in the light of the street lamps, and the air smelt of hot oil, and there was the Jag, waiting.

'In!' cried Pete.

They piled in. The Jag roared away. Something huge and white loomed in the headlights: something the size of an articulated lorry. Bigger than a lorry.

'Bleeding white van,' said Pete.

It was indeed a white van. A huge white van, doors open, great ramps down, the bonnet open, two ladders propped against it. 'It's broken down!' cried Daisy.

'More 'n likely,' said Pete. 'Now, then, Death, where to?'

'They knocked the house down,' said Daisy, dazed.

'We got plenty more,' said Death Eric.

'Masses,' said his kids.

So the nannies dropped them off at their penthouse flat in the middle of town, and returned to the *Kleptomanic*.

'Did you get it?' said Daisy, in the cargo net.

'Jewels,' said Pete. 'Nice little mandolin, cufflinks, nose rings –'

'The right leg of the Royal Edward?'

There was a short but well-filled silence. 'Not as such,' said Nanny Pete.

'So the white van people have.'

Pete sighed. 'More than likely,' he said.

'Not a disaster, though,' said Daisy.

'That's what you think,' said Pete.

After that, the silence went on and on. Finally, Daisy said, 'What is it about the Royal Edward?'

'Valuable bear.'

That old thing again.

*

Primrose was having a brilliantly experimental time in the kitchen. She had spent the afternoon with a kind lady called Sophie Nickit, working on a recipe for Sleepy Cake. Sophie was mixing away at a great bowl full of soothing blue mixture, and chattering as she worked. 'Yes, dear,' she said, batting her queen-sized lashes. 'I used to be a vamp and a roller.'

'Papa and Secretary Mummy have got a Roller,' said Primrose. 'Do you think blue's the right colour?'

'Bit bright,' said Sophie. 'Not that kind of roller. I used to meet chaps and pinch their wallets. Then I thought I'd run away to sea, I mean it's normally chaps do that, but why shouldn't us girls? Do you think pink would be better?'

'You bet,' said Primrose. Sophie sighed, threw away the mixture, and started again, using powdered pink sleep-moth instead of blue. 'What do you mean, run away to sea?'

'This is a ship, you know.'

Primrose nodded, stirring. Actually she had just about forgotten. For her the *Kleptomanic* was kitchen heaven, full of extremely interesting people who let you follow up Lines of Culinary Enquiry. 'But why,' she said, 'have you not sailed away already?'

'Ask the Chief Engineer.'

'Wha?'

'I mean, we're not ready yet.' Sophie suddenly looked oddly confused, as if she had been caught with her hand on a vampee's wallet.

'Ah,' said Primrose, and changed the subject. When they tried the Sleepy Cake on the ship's hamster, the chubby rodent's wheel came to an immediate standstill, and it fell plunk to the cage floor.

But despite her enthusiasm for cookery, Primrose found it hard to keep her mind on the slumber of experimental animals. It was on other things, deeper and darker.

That evening, the little Darlings ate supper in the suite. It was another delicious repast, featuring lobster cocktail, toad-in-the-hole with tinned tomatoes, and five colours of yoghurt with maple syrup. Normally, these excellent provisions would have inspired a merry buzz of conversation. Tonight, there was only a preoccupied silence.

'So,' said Daisy. 'They're trying to get all the bits of the bear, but they haven't.'

'What I do not understand,' said Primrose, 'is why

they haven't just started up the ship and sailed away somewhere interesting.'

'Most disappointing,' said Cassian. 'She's in first-class mechanical order, of course.'

'Which is more than can be said for the white van,' said Daisy.

There was a silence.

Finally, Primrose said, 'In the Chief Engineer's room. In that glass case with the eagle thing on top of it, that first time we went down there. What did it look like to you?'

'Bear's head,' said Cassian.

'On a crimson velvet cushion,' said Daisy.

'Yup.'

A bit more silence. 'Funny looking chap, the Chief Engineer,' said Daisy. 'Distinctive.'

The three of them summoned up a picture in their minds; a picture of a face with a nose 10 centimetres long, a drooping lower lip, and wildly rotating chestnut-coloured eyes under the peak of his blue and gold spiked hat.

'Tell you what,' said Cassian. 'Let's go and have a look at a couple of things in the ship's library.'

'But it is way past our bedtime,' said Daisy.

'Daisy!'

Off to the library they went.

They sat round a leather-topped table, coughing in the clouds of dust that rose from the volumes of *Burke's Steerage*, the famous reference book of the world's fallen aristocracy. They leafed. They stopped leafing, and read. Daisy made a note. Then out of the library they trooped, on to the grand staircase.

'To the bridge,' said Cassian.

'Hist!' said Daisy, raising a finger.

Through the quiet spaces of the ship there flowed a stream of music. The Darlings followed that stream to its source. They found themselves in the shadows on the fringes of the ballroom. A single spotlight shone on the grand piano on the stage. At the piano sat the Captain in her red dress, transported.

The music wound to its end. The Darling children stepped forward as one child.

'Why!' said the Captain, with a brilliant smile. 'You were listening. How sweet!'

'Not sweet,' said Daisy, over whom a nanny-like hardness had once again swept. 'Not listening. Waiting.'

'Ah,' said the Captain, closing the piano lid. 'What for?'

'Here,' said Daisy. Cassian pushed a chair to the

piano. Daisy climbed on to it. Primrose handed her the volume of the *Encyclopaedia Kleptomanica* they had brought from the library. Daisy flopped the book open. Dust rose. 'And what does this say?' said the Captain, putting a long red fingernail on the place on the page where it said 'For Reference Only – Not to be Removed.'

'Nicked it, dint we,' said Primrose.

'Well *done*,' said the Captain, beaming.

'Look at this,' said Cassian.

They all looked, in the earnest way people do look when they know what they are going to see because they have seen it already.

There was a picture of a man and a woman. Both of them were wearing crowns, and sitting on thrones made of some kind of dark rock, possibly volcanic. They wore the ribbons of Orders, on which were pinned silver reproductions of large fish. In the background, a volcano seemed to be erupting. The faces were long and blobby. The noses were 10 centimetres long. The eyes, which were chestnut-coloured, were looking in four different directions, as if the photographer had caught them in mid-whirl.

'Remind you of anyone?' said Cassian.

'Weeell . . .' said the Captain.

'Clue,' said Daisy. 'Somewhere under your feet.'

'Sulking,' said Primrose. 'Sulking a lot.'

'Er . . .' said the Captain, putting a red nail on her red lower lip.

'Spell it out, Daisy,' said Primrose.

'Your chief engineer,' said Daisy, 'is Crown Prince Beowulf of Iccland. And he is in a terrible sulk because someone has taken away his teddy.'

'And part of this sulk is that he will not start the engines on this ship until someone gives him his teddy back.'

'Which I would be well happy to do having sewed it together with my busy needle,' said Primrose. 'Except that it strikes me that you do not have all the bits, am I right or am I right?'

The Captain gazed upon them fondly, drawing a great rippling arpeggio from the keys. 'Darlings, you are *so* right,' she said. 'And I am *so* proud of you!'

Normally, this kind of talk would have turned the thoughts of the little Darlings towards violence of a subtle but extreme type. But this time, they felt unaccountably happy. They sat smiling like idiots, waiting for the explanation.

'Well,' said the Captain, getting up. 'Way past my bedtime, I think.'

'Er . . .' said Cassian.

'But . . .' said Primrose

Daisy folded her lips. 'You will sit here until you have quite finished telling us everything there is to know!' she cried.

The Captain blinked. Her eyes went glassy. 'Yes, Nanny,' she said. She frowned. 'Goodness. Where am I?'

'Here,' said Cassian.

'Now,' said Primrose.

'Telling us what you know about the Chief Engineer,' said Daisy. 'Like a good girl, who was brought up by a Nanny Who Knew Best.'

'How did you know?' sighed the Captain.

'One presses the button,' said Daisy. 'One watches the victim light up.'

'So shoot,' said Primrose.

The Captain shot.

'All right,' she said. 'But it's not a happy story.'

'Happiness?' said Daisy. 'What would that be?'

'Poor little Darlings,' said the Captain, and began.

'The revolution,' she said. 'A terrible thing, which I shall not begin to describe. Suffice it to say that Crown Prince Beowulf of Iceland escaped an outbreak of civil unrest by running away on a trawler bound for Aberdeen. But when going through his luggage at bedtime after his first dog-watch, he found that his treasured Gustav, the Royal Edward, was missing. Imagine,' said the Captain, 'the horror of this poor, deprived person. His kingdom gone. His icy, fishy, volcanic heritage snatched away from him.

And now his bear Edward – for at the end of it all, Gustavs are only bears, royal or not – snatched away. The bear he had sniffed and dribbled on ever since he had been a tiny baby –'

'Revolting,' said Daisy.

'Sad,' said Primrose.

'But entirely probable,' said Cassian.

'– snatched away from him by the hand of an unrelenting nanny.'

'A nanny?'

'It was the royal nanny who stole it. Seeing, one presumes, her pension going up in smoke as the mob ransacked the palace. Actually,' said the Captain, 'I think that the Iceland situation was what gave me the idea of starting a nicking nanny crew. But that is another story. Any road,' she said. 'The Royal Edward came up as a prize at the LORP's tombola, as you know. Actually, I was there.'

'How was that?' said Cassian, frowning.

'Very nice evening, if you like rich people.'

'He means, how did you come to be there?' said Primrose.

'Someone drove me,' said the Captain.

'Excuse me,' said Daisy, 'but could you give a straight answer to a straight question?'

'No,' said the Captain. 'Anyway. The Edward had been sold to a rich family by the ex-nanny of the royal family of Iceland. The rich family had got bored with it, had a moment of fashionable repentance –'

'What's that?' said Primrose.

'It's like going on a diet or going to a charity ball to help the homeless, all that,' said Daisy. 'Then you feel all right about making a pig of yourself or buying a lot of houses you don't need. Papa and Secretary Mummy do it all the time.'

'They say it's like being reborn,' said the Captain. 'So anyway there was this sort of raffle, and all these rich people loved the Edward, and of course I recognized it instantly, only one of its kind in the world. Then there was a riot, and seven people started to fight over it. I sort of got the head while nobody was looking.'

'But what were you doing at this tombola?'

'Playing the piano,' said the Captain. 'Looking for suitable burglary victims. Anyway, a bit later I found this ship. I tracked the Crown Prince down, because he's an utterly brilliant engineer, thinking he'd be happy to have at least part of his bear, one does so like to spread a little happiness, you know.

So I gave him the head. But it didn't work. Quite the opposite, actually. Every time he looked at it it made him sad and mad, and reminded him of the horror of his exile. So he's decided he won't start the engines until he gets the rest of it back.'

'All of it?'

'All of it.'

'And how much of it have we got?'

'Some of it.'

'But we are missing . . .'

'The arms. The right leg. The torso.'

'Where were they?'

The Captain smiled, the sort of smile a monkey might give you if you stood on its foot. 'There are,' she said, 'certain bits in the possession of . . .'

'White Van Dan,' said three voices at once – belonging (in reverse order of height) to Primrose, Daisy and Cassian.

'And,' said the Captain, 'I expect you would like to know about White Van Dan, too?'

The Darlings smiled at her sweetly. 'We are sitting comfortably. Do please begin, Captain dear.'

'Oi,' said a voice in the shadows. 'No way.'

'Pete,' said the Captain, and it was indeed none other than Nanny Pete Fryer, wearing nanny uniform and a deep scowl of loyalty. 'It is all right. These are clever children, and I must tell them what I know.'

'If you must you must,' said Pete.

'Well,' said the Captain. 'Let me take you back to the tombola that saw the division of the Edward. It was a large room, gracious, with a mighty chandelier, in a house on Avenue Marshal Posh. The myriad flames of the chandelier made rainbows in the jewellery of the assembled plutocrats. There was Bulgari, Yves Saint Laurent, Balenciaga, lashings of Versace, yes, Cassian, I shall get on with it if you stop yawning. And above it all, through a hole in the ceiling, there glittered a single eye. A bloodshot eye, children, an eye made sore by brick dust and fag smoke. The eye, in fact, of the bodger known as White Van Dan, who was patching a roof leak with a copy of the *Girls of the World*, which would stop the water as long as it did not rain, but what did he care?'

'Not a fig,' said Primrose.

'Exactly,' said the Captain. 'He watched the women with their jewels, and the men with their diamond Rolexes. He meant to nick them all. He was not interested in the tombola. As far as he was concerned, the bear was a dusty old freak. He built his machines, and started flattening houses to get at jewels. It was only later, when the machines began to break down, that the Edward became his life's obsession.'

'Why?' said Cassian.

'For no very good reason you may be sure,' said the Captain. 'For a bad one, indeed, and to understand it you have to know where White Van Dan comes from.

'They trace their ancestry to a certain Cesare Bodger, in Renaissance Italy. Cesare built many villas and churches. They all fell down, but Cesare did not care, because he made sure he got the ducats before the collapse. Generation followed generation, but the family traditions did not change. Until the present generation, when the evil genius White Van Dan discovered that instead of actually having to go somewhere and build something before he and his firm got their money, it was just as easy – nay, easier – to attack the houses of his clients with a digger, a dozer, and a dumper, and scratch the loot out of the rubble, then secure the rebuilding contract.' The Captain shuddered delicately. 'A coarse approach, without finesse,' she said, and paused, gazing at scenes that by the look of her face were faraway and painful.

'I do not understand,' said Daisy, 'why such awful villains would be troubling themselves with a teddy bear.'

'Bodger by name, bodger by nature,' said the Captain. 'White Van Dan and Hilda, his mate, designed and built a hugely sophisticated gaff-destroying tool, known as the White Van. At least, they think it's sophisticated. And it is, if your idea of nicking is to flatten gaffs and batter the loot. They are very, very stupid people.'

'There is no excuse for stupidity,' said Daisy.

'Except lack of brains,' added Cassian.

'Quite. Anyway, they made this machine out of low-quality materials and old coat-hangers, so it breaks down. They need an engineer of genius to maintain it and to help build a better one. The only great engineer they know of is our own Beowulf, ex-Crown Prince of Iceland. So they approached him with great blandishments, because they saw in him a chance not only to get their machines mended, but to gain effective control of a North Atlantic island surrounded by luxury-grade cod and studded with excellent volcanoes. They promised him that they would help restore him to the throne of Iceland, and that they would build him a palace there. And most importantly, that they would restore to him the missing parts of the Royal Edward. Naturally they had forgotten who had taken the parts home after the tombola brawl. So they took to following us around in the hope that we would lead them to bear parts.' The Captain looked grim. 'With, I am sorry to say, some success.'

'But you have nearly half the parts. The bum, the left leg, the head –'

'It is the Chief who has the head. He claims that it is now the property of the kingdom of Iceland. Whoever restores unto him the other parts of the bear secures his services. Frankly, I think he longs to get his hands on all that rotten site machinery. He is a real enthusiast.'

'Bravo!' murmured Cassian.

'Fie!' cried Daisy, her hand on her heart. 'So we have only two bear bits out of a possible six. And whoever gets the parts and reassembles the Edward gets the Chief?'

'Exactly so.'

'And whoever loses . . .'

'Never say it!' cried the Captain. 'On the one

hand, our kind and resourceful burglars. On the other, a bunch of builders who hate children and will fail to turn up to build a new loo for their granny if she is stupid enough to pay them in advance. The old, old battle, good against evil.'

'I say,' said Cassian. 'How awfully sporting. Why,' he said, a little later, 'are you all glaring at me like that?'

'We just are,' said the Captain, Primrose and Daisy.

'So what,' said Cassian, somewhat red about the ears, 'are you going to do about it?'

'Good question,' said the Captain. 'There is an answer. But first, we must complete the collection of the bear bits.'

'How many to go?'

'We must assume that we lost one tonight. To recap: we have the bum and the left leg.'

'And they have an arm and a leg.'

'Correct.'

'Goodness me,' said Daisy, whose head was spinning in a slow, whirling manner. 'And what if we wind up even Steven, three each, and neither side wishes to concede?'

'According to the Statutes of Larceny, the side

with the majority of bits has the opportunity to buy the other side's bits for the other side's nominee's weight in loot.'

'And if you have equal numbers?'

'There will be a Challenge.'

'Well, then.'

'But that will not be necessary.'

'How not?'

'Because I know where another arm is.'

'Where?'

'In the house of Cosmo Stuff, Minister for People.'

'Wow,' said Cassian. 'A politician.'

'Exactly so.'

'Our papa knows him,' said Cassian. 'I have seen his cars. Nasty pieces of American junk they are too.'

'Cassian!' said Daisy. 'No emotions here, if you please.'

'Frightfully sorry.'

'But the thing is,' said the Captain, 'we can't just sit around and wait for the Stuffs to ring up, because it might never happen. Of course they're on the nanny blacklist. But the nanny they've got at the moment has done seven years in the SAS, then three for GBH. What she doesn't know about violence and sarcasm is not worth knowing, and she will be hard to shift.'

'One is always anxious to persuade such authorities to pass their knowledge on,' said Daisy, simpering horribly.

'And a nanny is often partial to a cup of tea and a home-made bun,' said Primrose. 'What eh Daise?'

'Nice one, Primrose,' said Daisy. 'Off you go to your kitchens!'

'What is going on?' said the Captain.

'Wait and see,' said Daisy.

The Captain smiled. 'Really, darlings,' she said, 'you are so reassuring!'

There was a man with a pickaxe in a trench, hacking away. He neither knew nor cared what the trench was for. All he knew was that he had been digging it for a week, and that it was a short trench, and he had nearly gone down into the ground as far as the tops of his boots. The man took two more swipes, then leaned on his pick, looking down the street of large suburban houses peeping whitely from among their swimming pools and shrubberies. As he watched, a black Jag hurtled past him, jammed on the anchors, and came to rest outside the gates of a house that looked as if someone had grafted bits of Ancient Rome on to bits of Merrie England.

The man in the trench pulled out a phone, and dialled. 'Dick the Pick,' he said. 'Alert. Alert.' Braced by this exciting event, he spat on his hands, hefted the pick, and took a giant swipe at a cylindrical object running across the trench. There was a hiss and a roar, and a white jet shot 30 metres into the air. 'Water main,' said Dick the Pick, somewhere in his slow head. 'Nice one.' He sat down, took a thermos out of his bag, and poured himself a cup of tea. He felt he deserved it.

Daisy closed the Jag door, straightened her bowler and took the pram out of the boot. There was a bit of a racket coming from down the road, where a small saloon car seemed to be dancing on a large fountain that had suddenly come into being alongside a striped builder's tent. But Daisy in nanny mode had more important things than fountains on her mind. As Nanny Pete drove the Jag away, she began to push the pram slowly down the pavement.

It was three o'clock in the afternoon, an hour at which (Daisy calculated) children would have finished their Afternoon Sleeps whether they liked it or not, and would be on the point of being dragged out for a Nice Walk Before Tea. Sure enough, she had not gone far with her pram when she heard the crunch of brogues on gravel and the whimper of tiny voices. She slowed the beat of her own brogues, and leaned forward, adjusting the pink balaclava that concealed the face of the doll in the pram.

'Mush!' said a powerful, grating voice behind her. 'Git along, ye hounds of hell!' Fixing a sweet smile to her face, Daisy looked over her shoulder. And there were a little girl and a little boy wearing overcoats in regulation pink and blue, with little velvet collars and little white socks. On top of the overcoats were harnesses decorated with sweet bunnies. Holding the reins of the harnesses was a large and terrifying nanny, with a bowler hat pulled far down over her ears, hollow cheeks and a hatchet nose.

'Afternoon, Nanny!' said Nanny Daisy.

'Afternoon, Nanny!' said the nanny with the nose. Then, to the children, 'Giddap, ye miserable sinners.'

'Noooo!' wailed the little children.

'Sprigs of damnation,' said the nanny. 'Didn't finish up their nice lunches. Very very wrong.

Their poor mummy and daddy. Work their fingers to the –'

'Tch, tch,' said Daisy, wagging her own bowler. 'Ingratitude is a shameful thing. So that's you in there, is it?'

'With Sir Cosmo and Lady Stuff,' said the nanny, who seemed to be slightly Scots. 'Ai am Nanny Pierrepoint. And you?'

Daisy simpered. 'I hope through diligent niceness and cruelty to work my way up to your dizzy heights. Nowadays we are at Mrs Cringe's.'

'Ai don't think we know Mrs Cringe.'

'Not entirely suitable,' said Daisy, sniffing. 'But we have hopes.'

Nanny Pierrepoint gave her a nod in which superiority was mixed with respect for the decent ambitions of the younger generation. 'Never give an inch,' she said.

'Just what I always say,' said Daisy. 'Thank you for your excellent advice!'

'Hoot, toot,' said Nanny Pierrepoint. 'We must all start somewhere, I think.'

'Nanny!' said the little girl. 'I need to –'

'Speak when you're spoken to!' snarled Nanny Pierrepoint.

Daisy decided that she had had about all she could stand of this villainous battleaxe. 'Shall we sit down?' she said. 'You could give me some tips. And I have a tiny little basket of tea and cakes.'

'The children do not eat between meals,' said Nanny Pierrepoint.

'Who said anything about children?' said Nanny Daisy.

Nanny Pierrepoint's hand smote her a mighty blow between the shoulder blades. 'That's my gal!' she cried. 'Whoa there, reptiles! Let's sit on this bench!'

They sat. Nanny tethered her charges to a bench leg. Daisy hauled from under the pram a basket covered with a cloth embroidered with fuchsias, larkspur, and (she saw, to her horror) a skull and crossbones. 'Sweet cloth,' said Nanny Pierrepoint. 'Fuchsias, larkspur, and —'

'Tulip bulbs,' said Daisy, hiding the cloth quickly — really, burglars were hard to trust, even with embroidery needles. 'One lump or two?'

'One,' said Nanny, accepting the delicate china cup.

'Cake?' said Daisy, offering a tin of Primrose's sleepy fairy cakes, with pink icing.

'Oo,' said Nanny Pierrepoint, slavering. 'Don't mind if Ai do.' She took a cake and ate it with the ends of her teeth, like a vast, bony squirrel. It vanished in no time.

'Another?' said Daisy.

'Och, I shouldn't really,' said Nanny Pierrepoint, simpering horribly and taking two.

'Us,' whimpered the little boy, stirring at the end of his leash.

'Not suitable,' snapped Nanny Pierrepoint.

Daisy held her breath. Primrose had been quite definite. One cake for a doze. Two for a sound sleep. Three for a two-week holiday in Dreamland . . .

Nanny Pierrepoint's eyes rolled up in her head, and she crashed to the ground like a nasty old tree. Daisy searched her, found her keys, and rolled her into the bushes. Then she untied the poor little children, put the lid on the Sleepy Cake tin, and opened another, full of Primrose's best Archangel Cakes, acknowledged by all lucky enough to consume one as the most delicious things in heaven or earth. 'Well,' said Daisy. 'I'm Nanny Daisy, darlings. So dig in, and then we'll go home.'

'Hooray for Nanny Daisy!' cried the tinies,

punching their little fists in the air. They scoffed the cakes with amazing swiftness. 'Thank you, Nana,' they said, the joy of snacks shining from their poor little eyes.

'Now, then,' said Daisy. 'Off we go, and you can watch TV, if you like.'

'We're not allowed,' said the little boy sadly.

'You are today,' said Daisy. She found she was beaming. It was not something she had done for ages, and it did not hurt her face as much as she had thought it would.

But there was serious stuff on hand, so she un-beamed, and fixed a small, smug nanny smile on her face. She followed the footprints in the gravel round the side of the house, and opened the door marked NURSERY. She shooed the children in, went after them into a small hall full of the smell of boiled cabbage, and headed towards the uncarpeted stairs that wound upwards, presumably towards the nursery floors. She hoped they had a TV in the nursery. People had broken enough promises to the little Darlings to make her very keen on keeping any she made.

A door swung open. Brilliant light streamed into the dingy hall. 'Nanny!' cried a huge, fruity voice.

'Come, and bring the children with you, if you would be so kind, damn you!'

The speaker was a man, with a shiny white smile and a shiny dark suit. His eyes were warm and twinkling, and it seemed to Daisy that he had known her for years. Then she realized that what he was seeing was not Daisy but a nanny, any old nanny, or possibly a voter, any old voter.

'Children!' she trilled. 'Daddy wants you!'

The children went into the hall, mumbling sullenly. They were too young to vote, and therefore expected no mercy. 'Here we are!' cried the daddy. 'My little ones! Torquil and Nevada!'

'Utah!' cried the little girl.

'Ha, ha!' laughed the daddy, catching the little ones by the hands and spinning them to face a man with a TV camera. 'Yes, I am passionately attached to my children. I think it is so important. Education begins at home. Speak to me in Latin, Torquil!'

'No,' said Torquil, sticking out a lower lip like a church doorstep.

'Brilliant!' cried the daddy.

'And where is Lady Stuff?' said the man beside the camera.

'Shopping,' said the daddy. 'Enjoying the fruits of my party's splendid economic revolution!'

Utah burst into tears. 'I WANT MY MUMMY,' she howled. 'SHE WENT OFF WITH THE MAN WHO TEACHES HER HORSE-RIDING AND SHE SAID SHE IS NEVER COMING BACK. I WANT MY—'

'Ha, ha!' chortled the daddy heartily. 'Kids, eh?' Then, in a lower voice, 'Lose 'em.'

'Where's their TV?' said Daisy, in a low hiss. 'And the left arm of the Royal Edward? They'd like to play with it.'

The political smile turned grim and stretched. 'Do your job,' he said.

'I'll argue.'

'You're sacked.'

'Later I'm sacked.' Daisy drew breath, turned to the camera, and opened her mouth.

'Noooo,' said the daddy. 'In there.' He pointed to a door. There was the noise of engines in the drive. The smile flicked back on to his face, and he turned to the camera. 'And here come a few neighbours, to tell me how much they love me and how they admire what I am doing for this great country of ours. A happy country is made of happy homes!'

Daisy shepherded the children through the door. There was an enormous TV, and a huge buttoned-leather sofa. She turned on the TV.

'What's that?' said Torquil.

'Cartoons, dear.'

'What's cartoons?' said Utah.

'That is.'

The children nodded, attempting to grasp this brand-new idea. Daisy found them some chocolates, poured them Cokes from the drinks tray, and looked about her. Her heart beat once, hard, under her apron. High on the wine-red wall was a polished shield. On the shield was the left arm of the Royal Edward.

Marvellous.

Outside the window the roaring of engines had grown louder. The neighbours, no doubt, popping round to admire Sir Cosmo Stuff's teeth and achievements.

The sound became a noise. It got louder. It turned into an ear-splitting roar. Daisy peeped out of the door, just in time to see a bulldozer come through the closed front door and grind to a halt in the hall.

'Aiee!' cried Sir Cosmo, turning white with terror. He tried to run away, but he fainted first.

The cameraman kept right on filming.

Daisy shinned up a set of bookcases and seized the shield with the arm. The tinies were clutching each other like the Babes on the Sofa. Normally, Daisy would have ignored the little brutes. But since being kidnapped by burglars, she had come to realize that kindness was a Good Thing, within reason. So she said, 'Who looks after you when Nanny Pierrepoint has been drinking gin?'

'Nelly.'

'Where's Nelly?'

'In her room. Knitting stuff. Will you take us there? We're frightened.'

Daisy scowled at the infants. There was a perfectly good window in this room, looking out on a nice dark shrubbery into which it would be easy to disappear. But even as she imagined disappearing, a face rose before her eyes: the face of the Captain, brimming over with kindness. Stop it, now, Daisy told herself. Be hard, be definite – but she found that there was a little hand in each of her hands. 'Come on,' she heard herself saying. 'We'll find Nelly, then.' And leaving the arm propped on the sofa, she dragged the little people across a hall full of noise and dust into the smelly back regions of the house, where they collided with a nice-looking girl with pink cheeks.

'Nelly!' shrieked the munchkins. Nelly folded them in a sickening hug. Elsewhere in the house, a wall crumbled with a roar.

'Bye!' cried Daisy, and rushed back into the hall. It seemed to be raining chandeliers. Thank you, nanny hat, she thought, as a blizzard of crystals rattled on her head. The bulldozer was halfway up the stairs. The cameraman was looking at the place where his camera had been, and no longer was. *Nicked*, thought Daisy. The wall of the TV room seemed to have vanished. She ran through it, to pick up the arm from the sofa . . .

The arm had gone.

She stood there with her mouth open.

She knew what had happened.

While she had been softly handing saucepan lids over to loving Nelly, the arm of the Royal Edward had fallen into the hands of White Van Dan.

Well, she would take it back.

Settling her bowler hat firmly on her head, she started back towards the dozer.

That was when the digger bucket came through the wall.

It was a miracle, really.

The bucket swiped the sofa. The sofa swiped Daisy. As if biffed by a huge leather boxing-glove, she sailed out of the window. She hit the ground, rolled, and was on her feet immediately. When she looked at the house, she saw clouds of dust and gaping holes. As she watched, the hall collapsed on itself with a roar.

There was no sense going back in there. She had failed. Wearily, Daisy began to trudge back towards the Jag, which was rolling down the street towards her.

She was miserable.

The White Van Mob now possessed more of the Royal Edward than the nanny burglars, and there was only the torso to go. Daisy caught herself shuddering to think how disappointed everyone would be. It was a most unusual sensation.

And now she came to think of it, there was another thing. She had failed in her errand because she had shown kindness and concern for little Torquil and Utah.

What was happening to her?

It was a nervous, worried Daisy who loaded the pram into the Jag boot, heaved herself into the passenger seat, emptied her pockets of loose jewels and gold cigarette lighters, and allowed herself to be driven home.

'Looka dat,' said Nanny Pete, as they headed back down the road. Daisy could tell she was being cheered up, but she looked anyway.

A figure was crashing around in the bushes by the bench at the end of the road. Branches broke, and birds flew out. From the wreckage emerged a wide, flat person in a green uniform with starched white collar and cuffs, a heavily stained white apron, and a brown bowler hat. It was Nanny Pierrepoint.

Daisy watched, awestruck, as the nanny zigzagged out into the road. Three of the sleepy cakes should have left her in the Land of Nod for many a rosy day, but here she was, up and about, almost as good as new – (Nanny Pierrepoint fell over) – except for a slight dizziness.

Now she was up again, dusting herself down, scowling around her, looking for little Stuffs to torment. But all she could see was a mushroom-cloud of dust rising over the Stuff residence. She stood and gazed fuzzily at it, her bulldog jaw meeting her hatchet nose, the glint of stupidity dim in her eye as she tried to work out what the blue blazes was going on.

'Minim,' said Nanny Pete, in a quiet, thinking-aloud sort of voice.

'I beg your pardon?'

'Minim and crotchet, watch it,' said Pete, absently.

A dim shape had formed in the dust cloud: the shape of a huge white van. The clash of gears reached them, and a dull booming, like a heavy gun or a huge engine backfiring. The boom became a roar. The dim shape became distinct. And down the road trundled the white van.

It trailed white smoke. Daisy knew, even without Cassian's help, that this meant its piston rings were shot to hell. At least two of its eighteen tyres seemed to be flat, and its huge bonnet was flecked with rust, as if it had iron measles. Twin fluffy dice bounced in its windscreen. It was a shocking sight.

Certainly Nanny Pierrepoint seemed to think so. She stood in the middle of the road, scowling, as if preparing to ask why in the name of all that was cuddly this vehicle had on it neither pink bunny rabbits nor pale blue jumbos. When it was nearly on her, she raised a raw-knuckled hand to stop it. The hand was still up as the white van smote her with its radiator, knocked her flat, and steamed away into the afternoon.

'Dearie me!' cried Daisy, for good children and nannies never swear.

'She's all right,' said Nanny Pete. 'Huge ground clearance, that white van. Didn't crunch her bones nor grind her limbs. Look, she's up!'

And indeed, Nanny Pierrepoint was sitting up. Her bowler hat was jammed down to her chin, and she was shaking her fist at a blackbird, which she had apparently mistaken for the white van. She was drenched in black sump oil from the white van's many leaks. 'AI RESIGN!' she cried. She got up, reeled into a thicket of rhododendrons, and was seen no more.

'Home, James,' said Nanny Pete to himself. The Jag shrieked away from the kerb and shot down the road, fishtailing wildly. Half an hour later, Daisy was climbing out of the cargo net on to the launch pad.

'Any luck?' said the Captain, svelte in dark-green satin that matched her eyes, holding a shaker of emerald-coloured liquid.

'Quite the reverse,' said Daisy. 'They got the left arm. I blame myself.'

'Never do that,' said the Captain.

'It is a great pity,' said Daisy, 'and if you permit me, I shall do what I can to put it right.'

'But of course,' said the Captain. 'Cocktail? No? Well, you know best, I expect.' And she disappeared into the ship.

Later, the Darlings heard the piano in the ball-room. '"Stormy Monday Blues",' said Daisy.

'Sounds like she's got the hump,' said Primrose.

'Startling tragic intensity,' said Cassian.

And Daisy knew that things were not going well, not at all.

Cassian was really getting to know the engine room. The machinery, from coal lump to safety valve, with a comprehensive list of the intervening bunkers, furnaces, tubes, pistons, con-rods, valves and condensers, sat in his head in all its steel and brass and perfect logic. He really thought he could have got steam up and started the engine without trying; except that only the Chief Engineer had control of the starting switch, and without the switch, there was just no way.

On the day that Daisy was foiled at the Stuffs', Cassian was sitting on a deckchair between two piles of coal, wiping his hands on a piece of cotton waste and thinking about low-pressure condensers, when he had a most peculiar sensation. It was as if someone was shining a torch at him, but a torch emitting a beam of no visible light. When he looked up, he saw the Chief Engineer's eyes, not whirling any more, but fixed upon him.

Cassian raised a hand and gave a sort of salute.

The Chief winked.

Cassian got up, and strolled among the coal heaps

to the control shed. Using a bit of stick he had in his pocket, he pressed the brass bell. The door opened immediately. 'Comming in,' said the Chief. 'You haf big mechanical aptitude, I am thinking. Cuppy tea?'

'Don't mind if I do,' said Cassian, looking around.

There were colossal banks of switches, whole families of brass wheels of all sizes, gauges and dials and something that looked like a model *Kleptomanic* beetling steadily across a sea of mercury. And there were the clocks, dozens of them, arranged by type, ticking out a frenzied cross-rhythm.

The two of them exchanged engine gossip for five minutes. Then the Engineer took an iron teapot and held it under a brass tap. Boiling water roared in. The Engineer let it brew, then poured one cup, added condensed milk, and passed it to Cassian. 'Aren't you having one?' said Cassian.

The eyes gave a small whirl. 'I hates tea,' said the Engineer.

'Delicious,' said Cassian, sipping.

'Delicious things also I hate,' said the Chief.

Cassian raised a polite eyebrow, wondering if there were any biscuits.

'I am hating just about everything,' said the Chief.

'I am hating first the schtarting-up valves here, zen ze regulators, zen ze valve controllers, and ze bearing oiler monitor gauges –'

'Would you mind repeating that?' said Cassian, slyly.

'Ja, I vould!' cried the Chief. 'You are coming in here for tea not to learn ship-schtarting procedure. I hate ship-schtarting procedure,' he said. The eyes were definitely whirling again. 'Plus I hate captain, crew, burglars, schtokers, my clothes, my feet, myself, damn rewolution, people, everything.'

'Ah,' said Cassian, noting the sulky jut of the Chief's lower lip, and realizing that any child with half decent nanny training could provoke a really spectacular tantrum here with no trouble at all. It would not be clever, of course. But once Cassian had discovered how something worked, he could seldom resist starting it up. He pointed to the bear's head in the glass case. 'So I suppose you hate the Royal Edward, too?'

'NOOOOOOO!' roared the Chief. 'I LOF HIM! HE ISS MY BEAR! SMELLINK GOOD, AND KIND, SO KIND!'

'So if someone found the rest of him and put him back together?'

'I vurship this person. I do vot he vant, forever and ever.'

'Jolly good,' said Cassian. He looked at his watch. 'Gosh, is that the time? Thanks for the tea, Chief.'

'Is nodings,' said the Chief. 'How I hates it, zis tea.'

As Cassian left, all the cuckoo clocks went off at once.

'We have got to get those bear bits for the Chief,' said Daisy.

'Why?' said Primrose.

'Because we can't stay alongside forever,' said Cassian.

'Why not?' said Primrose.

'Because it's a ship, and ships are supposed to move around the world.'

'Not necessarily,' said Primrose. 'I'm quite happy. So's Chef.'

'Have you ever asked yourself,' said Daisy, 'where the food comes from?'

'Out of the larder,' said Primrose. 'I'm not stupid, you know.'

'Quite the reverse,' said Daisy, tactfully. 'But it's not quite as simple as that —'

'Daisy, you are right, it is an awesome burden of responsibility,' said a new voice. It belonged to Nanny Pete, who had wandered into the warm place by number two funnel where the Darlings were sitting. 'There's only three of us nannies active, now. Great burden on us, really. Don't know how long we can go on.'

'Nanny burglary isn't the only way. What's wrong with breaking and entering?' said Cassian.

'And mugging and ram-raiding?' said Daisy.

'Haven't got the heart for it somehow,' said Pete. 'Fair to say that most of the people here are your kinder type of burglar. Then you kids demonstrated unto one and all the skills of civilization like, and well, it's frightening, really.'

'You mean it's our fault?'

'It is merely,' said Pete, 'that everyone thought we were vicious and villainous and similar. But since you came on board we realize we are mere amateurs and you are the real thing.'

'How very gratifying,' said Daisy, blushing pink.

'I should cocoa,' said Primrose.

'One feels very humble,' said Cassian.

'But we got a problem,' said Pete Fryer. 'We

are in need of the bits of the bear them builders have got, and the problem is, how to get 'em.'

'Just what we were saying. But the Captain will know,' said Daisy.

'Um, ye-es,' said Pete. 'Which is to say, of course she will.'

'So how?' said Cassian.

'Challenge, probably,' said Pete.

'Challenge?'

''Scuse me,' said Pete. 'I've got to go. Plus it's past your woodbird.'

'I beg your pardon?'

'Woodshed, bed. Birdlime, time.'

'Ah. Goodness me!' said Daisy, checking her watch. 'So it is!'

And off they went, good as gold.

Later, they lay in their gilded beds, watching the silver disc of the moon shining through the port-holes. 'You know what?' said Cassian. 'Something's funny.'

Primrose said, 'If you ask me, everything's funny.'

'What do you mean?' said Daisy.

'When did the Bear's Bum come into the nursery?'

'Always been there,' said Primrose.

'No,' said Daisy. 'You were born. But you were just a baby. Too young to notice much.'

'Was not,' said Primrose.

'Were!' said Cassian.

'Was –'

'Children!' cried Daisy, in a voice like the snap of a nanny's knicker elastic. 'What are you getting at, Cassian?'

'It's just odd, that's all,' said Cassian. 'I mean, I think it turned up at about the same time as Secretary Mummy.'

'After Real Mummy left, then.'

'I suppose so. Odd.'

'What?'

'That whole tombola business. I mean, clever of the Captain to notice who was bidding.'

'It's not the sort of thing you'd forget in a hurry,' said Daisy.

'You know how they go on,' said Primrose. 'Secretary Mummy, f'rinstance. Oh yes, it was a lovely evening. Lady Mortdarthur and Lord Cringe were there, and Lord Cringe said, "Look at that roast peacock, I'm going to eat it all up," and Lady Peachbottom laughed so much I thought she would burst, ha, ha, ha!'

'Ha, ha, ha,' said Cassian, gloomily.

'Ha,' said Daisy. Her sister was right, of course. 'I don't care,' she said.

'Best not think about it,' said Cassian.

'Exactly,' said Primrose. 'The main thing is to get our hands on the bits of the bear. I'll sew them up.' Daisy and Cassian nodded in the dark. Primrose's sewing was nearly as magical as her cooking. 'Then off we go!'

'Off we go,' said Daisy.

'Over the far horizon,' said Cassian. 'But first assemble your bear.' There was a silence, during which the moonbeams continued to fall on the brocade counterpanes. 'What do you think a challenge is?'

'Not challenge, Challenge,' said Daisy.

'No idea,' said Primrose.

Silence descended on the cabin. Then there was the odd snore. Then there was more silence. Then it was morning.

'Hoop-ha and hee!' cried Primrose, soaping up a storm in the gigantic bath. 'And what will today hold?'

'Plenty,' said Cassian.

And of course he was dead right.

*

Breakfast was an ingenious blend of porridge with ample maple syrup, Parma ham omelettes and tropical fruits. Much refreshed, the Darlings went about their daily business – Daisy to the ready-nanny room, Primrose to the kitchens, and Cassian to the engine room – familiar worlds, all of them.

But all of them seemed subtly to have changed. As she went to the ready-nanny room, Daisy was surprised to see a blur in the distance; a blur that turned out not to be in the distance at all but just to look like it, because of its minute size. Actually it was Nosey Clanger, skipping with such speed that the rope was a silvery fuzz like a bumble-bee's wings.

'What are you doing?' said Daisy, highly nanny.

'Falt, pepper, muftard, binegar,' said Nosey, with fearful rapidity. 'Playin' nifely on me own, N. Daify.'

'Ah,' said Daisy, and went on her way frowning.

Primrose was in the early stages of developing a biscuit known as Angel Devil Dream Surprise. Needing advice on the icing, she threaded her way through the stoves to visit her friend Sophie Nickit, who had spent the last week on a replica of the Sistine Chapel, ceiling and all, in sugar. But Sophie had left the Chapel aside for the moment. She had replaced her svelte roller gear with unpleasant grey warm-ups, and was whipping a batter.

'What is it?' said Primrose.

'Heavy cake,' said Sophie, with a grim set to her pretty jaw.

'But why?' said Primrose.

'When the going gets tough, the tough get going,' said Sophie. And would say no more.

Cassian arrived in the engine room to find the Chief Engineer sitting in the control room in a golden chair. The Chief's arms were folded. Over his head was a badly-painted placard, bearing the word, 'WON'T'.

'Won't what?' said Cassian.

The Chief pressed a button. The sign rotated. On the other side was written the word, 'SHAN'T'. The door slammed. Cassian sighed, and went off to re-grind the number two oil-cooler thrust-bearing bearing plate. On the way, he heard a swifter hammering noise, as if of an engine. But Cassian knew all the *Kleptomanic*'s engines, and he had not heard this one before. So he went to investigate.

The hammering was not an engine. It came from Giant Luggage's fists. What Giant Luggage was hitting was a huge sack of coal, hung from an overhead girder. There was a hole in the sack, from which dribbled a stream of fine coal dust as Luggage beat the lumps to powder. There was quite a pile there.

'What are you doing?' said Cassian.

'Hur, hur,' said Giant Luggage, grinning bashfully.

Well, the man had been breaking coal. But why with his fists, and not the hammers provided? And why to useless slack? Cassian was about to enquire further, because he liked to get to the bottom of things. But suddenly a fearful rhythmic squawking came from the tannoy. 'ALERT,' said the metallic voice. 'FIVE ALARM NANNY EMERGENCY. GIANT LUGGAGE, CASSIAN, AND DUTY NANNIES TO THE LAUNCH PAD, CLEAN AND THAT MEANS BEHIND YER EARS AN' ALL. DRIVE, DRIVE, DRIVE.'

Cassian and Giant Luggage began to run.

12

'Daisy,' said the Captain, at the end of the briefing. 'I am putting you in overall command of this operation. It is the last chunk of the Edward, and we need it desperately.'

'But we can't just turn up,' said Daisy. 'They haven't asked us. You know what nannies are like. Territorial. Like wolverines.'

'I gave this one a ring,' said the Captain. 'Yesterday.'

'Oh?'

'Bit of a one for the horses, Nanny Magnum,' said

the Captain. 'I gave her a tip. Suggested she pinch Lady Smarte's tiara, pawn it, and put the proceeds on a horse called Staggery Jack for the 2.40 race at Lunchestown.'

'But how did you know Staggery Jack wouldn't win?'

'They almost never do,' said Pete. 'Plus your sister cooked up a batch of Slow Bran for the horse, and we sent Pygmy Eric over disguised as a stable lad, and he fed the horse the bran, and Bob's your mother's brother.'

'We hardly remember our mother,' said Daisy, sadly.

'Ah, well,' said the Captain, laying a hand on her shoulder. 'Into each life a little rain must fall, and she has my sympathy. But the important thing is, it is now 4.30 pm, and Staggery Jack is still running, and the rest of the horses are tucked up nicely in their boxes, and Nanny Magnum has had a bit of a breakdown, and you are in like Flint.'

'Flint?' said Daisy.

'Sort of stone,' said the Captain, vaguely. 'Oh, look, here come the rest of the Elite Squad. Off you go, now, and Godspeed!'

*

Cassian smelt slightly of soap, but he was still covered in engine oil; not that there was anything unusual in that, or anything anyone could do about it. 'It's the Big One,' said Daisy.

'Whuh?'

'Smarte Castle. The last limb of the Edward, or to be more precise, the torso. Our chance to draw level. It's not going to be easy, the Captain says. So we're the senior team.'

Cassian looked at the reflection in the Jag's gleaming black flank. Four figures. Four pairs of brogues, four pairs of thick stockings, four brown nanny dresses with white aprons, four stiff collars, four brown overcoats, four bowler hats.

They climbed into the Jag. It swung down to the quay, Nosey Clanger gibbering at them from the netting. Giant Luggage was driving, Nanny Pete in the rumble seat. Luggage gunned the engine. The Jag purred through the sliding doors and into the Port Quarter.

'Here they come,' said Cassian.

And sure enough, on to their tail, three blocks back, had turned a huge, rust-splotched white van.

'Go slow,' said Daisy.

'Hur, hur,' said Giant Luggage, lifting his size-eighteen accelerator foot. The Jag slowed. The white van slowed too. They crawled in procession out of town.

'What happens now?' said Daisy.

'The big-end bearings on that van go, by the sound of it.' Cassian took out a small notebook. 'What do they keep in it?' he said.

'Digger. Dozer. Dumper.'

Cassian's pen scuttled over the page, doing sums. 'Thirty-eight tonnes, velocity of light, mass at centre, expansion of the universe, let pi be 3.14, well, good enough . . . where's the nearest tree?'

They were in the country now. 'There,' said Daisy, perhaps a little tetchy. Really, Cassian could be so lazy sometimes. Could he not find his own trees?

'Wrong kind,' said Cassian, tetchy himself.

'Here we are,' said Nanny Pete. 'Smarte Castle.'

'Hur, hur,' said Giant Luggage, four-wheel drifting the Jag between two marble pillars with lions on top.

The van seemed to be speeding up. Daisy thought it might have crushing on its mind. 'What are you going to do?' she said.

Cassian's forehead looked faintly sweaty. 'Is there a river?' he said. 'An ornamental bridge, perhaps?'

'No ornamental bridge,' said Pete. 'No river.'

'It'll have to be trees, then,' said Cassian. The drive went through a wood. 'Slow,' he said. A track turned off to the right. 'Down the track.'

Giant Luggage swung the wheel. The Jag turned on to the track. The white van followed, roaring and belching smoke, its radiator grinning a rust-flecked grin that filled the rear-view mirror. The trees closed in on either side. 'He's catching up,' said Daisy, panicky. Then –

'He's stopped.'

'Not stopped,' said Cassian. 'Stuck.'

And when she looked round, there was the white van, firmly jammed between two oak trees.

'Nice driving, Luggage,' said Cassian.

'Hur, hur,' said Giant Luggage, giving the van a cheery wave out of the window. The white van waved back. Not cheerily, and not with a hand. Nastily. With a digger-bucket.

'He's using it on the trees,' said Cassian. 'He'll be out of there soon. Floor it, Luggage.'

Luggage floored it. The Jag hurtled on to a long,

straight drive across a rolling park, with deer. The turrets of Smarte Castle rose ahead. There was a puff of smoke on the battlements, and something whizzed over the Jag's roof. 'Stone me,' said Nanny Pete. 'Someone's shooting at us. With a cannon.'

Daisy's lips were a tight line. 'Hand guns are naughty but neat,' she said. 'Machine guns are wicked but sometimes understandable. But cannons are nasty and messy and inaccurate and thoroughly unspeakable. I do absolutely draw the line at cannons. Stop the car.'

She got out, and marched across the drawbridge and under the arch. From the battlements, childish eyes watched her suspiciously. A butler in a striped waistcoat opened the huge, nail-studded door. The shadows swallowed her up.

'There,' said Nanny Pete, 'goes a brave little woman.'

Hefting his socket set, Cassian trotted after his sister. Something told him she would be needing back-up. Giant Luggage parked the Jag behind a handy bunker. Then he and Nanny Pete crammed their hats over their ears, scooped up their swagbags, and went in too.

*

The inside of Smarte Castle was as Daisy had expected – snooty butler, stags' horns on the walls, diamond-crusted fire irons twinkling in a vast fireplace. 'Miss Henrietta is in the nursery,' said the butler, down his nose. 'Master Arthur is on the west battlements. Her ladyship asks me to remind you that Master Arthur is a delicate child in need of constant love and attention. His shooting at people with cannons should be interpreted as a cry for help.'

'And when will her ladyship be back?'

'Her ladyship did not say,' said the butler. 'Her ladyship and his lordship have naffed off to Scotland to chase wild animals. It normally takes a month or so. Sometimes longer.'

'Ah.'

'And if I might venture the observation,' said the butler, 'good luck, cocky, you are going to need it. They took Nanny Magnum off to the mental home at four sharp this afternoon and the shooting started straight after, need I say more?'

'I like a child with spirit,' said Daisy. 'Which way to the nursery?'

At the second landing, the stair carpet covering changed from thick Turkey carpet to linoleum. At the third, there were bare boards underfoot, and the air had that familiar soap pong. From behind a white door came the sound of someone practising scales on a piano. Daisy went in.

As she had guessed, it was the nursery. There were generations of teddy-bear portraits on the walls, and pictures of sweet children in flowery meadows, wearing puff skirts and velvet shorts and clean white ankle socks. Daisy and Cassian came to a halt.

There was a glass case containing something that looked like a mouldy bag of sawdust. The torso (realized Daisy, with bumping heart) of the Royal Edward.

At the piano sat a girl in a neat frock, with perfectly brushed hair in a blue velvet Alice band. Her socks were easily as white as the ones in the pictures on the walls. They matched her face.

'Nana!' she cried, bursting into a watery simper.

'You will be Henrietta,' said Daisy. 'Hetty for short? Or is it Etta?'

'Just Henrietta,' she said, and folded her lips primly. 'Thank goodness you are here. I would like to tell on Arthur. I know he is delicate but that is no excuse for blowing people up with cannons. I am shocked and so was Nanny Magnum, but she has gone and I do not understand why. Soon it will be time for high tea.'

'Nana will burn you some custard, then,' said Daisy.

The whey-faced idiot clapped her hands. 'Goody!' she cried.

Cassian said, 'But why do you like burnt custard?'

'Because it is good for me!' The girl stared at Daisy like a dog expecting a bone.

'Good girl,' said Daisy, wincing. 'Now let us hear you practise your scales.'

The clean little fingers plodded up and down the keyboard, slowly, boringly, not rushing, not making a mistake. Cassian said, 'I may be sick.'

'Shame on you!' hissed Daisy. She rushed into the nursery kitchen and rustled up a dose of peaches and ice cream and unburnt custard from among the champagne bottles and caviar tins in the fridge that said, 'NANNIES ONLY – TOUCH AND DIE'. It only took three minutes.

Henrietta ate the lot. 'That was delicious,' she said, brightly. Then her face dulled. 'But there was something wrong with it.'

'Not burnt?' said Daisy.

Henrietta shrugged, confused, nearly in tears.

'What about eat-what-you-are-given?' said Daisy.

'But it tasted good!'

'In future, send back anything that doesn't.'

Henrietta's lip began to quiver.

'You just have to put your foot down,' said Daisy.

'But they make you stand in the corner. Kneel on dried peas. Go to bed without your supper. I couldn't.'

'Try.'

But Henrietta had begun to practise her scales again, slow, boring, mind-shatteringly loud.

'Listen,' said Daisy. 'You don't have to do what you're told –'

'LA, LA, LA,' sang Henrietta. 'NOT LIST-ENIN'!'

The sudden BANG of a cannon rattled the windows. Daisy took the torso off the wall, walked out of the nursery and closed the door quietly on the thundering scales within. 'Too far gone,' she said. 'It happens.'

Giant Luggage stood twisting his bowler hat into a pretzel. 'We can't just leave the poor mite,' said Pete, horrified.

'We have to,' said Daisy. 'She's doing what she

was told to do. She causes no trouble. A nice, quiet child.'

'But that's diabolical,' said Pete.

'That's nannies,' said Daisy. 'Have you learned nothing?'

'The battlements!' said Cassian.

The door on to the battlements was locked. Daisy had expected no less. 'Well?' she said to Cassian, who had followed.

'We could use a chainsaw, but that would be rather noisy,' he said. 'And he'll have the door covered.'

Pete said, 'Luggage'll soup it.'

'Soup?'

But Luggage was already dripping a clear liquid gingerly into the keyhole. 'Nitroglycerine,' said Pete.

'Hur, hur,' said Luggage. He lit a fuse, straightened up and put his sausage fingers into his cauliflower ears.

'Light blue touchpaper and retire immediately,' said Pete.

There was a colossal explosion. Cassian and Giant Luggage sprinted through the smoke, keeping low.

On the roof a small child stood by an ancient cannon. The child was wearing a lace collar, velvet knickerbockers, white silk stockings and buckle shoes, and aiming a crossbow at Luggage's mid-section. Luggage made sentimental noises, sidestepping a bolt. He stretched out gigantic, welcoming arms.

The child began to snivel, knuckling its lovely blue eyes. Daisy said, 'Look out –'

But it was too late. Giant Luggage had stepped up to the infant and patted its golden curls. Quick as a cobra, the infant had sunk its teeth into the side of Luggage's hand.

'Aargh!' cried Luggage, shaking his hand, to which the child was still attached.

'Oi!' said Cassian to the infant. 'Arthur or whatever your name is. Stop thrashing about like that and I will show you how to lay this cannon because that shooting you were doing before was actually embarrassing.'

'Was not!' shrieked the child. But in order to shriek, it opened its mouth, and its teeth came out of Giant Luggage's hand, and Giant Luggage lurched back, bleeding.

'Look at this,' said Cassian, ramming in powder, wad, ball and new wad, and priming the touch-hole with gunpowder from the horn provided. 'Got your cross-wind, right?'

'Course,' said the child, sulky but listening now.

'Plus your elevation.'

'Teach your grandmother to suck eggs.'

'But have you got your humidity?'

There was a short but well-filled silence. Then Arthur said, 'Humidity?'

Cassian shook his head wearily. 'Crucial,' he said. 'Now forgive me, but if we were to want to hit . . . say that white van coming towards the castle at 110 mph, how would you do it?'

'Ten degrees depression,' said the child. 'Lay off 1.3 degrees for breeze.'

'Is that it?'

'' Course it is.'

'Nope,' said Cassian. 'Plus up one for humidity. Now do it. Fire.'

The cannon boomed. A large hole appeared in the centre of the white van's radiator. The white van slewed into the moat. Figures emerged, swimming clumsily. They struggled up the bank, staggered across the drawbridge, and began hammering on the door.

'And nobody hurt,' said Cassian.

'Awwwww,' said the child, disappointed.

'What shall we do?' said Daisy.

'Oh, I'll take care of them,' said Arthur. 'Got a light?' Luggage gave him some matches. He kindled a fire under a large cauldron of oil standing by a gulley. 'Fried builder,' he said. 'Very unhealthy.'

Daisy was most impressed. All children needed to make them happy and fulfilled was a little encouragement. She realized that this child's sister was in safe hands. She said, 'Is there a back entrance? Because I think you can take care of all this yourself.'

'I think I can,' said the child, simpering. 'Thanks for that stuff about humidity, it'll come in handy. By the way, you're not real nannies, are you?'

They stared at him.

'Only it's all round the county. You ring up emergency nannies and your house gets knocked down and everything gets stolen. But do swipe what you like on the way out. There's a Rolls Royce in the garage. I'll get the Jag back to you later, if I can. And if you see the coppers, tell them you're with Lord Arthur Smarte, and they'll leave you alone.'

'Yes,' they said, dazed. 'We will.'

Luggage and Pete wandered around the castle, doing a little looting. Then they proceeded to the garage, where the Rolls was waiting, as advertised. Daisy laid the Edward's torso tenderly on the back seat, and climbed in. The great car whispered out into the park and away.

'What a delightful child,' said Daisy, as they drove through the police roadblock, waving regally. 'And frankly, what a hideous bit of bear.' She held it up in front of her: a beige lump, loosely tacked to its shield. 'Lot of fuss about very little, really.'

'About a lot,' said Cassian.

Daisy tossed the shield on to the seat. Something rolled out of it and bounced on the carpet. Daisy picked it up, put it in her pocket and forgot all about it.

'Pity about the Jag,' said Cassian.

Giant Luggage said nothing. He was looking at his bitten hand. It was red and angry, and it hurt. It hurt a lot.

'Dear little Arthur,' said Daisy, as the derrick swung the Rolls off the quay. 'And his sister, so sweet.'

Cassian was getting rather bored with the way Daisy was going on. This nanny thing was all very well, but nannies were the enemy, and more and more often nowadays she seemed to be turning into one. He heard Pete say, 'How's the hand, Luggage?'

'Hur,' said Luggage, gnawing an agonized lip, and Pete frowned, looking worried.

Something was going on.

The wheelbarrow-men came. There were a couple of barrows of jewelled household stuff, bellows, fish slices, nothing much.

'Luggage!' cried the tannoy. 'Training!'

'Hurrrr!' cried Luggage, springing towards the gym deck. As he ran (clumsily, thought Daisy; a great lack of deportment) he tapped his hand against the door-frame. 'Aaargh!' he shrieked, clutching his wrist.

With one swift stride, Daisy was at his elbow. 'Show Nana,' she said.

'Grunt,' said Luggage.

'I shan't ask again,' said Daisy.

The hand came out. The red-spotted handkerchief came off.

'Just as I thought,' said Daisy, tutting. 'Really, I wonder when little Arthur last cleaned his teeth!'

'Hur,' said Luggage. 'Eek!'

For Daisy had prodded him again. 'It's antibiotics for you, Master Luggage, and a week in a sling,' she said.

'Grunt,' said Luggage.

Daisy folded her lips. She said, 'Be off with you now, and do what Nana says.'

'Daisy,' said Cassian, after Luggage had lumbered sheepishly away, 'you're not yourself.'

'Stuff and nonsense.' Her chin was up, her lips compressed, her eyes glassy. Cassian thought she looked . . . weird. He went into the wheelhouse and took the top off the kitchen voice-pipe. Five minutes later, Primrose came on deck. She said, 'Drink this.'

'My name is Nana,' said Daisy, in a strange, high voice. 'You will please mind your Ps and Qs. Children should be seen and not heard. A cup of tea is sometimes very welcome.' She took a deep draught. Then she coughed and spluttered. 'Ork!' she cried. 'What is this?'

'Pepsi Brown Cow. Pepsi and ice cream.'

'Where am I?' said Daisy. The glassy look had gone from her eyes.

'You were nearly lost in Nanny World. Now, men, hat off, and get the rest of the Brown Cow down you. It'll make all the difference.'

'Sigh,' said Daisy, downing the dregs of the delicious non-nanny drink. 'That's better.'

'Thought you were gone for a moment there,' said Primrose.

'Yeah. Thanks.' Daisy made a face. 'It was that

girl Henrietta. And bowler hats . . . after a while, they just start to bend your mind. Remember Elsie?'

'Sure we remember Elsie.'

Elsie had been a kindly girl who worked in the kitchen at Number One, Avenue Marshal Posh. She had always been ready to smuggle out the chocolates the ambassador refused to eat when he came to drinks. Then Nanny Hatchett had asked her to be sub-nanny. And as soon as the bowler hat had settled on her brow, she had started rapping out orders. She had knitted a really embarrassing baby hat for Primrose, tried to get Cassian out of welding and into Lego, and read aloud to Daisy from *Peter Pan*, which made Daisy actually sick. She had finally left in a hail of fire, and was now bringing up some little warlords and warladies on a mountain somewhere.

'It's definitely the hat,' said Daisy. She cast hers to the deck, and stamped on it with her brogue.

''Morning all,' said a voice. They looked up and saw the Captain: a new, different Captain, wearing a neat tailored suit and shoes with high heels. 'Sick of your hat?'

'A bit,' said Daisy, shamefaced.

'Responsibilities,' said the Captain, sighing. 'They can get on top of you. She looked tired under the make-up.

'Well, we've got the torso,' said Daisy, driven by a strange urge to cheer up this peculiar but nice person.

'Marvellous work,' said the Captain, with a strangely preoccupied air.

'Is everything all right?' said Cassian.

'Fine, fine,' said the Captain, waving an exquisite hand.

Daisy frowned. Things were clicking in her mind. 'So the Chief's got the head of the Edward. And you've got half the rest,' she said. 'And the builders have got the other half.'

'Quite,' said the Captain, giving her a smile that combined dazzlement with a sort of wistful sadness.

'How are you going to get the other half?'

'Oh, well . . .' said the Captain.

Daisy's spine stiffened. 'Speak up!' she cried. 'Spit it out! Tell the truth!'

'Daisy!' said Cassian, shocked.

'Sorry. Relapse,' said Daisy, her brow glistening with sweat. 'It's got to be a Challenge, hasn't it?'

'A Challenge?' said the Captain.

'Speak up!' cried Daisy. 'Spit it out! Tell –'

'Yes, yes, yes,' said the Captain, wearily. 'Yes. All right. It's a Challenge.'

'Please explain.'

The Captain looked astonished. 'Don't tell me you've never heard of it?'

'Hardly.'

The Captain sighed. 'Well, I don't know what they teach you nowadays, I really don't. It's in the Statutes of Larceny of the Worshipful Company of Burglars, Smash-and-Grabbers, Financial Service Engineers and Allied Trades. To settle questions of ownership. Basically, it's Trial by Single Combat.'

'Wow,' said Cassian, impressed. 'Like witches holding bits of red-hot iron and if they blister they're witches and if they don't they aren't?'

'Teacher's pet,' said the Captain, reprovingly. 'Nobody likes a know-all, and besides, you are thinking of trial by ordeal. But basically, yes. You have a champion from each side. They fight, with a police referee, on the challenger's manor. Winner takes all. In this case, the missing parts of the Edward, and hence the loyalty of the Chief.'

'Hence all this training,' said Cassian. 'Great!'

'You don't understand!' said the Captain. 'My

burglars are so sweet and kind and gentle. They abhor violence, except in the line of duty.'

Daisy tched. 'They nicked plenty of gear,' she said.

'But if we lose . . .' said the Captain.

'We won't,' said Daisy.

'Leave that to us,' said Cassian. 'Who's the champion?'

'Giant Luggage.'

'He wouldn't hurt a fly.'

'Yes, he would,' said Daisy. 'I've seen him. He cried afterwards, but Primrose can fix that. I'll go and deliver this challenge, never fear. They won't hurt me.'

'Probably not,' said the Captain, faintly. 'Oh, I did so hope it wouldn't come to this.'

'No use crying over spilt milk,' said Daisy.

'Daisy!' said Primrose.

'Sorry. Now then, I'll need a driver for the Rolls. And you can tell me the rules.'

'And I,' said Cassian, 'will need an elite corps of engineers and five burglars who can stoke boilers and twenty with dock experience.'

'What for?' said the Captain.

'When we beat the builders and reassemble the

Royal Edward for the Chief, do you want to hang around?'

'Of course not.'

'Well, then,' said Cassian.

'And it would be nice if you could give me four dozen eggs, some sugar, red wine, stinking hellebore, and 120 grams of toad warts,' said Primrose. 'Oh, and a needle and thread.'

'Of course,' said the Captain. 'But why?'

The children folded their lips, nanny style. 'You'll just have to wait and see,' they said.

Hilda the Builder put the fifth sugar into her tea and stirred, wheezing a little with the effort. Outside the window, a grey drizzle was falling on the yard – several hectares of rusty diggers and mixers, tumbled piles of concrete blocks, and a bungalow someone had started building and changed their minds about halfway. In the middle of the yard, a long black car had just cruised to a halt. Hilda said, 'Wozzat, Dan?'

White Van Dan looked up from his copy of *Daily Girls*. He was a wiry little person with a monkey face and tattoos all the way up his arms, so he looked like an ape wearing a skintight suit of ladies in bikinis. 'Woz wot?' he said.

'The car.'

'The Roller?'

'Yeh.'

'He's stopped.'

'I can see he's stopped.'

The Roller door opened, and a small figure climbed out. She wore a brown bowler hat, a long brown overcoat, and brown wool stockings. Her lips were pressed together in disgust as she picked her way between the puddles and the drifts of old burger boxes.

'Oozis?' said Hilda the Builder, swallowing a Mars bar whole.

'Search me,' said Dan.

It was Daisy, of course.

The caravan was green with mould. Black smoke oozed from its stovepipe, smelling of burning plastic. A sign over the door said D+H HIGH-CLASS BUILDERS. The sign was tilted to the left, because the nails that attached it to the caravan had come out, because they were too short, and had been hammered in wrong. Daisy splashed through the last black puddle and opened the rickety door. 'Mr Dan?' she said.

The wiry little man smiled, a smile that lit up his

sharp white teeth and his gold identity bracelet and watch, but not his eyes, which were grey as cement.

'And you must be Miss Hilda,' she said. 'How d'you do?'

The huge woman in filthy decorator's overalls frowned blubberily at the roll of foam-backed carpet she was feeding into the stove. There were full ash-trays and dirty teacups everywhere. The ceiling was varnished brown with the grease of many fry-ups.

'This,' said Daisy, 'is absolutely revolting.'

White Van Dan had been edging round behind her to cut off her line of retreat. Now he froze. 'What did you say?'

'You should be ashamed of yourself,' said Daisy, through tight lips. 'This is disgusting. It is quite unnecessary to live like pigs.' She put her hand in her overcoat pocket. Dan's hand went into his pocket, too, and his eyes narrowed. But Daisy's hand came out slowly, holding a long brown envelope with a red crest on the flap. 'Read this,' she said. 'I suppose you *can* read?'

Dan snatched it out of Daisy's hand and scowled at it angrily. 'What is it?' he said.

'It is what we call writing,' said Daisy sweetly. 'Words are made of letters. The one with a dot on top is "i". For "idiot." That one is "f". For "fool" –'

'I can read,' said Dan, rending the envelope.

'He can too,' said Hilda, admiringly. 'And nearly write, an' all.'

'So what shall I tell them?' said Daisy.

'About what?'

Daisy tutted and sighed, casting her eyes at the ceiling in an exceptionally annoying way. 'This is a challenge,' she said. 'The AAA Aardvark Nanny Agency presents its compliments –'

'Langwidge,' said Hilda.

' – and invites White Van Dan and Firm to select a champion to fight its own champion on board SS *Kleptomanic* tomorrow or other convenient date, for possession of the opposition's bits of the Royal Edward, winner take all. Usual rules apply.'

'Fight?' said Dan. 'No way.'

'Fraidy cat,' said Daisy.

'Am not,' said Dan.

'Is not,' said Hilda.

'Are. Prove it.'

'What,' said Dan, 'is stopping me dropping you in a great big pit of wet cement?'

'Don't be an utter baby,' said Daisy, nose high. 'Shall we say after tea tomorrow?'

'Too right, toffee-nose,' said Dan. 'We'll be using Dickie the Brickie.'

'Toffee-nose,' said Hilda, getting the idea. 'Toff –'

'Sticks and stones may break my bones but words will never hurt me,' said Daisy, and walked briskly through the drizzle to the Roller.

Hilda watched the great car glide silently away. She spooned extra sugar into her tea for the sake of her nerves.

'Cheek,' said Dan.

'Cheek,' said Hilda.

When they went out later to play with the bulldozer, they saw that near where the Roller had stood, an expanse of cement, wet earlier in the day, was covered in writing. HILDA IS A *, it read. But the * was not a *. In the cement, rockhard now, was the imprint of an enormous bottom.

'Oo,' said Hilda. 'Nasty.'

'Not as nasty as us,' said Dan. 'You wait.'

'You sure?'

'I'm always sure,' said Dan.

'But you were sure you could mend the van,' said Hilda.

'I am sure that when we get their Chief Engineer he will be able to mend the van, and build us a better one. And we can start up again in Iceland,' said Dan.

'Oh,' said Hilda.

'Say, "Brilliant, Dan",' said Dan.

'Brilliant, Dan.'

'Oh, I dunno,' said Dan, blushing.

Back on the *Kleptomanic*, the burglars were in a state of huge excitement. Quite a lot of these tattooed and hardened geezers had secretly thought it was undignified to go around dressed up as nannies. A good fight would make everyone feel much better. The training became intense. Ancient sacks were stuffed with ancient life-jackets, hung from chandeliers and pummelled until the dust hung in fat grey clouds. Ancient mooring lines were pressed into service as skipping ropes. All day long, Daisy and the Captain sat on the bridge, treating a succession of black eyes and bleeding noses and skinned knuckles.

'Tell me,' said Daisy, when they were alone for a moment. 'What makes you think that when the Firm lose the fight, they will stop causing trouble?'

'There are ancient traditions at work here,' said the Captain. 'I feel sure the Firm will respect them, and that their better nature will prevail.'

'Really?'

The Captain started filing her nails with anxious vigour. 'No,' she said. 'Actually not really, not at all. Sometimes I feel that we are too trusting, creatures from a kinder, older time. No smash, you know. And only the tiniest bit of grab.'

After lunch, one of the voice-pipes peeped. 'Cap'n,' said the voice. 'The Contender is doing his public training, should you be interested.'

'Extremely,' said the Captain. 'Come along, Daisy.'

A space had been cleared in the middle of the gym. A large punchbag hung from the ceiling. By the bag stood Giant Luggage, like a sack of bowling balls wearing knee-length shorts and boxing gloves.

'We are ready,' said the Captain.

'Hur, hur,' said Luggage, with a nervous half-smile. In Daisy's view, the smile fell some distance short of the sabre-toothed grin of an assassin.

'Train ho!' cried Nanny Pete, stopwatch in hand, dancing from foot to foot in a sweatsuit and trainers.

Luggage launched himself on the bag and started to pound it with horrid vigour.

Actually, with not very horrid vigour.

After ten seconds he stopped. 'Hur,' he said in

a small voice. He pushed the bag away from him with a large, disgusted shove, turned round and faced the Captain, spreading his hands, fumbling with the laces of his right glove.

The bag swung back and smote him on the back of the head. He went down like a building.

There was an awful silence.

Then Pete was on his knees by the body, taking off the right glove. And there was Luggage's main punching hand, red, large, and horribly painful, thanks to the unbrushed teeth of Lord Arthur Smarte.

Daisy frowned. 'Off games for a week,' she said.

'But –'

'It is not a good sign,' said Daisy, 'when the challenger is knocked out by his own training equipment.'

That was true, of course.

'Very well,' said the Captain. 'Substitute procedure initiated, if you please. Nanny Pete?'

'It would be a kebab.'

'I beg your pardon?'

'Kebab, doner, honour,' said Pete, eyes twinkling and chest swelling visibly.

'Ah,' said the Captain, reeling a little. 'Well, be

that as it may, congratulations. You are our new champion.'

Daisy and the Captain returned to the bridge. 'Dear Pete,' said the Captain. 'But perhaps too kind, and not really big enough for a champion. Dickie the Brickie is . . . well, a behemoth.'

'What?' said Primrose.

'A monster. As in very big and very ugly.'

'Relax,' said Daisy. 'Everything is under control.'

The Captain looked anxious. 'Do you think so?'

'Leave it to us,' said Daisy, and explained.

When she had finished, the Captain was still looking anxious. 'It's a bold plan,' she said. 'Daring, I grant you. But are you sure it will work?'

'We were brought up by nannies,' said Daisy. 'Real nannies. With respect, you burglars have had it easy.'

'*Such* a comfort,' said the Captain, hugging her. 'Daisy, you are *perfect*.'

'One does one's best to do one's bit,' said Daisy awkwardly. 'Now, I must pop off and make plans.'

She went. Watching her trim, sturdy figure march about its business, the Captain brushed away a tear.

She had become most attached to Daisy. It was

just another thing to worry about.

There were so many.

A bit later, the Darlings were having a meeting in the suite.

'Everyone clear?' said Daisy.

'Sorted,' said Primrose.

'As crystal,' said Cassian.

'Background, please,' said Daisy.

'They were talking about the substitute procedure in the kitchen,' said Primrose. 'By the terms of the Parkhurst Convention, Dickie the Brickie is blindfolded. He comes on to the ship. In the absence of the nominated champion, he gets to fight the first person he sees when they take the blindfold off him.'

'And if it's the ship's cat?'

'It'll make a change from mice. But it is accepted that the Captain sets things up so the first person he sees is a good challenger.'

'Good. So what have you been doing?'

'Cooking.' Primrose smiled shyly. 'I think it'd be best if Dickie lost the fight.'

'Oh, I dunno,' said Cassian.

'What?' shrieked both his sisters at once.

'Life moves on,' said Cassian, irritatingly.

So of course Daisy told him he had a smudge of oil on his nose, and asked him why he was so dirty. And he smiled a superior smile.

'Up to something,' said Primrose. 'Definitely.'

'Mischief, I'll be bound,' said Daisy.

'Daisy!'

'Oops. Sorry. Any more nanny stuff, put a bucket of water over me.'

'With pleasure!' said Primrose and Cassian, together.

'Anyway,' said Daisy. 'We stand on the brink of a new and strange world. Our first home has been flattened by burglars. Our parents have vanished. We are in the power of a self-professed lady burglar, delightful, I grant you, but a woman of unknown motives. And even now our new home is in the balance. Everything may be won or lost on the slug of a criminal fist. This time tomorrow, who knows? We may be engineerless, running from the vengeance of the White Van, or triumphant. It will be strange, and lonely, and rootless. It will in short be dead weird.'

'Fantastic!' said Primrose.

'Wonderful!' cried Cassian.

'Quite so!' said Daisy. 'Now, onwards!'

14

The day of the big fight dawned bright and clear.
The Rules of Challenge had been agreed and, as
per routine, signed in blood by both parties. Nanny
Pete Fryer's selection as champion had been a move
popular with the burglars, who had said he was a
diamond and given him three hearty cheers. Giant
Luggage was rattling with powerful antibiotics. Half
an hour before fight time Pete was on the Jag deck,
dressed in satin shorts, killing time by shadow boxing
as he awaited transfer to the Meeting Room.

Meeting Room?

Sorry.

As outlined earlier, the Rules of Challenge stipulate that the Champion of the Challenged Firm comes to the Challenging Firm's base, den or lair, in a blindfolded state. The first person the Challengee sees after blindfold removal will be his opponent in the Fight. It is generally accepted that to avoid nasty accidents (like the time when Bruiser Jago clapped eyes on Conchita, the Bandit Queen's chihuahua, before Deathstar McMurtrie, the true Challenger, caught Mexican rabies, and died horribly soon afterwards) the meeting is rigged. The Meeting Room is a sort of cell, in which the fighters are shut up together with brown paper bags on their heads, and then revealed to each other in total privacy. In the case of the *Kleptomanic*, the Meeting Room had been established in the base of funnel three. 'All ready?' said the Captain to Nanny Pete.

'Ready,' said Nanny Pete, through his gumshield.

'Beft of luck!' shouted tiny Nosey Clanger, who only reached up to his knee.

'Ta, Nosey,' said Nanny Pete, polite as always. The crane hooked his harness. He went up, up, up into the spider-web rigging and down, down, down into the funnel.

The crane hook came back empty. There was a rumble and clash of sliding doors. The ship's clock struck the hour. Silence fell, broken only by the teeny thump of Nosey Clanger's feet on the deck, for Nosey was very excited, and had to be leaping continually to and fro. There was also the sound of an engine. The white van (a new, small version, mechanically even more dreadful than the previous one) arrived on the quay with a sickly clatter. Leaning over the side, Daisy saw Hilda the Builder emerge from the exhaust smoke. Hilda stood for a moment, waiting for the wobble of her outer reaches to steady. She took a pat of lard from her overall pocket, and ate a few strengthening mouthfuls. Then she waved away the crane hook, and started to walk up the gangway. Ten minutes later she was standing on the Jag deck, puffed and wobbling, a pool of sweat spreading round her feet. With her in her personal pond were White Van Dan, Dickie the Brickie with the traditional brown-paper bag over his head, a couple of hundred of the Firm, and, in an old sack, the arms and right leg of the Royal Edward.

Daisy, standing to one side, smelled that smell of

burned carpet and old grease and ancient, ancient
fags. Really, how quite unsuitable, she thought.
What if a child were to see them . . .

She shook her head to clear it. Beside her, a small
voice said, 'If it waf me I'd fpifflicate 'em.'

She looked down. There at waist level was Nosey
Clanger, looking ferocious. 'Quite so,' she said, and
for a moment she did feel very, very annoyed with
these horrid building people who wanted to upset
these poor, nice burglars and knock down houses
and cause fuss and dust and general mess.

The builders and the Captain were going into the
wheelhouse. During a brief but moving ceremony,
the shields containing the bits of the Edward were
hung on the wall, so they made an exploded bear,
headless.

'Even Steven,' said Hilda the Builder, according to long established usage. 'I say this is a correck
Challenge.'

'Nice one,' said the Captain, with all due
formality. Hilda and the svelte Captain returned to
the Fighting Deck.

Daisy knew she should have been concentrat-
ing on the ceremony. But at that moment, out of

the crowd, there leaped the face of her brother. A surge of nanny spirit rose in her. So dirty, that face, peering round the striped jersey of a stout burglar. Covered in oil, nearly as bad as a builder. She opened her mouth to give him a sound ticking off. But suddenly he was gone.

'I'd give that Dickie fuch a feeing to,' said Nosey, down there.

The frustration of seeing her grubby brother was seething in her. 'Oh, for goodness' *sake*,' she snapped. 'You're too small. And too silly. Why don't you find someone your own size? Like a smelly *mouse* or something.'

Nosey's toothless mouth fell open. He seemed for a moment speechless. Then in tones of gigantic scorn, he said, 'Ha!'

Daisy had never seen so many hurt feelings crammed into such a tiny person. She knew that the last shreds of nannyishness had led her to say something absolutely awful. She began saying she was sorry, sorry, sorry.

Too late.

The minute space Nosey had occupied was now empty, and she was apologizing to empty air. From high above, she could hear a thin voice crying,

'Small? Small? SMALL?' and a peal of tiny but hideous laughter.

'You bust our van,' said Hilda the Builder, at the outdoor tea that preceded the Challenge.

'Dearie me,' said the Captain sweetly, pouring a cup. 'Milk?'

'Five sugars,' said Hilda the Builder, who was standing next to Dickie the Brickie, who had a brown paper bag over his head.

'Oi,' said Dan, and there was something nervy in his bounce. 'What about the fight?'

'Our boy is waiting in the Meeting Room, bless him,' said the Captain.

Suddenly a cranc hook whizzed out of the sky. It caught in the back of Dickie's dungarees. 'Ooer,' said Dickie.

'Doesn't he like heights?' said the Captain.

'Loves 'em,' said Dan.

Dickie the Brickie nodded. He was two metres tall and a metre wide. In the pockets of his enormous dungarees he carried a couple of dozen bricks, without noticing the extra weight. It was his habit, when peckish, to munch one. Even now, a dribble of red dust was filtering down his dungaree bib under the paper-bag rim.

'Up he goes,' said the Captain.

And up went Dickie the Brickie into the cable-webbed void.

Not quite a void. Voids are empty. And a space is not empty if it contains anything at all. Even something tiny. Even something as tiny as Nosey Clanger.

There was a slithering noise above Dickie's head, as of a light weight slipping down a heavy cable. Something small but surprisingly heavy landed on Dickie's shoulder. A tiny voice hissed in his ear, 'Villin!' Minute hands grasped the edge of the paper bag and ripped it in twain. Dickie the Brickie found himself gazing into the tiny tattooed features of Nosey Clanger, twisted into a grin of pure spite. 'Challenge!' cried Nosey. 'You will periff miferably!'

'Not as miferably as you will,' said Dickie, in whose pea-sized brain a light was slowly dawning. 'Oi!' he cried, directing his voice between his feet at the now tiny deck. 'I seen one!'

'Challenger!' cried White Van Dan, according to ancient ritual.

The Captain looked up, shaking her head. The

ritual could not be changed. The die was cast. 'That is the first of us seen, and therefore let him be our challenger,' she said. And Daisy, standing next to her, saw the long red nails sink into the palms of the long white hands.

Things had gone badly wrong.

Cassian had every confidence in his errand. He normally did, when there was something mechanical to be dealt with. He whizzed down the ladders to the engine room, and said, 'Progress report, please.'

'The boys on the gate say tickety boo,' said one of the stokers. 'Any minute now, they said. Tide's right for the next hour.'

'Check,' said Cassian. He trotted along the ranks of engineers. The furnaces were glowing. The safety valves were hissing. Boilers one, two and three were up to pressure. All that was required was for the Chief to pull the great knife-switch that activated numbers one, two and three entry-valve servo motors . . .

But this is foolishly complicated stuff, best left to Cassian. The point was that the *Kleptomanic* was ready for sea.

All he had to do was persuade the Chief to throw the switch.

He made a last-minute adjustment to a pressure valve, and gave a word of fatherly advice to a stoker whose trimming showed room for improvement. Then, removing his length of wood from his overall pocket, he pressed the electric bell by the control-room door.

It opened a crack. There seemed to be five chains on it. 'Vot?' said the Chief.

Cassian noted that the eyes were whirling, and the voice was distinctly hostile, to say nothing of the chains. But as an engineer, Cassian had a high regard for pure logic. He had made a resolution based on the fact that the Chief, at the core of his being, must feel similarly. Engines ran by pure logic. Logic was logic, and left no room for sentiment.

Which shows how much Cassian knew about people.

'Chief,' he said, 'it is like this. There is a Challenge going on up there for your bear –'

'Mein Edward!' cried the Chief, the eyes whirling like Dutch windmills.

'– but it is in your power to prevent all this bloodshed, and get your Edward back.'

The eyebrow rose on the Chief's moon forehead. 'Ja?' he said.

'Easily,' said Cassian. 'You will observe from your dials that we have steam up and are in all respects ready for sea.'

'So?' said the Chief.

'Also, I have the dock gates ready for immediate opening, and the tide is right for a safe, nay, a dignified exit. To sum up: your bear is here, the ship is ready, the gate is open, the tide is in our favour. Let me beg you to throw the switch, so we may boldly go where –'

'SCHTOP!' cried the Chief. His eyes had stopped whirling. They now focused on Cassian with an unnerving vibration. 'I cannot. I am of the Blood Royal. A Challenge is a Challenge. Honour demands that until I receive my bear by fair and legitimate means from the vinner I can make no svitch movements.'

'So you would rather live in the mud and mend filthy diesels for White Van Dan and the Firm?'

The long chin jutted. The floppy white hand dashed a tear from the eye. 'Avast, tempter!' cried the Chief. The door slammed.

And that, thought Cassian, looked distressingly like that.

Well, there was much to do.

The fight ring had been built between the front two of the *Kleptomanic*'s four funnels. It was a square of canvas, surrounded by a velvet-covered rope. The rope was a metre off the ground. Dickie the Brickie stepped over it without effort. Nosey walked under it without ducking. The crowd roared.

Above the ring had been installed a mighty clock, the hands set to twelve noon. In each of two opposite corners of the ring was a wooden stool. Dickie the Brickie sat down on his. Giant Luggage and Nanny Pete, who had been brought blinking out of the funnel to serve as seconds, helped Nosey up on to his. The referee, Superintendent Bent Larsen of the Freeport Constabulary, entered the ring himself. 'GOOD morning, ladies and gentlemen!' he cried. 'And a fine bright morning it is –'

'Move it, copper!' cried the crowd.

(And it was a crowd. Up and up it stretched, like the crater of a volcano made of people. There were burglars in masks, burglars dressed as nannies, burglars in red and black striped jerseys, and of course burglars dressed as builders, or builders dressed as burglars – it was hard to tell the difference, assuming there was one.)

'Orright!' roared Superintendent Bent. 'Inna red corner, Dickie the Brickie! Inna other red corner, er . . . anyone got a magnifying glass, hur, hur! Aargh!' The Superintendent began to hop round the ring, screaming. For Noscy Clanger had shot out and bitten him sharply in the leg.

There was an enthusiastic rumble from the crowd; violence was always highly acceptable. Dickie the Brickie locked his salami fingers and cracked his knuckles with a sound that sent seagulls squawking from their nests in the ledges of the ship.

Watching from a porthole high above, Daisy turned to Primrose, who had just returned from the kitchen. She said, 'We're in trouble.'

Primrose just smiled a large, calm smile, and hugged the Safes of the World cake tin she had in her arms.

'But look at the size of him!'

'You wait till he has a sip of water.'

Daisy looked at her sister sideways. 'Not normal water?' she said.

Primrose raised her eyebrows, sweetly innocent.

'Like Nana says,' she said. 'What you don't know can't hurt you, dear.'

Daisy snarled at her.

'Temper,' said Primrose.

'And now!' roared Superintendent Bent, 'as is traditional, seconds will swop water bottles, just to make sure there's no dodgy dealing.'

'Oh, dear,' said Primrose. 'I hadn't thought of that.'

'Problem?' said Daisy.

'Disaster,' said Primrose. She explained.

'I'll find Cassian,' said Daisy.

The water bottles were swopped. 'Seconds out!' cried Superintendent Bent. 'No gouging, no biting, no tactical missiles or other fire weapons. Otherwise anything goes. Round one!'

Bing, said the bell. And high overhead, the *Kleptomanic*'s great clock began to tick.

Primrose struggled through the crowd to the clear area round the red velvet ring. She started across it. A rural burglar grabbed her arm. 'Can't go there, liddle missy,' he said.

'But something terrible will happen!'

'Can but 'ope,' said the burglar, with a happy, rustic, scarfaced grin.

'I must get in!'

'Now lookie yur,' said the rural burglar, who had specialized in twocking tractors before he had run away to ship. 'I knows that you nanny folks is crool 'ard. But we is burglars and we has got standards. Because we breaks the lor for a living and before you breaks the lor you got to know where it lies, be it the Lor of the Land or, as in this case yur, the Lor of the Jungle. If you follow.'

There were nods and growls all round.

'Why don't you watch with me,' said the Captain, who had appeared at her side.

Up in the ring, Dickie the Brickie was lumbering in circles, trying to grasp Nosey Clanger, who was launching small but apparently painful kicks at his ankles. It was going better than Primrose had expected. Just as long as Nosey did not drink the water . . .

Primrose had worked long and hard at that water. She was proud of the result. It had henbane for illness, bat kidneys for sleepiness, eggs for sloshing and cake for clumsiness. It was in a base of her own devising, made of river foam and fish bladders, that made it taste exactly like water, only slightly thicker. And it contained a secret delay ingredient, made from the temporal lobes of snail brains, which meant that its effects took a minute to kick in.

The clock ticked round to three minutes. *Bing*, went the bell. The fighters returned to their corners.

'How do you think it's going?' said the Captain to Daisy, who had finished a certain mission and come alongside.

'Fine,' said Daisy. Her face felt as if it was made of wood. 'Can we knock over the water bottle?'

'Against the rules.'

'Blast the rules!'

'Not very nanny,' said the Captain.

'Don't care.'

'The rules are the rules,' said the Captain. 'They have been put in place to avoid a general battle.'

'In that case,' said Daisy, 'we are going to have to make the bits of the bear vanish.'

'The rules –'

'What the eye don't see, the heart don't grieve over,' said Daisy.

'Besides,' said the Captain. 'The bits are heavily guarded.'

'We've thought of that,' said Primrose, clutching her cake tin.

'So be good and hope for the best. It's all we can do, Primrose, dear. Primrose?'

'She's gone,' said Daisy.

And she had.

There were two nanny burglars and two builders in the wheelhouse. They were sitting on opposite sides of the chart table, glaring at each other. Behind them on the wall were the six shields that bore the Bits of the Bear. When the door opened, they looked round. A little girl was standing there. She was wearing a pink gingham dress, white socks, and dear little black patent-leather pumps. Her hair was yellowish blonde, scraped back under a pink Alice band. And her eyes were pale blue and blinked a lot. In her hand was a Safes of the World cake tin. 'Hello Mr Big Person,' said Primrose, and gave a high giggle. 'I brought you some cakes.'

'Oo,' said the builders. 'Thoughtful. Where you gone, ship burglars?'

'Down here under the table,' said the burglars, who knew how truly dangerous she was.

The little girl took the lid off the tin. 'Don't your friends want some?' she said.

'No,' said a voice from under the table.

'All the more for us,' said the builder.

His mate looked into the tin. It contained four delicious looking cakes, pink, with real cream, tutti-frutti sprinkles and chocolate icing. 'Sloo,' he said.

'Yeah,' said his mate, grabbing with unwashed hands. 'Cheers, little girl. Yum.' Down went the cakes.

'That's it, then,' said the builders. 'Scarper, kid.'

But the kid did not scarper. She stood there blinking and smiling her watery smile. She had never seen anyone eat a double dose of her Extra-Fast-Acting Sleepy Cakes before, and she wanted to see what would happen.

There was a noise like two sacks of potatoes being dropped from a height. ''Scuse me,' said Primrose, stepping over the bodies. 'I'll take that.' She started unhooking the bear-part shields from the wall.

'Oi,' said the nanny burglars, nervously.

'Oh do be quiet,' said Primrose. 'There's a really interesting fight outside. Why don't you have a butcher's?'

The Nannies crowded to the wheel-house windows.

'Well, then,' said Primrose, gathering up the bear bits. 'Bye!'

232

And she slipped away.

It was busy needle time.

'Seconds out!' cried Bent, by the ring. 'Round two!'

And Nosey Clanger went in.

He buzzed towards Dickie the Brickie like a hungry mosquito. Dickie tried to clap one of his hands on each of Nosey's ears. But Nosey was too quick for him. The great palms came together behind him with a sound like bricks colliding. And Nosey was through, biting Dickie sharply in the leg as he passed.

The round went on.

The second part of the round consisted of Nosey, pawing at his opponent's mouth, sprinting round the ring, while Dickie lumbered after him. Nosey took to ducking under the ropes, probably in the hope that Dickie would trip up as he chased him. Now it was the white van's turn to boo. Nosey's leg nips had slowed Dickie down, but not enough. Swat, went his mighty fist. The wind of it blew Nosey's face out of shape, and he stumbled. The next fist hurtled towards him –

Bing, went the bell.

Nosey dropped to the ground. The fist missed.

'Phew,' said a couple of hundred burglars.

Nosey crawled to his corner. He picked up the water bottle.

Daisy stood frozen with horror.

He rinsed his mouth out and spat.

Daisy let out her breath.

Nosey took another swig.

'Oops,' said Daisy.

Nosey swallowed.

Daisy's mouth hung open, and she forgot to breathe.

'The leg bone connected to the bum bone,' sang Primrose, her sewing hand a blur. 'The other leg connected to the, er.' Even a bear as smart as the Royal Edward did not have actual bones, so the song was pretty useless really, and Primrose had no time for useless things, including songs.

She chewed her lower lip, and stitched on the other leg. She sewed the bear's bum to the bear's tum. She sewed the arms to the torso. It was a fantastically neat job, done at the high speed she had learned while sewing nanny skirts to nursery curtains behind nanny backs in earlier life. After two and a half minutes, the Royal Edward was all there, except for the head: a dumpy beige bear, moth-eaten, giving off a slight, sour smell of royal and ancient dribble.

Primrose ran for the iron ladders that plunged into the oily deeps.

'Cassian!' she cried. 'CASSIAN!'

But Cassian was elsewhere, doing other stuff.

At first, the special water seemed to revive Nosey. He did a couple of press-ups and danced on the rope. But inside him, Daisy knew, the henbane, raw eggs, cake, fish bladders, river foam and snail brains would be doing their deadly work. In precisely sixty seconds, the fight was going to take a turn for the worse.

And there was nothing anyone could do about it.

'Round three!' cried Bent.

Bing, said the bell.

The fighters leaped from their stools and headed for the middle of the ring.

Daisy could now see that the mixture was definitely working on Nosey, but not, perhaps, in the way Primrose had intended. He skipped confidently across the ring. His gums were no longer bared. His eyes were fixed on the point of Dickie's square, stubbly chin. They had a weird glitter.

The crowd could definitely feel something was going on, and they liked it. 'Bop 'im!' they cried.

For a moment, Nosey stood perfectly still. Then he leaped backwards, landing on the red velvet rope. The rope stretched under his boots like catapult elastic. Then it shot him through the air, fists out, straight at Dickie the Brickie. Daisy caught a glimpse of Nosey's tiny face. The eyes were closed, and it wore a blissful smile. As he hurtled towards the delivery of his killer punch, Nosey was already fast asleep.

Asleep or not, things now happened extremely fast.

Dickie had been standing there with his mouth open. As Nosey's gloves hit his chin, his teeth came together with a click. He went down flat on his back, seeing stars. Nosey landed flat on his face next to him, and lay snoring peacefully.

A flicker of movement caught Daisy's eye, high up by the clock. A figure was up there, carrying what looked like a petrol can: stocky, with thick black hair and oily overalls. Cassian.

The crowd was going barmy. Bent scratched his

chin. A double knockout was against the rules, and Bent never broke the rules, unless of course someone paid him to do it.

Dickie's eyelids fluttered. He groaned, pushing himself on to one knee. The sweat of relief poured down Bent's forehead. Dickie got up, and leaned on the ropes. 'ONE!' cried Bent.

High among the cogs of the clock, Cassian poured the last drops from his tin into the giant springs and balance wheels. It was a blackish, gooey liquid. Where it touched the metal surfaces, it made strings, like chewing gum or extra sticky toffee (both of which were in the mixture). A weird groaning was coming from the machinery as the treacly goo spread through it. You would have said the cogs were moving more slowly.

You would have been right.

Cassian threw the tin into the works, and slid down a funnel-stay towards a dark hatch leading into the bowels of the ship.

There was much to do, and little time.

Primrose marched across the engine-room floor, clutching the Royal Edward to her pink gingham chest. It seemed hotter than usual down here, with more steam, and bigger mechanical thumpings, and hollower clangings. She clutched the Royal Edward more tightly – even headless, he was a comforting bear. Kitchens were fine, but she was not so sure about engine rooms.

Too late to worry now.

She was at the door of the control room. Cassian had told her about the bell push. Using the paw of the Royal Edward, she gave the bell a prod.

'NOOO!' cried the voice from within. A pair of whirling brown eyes appeared in the holes in the glass. Primrose held up the bear.

There was a moment of silence, as far as silence was possible in the engine room. Then: 'YEEEES!' cried the voice from within. There was the sound of five chains coming off, a dozen locks unlocking. The Chief stood there, jaw swinging, getting ready to say something fantastically stupid.

Primrose got in first. 'Listen up, you big palooka,' she said. 'This is your bear, but as even you should be able to see, it has got a bit of a head shortage. And I cannot tell a lie, we nicked the bits we didn't have. But of course it is your bear and has been all along, so in my view this whole Challenge business is just a load of nonsense. I'll put it back if you want to be all silly and royal and sporting. Or I can sew it back together good as new with my busy needle. And then we can forget about this Challenge nonsense and you can do what our Cassian wants. Right?'

The Chief fiddled with his fingers, racked between love and duty. 'Smellink so good,' he mumbled. 'Rules is rules, but schtolen from me by rewolution men and poor sing, no head. IN EWENT OF EMERGENCY, BREK GLESS!' Picking up a hammer, he took a mighty swing at the glass case containing, under its gilt wrought-iron crown and eagle, the head of the Royal Edward.

Glass flew everywhere. The head rolled free. Primrose scooped it up. 'Moment,' she said, one eye screwed up, threading her needle against an arc lamp.

It was done in a trice.

'There you go,' said Primrose, tossing the Chief his bear.

'Not to throw poor him!' snapped the Chief. Then the tidal wave of emotion smote him.

Reader, it was a fearful sight. That enormous man in blue and gold kissed his teddy. He hugged it. He sniffed it, drooled on it, and hugged it a bit more. Primrose was forced to look away.

And saw Cassian, one eyebrow up on his oily forehead, wearing an expression of bright hope and expectation –

'NOOOOO!' bellowed the Chief. 'NODINGS HAPPEN!'

'I beg your –'

'I AM PRESSINK TUMMY,' howled the Chief, pressing it. 'MY ALGERNON IS SUPPOSED TO SAY, "GOOD EVENINK, YOUR ROYAL HIGHNESS, I VISH YOU MANY CODFISH AND ABSOLUTELY NO VOLCANOES." But I PRESS and I PRESS and NODINGS I get. Not a SPRAT. Not a GEYSER –'

'Oops,' said Primrose. 'Wrong bear.' And before the Chief knew what was happening, she had twitched the mouldering beast out of Prince Beowulf's hands and darted into the coal-heaps.

'What's wrong?' said Cassian. 'We haven't got much time.'

'Hold it,' said Primrose. 'I need to talk to Daisy. Stay by the ventilator.'

'But –'

But Primrose was gone.

15

The clock's second hand seemed to be moving too slowly. 'Am I going crazy?' thought Bent Larsen, the referee. During the first second of the count, he took a cheese sandwich from his pocket and ate it. Slowly. He said, 'I don't believe that clock.'

'Ship's time is ship's time,' said the Captain's voice, elegant but nautical. Another voice said from the crowd, 'DO WE BELIEVE IN THE SHIP'S CLOCK?'

'YEEEES!' roared many voices.

'Then COUNT!'

'TWO!' roared the crowd. Bent ate the other half of his sandwich, even more slowly than the first, while weird groanings came from the clock. '. . . and . . . THREE!'

Another long pause. 'Next time, louder!' cried a voice. Daisy's voice. Nosey needed to be woken up, and a good shout might do it.

'F . . .' hissed the crowd.

'Not yet!' cried Daisy. Cassian had overdone the clock goo. A huge syrupy strand was hanging from the hour hand. Hilda the Builder's moon face and button nose turned up at it, frowning.

'. . . OUR!' cried the crowd, as the second hand crawled round.

'FIXX!' cried Hilda.

'Gerroff!' cried the crowd. 'Gerraway!' There was a general soup of roaring. Fights broke out. Someone fried an egg and ate it.

'FIVE!'

'Up, Nosey!' cried Daisy. 'Up!'

But it was not Nosey who was up. It was White Van Dan, swinging skyward like an awful ape on one of the taut hawsers supporting the funnel, heading for the clock. The crowd watched him, mouths open. The strand of goo from the clock stretched like chewing gum, and fell into the gigantic mouth of Hilda the Builder. 'Treacle!' cried Hilda, slobbering delightedly. 'Yummmmmmmmmmm!' And could say no more, because the go-slow goo had got its deadly grip on her jaws, and stuck them together sure as superglue.

High above, Dan had reached the clock. He scooped a sample of goo into his tobacco tin, got some on his hand, and wiped his nose on the back of it.

'SIX!' cried Bent Larsen, and chorus, far below him.

'FIX!' yelled Dan, or meant to. But the goo had spread from the back of his hand to his nose, and from his nose to his lips, so the sound came out, 'FXXXXXXXX,' like an escape of steam. He hung there, lips sealed, gibbering.

'He looks,' said Daisy, 'like a sloth.'

'Only slower,' said the Captain. 'Goodness.' Her ruby lips were pressed together, her knuckles the colour of ivory. 'If he can claim the fix, with evidence, before the end of the countdown, he automatically wins. There will be a debate over ship's time, of course, but –'

'Nosey blinked!' cried Daisy. 'He definitely blinked!'

And indeed, there on the canvas, the tiny shell-like eyelids of Nosey Clanger had moved.

'Not long till he wakes up,' said Daisy.

The Captain sighed. 'But then what?' she said.

High on his wire, White Van Dan was hard at work. His lips were still sealed. But he had taken from his dungarees pocket a small pointing trowel. With this tool he had scraped go-slow goo from his baccy tin and smeared it on his boots. Then he stood up on the hawser and let himself fall forward until he was hanging head downwards, directly above the ring. The crowd gasped. Very slowly, White Van Dan descended on twin strings of goo towards the tiny figure sprawled on the canvas. And all the time, he was doing something with his thick, tattooed hands.

Someone was tugging at Daisy's sleeve. 'Oi!' hissed a voice. Primrose's voice.

'What?' said Daisy, impatiently.

'The bear's squeak,' said Primrose.

'What are you talking about?'

'It's missing. It used to be in its tum. It isn't any more.'

'Oh,' said Daisy, and thrust her hands into the pockets of her nanny coat, the better to think.

Her hand met something metallic and drum-shaped. She pulled it out, frowning. It looked like a miniature concertina. It could almost have been a weird, elaborate, massively over-complicated . . .

(She remembered something falling on the Roller's floor; falling from the torso, in fact; picking it up; putting it in her pocket . . . from the torso.)

. . . bear's squeak or voice box. She gave it to Primrose.

'Ahem,' said Primrose. 'Captain?'

'What?'

'I need a burglar who can throw.'

'Of course, of course,' said the Captain, dis-tractedly. 'Bruce used to play cricket for Australia. Expert at stealing runs. Bruce!'

Bruce came over. Primrose gave him his instruc-tions. Bruce scratched his head. 'That ventilator?' he said, pointing.

'That ventilator.'

Bruce took the voice box of the Royal Edward, wound it up, and threw. The little silver drum soared into the air, went dead centre into the red mouth of the ventilator, and disappeared from view.

'SEVEN!' roared the crowd.

'SEVEN!' said the ventilator pipe far below. Cassian looked up. There was a rattle and a clatter. And out of the ventilator pipe there clattered a small silver drum.

Cassian caught it before it could hit the deck, stuffed it into a slot he had cut in the bear's middle, and ran across to the control room. He held up the bear. The Chief's eyes whirled. Cassian pressed the bear's stomach. 'GOOD EVENINK, YOUR ROYAL HIGHNESS,' said the bear. 'I VISH YOU –'

The door crashed open. Loving hands snatched the Royal Edward. 'VELCOME HOME!' cried the Chief, embracing his old pal.

'And now,' said Cassian, 'your side of the bargain.'

'What's he doing?' said Primrose.

'Dread to think,' said the Captain, as if she already had thought, and did not like it.

'What's that?' said Daisy.

Everyone suddenly stood very still. For a second, a hush fell.

For deep, deep under the steel deck on which they stood, something had moved. It might have been a tiny earthquake, or a door slamming far away in a house.

Then it stopped, as if it had never been.

'Just settling,' said the Captain. She really was very, very pale. 'By the way, where's your brother?'

Daisy found it easy to like the Captain. Which was odd, because Daisy did not like anyone, much, except her brother and sister. It was a most peculiar feeling. Because she was not used to it, it took the form of worrying about all the work that would go on, the misery and suffering that would result if the poor kind nanny burglars had to leave their ship or got arrested or something because of a Challenge that had gone wrong . . .

Goodness, thought Daisy, who thanks to years of nannies was used to taking the blame. It is practically my fault.

She found she was holding the Captain's hand, and the Captain was holding hers back.

'EIGHT!' roared Bent Larsen.

Up there on the canvas, Nosey Clanger rose on one tiny knee.

'Oo!' cried the crowd.

Nosey fell down again.

'Aa!' cried the crowd.

Far below, in the *Kleptomanic*'s engine room, Cassian stood at a huge console gleaming with polished brass. Around him stood his hand-picked henchmen, all of them with high mechanical qualifications – safe-crackers, train-robbers, bank-vault tunnellers. Beside him beamed Chief Engineer Crown Prince Beowulf of Iceland, the Royal Edward in his arms.

'Report,' said Cassian into the speaking-tube at his ear.

'Water levels equal, guv,' said a voice.

For Cassian, this was the culmination of much work. Naturally he knew all about liners, having read the Arthur Mee *Books of Knowledge* from C to shining Zee (A and B had been destroyed in an experiment).

This is his master list:

1. Oil everything
2. Trim bunkers, specially number 9, redistributing

contents in nos 2, 3, 4 and 7 for optimum stability (port bunkers odd, starboard bunkers even)
3. Check speaking-tubes
4. Check oil, water, other fuels, generators, food, sheets, blankets, lifeboats, butter, cheese and all ancillary machinery
5. Check speaking-tubes again, also engine-room telegraphs
6. Check lock gates
7. Light boilers
8. Persuade Chief Engineer to throw master switch
9. That's it.

All those years, the *Kleptomanic* had been sitting in a dock – a huge basin of water with a gate at one end, so no matter whether the tide was high or low outside, inside it would always be at the same level. This morning, Cassian had sent his dock gang out on to the sluice gates to open the hatches that would make the water level inside the dock the same as the water level outside. Stealthily, the levels had equalized, and the gates had swung open in a sullen swirl of black water, leaving the *Kleptomanic* pointing at the open creek.

After the restoration of the Edward, Cassian

had gone to the console. 'Mornin', Fingers,' he said.

'Mornin', Chief.'

'Steam up?'

'Steam up.'

Earlier that morning, he had given the order to get up steam. From nooks and crannies and black beds in the bunkers the stokers had poured – gold-diggers, grave robbers, treasure hunters and other low forms of criminal life, good for nothing but shovelwork. A couple of arsonists had got sticks and paper going in the cavernous hearths. Then the coal started to rain down, caught, glowed, and the heat rushed round the boiler tubes and the water boiled and turned to steam, and waited behind its valves to push up the huge pistons linked to the shafts that plunged through the ship's back end and turned the five-metre bronze propellers that had once driven the ship across the Atlantic in a breathtaking six days.

Now, two hours later, the needles on the pressure dials were crawling up to the red line.

Cassian uncapped a speaking-tube. 'Report,' he said.

One of the tubes was saying, with several hundred voices, 'FIIXXX!' Another, the one Cassian was listening to, said, 'Gates open, guv. Ready when you are.'

'Check,' said Cassian. 'Test drive train.'

'All systems nominal, guv,' said Fingers.

'Bridge?' said Cassian into a speaking-tube.

'All present and correck.'

'Same here.'

'Dead slow astern, then,' said the bridge.

'FIIXXXXX,' roared the faraway crowd.

Ding, went the telegraph.

Steam whooshed into the cylinder. The gleaming cams shifted. The great shaft turned and kept turning.

And all the time, White Van Dan was descending on his slow ropes of goo. Now the people below could see what he was doing. He had pulled the pencil from behind his ear. Fighting goo at every letter, he was writing on the slab of four-by-two that he always carried in the back pocket of his filthy, low-slung jeans. Below him, the ring was a white square, Dickie the Brickie in his corner, dribbling brick dust down his fearful jaw as he snacked; Bent Larsen stooped over the tiny flat-out figure of Nosey Clanger, whose eyes were once more closed.

Whose eyes were suddenly open.

The eyes looked straight up, the whites showing all the way round the irises. They focused straight-away on descending Dan. Bent Larsen, following his gaze, looked up.

And saw, in reverse order, this: the clock, the string of goo, White Van Dan, and the length of four-by-two in Dan's hand. And on the four-by-two, words, scribbled in huge ignorant writing: FIX. OFISHUL PROTETS.

Give or take a bit of spelling, it was the correct formula.

'STOP THE FIGHT!' roared Bent.

The *Kleptomanic* moved again.

This time, it did not stop.

The crowd stilled. A cloud of gulls rose from the upperworks. They were already nervous from all the shouting, and now they wheeled and shrieked and watched with their mad yellow eyes as some-thing the size of a city block slid ponderously from between the piers and warehouses. They sailed, bright white against the blue as it stopped going backwards and started going forwards, pointing its nose out of the long black creek towards the sea.

The gulls thought about going to sit on the ship again. They soared among the black plumes billowing from the funnels, nervous, not quite liking to perch.

A gull's life is hard and uncertain. Gulls get good at smelling out trouble before it happens.

16

Hilda the Builder had just managed to wrench her huge lips apart, using both hands. 'Oi!' she cried, in a voice still goo-muffled. She began puffing and wobbling through the crowd towards the Captain. 'Dickie!' she yelled over her bloated shoulder. 'Get Dan!'

Dickie the Brickie reached up, grabbed White Van Dan, and hauled him down into the fight ring. Dan took his boots off. The smell floated across to Nosey, who sat up suddenly. 'Have I won?' he said.

Dan shook his head, lips still stuck.

'Oh,' said Nosey, disappointed, 'Phwoar. Your feet fmell awful.'

Dickie the Brickie produced a nasty grinding sound. 'Cheeky,' he said, blowing a cloud of brick dust. 'Pygmy boy.'

Things then began to happen fast. Nosey, refreshed by his short sleep and still sensitive about his height, bit Dickie in the leg. Dickie picked up Nosey, swung him twice round his head, and threw him into the sea.

Nosey cried, 'I can't fw i
          i
            i
              i
                i
                  i –' The word ended in a small white splash in the broad black creek.

'Oi!' cried Bent Larsen, blowing his ref's whistle. But the sound was drowned in a great roar of burglarious rage as AAA Aardvark Childminding and Security fell on the Firm.

'Oi, sunshine, your boy is well out of order,' said the Captain to White Van Dan in fluent Criminal. 'It was a fair cop. There was a fix, granted, which I hereby admit as per the rules, clause 14 section Q (i).

But we have, as it now appears, got the Edward. And possession being nine points of the law, plus it was the Chief Engineer's bear anyway, what you going to do about it?'

White Van Dan's face was hard as cement. He made no answer.

'Can you, frinstance, drive a ship?' said the Captain. 'It means turning up on time, and not stopping for tea every ten minutes.'

'Fine,' said Dan. 'See what you mean. You win.' His face now looked like cement in a mixer, sloshed around by strong paddles of emotion. 'But wot am I gunna tell the boys? And Hilda?'

'We keep the Chief. You wouldn't like him. Or Iceland. If anyone asks, you have won, and I shall give you a certificate. We are off, under clause 28 section B, viz. in the event of a fix the fixer will leave the manor, no error. There is no call for nastiness or unpleasantness. We shall put you ashore in one of the lifeboats.'

'Fair doos,' said White Van Dan.

'Daisy,' said the Captain over her shoulder. 'Could you ask Cassian to arrange this?'

Silence, except for the ear-splitting roar of fighting burglars.

'Daisy?'

But Daisy seemed to have vanished.

Then a small, clear voice shouted, 'Over there!'

It cut through the roar like a knife, that voice. For a moment the world hushed. The moment spread, became a second, then a minute. All eyes were directed over the side.

This is what they saw.

They saw Daisy, now wearing shorts and a T-shirt, loping with a ballerina's grace to the far outside end of the *Kleptomanic*'s bridge, where it hung over the water like a diving board. They saw her arms go forward, out, forward again. And as they went forward for the last time, she launched herself into space, arms outstretched, body arched back in a perfect swallow dive, down, down, down, until she entered the creek with the smallest feather of a splash. There was a rattle of applause. '*Neuf points!*' cried the Captain.

'Do what?' said White Van Dan.

'Shut it and get in the lifeboat, concrete features,' said Pete Fryer, who was standing close at hand.

'Manners!' said Dan, sniffily. He had never had

a nanny, so no one had ever in his long life of crime spoken to him in that tone of voice.

But he went down the ladder and squeezed into the lifeboat next to Hilda the Builder. Dan had made a decision. He would stop all this building nonsense, and go into the security trade. There would be uniforms, of course: boiler suits with gold badges, truncheons instead of hammers. They would get paid for hanging around drinking tea near banks and jewellers. Pickings in the security industry would be astonishingly rich.

The future looked bright.

Daisy went down and down, until the waters of the creek were as black as the blackest midnight. She was not worried, though. She was thinking how upset poor Nosey must be, floundering tinily after all that brilliant fighting. It was as if something ancient and powerful was driving her on. Nosey felt like part of her family.

Part of her *what*?

Deep under the surface of the creek, she was suddenly very confused. She had been looked after by nannies for so long that the idea of families was strange and distant. Now, weirdly, it made her think of the Captain, and of course her dear brother and sister, with somewhere in the background, small and wobbly, Papa Darling . . .

Here she stopped thinking. Because far above, in a twinkle of white water, she saw two of the smallest legs in the world, kicking.

Kicking frenziedly, to keep their owner afloat.

And failing.

Daisy whooshed up to the surface and took a deep breath. The *Kleptomanic* rose above her like a cliff. Builders who had failed to get places in Dickie and Hilda's lifeboat were falling down the side like fruit off a tree. Eyeing them with a diver's scorn she turned away, looking for Nosey. The water slopped black and empty and cold.

Ten metres away from her, bubbles rose.

She dived after them.

The line of bubbles rose silvery and wobbling, pointing at a tiny white frog drifting down, down towards the mud and old fridges of the creek bottom. A frog wearing huge boxing shorts. Nosey.

Daisy had never done any lifesaving before. But she knew exactly what to do. She kicked firmly downwards, grabbed the frog by its shorts and headed for the surface. Her head broke water. 'Help!' she cried.

And from all along the rail of the *Kleptomanic* there rolled a long, delighted cheer.

It was pretty straightforward after that. A rubber dinghy with Pete Fryer at the helm picked them up. Held upside down, Nosey gurgled forth a great deal of water and started snoring. Many builders passed, vacating the ship as per agreement with the Captain, heading for shore in lifeboats and making gestures of the rudest type. Daisy put her nose in the air. 'Sticks and stones may break my bones but signs will never hurt me,' she said.

'Quite fo,' said Nosey, opening his eyes.

'You're better!' cried Daisy, pink with delight.

'I had him right where I wanted him,' said Nosey. 'I waf robbed.'

Then they were alongside, and the crane was coming down, and up they soared to the Jag deck, where the Captain was waiting with Primrose and Cassian. 'Darlings!' said the Captain.

'It waf nuffink,' said Nosey, beaming modestly from knee level and not noticing that he was by no means the centre of attention. Red Crook burglars hustled him away to the sick bay. The Captain smiled sweetly at the departing stretcher, and pulled out a telescope.

The creek was much wider now. The *Kleptomanic* was heading straight for the open sea. 'Steady as she goes,' said the Captain. 'Now, Daisy. I want a word. Ah, well done, children.' For Cassian had brought up a giant fluffy towel from the First Class Airing Hall, and Primrose had whipped her up a large, dark cocoa strong enough to blot out the taste of the creek.

'A good job well done,' said the Captain. 'I had no idea you were such a splendid lifesaver.'

'Nor me,' said Daisy. The creek had washed away the last traces of nanny attitude. Now she was grinning in the modest way she had seen girls grin in the *Nice Big Book for Girls*. 'It's in the blood, I suppose.'

'The blood?'

'I don't know if you've ever heard of Grace Darling?' said Daisy. 'Daughter of the keeper of the Longstone Light. On a hideous stormy day she rowed out with her dad and rescued a lot of people from the sea in Scotland. Her dad was my great-great-great-grandpa. So I suppose you could say it was in the blood – Are you all right?'

For the Captain had gone white as a gull's stomach, and was swaying on her ten-centimetre heels. She said, in a strange, breathy voice, 'So what's your name?'

'Darling.'

There was a silence. Then Daisy said, 'Timberrrrrr!' And Cassian and Primrose, practised in teamwork after years of nanny torture, stepped behind the Captain and caught her just as she went down like a tree, spark out.

'Uh?' said Cassian.

'I've got a funny feeling about this,' said Primrose.

So had Daisy.

Daisy was looking at her brother and sister, one on either side of the Captain's pale, unconscious face, so there were three faces in a line.

Give or take a bit of age and make-up, the three faces were alike. Three peas in a pod, was the expression that came to mind.

'Bring her round,' said Daisy, grimly.

They poured a bucket of water over the Captain. The eyes opened. They did not look sleepy. In fact, Daisy thought, they looked as if she had been faking, to give herself time to think about what she was going to say.

But when the eyes settled on the children, they filled up with tears.

'Oi,' said Daisy. 'Was there something you wanted to tell us?'

'Don't,' said soft-hearted Primrose, holding the Captain's hand. 'Not till she's had some eggnog or something.'

'Wha –?' said Cassian.

'Idiot!' said his sisters. 'Don't you understand *anything*?'

Cassian scowled. 'What is it?' he said.

'Curiosity killed the cat,' said Daisy.

'Question and answer is no substitute for conversation,' said Primrose.

''Scuse me,' said Fingers, Chief Stoker, 'but we've got a bearing running hot on number-two shaft, and Chief says he's busy talking to his bear.'

'Coming,' said Cassian. He went.

'Are you sure?' said the Captain to the two sisters, when their brother had left.

'As eggs is eggs.'

'But –'

Both sisters sniffed.

The Captain fell silent.

None of them noticed they were all holding hands.

It was a tough three weeks.

Cassian was awake at all hours, supervising the engines as they screwed the ship ever south and west. Having moved his mattress to a warm corner of the stokehold, he made it absolutely clear that he did not want to talk to any girls about anything, not even if it was extremely important. So naturally his sisters let him stew in his own juice.

As the weather got hotter, Primrose found the Chef, used to chillier northern climes, sitting tomato-faced in a pool of sweat by his ranges. So she took over the kitchens. Sea air makes people hungry. The burglars were organized into two teams or watches (the breaking watch and the entering watch) because a ship never stops, day or night, so there must always be someone awake, even if it is only to bring flying fish downstairs for frying. And if someone is awake, someone is hungry. So if it is not huge lunches, it is midnight feasts. It never stops, and nor did Primrose.

As for Daisy, she spent a lot of time talking to the Captain.

*

On the twenty-second day, Nosey Clanger, who because of his extreme lightness could get further up the mast than anyone else, cried, 'I fee land!'

Nobody paid any attention. Nosey had said the same thing three times a day for two weeks, having decided after his near-drowning that he was a salty son of the sea who could see a black dog in a coal cellar, from outside. But if you keep on saying the same thing often enough, sooner or later you will be right. And on this day, half an hour later, a small, palm-fringed shore did indeed loom above the horizon. Not long after that, the *Kleptomanic* glided through the entrance to a lagoon, and her anchors roared down into water as clear and bright as emeralds.

'Finished with engines,' said Cassian, who was on the bridge. 'Good grief. What's that?'

The *Kleptomanic* lay deep in a horseshoe of white beach. Behind the beach was thick tropical forest, from which rose a slim thread of smoke, perhaps from a camp fire. On the beach, hopping up and down and waving at the city-block-sized ship lying rusty black in the lagoon, was a man. A large man, dressed in rags. Rags that might once, in another life, have been gents' formal evening wear. Except that now the bow tie was tied round the head to keep the filthy hair out of the crusty eyes, and the sleeves had been hacked off the jacket, whose pockets were now full of wild bananas, and the trousers ended just below the scabby knees.

Cassian focused the telescope. 'Goodness me!' he cried. 'It's Papa!'

Daisy cleared her throat nervously. 'Yes,' she said. She took the Captain by the hand. 'And this,' she said, 'is our own dear, true Mama.'

'Who is *so* proud of you,' said the Captain.

This time it was Cassian who fainted.

At this point in the average book, the author dips his pen elbow deep in the old golden syrup, and there are a couple of pages of tears and laughter, after which all and sundry live happily ever after, except the bad guys, who lose limbs.

It was not like that on the *Kleptomanic*. Not quite, anyway. In fact, Papa Darling and the Captain sat on opposite sides of the chart table, and seemed to be having some trouble thinking of things to say to each other. Cassian, having received a bucket of sea water in the face from his unsympathetic sisters, sat groggy on the floor with his back against the wall. 'Out,' said Daisy. She and Primrose dragged him by the legs on to the Jag deck.

'Away,' said Daisy, shooing off Giant Luggage and a gaggle of emotional burglars who were staring in at the bridge windows, hankies at the ready.

The Caribbean air soon brought Cassian back to his full wits. 'How come she didn't know it was us earlier?' he said.

'Secretary Mummy changed our names to make us sound richer. We're really called Jane, Mary and John. And Papa moved house to Avenue Marshal Posh after Captain Mummy left, and it was Secretary Mummy who lost her temper and ripped up the bear and brought the bum back.'

'Silly fool,' said Primrose. 'By the way, we're not changing back.'

'Hardly worth it,' said Cassian. 'So what now?'

'They thrash it out.'

'What?'

'It. Us. Life. All that. I think.' They were walking down towards the engine room now. There was a silence, broken only by the clatter of shoes on iron ladders. 'None of our business,' said Daisy.

'Yes it is,' said Cassian.

'No it –'

They had arrived at the Chief Engineer's console. 'Listen,' said Cassian. 'Even burglars are interested in this kind of man and woman and children stuff. So there's no reason why we shouldn't be either.'

'Yes there is.'

'Why?'

Silence.

'Why?' said Cassian.

'Because Nanny says so,' said Primrose.

Silence. A long, horrid silence. 'But we never pay a blind bit of notice to anything Nanny says,' said Daisy.

'Yep,' said her brother and sister.

'So.'

Cassian took the lid off the voice-pipe marked, 'BRIDGE'. A voice floated into the hum of the engine room. Papa Darling's voice.

'Well?' he was saying. 'Where did you go to, all those years ago?'

'I left.'

'I am acquainted with the central dynamic of your thesis,' said Papa Darling.

'And on what date did I leave?'

'You will kindly refrain from using judgemental speech patterns with regard to myself.'

'Allow me to remind you, Papa Darling,' said the Captain's voice, 'that I have rescued you and that at any moment I could unrescue you, with the assistance of my 200 loyal burglars, trained in violence, larceny and nanny skills.'

There was a silence, in which the children could practically hear Papa go pale.

'So. On what date did I leave?'

'Ninth of August. Ten years ago.'

'Wrong.'

'But I wrote it down in my diary.'

'It was the seventeenth of July. It took you three weeks to notice.'

'What?'

'Our life together. You got up in the morning, read the newspaper at breakfast, went to the office, got back at eight if you got back at all, nodded a lot at dinner, made transatlantic telephone calls till midnight, and went to bed. Every day, weekends included, except when you were on a business trip. You never seemed to notice whether I was there or not, and you always insisted on those ghastly nannies. So one day I was watching the horse-racing on the wide screen TV, you know, the one you gave me to shut me up, and a chap came in, black mask, striped jersey, bag marked 'SWAG'. He said he was a burglar, poor simp, as if I hadn't guessed. And of course he was absolutely hopeless at it. So my heart went out to him, really, I mean I was a bit short of people to look after, and he was so useless. So I helped him with the burglary and he introduced me to all these diamond geezers and we found the ship and I started the agency and looked after him and his friends, and you may say it is wrong to burgle, but if you have got a nanny agency full of burglars it makes sure that you only burgle people who are big enough idiots to use nanny agencies, and most of them deserve it.'

'Tosh,' said Papa. 'You done a runner, with a thief.'

'Talking about thieves,' said the Captain, 'what exactly is it you do at Darling Gigantic?'

'Property development. Enhancement of land values by subdivision and the creation of dwelling units.'

The Captain sighed. 'Translate into English, if you please.'

'Buying land –'

'Nature reserves.'

'Sometimes.'

'And building millions of cheap and nasty houses on them.'

'People gotta live somewhere.'

'Strikes me,' said the Captain, 'that you are a large-scale thief yourself and that you do your nicking from people who are not all that rich in the first place.'

'Wouldn't know,' said Papa, and now there was definitely a sulky note in his voice.

'Kev,' said the Captain, 'you know this to be true.'

'Don't call me Kev,' yelped Papa Darling. 'Nobody knows I'm called Kev. In the business, they call me Colin.'

'But you're not in the business any more,' said the Captain, sweetly. 'That secretary woman with the jewels has got all the loot. She made sure of that when she left you here. Didn't she?'

'Yep,' said Papa Darling, in a tired voice the children had never heard before. 'It's true. By gum, you're still a fine-looking woman, Queenie. But don't call me Kev, all right?'

'We'll see,' said the Captain. 'By the way, you

don't look so bad yourself. Bit porky, mind. But if we put you on first-floor drainpipe and fire-escape training for a month or two, that'll sort itself out.'

There was a pause. Then Papa Darling said, 'Thanks, Queenie.'

'Don't thank me,' said the Captain. 'Thank the people who made it happen.'

'Who?'

'The children. Brilliantly trained in violence, cookery, engineering and sabotage.'

'Stone me,' said Papa, right out of his depth.

'They saved my ship,' said the Captain. 'They are a credit to their parents. And now their parents must show them love.'

'Does this mean,' said Papa, sounding hopeful, 'that you and me might, you know, get back together again? Because I'm up for it if you are –'

'As far as I am concerned, Colin,' said the Captain, and even via the voice-pipe the children heard Papa wince, 'you are just another first-year first-storey man, on extra lav-cleaning duties. Other than that, we shall see.'

Then there was silence.

Cassian and Primrose stared at Daisy in horror. 'Love?' they said.

'Grim, I grant you,' said Daisy. 'But I have a feeling that things are going to get better.'

'Hmm,' said her brother and sister. Both of them could feel, however, that there was indeed a strange optimism in the air.

They sat for a while in silence. It was indeed most puzzling. Then Primrose said, 'What's that?'

For from another of the speaking-tubes there suddenly came the sound of music.

'The ballroom,' said Cassian.

'Come on,' said Daisy.

They went.

OK. Golden-syrup time.

The gallery of the ballroom was thronged with burglars, some of them sobbing openly into hankies. They were watching the dance floor.

By the side of the floor stood the huge grand piano. A woman in a red velvet ball gown was playing it. The tune was 'Stand by Me'. A man was singing the song: a man wearing the tattered shreds of formal evening wear. The woman was the Captain. The man was Papa Darling, obliging with a few bars of the old favourite before reporting for bog-cleaning duty.

Pete Fryer was standing next to the children.

'Aah,' he said, with a catch in his voice. 'In't it Rolls?'

'I beg your pardon?'

'Rolls Royce, choice.'

The children made no reply. They had the impression that if he had closed his eyes, tears would have rolled out. And those eyes seemed completely attached to the Captain. Daisy understood. A skilled and charming burglar like Pete could not spend so much time so close to an clever, elegant criminal mastermind like the Captain without an attachment developing. She sighed. She said, 'The saddest words, Nanny Pete: "What might have been."'

'Huh?' said Cassian. 'Wha?'

'Poor baby,' said Primrose, squeezing Pete's hand.

'Cor stone me strike a light what on earth are you going on about I do not know, a load of old cobblers I am sure,' said Pete, not at all convincingly. 'Well, the Caribbean, eh? Nice warm place to go robbin' of an evening, or so I hear. Eh? What? Don't you think?'

'And close to America,' said Daisy, to help Pete recover his composure. 'There are many openings in America, one hears.'

'Well, we'll be through 'em, doesn't matter what

floor they're on,' said Pete, drying his eyes and laughing heartily. 'Well, love is love and cannot be denied, but now it is time for my pint of stout.'

And the *Kleptomanic* surged on under the fiery tropical sky, carrying the Darling family – parents, children and nanny burglars – towards Miami, Florida, home of millionaires.

Stay in your beds little Darlings,
don't wander about in the night,
for millions of 'orrible villains
is waiting to give you a fright.
You may fink that you're sleeping in safety,
wiv all of your toys shut up tight,
but millions and millions of villains
will be there if you turn on the light.
Ohhhhhhhhhhhhhh . . .
you may chain up your cycles
and lock up your fings
but they'll bite off your fingers
and 'alf-inch your rings –

Read more in Puffin

For complete information about books available from Puffin – and Penguin – and how to order them, contact us at the appropriate address below. Please note that for copyright reasons the selection of books varies from country to country.

www.puffin.co.uk

In the United Kingdom: Please write to Dept EP, Penguin Books Ltd, Bath Road, Harmondsworth, West Drayton, Middlesex UB7 ODA

In the United States: Please write to Penguin Group (USA), Inc. P.O. Box 12289, Dept B, Newark, New Jersey 07101–5289 or call 1–800–788–6262

In Canada: Please write to Penguin Books Canada Ltd, 10 Alcorn Avenue, Suite 300, Toronto, Ontario M4V 3B2

In Australia: Please write to Penguin Books Australia Ltd, 250 Camberwell Road, Camberwell, Victoria 3124

In New Zealand: Please write to Penguin Books (NZ) Ltd, Private Bag 102902, North Shore Mail Centre, Auckland 10

In India: Please write to Penguin Books India Pvt Ltd, 11 Panscheel Shopping Centre, Panscheel Park, New Delhi 110 017

In the Netherlands: Please write to Penguin Books Netherlands bv, Postbus 3507, NL–1001 AH Amsterdam

In Germany: Please write to Penguin Books Deutschland GmbH, Metzlerstrasse 26, 60594 Frankfurt am Main

In Spain: Please write to Penguin Books S. A., Bravo Murillo 19, 1° B, 28015 Madrid

In Italy: Please write to Penguin Italia s.r.l., Via Felice Casati 20, I–20124 Milano

In France: Please write to Penguin France S. A., 17 rue Lejeune, F–31000 Toulouse

In Japan: Please write to Penguin Books Japan, Ishikiribashi Building, 2–5–4, Suido, Bunkyo-ku, Tokyo 112

In South Africa: Please write to Longman Penguin Southern Africa (Pty) Ltd, Private Bag X08, Bertsham 2013

On Friday morning, November 28, the day after Thanksgiving, Matthew Hope went to see Carlton Barnaby Markham at the county jail.

According to the Grand Jury's indictment, he had "coldly, calculatedly, and premeditatedly" murdered his wife Prudence "in an especially heinous, atrocious and cruel manner".

"Did you kill her?" Matthew asked.

"No, I didn't kill her," Markham said.

"So why'd they arrest you? Why'd they charge you?"

Markham was silent for several moments.

Then he said, "The blood was the main reason."

"What blood?"

"On my clothes."

Also by Ed McBain in Sphere:

CINDERELLA
JACK AND THE BEANSTALK
SNOW WHITE AND ROSE RED
THE SENTRIES

Puss in Boots

ED McBAIN

SPHERE BOOKS LIMITED

SPHERE BOOKS LTD

Published by the Penguin Group
27 Wrights Lane, London w8 5tz, England
Viking Penguin Inc., 40 West 23rd Street, New York, New York 10010, USA
Penguin Books Australia Ltd, Ringwood, Victoria, Australia
Penguin Books Canada Ltd, 2801 John Street, Markham, Ontario, Canada l3r 1b4
Penguin Books (NZ) Ltd, 182–190 Wairau Road, Auckland 10, New Zealand

Penguin Books Ltd, Registered Offices: Harmondsworth, Middlesex, England

First published in Great Britain in hardback by Hamish Hamilton Ltd 1987
Published by Sphere Books Ltd 1989
10 9 8 7 6 5 4 3 2

Printed and bound in Great Britain by
Richard Clay Ltd, Bungay, Suffolk

This is for George Greenfield

PUSS IN BOOTS

She thought she heard a sound.

She looked up sharply from the flatbed, listening.

The palm fronds outside the studio rattled with a fierce November wind. A bird called inanely to the night.

Nothing more.

She kept listening.

Lots of expensive photographic and sound equipment in here, you had to be afraid of junkies breaking in. The heavier stuff like the Bell & Howell projector, synched to the mag recorders and dubbers, would be difficult to haul away unless you backed a truck in. But all the lenses and all the smaller cameras like the Nikons and the Hasselblads, even the Pageant projector could be packed easily into the back of a car, driven up to Tampa or St. Pete, sold there in a minute.

Kept listening.

The wind again, palm fronds whispering.

A car going by, tires hissing on asphalt.

Hardly any traffic, this time of night. This was cattle country, or used to be. The studio was set back some three hundred yards from what was still called Rancher Road, surrounded on either side by acres of land already yielding to the developers' bull-dozers. Ten o'clock at night, you'd think it was two in the morning, everything as still as death except for the bird again, calling, calling, and the wind, and the clicking whisper of the palms.

She shook a cigarette free from the package of Benson & Hedges on the blue Formica surface of the flatbed editing machine. The Steenbeck was worth at least twenty thousand, but nothing a junkie could pack in a duffel bag. She picked up a plastic lighter the color of the cigarette package, and thumbed it into flame. She took several puffs on the cigarette, and then immediately stubbed it out. There was work to be done.

She'd shot a bit more than nineteen thousand feet of film in twenty-eight days, figuring a burn ratio of six-to-one in order to get the ninety-minute finished film she was going for. The dailies came back from the lab in New York on eight-hundred-foot cores that fit onto the Steenbeck's revolving stainless steel plates. She'd carried two of those cored rolls to the studio tonight, and had already run one of them through the machine several times, taking notes, marking film and magnetic sound tracks. The second roll was now on the machine, together with her A and B tapes. She checked her synch marks again, to make sure the film and the mag tracks were in absolute synch, and then moved the control lever to roll all three at twenty-four frames per second.

One of the two screens above the editing surface flashed the first image.

The speakers on either side of the screens erupted with sound.

It was almost ten-thirty when the last frame of film rolled through the machine.

She lighted another cigarette, threw the control switch to fast reverse, and sat there smoking while the work print and the mags whirred back through the machine, savoring the cigarette this time, a satisfied smile on her face, pleased with what she'd seen but realizing there was still a great deal of work to be done before the first of the month.

The negative was what she'd be taking with her to Mexico. Plus the workprint and the synchronized sound tracks. Find a lab down there to do the rest of the work. Plenty of work down the road. Assuming all went well. Assuming Jake came up with what she needed down there. Assuming Henry didn't start getting . . .

Well, no sense getting itchy herself.

This was no time to panic.

She stubbed out the cigarette, lifted the cores from the plates, made sure film and sound rolls were tightly wound, and then taped their ends. She put the two cores of film in a sixteen-millimeter film can, one on top of the other, put the lid on it, and closed it securely. She packed her four sound rolls in plastic bags, and then put them into an aluminum carrying case together with the can of film. She carried the case to the back door, set it down just inside it, and then went around the studio turning off all the lights except the one just inside the door.

She picked up the carrying case.

She hesitated near the light switch.

Went back to the flatbed to make sure she'd put out her cigarette.

Went to the door again.

Looked back into the studio, her hand on the burglar alarm panel beside the door.

Put down the carrying case for a moment while she searched in her shoulder bag for her keys.

Picked up the case again, hit the three-digit code on the alarm pad, opened the door, snapped out the last of the lights, and stepped outside.

It was twenty minutes to eleven.

A light bulb in a cage hung over the back door to the studio.

It cast her long shadow on the white gravel of the parking lot.

She locked the door, located her car keys in the illumination afforded by the light bulb, and was walking toward the car when she saw a second shadow on the ground.

She was turning, starting to turn, when the knife plunged into the meaty part of her back, just above the shoulder blade.

She felt only searing pain as the blade penetrated.

She screamed.

And then she was turning, *being* turned, a hand clasping onto her right shoulder and spinning her around to meet the knife as it plunged again. She dropped the aluminum carrying case. She screamed again. The knife kept coming at her. She screamed as blood bubbled into her mouth, spit blood as she screamed, kept screaming until she could no longer scream, the front of her yellow blouse covered with blood welling from her wounds, her face covered with blood, her throat, her hands covered with blood as she fell to the white gravel and the gravel turned red.

And she stared up sightlessly at a star-drenched Florida sky while the palm fronds whispered and the blood continued to run from her torn and lifeless body, touching at last the aluminum carrying case with its cores of film and sound tapes.

At eleven-thirty that night, in a bar called the Goat's Head, some sixty miles north of where Prudence Ann Markham leaked her blood onto a white gravel driveway, two girls in aerobic costumes were playing darts and drinking beer. One of the girls was a blonde and the other was a redhead. The blonde was wearing black tights, a yellow leotard and yellow leg warmers. The redhead was wearing blue tights, a green leotard and green leg warmers. They were both nicely color-coordinated. Neither of

4

the girls was wearing aerobic shoes. They were both wearing shoes with extremely high heels. Black patent leather on the blonde, blue patent on the redhead. The snug costumes, the leg warmers, the stiletto heels made them look like Bob Fosse dancers.

Or hookers.

The girls had just come from an aerobics class, though they probably hadn't been wearing the high heels while they exercised. They kept talking about the class being too crowded, and there being hardly any space near the mirror, meanwhile throwing darts at the board and occasionally hitting it. Each time one of their darts flew out of control, they wiggled their pert little asses and giggled. They were making a big deal out of playing darts like beginners.

Tick and Mose figured the show was for them.

They had been coming on with the girls for the past half-hour now, from the minute the two of them pranced into the place like racehorses. So far, Tick and Mose were batting approximately zero. This was because they had started off by telling the truth. They had told the girls they were in the movie business. The girls thought this was a line. The girls were both in their early twenties and hip to the ways of the world. You met two guys in a Tampa bar that looked like an English pub—all mahogany and brass and leaded windows—they told you they were in the movie business, you had to figure they were full of shit. That had been the first mistake Tick and Mose made, telling the girls the truth about their line of work. They should have said they were in the construction business. The next mistake was giving the girls their true and proper names, which the girls thought were phony.

George Ticknor had said, "My name is Tick."

The blonde girl had said, "What's your friend's name? Tock?"

"Mose," Mose had said. His full name was Mosely Jones, Jr.

His father was also in the movie business, in Atlanta where Mose was born, but he didn't think it was wise to bring up the movie business again.

"What do you girls call yourselves?" Tick asked.

"*Women* is what we call ourselves," the blonde said, and bent over to pick up another dart, exhibiting her fine feminist ass and causing Tick to wet his lips.

For the past half-hour, they'd been making a game of trying to wheedle the girls' names from them. The girls kept playing darts and wiggling and giggling. Tick and Mose sat at the bar, watching them, trying to make conversation over the noise of the TV set blaring the late night news.

"I'll bet your name is Trudy," Tick said to the blonde.

"Ick, Trudy," she said, and pulled a face.

"But close, right? Judy?"

"No way."

"I'll bet you ten dollars your name has an 'oooo' sound in it."

"My mother taught me never to gamble with strangers."

"Who's a stranger?" Tick said. "I already introduced myself."

"Tick, right," she said skeptically, and pulled another face.

"You're ticking us off, Tick," the redhead said. "Take a walk, okay?" But she wiggled her ass again.

"You must be Eileen," Mose said to the redhead.

"Nope."

"Or Maureen."

"Nope."

"Or Colleen. All redheaded girls have Irish names."

"Wrong," the redhead said.

"So what's your name?"

"Revlon," she said, and threw a dart.

The dart missed the board by a mile. It almost missed the *wall*.

"Revlon?" Mose said.

"Figure it out," the redhead said.

Mose tried to figure it out.

"So you guys are in the movie business, huh?" the blonde said.

"That's right," Tick said. At *last*, he thought. A little fucking progress at last.

"Big movie producers, huh?" the redhead said.

"Directors," the blonde corrected. "Looking for starlets. How come you don't have your casting couches with you?"

"I'm a sound man," Mose said. He was lying now. He was a grip.

The blonde picked up her beer mug and licked at the foam, unimpressed. There was a fine sheen of perspiration on her face and on the sloping tops of her breasts. Tick wet his lips again.

"I'm a gaffer," he said. He was lying, too. They were both grips.

"Oh?" the redhead said. "And what's a gaffer?"

"I do the lighting," he said.

"Lights, camera, *action!*" the redhead shouted, and pointed her finger at the blonde, legs spread, ass jutting, one hand on her hip. Both girls giggled again.

"That's not the way it works," Tick said.

"That's not the way *what* works?" the redhead asked.

"Lights, camera, action. That's not what a director says."

"I told you," the blonde said. "He's a director."

"No, I'm a gaffer," Tick said.

"Okay, so tell us what a *director* says," the redhead said, and winked at the blonde.

"First tell us your names," Tick said.

"Should we tell them our names?" the blonde said.

"I already told them mine," the redhead said. "You figure it out yet?" she asked Mose.

"Sure. Revlon."

"Sure *what*?" the redhead said.

"Revlon," Mose said, and shrugged.

"Come on," Tick said. "How we gonna get to know each other if you won't even tell us your names?"

"Who says we *want* to get to know you?" the blonde asked.

"Well, we're talking here, that's getting to know each other, isn't it?" Tick said. "Come on, what's your name? I'll bet it has an 'oooo' sound in it."

"No, it's Rachel," the blonde said, almost shyly.

"What's your friend's name?"

"Gwen."

"Nice to meet you both," Tick said, and got off the bar stool and walked to where the girls were standing near the dart board, hands on their hips.

"Is your name really Tick?" Rachel asked.

"For Ticknor," he said, and nodded.

"Actually, that's kinda cute," she said. "Tick."

"So what does a director say, Tick?" Gwen asked.

Tick was trying to figure out which one he wanted. The blonde had bigger tits, but the redhead had legs that could make a grown man cry. She reminded him a lot of Connie. The red hair, those spectacular wheels. But no one in the world was like Connie.

"Well," he said, "first your A.D. yells for quiet. He'll say . . ."

"What's an A.D.?" Gwen asked.

"Assistant director," Tick said.

"Okay, he yells for quiet."

"'Quiet, please,' something like that."

"Then what?"

"Then the director says, 'Stand by . . .'"

"Okay."

"And then, 'Roll camera . . .'"

"Which is when your cameraman starts the film running," Mose said.

"'Rolling,' is what he says," Tick said.

"The cameraman," Mose said.

8

"Then your director says, 'Roll sound . . .'"

"Which is when your sound man starts his recorder and says, 'Speed.' Me," Mose said, "I'm a sound man." Still lying.

"Then your A.D. says, 'Mark it,'" Tick said.

"For the guy on the clapstick."

"And *that's* when the director yells, 'Action,'" Tick said.

"So at least I was right about the action," Gwen said, and looked them over with what Mose hoped was new respect. "So you're really in the movie business, huh?" she said. "A sound man and a . . . what'd you say you were?"

"A gaffer," Tick said.

"What the hell's a gaffer?" Rachel said.

"I told you. A lighting director."

"Well, at least you're *some* kind of director, right?"

"I'm a whiz with lights," Tick said. He had decided she was the one he wanted.

"Listen," Mose said, "we're gonna be perfectly honest with you."

"Go hide the silver, Rach," Gwen said.

"No, seriously," Mose said.

"He's being serious, Rach."

"I am."

"Weren't you being serious before?"

"Well, yes, but . . ."

"Or honest?"

"What he means . . ." Tick said.

"You figured out where the Revlon comes from?" Gwen asked Mose, playing to him. Good, Tick thought. No problems about who gets who.

"Of course I figured it out," Mose said.

"So where'd it come from? The Revlon."

"Where'd it come from?" Mose asked.

"A bottle," Gwen said.

Mose looked at her.

"He still doesn't get it," Gwen said.

"I get it, I get it," Mose said.

"You were talking about redheads, remember?"

"Sure. Listen, I get it."

"So what is it?"

"Revlon," he said, and shrugged. "Listen, I get it. Revlon."

"I think I picked the dumb one," Gwen said. "So let's hear your big honesty pitch, okay?"

"Well, the minute you girls walked in, I said to Tick here . . ."

"Wait, let me guess. You said we oughta be in pictures."

"No. I said you were gorgeous. Both of you."

"We are," Gwen said. "So?"

"I know you are. That's what I told Tick."

"So?"

"Let me take it from here, okay?" Tick said.

"Here comes the whiz with lights," Rachel said.

"I'm gonna give this our best shot, okay," Tick said, "and if you tell us to walk, we'll walk. But we'd like to get to know you better. I've got a nice place right nearby here, with a good stereo system and some very good pot, and if you'd like to come there with us, I think we can maybe have a good time together. If you say no, we'll thank you for your kindness in listening to us and go our merry way, sadder but wiser. So that's it, our best shot," he said, and smiled in what he hoped was a boyish manner.

"What are you?" Gwen asked. "The dumb one's agent?"

"We're just two nice guys hoping to spend a little time with two nice girls."

"He thinks we're hookers," Rachel said.

"I do *not*!" Tick said, sounding offended, but wondering about it nonetheless.

"We're not, you know," Gwen said.

"I didn't think you were."

"I mean, we're *not*."

"So what do you say?" Mose said.

"Listen to Speedy here," Gwen said. "It's a good thing you're handsome because you sure are dumb." She turned to Rachel. "What do you think?" she asked. "You want to go listen to some stereo with these two nice guys who're hoping to spend a little time with two nice girls?"

"Gee, I don't know," Rachel said. "I'm a little stiff from exercise class."

Tick held his breath.

The girls exchanged glances.

Tick waited.

It seemed to take forever.

"Well," Gwen said at last, "I'm game if you're game."

"Well, maybe for a few minutes," Rachel said.

"Good," Tick said at once. "Let me settle the tab, and we'll . . ."

And that was when he heard what the television announcer was saying.

The television announcer was saying that a woman identified as Prudence Ann Markham had been found stabbed to death outside a movie studio in Calusa, Florida.

Tick looked at Mose.

Mose was staring open-mouthed at the television set over the bar.

"So are we getting out of here or what?" Gwen said.

On Friday morning, November 28, the day after Thanksgiving, Matthew Hope went to see Carlton Barnaby Markham at the county jail. Markham was wearing dark blue trousers, a pale denim shirt, black socks and black shoes. A handsome man—

lean and muscular, with blond hair and blue eyes—he was rendered anonymous by the institutional clothing he wore and the jailhouse pallor he'd acquired in the four short days since his arrest.

Markham had been charged with violation of Section 782.04 of the Florida Statutes which read: "The unlawful killing of a human being, when perpetrated from a premeditated design to effect the death of the person killed . . . shall be murder in the first degree and shall constitute a capital felony, punishable as provided in Section 775.02." In Florida, even a person accused of a capital crime was entitled to bail, the State Attorney's burden being to oppose bail by showing that the evidence in hand was legally sufficient to obtain a verdict of guilty. The Court, in its sole discretion, had the right to grant or deny bail.

Markham had been denied bail.

According to the Grand Jury's indictment, he had "coldly, calculatedly, and premeditatedly" murdered his wife Prudence "in an especially heinous, atrocious and cruel manner," the latter language setting up for the State Attorney a request for the death penalty as defined in Section 775.02.

"Did you kill her?" Matthew asked.

"No, I didn't kill her," Markham said.

Important to Matthew in that when he'd decided to specialize in criminal law, he'd also decided he would never take on anyone he believed was guilty. Since July, when he'd begun his new career (*some* career, so far) he'd represented only two clients (well, almost two) who'd been charged with criminal offenses. The first was a lady schoolteacher who'd been arrested for violation of Section 316.193 of the Florida Penal Statutes, defined as "Driving, or being in physical control of, a vehicle while under the influence of alcoholic beverages or a chemical or controlled substance, or with a specified blood alcohol level" and commonly referred to as DUI, for "driving under the influence." The violation was a misdemeanor that could net a $500 fine and up to six months in jail for a first conviction.

There were four county court judges in Calusa, and two of them had come up with an innovation regarding punishment for a DUI conviction. If an offender was placed on probation, a bumper sticker was affixed to his automobile and the sticker read:

CONVICTED DUI
Restricted License

The license restriction meant that the driver could only use his automobile for business purposes or for routine chores like grocery shopping or visits to the doctor. Matthew had argued the case unsuccessfully: the lady was fined $250, and her car wore the DUI bumper sticker for the full six months.

His second client—the *almost* client—was a man charged with violation of Section 893.135, "trafficking in cannabis," a first-degree felony punishable by three years in prison and a fine of $25,000. He admitted to Matthew, up front, that when he was arrested he was indeed carrying in his pickup truck five hundred pounds of very good Mexican gold, but he insisted that a good criminal lawyer should be able to beat the rap. Matthew had no reason to believe he was a good criminal lawyer who could beat the rap; he would have refused the case, anyway, because the man had already admitted his guilt. (He also called Matthew a no-good turd as he left the office in high dudgeon, but that was *after* he learned Matthew wouldn't represent him.) One and a half clients since July. Back to real estate closings, divorce settlements, will probations, property liens—until Carlton Barnaby Markham called from the county jail.

"Want to tell me why they arrested you?" Matthew said.

"They arrested me because they couldn't find anybody else to arrest," Markham said.

Somewhat petulant mouth, sudden anger flashing in the blue eyes, as though he suspected Matthew of having baited a trap. Voice tinged with a faint Southern accent. Probably born right here in Florida. When you thought of Florida, you visualized beaches and water and sailboats and cloudless blue skies, and palm trees and oranges, you conjured a *resort*. The resort, though, was a part of the Deep South—as far south as you could go, in fact, without falling off the continent—and there were millions of people here who weren't on vacation, and who knew damn well that this was Dixie.

"Even assuming the police were wrong . . ." Matthew said.

"They were."

"Even so, the State Attorney wouldn't have gone to the Grand Jury without what he believed was sufficient cause for indictment."

"I'm sure he thought he had a strong case."

"And so did the Grand Jury when they returned a true bill, and so did the circuit court judge when he denied bail. Mr. Markham, why were all these people so sure you killed your wife?"

"Whyn't you go ask *them*?"

"Because you're the one who's asked me to represent you."

"What do you want me to tell you? Why it *looks* like I killed her?"

"If you will."

"Whose side are you on, anyway?"

"Nobody's. Not yet."

"All they've got is circumstantial evidence," Markham said.

"Well, that's all they *ever* have, unless someone's caught in the act, or unless someone else witnessed the actual killing. They didn't catch you in the act, did they?"

"Of course not!"

"And I'm assuming no one witnessed the murder."

"Only the killer."

"So why'd they arrest you? Why'd they charge you?"

Markham was silent for several moments.

Then he said, "The blood was the main reason."

"What blood?"

"On my clothes."

"There was blood on your clothing?"

"Yes."

"*Her* blood? Your wife's blood?"

"So they say. Her *type* blood."

"You were wearing this clothing, with your wife's blood on it—her *type* blood—when they arrested you?"

"No, I was asleep in bed when they came to the house with their warrant. I was wearing pajamas."

"When was this?"

"Four days after the murder."

"They came to the house with an arrest warrant . . ."

"Yes."

"What time of night?"

"A little after eleven."

"And you were in bed, wearing pajamas."

"Yes."

"Then what?"

"I got dressed, and they took me downtown and questioned me."

"Who was present at the questioning?"

"A detective named Sears, from the Sheriff's office, a police detective named Morris Bloom, and a man named Arthur Haggerty, from the State Attorney's office."

"If they requested someone from the State Attorney's office, then they already thought they had real meat. Did they show you this clothing with bloodstains on it?"

"Yes. They asked me if I recognized it."

"Did you?"

"Yes. It was mine. A jacket and a shirt and a pair of pants. And my shoes and socks."

"The clothing belonged to you."

"Yes."

"And there was blood on it."

"Yes. Well, *dried* blood. And a lot of dirt."

"Dirt?"

"Earth."

"Did they say where they'd got this clothing?"

"They dug it up in my backyard. They came to the house the day after the murder—with a search warrant. They began digging, and they found the clothes and the knife."

"A knife? What do you mean? You didn't mention a . . ."

"A butcher knife. They said it was the knife I used on Prue."

"Had you ever seen that knife before?"

"Yes."

"Where?"

"In my kitchen."

"It was *your* knife?"

"Well, *our* knife. It was a kitchen knife. A butcher knife. It hung on a rack in the kitchen."

Matthew stared at him.

"Mr. Markham," he said, "I guess you realize that's pretty strong circumstantial evidence. Even if they've got nothing else . . ."

"They know the clothes were stolen," Markham said. "The knife, too."

"Stolen?"

"Someone broke into the house and stole them. Took a lot of other things besides."

"When?"

"Ten days before the murder."

"Did you report the burglary?"

"I did."

"To the police?"

"Well, of course to the police."

"Did they investigate?"

"They sent some detectives around. Bloom and his partner, a black cop named Rawles."

"And this burglary took place ten days before the murder?"

"Yes."

"Where were you when it happened?"

"At a friend's house. My wife was working, she's a . . ."

He hesitated, catching himself.

"She *was* a filmmaker," he said, switching to the past tense. "She made commercials, industrials, an occasional documentary."

"Here in Calusa?"

"Well, all over. But she rented studio facilities here. She was working out on Rancher Road the night of the burglary. And also on the night she was killed."

"Working?"

"In the studio there."

"Doing what?"

"Editing."

"Editing a film?"

"Yes."

"What kind of film?"

"I don't know."

"Well, was it a documentary, a commer . . . ?"

"She didn't tell me. She got that way sometimes."

"What way?"

"Secretive about her work. Protective of it."

"So . . . she was at the studio on the night of the burglary."

"Yes."

"And you were at a friend's house."

"Yes."

"From what time to what time?"

"Oh, just for a few hours. We were planning a fishing trip. I got there at about nine, it must've been, and left at eleven."

"Got home and found the house burglarized."

"Yes. Around eleven-thirty."

"Was your wife home yet?"

"No. She was still out at the studio. Didn't get home till around one, one-thirty. The police had already left by then."

"What else was stolen that night?"

"A clock-radio, and a camera, and a small television set."

"In addition to the clothes they later found buried in your yard."

"Some other clothes, too. Some of Prue's clothes."

"And the knife."

"Yes."

"Just the one knife?"

"Yes."

"Did you list these missing items for the police?"

"Yes."

"During the interrogation—after they arrested you—did anyone mention this burglary?"

"Yes, I did. I told them those clothes and that knife had been stolen from the house."

"Did anyone make any comment about that?"

"Haggerty said, 'That's *your* contention, Mr. Markham.'"

"It's more than just that," Matthew said. "A burglary *did* take place and you reported it to the police. If the clothes and the knife were stolen from your house ten days *before* the murder . . ."

"They were."

"Then what the hell are they hoping to prove?"

"That I killed her," Markham said. "You see . . . I have no alibi for the night of the murder."

"Where were you *that* night?"

"My wife had work to do. That's what took her to the studio. I went to the movies alone."

"Which theater?"

"Twin Plaza I. In the South Dixie Mall."

"Meet anyone you know?"

"No one."

"In the theater?"

"No."

"In the mall?"

"No."

"What time did the movie start?"

"Eight o'clock."

"What time did it end?"

"Around ten-thirty."

"Did you go directly home after the movie?"

"No. I wandered around the mall for a while, and then went to a bar named Harrigan's."

"What time did you get there?"

"Around ten to eleven."

"How long did you stay there?"

"I just had one drink."

"What'd you drink?"

"A Tanqueray martini. Straight up. Very dry. With two olives."

"How long did it take you to drink that?"

"Well, I was watching television. There's a television set over the bar."

"So you left the bar when?"

"Around . . . twenty to twelve? A quarter to twelve?"

"And got home when?"

"Around midnight. The police got there about twenty minutes later." Markham sighed deeply. "I know how it looks. I've got no real alibi for where I was when somebody was stabbing her, and the police have only my word for the burglary." He shook his head. "So if you don't take the case, I can't blame you much. I can only tell you again, I didn't kill her."

"I believe you," Matthew said.

Matthew's demand for discovery listed twelve essentially boiler-
plate items—plus an added typewritten one for "any police reports made in connection with this case"—and concluded with
the words, "WHEREFORE, said Demand for Discovery by the
Defendant being material and relevant to the proper defense of
Defendant under applicable rules, cases and constitutional provisions, Defendant requests that this demand be answered in all
respects."

The demand was delivered by hand to the State Attorney's office on the first day of December.

On Wednesday morning, December 3, Arthur Haggerty, the
Assistant State Attorney who was handling the prosecution's case,
had his response delivered by hand to Matthew's office.

It read:

IN THE CIRCUIT COURT OF THE TWELFTH JUDICIAL
CIRCUIT IN AND FOR CALUSA COUNTY, FLORIDA

STATE OF FLORIDA
                            CASE NO. 84—2207—CF—A—S9
         VS.
CARLTON BARNABY MARKHAM

STATE'S RESPONSE TO DEFENSE DEMAND FOR DISCOVERY

1. *Names and addresses of persons with
    information relevant to offense: 3.220 (a)
    (1) i.   See attached
    witness list.
2. *Written or taped verbatim witness
    statements made to police: 3.220 (a) (1) ii.
                               See attached.
3. Defendant's oral, written, or taped
    statements: 3.220 (a) (1) iii.
                               See attached.
4. Co—defendant's oral or written statements:
    3.220 (a) (1) iv.   Not applicable.
5. Grand Jury testimony of accused: 3.220 (a)
    (1) v.   See attached.
6. Tangible papers (objects obtained from
    defendant): 3.220 (a) (1) vi.   None.
7. Whether State has confidential informant:
    3.220 (a) (1) vii.   None.
8. Whether State has used electronic
    surveillance: 3.220 (a) (1) viii. None.
9. Whether there has been a search and seizure
    (with documents, if any): 3.220 (a) (1) ix.
                    Yes.   See attached.
10. *Expert reports and statements: 3.220 (a)
    (1) x.   Yes.   See attached.
11. **Tangible papers and objects to be used at
    hearing and trial: 3.220 (a) (1) xi. Knife,

clothing, photographs, autopsy report, diagrams of scene, statements, cassettes.

12. Similar fact evidence. Florida Rule of Evidence 90.404 (must be provided at least 10 days prior to trial.)
13. Police reports made in connection with this case: 3.220 (a) (1) xii. See attached.

*Defense must reciprocate within 7 days.
**Defense must reciprocate within 15 days.

The prosecution has (   ) has no (X) knowledge of evidence tending to negate defendant's guilt.

   I HEREBY CERTIFY that a true copy of the foregoing has been furnished by hand to: MATTHEW HOPE, ESQ., Summerville and Hope, 333 Heron Street, Calusa, Florida on this 3rd day of December, 1986.

> SKYE BANNISTER
> STATE ATTORNEY
>
> by *Arthur Haggerty*
> ARTHUR HAGGERTY
> Assistant State Attorney

Matthew had his work cut out for him.

"I have to tell you frankly," Frank Summerville said, "I don't appreciate your having taken on this case."

"It's the first real case I've had since July," Matthew said.

"By that, I assume you mean the other petty little legal matters that have been occupying your time here are all *fake* cases."

"Frank, this is an important one."

"Every case we handle is important."

"Yes, I recognize that preparing eviction papers for the owner of a condominium . . ."

"His tenant stopped paying the rent. In that respect, the eviction papers are important to him. And if something is important to a client, it's important to us."

Matthew knew many people who maintained that he and Frank looked alike. He figured these were the same people who insisted that married couples of many years standing (or sitting, or lying abed) resembled twins. Actually, he could see no resemblance between him and Frank but their dark hair and brown eyes.

Matthew was thirty-eight years old. Frank had just turned forty. Matthew was an even six feet tall and weighed a hundred and seventy pounds; his partner was two and a half inches shorter and twenty pounds lighter. Frank's face was round—what he himself called a "pig face"—and Matthew's was narrow, a "fox face" in his partner's lexicon. Moreover, Frank was originally from New York, and Matthew's home town was Chicago.

"Suppose you lose it?" Frank said.

"I don't intend to lose it."

"What'll you do then? Take an ad in the paper? Matthew Hope, Attorney at Large, desperately seeks clients charged with sundry misdemeanors or felonies . . ."

"No, I won't take an ad in the paper."

"Why not? Desperate dentists take ads," Frank said.

"I'm not a dentist. Desperate or otherwise."

"I know. You're a *criminal* lawyer." The emphasis was on the word "criminal" as though Frank felt there was something criminal about being a criminal lawyer. "Even unemployed actors take ads," he said. "In *Variety*."

"And *remain* unemployed," Matthew said. "And I'm not unemployed. And when did you start reading *Variety*?"

"Leona subscribes to it."

Leona was Frank's wife. Another difference. Matthew was divorced.

"Well, I'm not going to lose it, so I won't have to take an ad," Matthew said. "In *Variety* or anyplace else."

"Zack Norman takes ads in *Variety*."

"Is Zack Norman a dentist?"

"He's an actor. The point is, Matthew, if a person suddenly decides—for no apparent reason that I can discern—that he wants to specialize in *criminal* law . . ."

"I didn't *suddenly* decide," Matthew said.

"That's right, you were dabbling . . ."

"Not dabbling."

"That's right, *flirting* would be the more appropriate word. Flirting with murder cases that took you away from real estate, and probate, and all the other petty concerns of the legal profession which, I'm sure, must seem terribly humdrum to Mr. Perry Mason."

"Is Perry Mason a dentist or an actor?"

"Matthew, I'm trying to make a point here," Frank said. "You may think it was enough to start studying the Criminal Laws and Rules book as if it was the Bible . . ."

"*Were* the Bible . . ."

". . . and having lunch with every criminal lawyer in town, picking their brains . . ."

"Picking *his* brain . . ."

". . . but just between you and I . . ."

"You and *me* . . ."

"Well, all right, if you want to repeat everything I say instead of listening to me . . ."

"I *am* listening to you, Frank. And I hear what you're saying. I have not been a raging success, I know that."

"That's right."

"But this is a big one . . ."

"Homicide? No kidding? A big one?"

"And if I can get Markham off . . ."

"I'm concerned about what might happen if you *don't* get him off. What repercussions will that have for the firm, Matthew? Will a potential client automatically assume we're lawyers who *lose* cases? Lawyers who *lose* cases don't make money, Matthew."

"If I wanted to make money, I'd become a dentist," Matthew said. "And take an ad in the paper."

"All of a sudden, money doesn't matter to him," Frank said to the air. "All of a sudden, he doesn't care about alimony payments, or the private school for his daughter, or his tennis club, or his . . ."

"I care about *all* those things, Frank. But . . ."

"*All* of a sudden, those of us who are concerned with the finer things in life are all of a sudden crass and grasping . . ."

"You said it, not me."

"Matthew, listen to me, okay? Ask Benny Weiss to take over, okay? Or Jim Willoughby. They're both fine criminal lawyers, and I'm sure either of them would *love* representing a pauper who . . ."

"Markham isn't a pauper."

"From what I understand the man owns a *clock* shop."

"Clocks are important, Frank. Everybody has to know what time it is."

"In Calusa, nobody gives a *damn* what time it is. Calusa isn't New York, Matthew."

"Noplace is, Frank. We all know that."

"In New York, it's important to know what time it is. In Calusa, does anyone take a clock to the beach? Selling clocks in Calusa is like selling ice cubes in Nome, Alaska."

"Or refrigerators."

"Or refrigerators, right. What I'm saying . . ."

"I know what you're saying."

"What am I saying?"

"You're saying don't lose it."

In Calusa, there are two local law enforcement agencies. The Calusa Police Department handles any crimes committed within the city limits. The Calusa County Sheriff's Department handles any crimes committed beyond the city limits but still within Calusa County. Uniformed Police Department fops are called officers. Uniformed Sheriff's Department cops are called deputies. Plainclothes detectives from either department are called just that: detectives.

Carlton Barnaby Markham lived in the city of Calusa, but his wife had been slain out on Rancher Road, well beyond the city limits, and the homicide had been investigated by the Sheriff's Department. Among the discovery papers supplied by the State Attorney's office was a report written by a Sheriff's Department detective named Jonas Crier:

INVESTIGATIVE REPORT
Calusa County Sheriff's Department

INVESTIGATION AT: Calusa County, FL	DATE THIS REPORT: 11/20/86
TITLE: Prudence Ann Markham 1143 Pompano Way Calusa, FL	**CLASSIFICATION:** MURDER
	FILE: 86-51175

SYNOPSIS:

Writer, the on—call detective supervisor on 11/20/86, was phoned by Det. Sears at 2307

---

hours, and advised that he was responding to a stabbing incident at 8489 Rancher Road, Calusa.

Writer did respond to the incident location and met with Cpl. Gandy and Det. Sears at 2315 hours.

Stabbing victim was DOA white Caucasian female, app. age 30–35, app. height 5'7", app. weight 125, hair blonde, eyes blue, wearing yellow skirt and blouse, brown sandals, no handbag, no identification.

Victim was lying on back in gravel parking lot outside Anvil Studios at above address, 15'6" from entrance door. Door locked, burglar alarm activated, no sign of forced entry. Caged light over door only illumination in parking lot. Blue 1985 Honda Civic locked and parked 12' from body parallel to cyclone fence surrounding studio. (Sketches of scene attached.)

Medical Examiner J.E. Ritzig pronounced victim dead at 2331 hours, probable cause multiple stab and slash wounds.

Ford Econoline van from Criminalistics Unit on scene at 2335 hours.

Radio call at 2340 hours yielded Honda registered with Div. Motor Vehicles by Prudence Ann Markham, 1143 Pompano Way, Calusa.

Phone call at 2345 hours to number listed in Calusa directory under name C.B. Markham, 1143 Pompano Way, yielded no response.

Body removed to Southern Medical mortuary at 2350 hours.

Writer, in company of Det. Sears, arrived 0020 hours, 11/21/86, at 1143 Pompano Way in subdivision named Sunrise Shores. Mr. Carlton.

Barnaby Markham answered door, agreed to accompany Sears and writer to Southern Medical for possible identification victim.

Positive ID made at 0050 hours, victim Prudence Ann Markham, wife of Mr. Markham, age given by him as 28 years old.

Mr. Markham stated his wife was working on a movie, renting editing space at Anvil Studios. Last saw her alive when she left house at 1900 hours. Stated that he himself left house a half-hour later, 1930 hours, drove to Twin Plaza I, where he saw motion picture starting at 2000 hours. Movie let out at 2230 hours. Markham says he wandered mall, went to a bar named Harrigan's for a drink, drove home from there, arrived at ''a little before midnight.''

(See transcribed statement for exact details of statement.)

Writer did then respond back to Calusa P.D. and met with Det. Morris Bloom where together the attached P.C.A was drafted.

Writer did then give Det. Bloom taped statement described above.

Writer has had no further involvement in this case and/or investigation other than what is described above.

COPIES TO: Det. M. Bloom, Calusa P.D.

REPORT MADE BY: Det. J. Crier #53, Deputy Sheriff Calusa County, Calusa, Florida.

REPORT APPROVED BY: Gregory Younger, Sheriff of Calusa County, Calusa, Florida.

At ten o'clock on a bright December morning, it was difficult to believe that the parking lot at Anvil Studios had been the scene of a violent stabbing not two weeks earlier. The white gravel driveway glistened like snow in the sunshine, the pink stucco building behind it reflecting a hue that touched the ground like a blush, echoing more deeply in the hibiscus bushes and bougainvillea that crowded the walls. The words ANVIL STUDIOS, fashioned of wrought-iron letters, were affixed to the front side of the building above a wrought-iron, black anvil logo. Matthew parked his Karmann Ghia in a space just below the anvil, and then walked to the front door and opened it.

Wood-paneled reception area, bookshelves on one wall, white Formica-topped conference table, four black vinyl covered chairs around it, white decorator filing cabinets on another wall, a small decorated Christmas tree in a stand on top of one of them. A young girl sat behind a desk just inside the door, telephone receiver to her ear. She looked no older than seventeen, a round-faced brunette with a stunning figure, sparkling blue eyes, and hair cut in bangs on her forehead and molding her head like a sleek black helmet.

"Yes," she said into the phone, "I understand that," and rolled her eyes at Matthew, taking him into her exasperated confidence. "But we ordered the stock two weeks ago, and if we don't have film we can't shoot, now can we? Wouldn't you agree with that? That a person can't load a camera with promises of delivery?" She rolled her eyes again. "No," she said, "we're not Twentieth Century-Fox, that's true. Why? Is Twentieth Century-Fox one of your customers? Oh, I see, I didn't think so. We're just an itty-bitty little film company here in teensy-weensy Calusa, and all we're shooting is a ninety-second commercial for a furniture store on the Trail, but you guaranteed delivery by the first, Mr. Peyser, and today is the third, and it'll be Christmas before you know it, Mr. Peyser, so when are you going to deliver the fucking *stock*?" She looked at Matthew, shrugged elaborately, and then said into the phone, "Oh, forgive me, I didn't realize you were perhaps a Baptist minister. I thought you were perhaps a person accustomed to dealing with eccentric motion-picture types who occasionally pepper their speech with obscenities especially when they are so fucking aggravated they could *scream*! Just tell me when we're going to get the stock, okay? Give me an exact date and an exact time." She picked up a pencil and began writing. "Okay," she said. "Thank you ever so much, Mr. Peyser, and it had better be *here* by then." She slammed the receiver down onto the cradle, looked at Matthew, grinned angelically, and said, "So. What can I do for *you*?"

"I have an appointment with Mr. Andrews," Matthew said. "My name is Matthew Hope."

"I'll buzz him," she said, and lifted the receiver and hit a button on the base of the phone. "Mike," she said, "there's a Mr. Hope here to see you." She listened a moment, said, "Right," and then put the receiver back on its cradle. "You can go right in," she said. "It's right through the door there, you go into this big room looks like a mausoleum. He's in the projection booth." The phone rang. She picked up the receiver, said "Anvil Studios," and then waved him on toward the door at the far end of the reception area.

The room Matthew entered was perhaps forty feet wide by sixty feet long. He had never been inside a movie studio before, but this one couldn't possibly be mistaken for anything but what it was. Hundreds of film cans were stacked on shelves lining the room, each can bound with a white adhesive strip upon which a title had been lettered with a black marker. Two huge angled consoles with buttons, switches and dials on their faces sat before a glass-paneled room containing what Matthew guessed was sound equipment. Open boxes of cables were strewn everywhere on the floor. Aluminum carrying cases were stacked against the walls. Several cameras on wooden tripods stood in the underfoot debris like wading birds in shallow water. A large white screen dominated the far end of the room. The projection booth faced it. Matthew climbed a short flight of steps, knocked on the closed door, and then opened it.

A man in his early thirties was sitting behind the projector, rewinding a reel of film. The film came off the takeup reel, its leader flapping. He put his hand up to the still-moving reel, slowed it with his palm, removed the reel from the spindle, put it in a can, and only then turned to face Matthew.

"Mr. Andrews?" Matthew said.

"Yes." He rose, extended his hand. "Pleasure to see you."

His face was square, the cheekbones high, the nose a trifle too large. He had long curly red hair that sat on his head like a fright wig. He was wearing wrinkled lime green trousers, white high-topped sneakers with red stripes on them, a purple shirt with narrow yellow stripes, a tiny blue clip-on bow tie, and a pink polyester jacket flecked with random black tufts of fabric.

If he'd stepped out of a tiny automobile, he could have been a circus clown. If he'd stepped off a banana boat, he could have been an immigrant. But his eyes were the eyes of a robot programmed to kill. Pale blue. An eerie feeling of transparency about them, suggesting that if you looked hard enough you might see through them into the circuitry buried in the skull. The mouth, too, seemed etched onto the emotionless face, a thin line that attempted a smile as he shook hands with Matthew—but the smile was programmed and it came over as false.

"It's an honor to meet one of Calusa's most illustrious criminal lawyers," he said. The words may have been spontaneous, but they sounded rehearsed. Moreover, Matthew was *not* one of Calusa's most illustrious lawyers, criminal or otherwise.

"It's good of you to make time for me," Matthew said. "I know you must be busy."

"I'm usually here from seven in the morning till ten at night," Andrews said, and sighed heavily. "It's a long day, believe me, but hard work never killed anyone. I sometimes think my partner and I inadvertently chose the correct name for our little enterprise. Anvil Studios. In that we keep hammering away against steely resistance in an attempt to forge some small appreciation of quality here in the boondocks."

The thin false smile again.

Matthew was sure he'd spoken those very same words a thousand times before. Hit the robot's HARD WORK button and out came the anvil metaphor.

"Actually," Andrews said, "the name is an acronym of both our surnames. My partner's name is Peter Villiers, he's of French ancestry. We put together the first two letters of my name and the first three of his, and came up with Anvil. It's fortuitous that our names aren't Sheen and Itkin."

Again the narrow smile.

Again, the feeling that he'd told this same little anecdote many times before.

"Mr. Andrews," Matthew said, "I have the Sheriff's report made on the night Prudence Markham was murdered . . ."

"Terrible shame," Andrews said. "An extremely talented person, hard to come by here in Crackerville, U.S.A. Cultural pretensions abound in Calusa, Florida, but everyone here spells culture with a K, as in cat. A wonderful person, Prue. I'll miss her."

"Did the police contact you that night?" Matthew asked. "There were no reports in the file . . ."

"Well, I wasn't here," Andrews said at once.

"You weren't working your usual long hours that day, is that it?"

"My usual . . . ? Oh. Seven to ten. No. At the time of the murder, in fact, I was in bed with a little bitch from Sarasota."

The words irritated. More so in that they were accompanied by the android smile. There was about Andrews an air of self-importance entirely out of keeping with the fact that he was a small-time filmmaker in a city not particularly noted for such endeavor. One would have expected such a bloated attitude from a production chief in Los Angeles, though even there it might not have been tolerated. To find such an ego here in Calusa was unimaginable. To find it in someone so *young*—

"Then they didn't telephone you?" Matthew said. "To ask you to come out here?"

"No, they didn't. The building was locked and the burglar alarm on. The killer couldn't possibly have been hiding inside. Therefore, why the need to drag me out of bed? Elementary, my dear Watson," he said, and smiled again.

"Had you ever worked with Mrs. Markham?" Matthew asked. "You said she was extremely talented . . ."

"An exception here in Calusa. E*xtreme*ly talented. I should know. I'm a shrewd judge of talent and a man of little patience for dilletantism."

"Then you *did* work with her."

"On several films, yes. We did one, oh, it must have been six months ago, I would imagine . . . yes, in June sometime . . . at the beach on Sabal Key, an educational film for showing in schools, an attempt to introduce adolescent shit-kickers to the beauties of the omnipresent and largely ignored natural splendor surrounding them here in Florida."

Period.

Another rehearsed speech.

Or was he really so bright that his mind, computerlike, fashioned pearly strings of words and spewed them instantaneously?

"Were you working with her on her current project?" Matthew asked. "The film she was editing on the night she was killed?"

"No. On occasion, Prue adopted an air of unbecoming secrecy

about her work. My partner and I prefer *discussing* creativity, as did the American expatriates at Deux Magots in Paris all those years ago. You may consider it odd that I think of myself as an expatriate, when surely Calusa is within the territorial limits of the United States. But anyone here who is concerned with quality filmmaking *is* an expatriate, believe me. I often feel like Samson among the Philistines."

Or Hercules in the Augean stable, Matthew thought. Incessantly shoveling horse manure.

"She once did an educational film on child abuse," Andrews said, gathering steam. "A fine film, as it turned out. But you would have thought she was Woody Allen, the *security* surrounding that project! A closed set, just herself, the actors, a cameraman, a lighting man, a sound man, and a few grips—all of them sworn to secrecy. Edited the film here all by herself, at night, in a locked room. Never left a scrap of film around for anyone to see, God knows where she was hiding it, perhaps under her mattress. And then the unveiling! Ta-ra! Ran it right here in this room, this very projector, that very screen. A marvelous film, as I said, I believe it even won a small prize later on. But why such theatrics? I despise pretension in art."

"But you liked Mrs. Markham."

"Yes, very much."

"What was her new film about, do you know?"

"I thought I made it clear . . ."

"I'm sorry, I must have . . ."

". . . that she often worked in secrecy."

"Yes, but . . ."

"By extension, I was alluding to her new project as well. I had no idea what it was. A documentary about the horseshoe crab? An advertising campaign for one of Calusa's illustrious jewelry stores? She never said."

"Did you ask?"

"I knew better than to ask Prue anything when she was in her *auteur* mode."

"But she was using editing space here . . ."

"Yes. Renting it at a thousand dollars a month. My partner and I are forced to rent some of our space, the price one must pay for attempting to make films of distinction in a backwater village. Peter and I came here from Pittsburgh, we're both graduates of Carnegie Tech. We'd decided to forsake the Hollywood route, littered as it is with car chases and special effects. We decided instead to make quiet little films, establish our reputations *here* as quality filmmakers, and then move on when the establishment was ready to recognize the superiority of our work. But one must eat. Hence the rental of space. We have fine facilities here, and we're not above allowing lesser mortals to use them."

"Did you consider Mrs. Markham a lesser mortal?"

"I consider almost everyone a lesser mortal." The smile again. "But not Prue, no. As I said, she was extremely talented."

"Mr. Andrews, this editing room she was using . . ."

"Yes?"

"May I see it?"

"Why?"

"On the night she was murdered, the police found only her body and her automobile outside there in the parking lot."

"A terrible tragedy."

"The car was locked. Nothing in it. No handbag, no identification . . . certainly no film."

"I'm sorry, I don't seem to be following your drift."

"Well, she was here editing *film*, wasn't she?"

"I would assume so. I have no idea why she was here."

"Her husband says she was here editing film."

"Well, yes. But her husband is a murderer."

"I don't believe that, Mr. Andrews."

"Which, of course, is why *you're* here."

"Yes. That's why I'm here."

"But I still don't know why you want to see that editing room."

"Because if she was here editing film, there has to be film. Do you have a key to that room?"

"Certainly. But I don't like violating the privacy of anyone renting space here at Anvil."

"Mrs. Markham's privacy has already been violated," Matthew said flatly. "In the worst possible way."

"I suppose your point is well taken," Andrews said. "Let me get the key."

The editing room door opened onto a six-by-twelve-foot space with a fluorescent light centered on the ceiling. A machine Andrews identified as a Steenbeck occupied most of the room. A chair on wheels sat in front of the machine. Behind the chair was what appeared to be a canvas sack hanging from a metal frame. Andrews identified it as a film bin, and explained that film to be discarded was usually dropped into it. The bin was empty. So were the hangers over the bin, where Andrews said the editor usually hung film or sound tape he or she planned to use. There was nothing on the surface of the editing machine. Not a scrap of film, not a hint of tape.

"Any other keys to this room?" Matthew asked.

"Only the one Prue had. And the master I just used to unlock the door."

"Then where's the film? If she was editing film . . ."

"She may not have been editing, you know," Andrews said.

"Then why would she have rented . . . ?"

"She may have been looking at what she'd already shot, selecting the best takes, marking the film, deciding how she would cut it later on. *Part* of the editing process, certainly, but not editing per se."

"Even so, she needed film."

"Yes."

"So where is it?"

"Did the police check out the automobile?"

"Thoroughly."

"No film in the trunk?"

"Nothing."

"That's decidedly odd," Andrews said.

"Is there anywhere in the studio she might have stored the film? Before she left?"

"We do have a storage room," Andrews said, "but I was in there straightening up last night, and I didn't see anything that might have been hers."

"How do you know?"

"The reels are marked for identification," Andrews said. "A tape around the can, with the working title of the film lettered onto it."

"And all those titles were familiar to you?"

"All of them."

"Were any of the cans untitled?"

"None of them."

Matthew was silent for a moment. Then he said, "Do you have any idea how long she was here that night?"

"None."

"You weren't here when she arrived, were you?"

"No."

"What time did you leave the studio?"

"At around six. As I mentioned earlier . . ."

"Yes, your friend from Sarasota. Was *anyone* here when you left?"

"I was the last one out."

"Did you set the burglar alarm?"

"I did."

"And locked the door?"

"Yes."

"Did Mrs. Markham know the alarm combination?"

"Yes."

"I assume she had a key . . ."

"Of course."

"This film she was working on," Matthew said. "Would you know who was working with her?"

"I'm sorry, I don't."

"Who does she *normally* use? As cameraman, as grip . . . what's a grip?"

"A grip is a person who moves things around the set. Grips come and go, they're relatively easy to find. But Prue used the same cameraman, lighting director and sound man on most of her films."

"I'd appreciate their names," Matthew said.

3

Henry Gardella considered himself a man of exquisite taste.

"I want this to be tasteful," he'd told her.

"It will be," she'd said.

"That's why I came to you," he'd said. "There are hundreds of people in Miami who can shoot this movie, I could've gone to any one of them. I picked you instead."

"Thank you," she'd said.

This was back in September.

Very serious girl, he'd thought. Been shooting movies for years now, good reputation. Interested in making a buck, though, who wasn't? Move out of the penny-ante documentary shit she was doing into the big time. He was putting up a hundred and seventy-five grand to make the movie. Plus she'd be getting ten percent of the gross, which wasn't meatballs.

"A movie is like a bullfight," he said, "the same ritual each time out. Raw stock to dailies to assembly to rough cut to final cut to first answer print to second answer print to release print. Every day of the shoot, you ship your exposed film to the lab, and get back your one-lights the next day—everything you asked the lab to print. Ritual. Routine." He looked across the desk at her. "I could get this movie done for a hundred grand, maybe less," he said. He was lying. "I know guys in Miami who can grind it out in a week." Still lying. "But then I'd get the usual cheap product, and what I'm looking for is taste. I'm looking for something, if we do it right, it'll be like a first-class Hollywood production, not something we shot in some sleazy hotel room on Collins Avenue with a tattooed sailor and a couple of hookers. There are more hookers in this town than you can shake a dick at."

He smiled.

Prudence Ann Markham did not smile back.

Very serious girl. Sitting there in a gray skirt and a white blouse, low-heeled shoes, hands folded in her lap, blonde hair caught in a bun at the back of her head, looked like a minister's wife. He wondered what kind of panties she was wearing.

"I'm looking for style," he said. "Class. I want the kind of taste I saw in that movie you did on child abuse. Understated. Powerful."

"Thank you," she said.

"Don't misunderstand me," he said. "I want to see everything there *is* to see, we're not doing Donald Duck here."

"I know that."

"But there's a cheap way of showing sex, and there's a classy way, and I want the classy way."

"You'll get class," she said.

He wondered if she had blonde pubic hair.

"And style," he said.

"And style."

"And taste."

"Of course."

"Did you see *Behind the Green Door?*"

"No," she said.

"There's a slow-motion shot in it, that's the kind of thing I'm talking about. Very classy. The man ejaculates in slow-motion for what must be five minutes. It's like a snowstorm on the screen. Very beautiful. That's the kind of class I'm looking for. You should get the video, take a look at it."

"I will."

"You should also take a look at *Deep Throat*. That played in legit theaters, do you realize it? Grossed fifty million dollars. What you saw was this gigantic *edifice* on the screen, husbands and wives in the audience, guys with their girlfriends, a regular movie theater, not one of these cheap porn houses, and Linda Lovelace swallows it to the hilt. That's what I'm looking for, a tasteful movie like that, where maybe we have a chance at getting into a legit house. The video I'm not worried about. We'll make a lot of money on the video. Also, you'll do two versions—when you're cutting it, I mean. So we can sell the soft one later on to cable. Cable," he said, and shook his head sadly. "On cable, you never see any real action. You *know* what they're doing, but you never really see any close shots of what they're doing. I want a lot of close shots, there's nothing more beautiful in the world than two people making love, don't you agree?"

"Yes," she said.

"We can make a lot of money on this movie, if we do it right," he said. He paused, looked her dead in the eye. "Do you think you can do it right?"

"Oh, yes, I know I can."

Eager. Smelling the money. He was willing to bet her thighs were sweating under her serious gray skirt.

"Because a hundred and seventy-five thousand is a lot of money I'm putting up."

"I know."

"When can you start?" he asked.

"I thought the end of the month."

"And when can you deliver a final cut?"

"By Christmas?" she said.

A question mark. She wasn't even *sure* it would be Christmas.

"That long, huh?"

"Well, we want to do it right," she said.

"How many days do you figure? For the actual shooting?"

"I thought thirty-five."

"Make it twenty."

"Twenty?"

"Figure a four-to-one burn ratio . . ."

"I was thinking ten-to-one."

"Make it six-to-one."

"Still, twenty days . . ."

"That's all you should need."

"I don't see how . . ."

"Thirty-five days is out of the question. There are people could do this in ten, fifteen days."

"Twenty still feels . . ."

"All right, make it twenty-*five*, that should do it."

"Twenty-eight," she said. "Because, you see . . ."

"Okay, twenty-eight, I'm not gonna argue three days. Can you get the people you need in Calusa?"

"I don't want to use my regular people," she said.

Running scared already, he thought.

"Who will you get?" he asked. "I don't mean your actors, that's up to you, provided you don't use hookers."

"I've got some good people in mind," she said.

"And no junkies looking to make a fast buck unzipping their flies."

"No, no."

"I want this to look real. Real people doing it. With taste, of course. So who have you got in mind?"

"For the actors, do you mean?"

"No, I told you, that's up to you. I don't want to mess here with artistic control."

"I appreciate that."

"So who have you got in mind?"

"Some people in Tampa."

"Experienced movie people?"

"Oh, sure."

"Don't hire anyone in Miami. I've been running this dinner theater here for ten years now, I don't want word to get around that Henry Gardella is financing a dirty movie. Not that it'll be dirty."

"It won't, I promise you."

"And I don't want the boys to get wind of this, either. Do you know who I mean by the boys?"

"No. Who do you mean?"

"The boys," he said, and brought his fingers to his nose, and bent the nose sideways. "The ones who'll shoot you in the kneecap if they think you're moving in on their territory. Keep this quiet, keep it discreet, keep it tasteful."

"I will."

He wondered if she'd object to his throwing up her serious gray skirt, teach her what he meant by taste.

That was back in September.

Now, on the fourth day of December, he sat in his office at the Candleside Dinner Theater, and wondered what had happened to the goddamn film.

Prudence Ann Markham dead, and nothing to show for his money.

He'd personally budgeted the movie at a hundred and seventy-five grand. He'd figured five men—camera, lighting, sound and two grips—at twenty-eight days, a ten-to-twelve-hour day, for about thirty-five thousand. He'd figured another twenty-five for the actors. Renting the equipment would cost seventeen. The sixteen-millimeter stock, processed and printed, would cost about ten thousand, figuring a six-to-one burn ration, though Prue kept saying ten-to-one would be better. The quarter-inch sound stock would cost another six to seven hundred bucks. He had to figure something like ten bucks a day per person to feed the crew and the actors. Federal Express charges for shipping the negative to a lab in New York or Atlanta and the dailies back to Florida would come to something like fifteen hundred. All the later lab work—quarter-inch to mag, sixteen to thirty-five millimeter, opticals and so on—would be another forty to fifty grand. A hundred and fifty grand in all, give or take a penny here or there, with an additional twenty-five going to her as a bonus on delivery of the final cut.

Being dead was her own business. Dumb husband decides to kill his wife, who the hell knew why? Maybe she was playing around outside the marriage. You got these quiet, serious types, they turned out to be screamers in bed. Not their own beds. Always somebody else's bed. Screamed loud enough to wake up the whole neighborhood.

He'd written checks to her production company—The Prudent Company—each and every week of the shooting. Wrote the first one on the third of October, wrote checks every damn week after that, kept writing them right up to the Friday before she died.

So where was the film?

What the hell had she done with the film?

He figured he'd have to drive over to Calusa, do some looking around.

He didn't like the idea.

Calusa was boring, except when dumb cunts were getting themselves killed.

Matthew would have gone to Otto Samalson, but Otto Samalson was dead.

He would have gone to May Hennessy, the Chinese lady who'd been Otto's assistant at Samalson Investigations, but Otto's family had dismantled the business and sold off the furniture and equipment the moment his will was probated, and the last Matthew had heard, May had moved to Hong Kong.

There were only a dozen detective agencies in the city of Calusa, population fifty some-odd thousand, and so the choices were limited. The private detective he decided to use was a young black man named Warren Chambers, recommended by Benny Weiss who was indisputably the best criminal lawyer in town.

Warren had been a police officer in his native St. Louis, and had been living in Calusa for the past three years, where he'd done security work for several firms before opening his own agency. He was a soft-spoken man in his mid-thirties, his shy, reserved manner and his horn-rimmed glasses giving him the look of an accountant rather than what one imagined a private eye should look like. Beanpole tall, a former basketball player for the University of Missouri, which he'd attended for two years before joining the St. Louis P.D., Warren still moved like an athlete, and seemed uncomfortable in the lightweight business suit he wore to his first meeting with Matthew. His eyes were the color of his skin, as dark as loam, and they watched Matthew intently as he spoke. Matthew liked people who *listened.* Warren Chambers was a listener. Which perhaps accounted for his reputation as a careful and accurate investigator.

"The cameraman's name is Vaughan Turner," Matthew said. "The lighting man is Lew Smollet. The sound man is Mark

Wiley. That's the nucleus crew she normally used. Here are their addresses, they all live right here in Calusa." He handed a sheet of paper across the desk. "I'm also giving you copies of the State Attorney's witness list and the witnesses' statements—I'll need your help there, too. There are only two of them. Both of them live right next door to Markham. Velma Mason lives in the house on the right. Her statement says she saw Markham breaking the glass on his own kitchen door on the night of the burglary. Positive ID, she's been living next door to him for seven . . ."

"What kind of visibility that night?" Warren asked.

"That's one of the things I want you to find out."

"Okay, who's the second witness?"

"Man named Oscar Raddison. Lives in the house on the left. Claims he saw Markham burying something in the backyard on the night of the murder. That was what gave them probable cause for the search warrant."

"Where does our man say he was?"

"At the movies. Twin Plaza One, the South Dixie Mall. And later on at a bar."

"Got home when?"

"Around midnight."

"Is that when this guy saw him?"

"No, he saw someone at eleven-fifteen."

"Burying the clothes and the knife?"

"No, just burying *something*."

"Didn't identify the something as bloody clothing? Or a bloody knife?"

"No."

"Again, you want to know whether a positive ID was feasible. I'll get on that right away. Did the police find any bloodstains in Markham's car?"

"There's nothing in the lab reports about bloodstains in his car."

"How do they figure he drove all the way from Rancher Road to his house without leaving bloodstains in the car? I mean, if he was wearing these clothes soaked with blood . . ."

"I don't know what they have in mind," Matthew said. "They're not obliged to disclose how they plan to hang him."

"They'll have to work pretty damn hard to explain his car being clean."

"The best way to explain it is to say he didn't kill her."

"Anybody see him at the movies?" Warren asked. "Or later in the bar? In his *blood*stained clothes?" Light sarcasm in his voice. Matthew smiled.

"Not that he knows of."

"So we're still looking for an alibi."

"Anyone who might have seen him on the night of the murder, yes."

"That'll be like searching for a needle in a haystack," Warren said, "but I'll do my best. Do you have a picture of him?"

"Just this one," Matthew said, and opened the top drawer of his desk and took out an eight-by-ten black-and-white photograph of Markham standing alongside his wife on a beach someplace. "I had it enlarged from a recent snapshot."

"I wish we had one without his wife in it," Warren said. "Her picture's been all over the papers, it might scare off a potential witness. But let's say we *do* come up with somebody who'll say, 'Yes, I saw this fellow buying a ticket there at Twin One,' or 'I saw him eating a hot dog later there in the South Dixie Mall,' or having a drink in the bar . . . what's the name of the bar?"

"Harrigan's."

"What'd he drink? Did he tell you?"

"A Tanqueray martini. Very dry, straight up, with two olives."

"Just the one drink?"

"Just the one."

"So, okay, suppose somebody says, 'Yeah, I saw him.' I'm not so sure that'll stand up. The prosecution'll tear into him, remind him that the murder took place back in November and can he be *sure* this is the man he saw, can he be positively *certain* because we are dealing here with a brutal murder, sir, and I know you understand the gravity of the charge against the defendant. *That* kind of legal bullshit."

Matthew smiled again.

"Anyway, it's perfectly reasonable to believe that the man went to a movie alone because his wife was working, and stopped for a drink later, and *didn't* see anyone he knew or anyone who knew him. There's nothing wrong with that story." Warren picked up the witness statements, read both carefully, and then looked across the desk at Matthew again. "Judging from this lady they've come up with, they're gonna claim Markham *faked* the burglary," he said. "Lady saw him breaking into his own house, that's what they're gonna try to show. The man stole his own clothes and the knife because he planned to use them in a murder ten days later. Where'd he say he was on the night of the burglary?"

"A friend's house."

"From when to when?"

"Nine to eleven."

"And got home when?"

"Around eleven-thirty."

"And this lady says she saw him breaking in at *ten*-thirty, right?"

"According to her statement."

"So if we can show Markham was with this friend—what's the guy's name?"

"Alan Saunders, lives out on Whisper Key."

"Have you talked to him yet?"

"On the phone. He seemed vague about the exact time Markham left him."

"Uh-oh."

"Yeah."

"Okay if I take a run at him?"

"I'll give you his address," Matthew said.

"Because if we can nail down these times, we're home free regarding the burglary. Either that, or we have to find the burglar. Maybe if we find the burglar, we also find the killer."

"We're not obliged to find the killer," Matthew said.

"But it sure wouldn't hurt," Warren said. "Let me ask around downtown. I've got a few friends in the police department who enjoy shmoozing with a former big-city cop. Maybe I can come up with some other unsolved burglaries, same M.O., who knows? It's worth a shot. Who'll be talking to these two witnesses? You or me?"

"I planned to drop in on Mrs. Mason later this afternoon."

"Maybe I'll have something on what she could've seen or not seen by then. I'll check the papers, find out what the weather was like, what kind of moon there was, anything that might have affected visibility. I may even run over to the house tonight, see if there's a street lamp, or floods in the backyard, or a light over that kitchen door. Be nice if we could knock out her identification that way, wouldn't it?"

"There's something you should ask Mrs. Markham's crew when you talk to them," Matthew said.

"What's that?"

"What they were working on. And where she stored the film."

"Okay, let me get started," Warren said, and rose suddenly, unfolding the long length of his body from the chair. He extended his hand. "Let's keep in touch, Mr. Hope," he said, and smiled. "It's gonna be nice working with you."

They shook hands.

"Call me Matthew," Matthew said.

"And you call me Warren," Warren said.

CALUSA POLICE DEPARTMENT

WITNESS STATEMENT

Case No: 84–2207–CF–A–S9
Date: 11–21–86
Time: 0120 hours

I, Velma Judith Mason, residing at 1141 Pompano Way, Calusa, Florida, do hereby make the following voluntary statement to
Det. Morris Bloom #714 and _____ who have/has identi-
fied themselves/himself to me as Detective(s) of the Calusa Police Department.
I make this statement without having received any reward, nor have I been made
an offer of reward for making this statement. No threats, force or promise have
been made to induce me to make this statement.

Q: November 21st at 0120 in the morning. Would
you please state your full name?

A: Velma Judith Mason.

Q: Mrs. Mason, are you familiar with the people
who live at 1143 Pompano Way? That is the
house next door to yours, isn't it?

A: Yes, it is.

Q: Do you know the people who live there?

A: Yes. Prue and Carlton Markham. I know them.

Q: How long have you known them?

A: I've been living there for seven years now. I
met them shortly after I moved in.

Q: Seven years ago. You've known them all that
time?

A: Yes.

Q: And, of course, you would be able to recognize
either one of them . . .

A: Oh, yes.

Q: If you saw them on the street, or in a restaurant or . . .

A: Anyplace. They've been my neighbors for seven years. We were in and out of each other's houses all the time.

Q: Now Mrs. Mason, can you tell me in your own words what you saw on the night of November 10, that was a Friday night. Were you home that night?

A: I was.

Q: What were you doing at approximately ten-thirty on the night of November 10?

A: I was watching television.

Q: Do you remember what show you were watching?

A: Yes. A movie on cable. A murder mystery. I like murder mysteries.

Q: Where is your television set located, Mrs. Mason?

A: In the living room.

Q: Is your living room on the side of the house that faces the side door of the Markham house?

A: Yes.

Q: That would be the south side of your house, would it not? Facing the north side of the Markham house.

A: I'm not good at directions. My living room . . .

Q: Well, would it be correct to say that your living room windows open on the side of the Markham house where the side door is located? The door leading into the Markham kitchen?

A: Yes, that's correct.

Q: And if you looked through one of your living room windows, could you see the side door of the Markham house?

A: Yes, I could.

Q: All right, please tell me what you saw and heard on the night of November 10.

A: The first thing I heard was glass breaking. I thought it was coming from the television set, because there was a lot of action going on. But then I realized it was coming from outside.

Q: Outside your house?

A: Yes. The sound of glass breaking.

Q: What did you do when you heard the sound?

A: I went to the window and looked out.

Q: Looked out where?

A: Toward the Markham house.

Q: Toward the side door of the Markham house?

A: Yes.

Q: Are there glass panels on the side door of the Markham house?

A: Yes. Well, on my house, too. These louvered panels in the upper half of the door.

Q: Louvered glass panels.

A: Yes.

Q: Could you clearly see the side door of the Markham house from where you were standing at the window?

A: Oh, yes. It's only ten, fifteen feet away.

Q: And what did you see?

A: I saw Carlton Markham standing at the side door. With a hammer in his hand.

Q: Are you sure it was Carlton Markham?

A: Well, of course. I've known the man for seven years.

Q: What was he wearing?

A: Gray trousers and a blue sports jacket. And a hat. One of those little straw snapbrim fedoras.

Q: What color was the hat?

A: Same color as the jacket. Blue.

Q: What was Mr. Markham doing?

A: Just standing there. At least for a minute or so. Then he reached into where the louvered panels were broken, reached inside the house . . .

Q: When you say the panels were broken . . .

A: That must've been the glass I heard breaking.

Q: But could you *see* the broken panels on that side door?

A: Oh, yes.

Q: And you say Mr. Markham reached in where the panels were broken . . .

A: Yes. Reached in with his hand.

Q: Was he wearing gloves?

A: No. I didn't see any gloves.

Q: What happened after he reached in?

A: He opened the door.

Q: And then what happened?

A: He went into the house.

Q: Did you see any lights go on after he went into the house?

A: No, I didn't.

Q: Did you see Mr. Markham *leaving* the house?

A: No. I went back to the movie. I figured he'd lost his key or something and had to break the glass to get in.

Q: You didn't call the police, did you?

A: No, why should I? It was Carlton going inside his own house.

Q: But there *were* police cars later on, weren't there?

A: I don't know. I understand there was a burglary, but I went to bed right after the movie went off. I didn't see any police cars.

Q: Okay, thank you, Mrs. Mason. (tape stops)

Signature: *Velma J. Mason*   Witnessed by: *Det. Marvin Bloom*

Time completed: *0145*   Witnessed by: *Det. Cooper Rawles*

Christmas in Florida never felt right to Matthew. They decked out Main Street in holly and pine, and hung a big Santa Claus in a sleigh over the three-way intersection at the Cow Crossing—which actually *had* been a cow crossing back when the town was incorporated—but without snow it didn't mean a damn. He realized the very *first* Christmas was celebrated in a climate not too much different from Florida's, but to *his* way of thinking Christ should have been born at the North Pole. Today was the fourth day of December, and Velma Mason's house was already decorated for Christmas. Wreaths in the windows facing the street, lights strung in the Norfolk pine on the front lawn, little plastic Rudolph the Rednosed Reindeer sitting alongside a small hibiscus bush. She answered the doorbell on his third ring, stood just inside the closed screen door, peering out at him.

"Mrs. Mason?" he said.

"Yes?"

Woman in her late sixties, he guessed, wearing eyeglasses, a flowered housedress, and sandals. She looked startled. Faded blue eyes opening wide behind the thick-lensed glasses, the better to see you, my dear. Behind her, a Christmas tree winked its lights near a screened lanai at the back of the house, and Matthew heard a television set blaring a game show at four in the afternoon.

"My name is Matthew Hope," he said. "I'm the attorney defending your neighbor."

"Yes?"

Still defensive. Screen door closed. Arms folded across her chest now. Keep the big bad lawyer out of the house.

"I've read the statement you made to the police . . ."

"Listen," she said, "have you got some kind of identification?"

Matthew took out his wallet, opened it, and extended his card to the closed screen door. Mrs. Mason opened the door, took the card, and squinted at it. On the unseen television set inside the house, someone seemed to have won six thousand dollars.

"All right to come in and ask you a few questions?" he said.

"I guess," she said, and opened the screen door wider. She did not give him back his card.

He followed her into the house. It smelled of Florida mildew, old age, and stale cigarette smoke. The Christmas tree near the lanai looked pathetically scrawny and severely underdressed. Rattan furniture. Soiled throw pillows. Beyond the lanai, another house in the development was scarcely hidden by bougainvillea. Mrs. Mason looked at the television screen, her back to him, and then turned off the set.

Silence.

"Well, have a seat," she said, managing to sound reluctant, suspicious and rude, all at the same time.

He sat.

"I want you to know right off," she said, "that I think Carlton killed her. I also want you to know that what I told the police is the absolute truth." She hesitated, and then said, "I liked Prue a lot." She took a package of cigarettes from the pocket of her dress, shook one loose, lighted it—nicotine-stained fingers, Matthew noticed—and let out a stream of smoke. "So what do you want to know?" she said. "I'm not about to go back on anything I told the police, if that's why you're here. I can never understand why lawyers take on cases defending murderers, anyway," she said, and shook her head.

"Well," Matthew said, "everyone's entitled to a fair trial with a proper defense. Which is why we have to ask these questions, even though you've already answered most of them."

"Yes, well, let's just get it over with," she said, "I don't want to miss any of my shows."

"Yes, ma'am, I'll be as brief as possible," Matthew said, and immediately opened his briefcase and took out his tape recorder. In what he felt was a seamless introduction, he said, "I know you're familiar with these gadgets," and smiled, and started the tape going, and immediately said, "Mrs. Mason, on the night of the burglary at the Markham house, did you . . . ?"

"There wasn't any burglary," she said.

"Well, a burglary was reported to the police," Matthew said. "Did you happen to . . . ?"

"That doesn't make it a burglary," she said, "it being reported."

"Did you talk to any policemen that night?"

"No, I did not."

Defiantly. Aiming her words straight at the recorder, chin jutting. Good, he thought.

"A detective named Morris Bloom didn't interview you that night, did he?"

"No, he did not."

"So you didn't have an opportunity to discuss what you'd seen until much later, is that right?"

"Not until the night of the murder."

An assertive nod. Another puff on the cigarette.

"Were you questioned here at the house?"

"Well *first*, yes. Then I went downtown with Detective Bloom, and he taped what I'd already told him here."

"Did you *volunteer* information about what you'd seen on the night of the burglary?"

"No, Detective Bloom asked me about it. And it wasn't a burglary."

"He knew a burglary—or whatever you choose to call it—had taken place, is that right?"

"That's right."

"And asked you if you'd seen or heard anything that night?"

"Yes."

"Before that—before Mr. Bloom asked you about it—had you discussed what you'd seen with anyone else?"

"No. I knew there'd been some kind of fuss next door, but I supposed Carlton had straightened it out with the police who came around. I mean, explaining to them it was him breaking into his own house."

"You're sure it was Mr. Markham?"

"Positive."

"You saw him clearly?"

"Plain as day."

"He was standing at the side door, is that right?"

"Yes."

"With a hammer in his hand."

"Yes."

"He'd just broken the louvered glass panels, isn't that what you said?"

"Well, if you hear the sound of breaking glass, and you look out your window, and you see someone standing at the door with a hammer in his hand, then you've got to figure he's the one who just broke the glass, don't you?"

"And that's just what you figured."

"That's just what I figured."

Another nod. Pleased with herself, pleased with the way she was handling this.

"Did you call over to him?" Matthew asked.

"What do you mean?"

"Did you open your window and call over to him?"

"No. Why should I? It was a man getting into his own house. I knew who he was, it was none of my business."

"You didn't open the window?"

"No."

"The window was closed, is that right?"

"Yes, it was very chilly that night. It started getting cold down here in October, the end of October. All my windows were closed."

"But you were able to hear the sound of breaking glass? Even with all your windows closed?"

"I have very good ears, thank you."

"So when you looked through this closed window, you saw a man facing the door, is that right?"

"I saw Carlton facing the door, yes."

"With a hammer in his hand."

"Yes."

"And he was wearing gray slacks and a blue jacket and a blue straw hat."

"Yes."

"Had you ever seen him wearing those clothes before?"

"Except for the hat."

"You saw him wearing gray slacks and a blue jacket."

"Oh, sure. Lots of times."

"Did you ever see him wearing a blue hat?"

"No."

"Or *any* kind of a hat?"

"I really can't say. I didn't watch Carlton day and night to see what he was wearing."

"Did you notice the color of his hair?"

"No, he was wearing a hat. I just told you."

"You know that Mr. Markham is blond, don't you?"

"Of course I know. I've lived next door to him for seven years."

"Was this man blond?"

"I told you, he was wearing a hat. But he was Carlton, all right. I ought to know Carlton."

"How can you be so sure it was Mr. Markham?"

"His build, his height, his weight, his posture, the way he was standing, the way he moved . . . it was Carlton, all right."

"Did you see his face?"

Mrs. Mason hesitated. She stubbed out her cigarette, lighted a fresh one, blew out a stream of smoke.

"Mrs. Mason? Did you see his face?"

"Yes," she said.

"When?"

"What do you mean when? I saw him standing there . . ."

"Yes, but you said he was facing the door, didn't you? He'd just broken the glass louvers, and was facing the door. I'm assuming that when he reached in to unlock it, he was still . . ."

"I know I saw his face."

"When?"

"It was Carlton."

"Mrs. Mason, did he turn away from the door at any time? Did he turn to look at you? While you were standing at the window?"

"I know it was Carlton."

"Mrs. Mason, at any time while you were looking at this man, did you clearly see his face?"

"I saw him clearly *all* the time. He was standing about where the Christmas tree is, only about that far away."

"I asked if you had clearly seen his *face*."

"If I recognized him as Carlton, then I must have seen his face, isn't that so?"

"Are you asking *me* whether or not you saw his face?"

"I'm just saying it's common sense . . ."

"You're saying if you identified the man as Mr. Markham, then you must have seen his face. You're not saying . . ."

"That's right."

"You're *not* saying that you saw his face and were therefore able to identify him as Mr. Markham."

"That's the same thing, isn't it?"

Not the same thing at all, Matthew thought. "Mrs. Mason," he said, "were you wearing your eyeglasses while you were watching television?"

"Yes. And I was wearing them when I saw Carlton, too."

"Didn't take them off when you went to the window, did you?"

"I *never* take them off. They're bifocals."

"Are they new glasses?"

"New? I've been wearing glasses since I was twelve years old."

"A new prescription, I meant."

"If you're trying to say these are new glasses I wasn't used to or something, then you're barking up the wrong tree. I've been wearing these same glasses for the past three years now. And I see fine with them, thank you."

"Mrs. Mason, do you remember if there was a light burning over the Markham kitchen door on the night of the burglary?"

"First off, there *wasn't* any burglary. It was Carlton going into his own house. And next, they *always* left a light on over that door. That's the door they usually went in by. There's no garage, just the carport, and they walked right from there to the side door."

"Is that what Mr. Markham did on the night of the burglary?"

"What do you mean?"

"Walked from the carport to the side door?"

"I don't know what he did. I only saw him when he was standing there outside the door. And it wasn't a burglary."

"Did you see his car? In the carport?"

"I didn't look for his car."

"Well, you would have noticed a car if it was there, wouldn't you?"

"I didn't notice a car. I wasn't looking for a car."

"Not Mr. Markham's car or anyone's car, is that right?"

"Not any car at all. I heard glass breaking and I looked out toward the side door. I didn't look toward the carport."

"Which is close to the side door, isn't it?"

"Close enough, but I wasn't looking for a car. I was looking to see who it was broke the glass on that kitchen door."

"What time did you go to bed that night, Mrs. Mason?"

"Right after the movie went off."

"Which was when?"

"I don't know when. It was when the movie went off. Eleven o'clock, I guess."

"You went directly to bed at eleven o'clock, is that right?"

"Directly to bed, yes."

"Did you hear a car coming into the Markham driveway at any time after you went to bed?"

"No, I didn't. I'm a sound sleeper. Fall right off to sleep, and stay dead to the world till morning."

"You were asleep at eleven-thirty?"

"*Sound* asleep."

"Then you wouldn't have heard Mr. Markham if he came home at that time."

"He *didn't* come home at that time. He came home around ten-thirty. And broke the glass on his side door. And went into the house."

"Did you hear any police cars arriving later that night?"

"No."

"Did you hear Mrs. Markham's car when she got home later that night?"

"No."

"All you saw or heard, then, was the sound of breaking glass and a man entering the . . ."

"It wasn't just *any* man," Mrs. Mason said firmly. "It was Carlton Markham."

Whose face you never saw, Matthew thought.

4

A sure indication of progress in the city of Calusa, Florida was the new sign outside the Public Safety Building. It stated—in bold white letters on a blue field—that this was the POLICE DE-PARTMENT, a blunt admission for staid Calusa, whose citizens chose to believe their elected place of residence was as crime-free as Eden had been before the serpent did his number.

Nor was the large sign hidden, as had been its smaller prede-cessor, by the leaves of the pittosporum bushes that flanked the brown metal entrance doors of the building. It stood on a metal post close to the sidewalk and perpendicular to the building, so that it could be seen from either direction of approach, clearly visible during the day and illuminated at night. POLICE DEPART-MENT, it shouted. Here we are, folks. You got troubles, come on in. Matthew had troubles. He nodded in brief approval, and then walked into the building and directly to the elevator bank.

Detective Morris Bloom was waiting for him on the third floor.

Today was the eighth of December. The men hadn't seen each other since the end of last May, a long time between drinks. Their handshakes, their smiles of greeting were genuinely warm. It wasn't until they were seated in Bloom's office (hung with photographs of his derring-do in Nassau County, where he'd worked before moving south) that Bloom said, "I hear you had a run-in with Rawles." He was referring to some heated words exchanged between Matthew and Bloom's colleague, Cooper Rawles, back in June while Bloom was on vacation.

"I guess you might call it that," Matthew said.

"I'm sorry to hear that," Bloom said.

He did look extravagantly sorry. Then again, he always looked sorrowful, his mournful brown eyes—overhung by shaggy black eyebrows and straddling a nose that had been broken more than once—seeming perpetually on the edge of tears. Bloom dressed as though he were an undertaker in a cold climate, favoring dark suits that hung forlornly on his huge frame. He was an inch over six feet tall, and he weighed easily a solid two-twenty, with broad shoulders and the oversized knuckles of a street fighter. Matthew had learned only recently that he'd worked as a detective out of New York's Ninth Precinct, no garden spot, before he'd moved to Nassau County. He could visualize Bloom tossing Alphabet City dope dealers on their asses. Bloom had taught him everything he knew about the so-called "manly" art of self-defense. Matthew now knew how to break someone's arm without working up a sweat. Maybe that was manly. In any event, he would have entrusted his life to Bloom without a second thought.

"Coop told me you were sticking your nose in a narcotics case, is that right?" Bloom said.

"A good friend of mine was killed, Morrie. I was trying to find out why."

"Well, I don't want to compound the felony, Matthew, but . . ."

"Then please don't."

"But investigating homicides is police business."

"So I was informed."

"You're getting sore again, right? Don't. I'm your friend. But Coop's a friend, too, and I wish you two would get along better."

"He's going to like me even less after today," Matthew said. "I'm about to stick my nose in again. Officially, this time."

"The Markham case, right? I hear you've taken him on."

"I have."

"I wish you hadn't. He's guilty as homemade sin."

A Southern expression. Detective Morris Bloom was going native.

"Morrie, I have a few questions to ask you."

"Shoot," Bloom said.

"The Markham murder took place in Calusa County . . ."

"It did."

"But not in the city of Calusa."

"That's right."

"The Sheriff's Department detective who filed the original report was a man named Jonas Crier."

"Good cop," Bloom said.

"And his report indicated that he met with you here at the Public Safety Building after he'd taken Markham's statement on the night of the murder."

"He did."

"And that he gave you a taped copy of that statement."

"True."

"Why?"

"Because we were investigating a burglary that had taken place at the Markham house ten days before the murder."

"How did he know that?"

"I told you. He's a good cop."

"Come on, Morrie."

"Okay. One of our cars was patrolling Sunrise Shores on the night of the murder. Saw a Sheriff's Department car in front of the Markham house, stopped to see what the trouble was, thought an assist-officer might be called for. He spoke to Crier, mentioned there'd been a burglary there a week or so ago. Crier picked up on it, called me, and then came to see me after he'd talked to Markham."

"Did he turn the homicide investigation over to you at that time?"

"No."

"Did he turn it over to you at *any* time?"

"No."

"Morrie, you were present at the Q and A on the night Markham was arrested . . ."

"Together with Haggerty from the State Attorney's office, and Detective Sears from the Sheriff's Department."

"The one who caught the initial squeal out on Rancher Road."

"Yes. Crier was his supervisor. When Sears figured he was looking at a homicide, he called back home, asked Crier to come on out."

"Was Sears officially in charge of the investigation?"

"Right."

"Then why were you present at the Q and A, Morrie?"

"Because I was the one who handled the burglary investigation."

"Why was your presence so essential? No one even *asked* my client about the burglary."

"He volunteered the information, that's correct. I was there to ask specific questions if it came to that."

"But it never came to that."

"No, it never did. What are you looking for, Matthew? A technicality? I had every right to be there at the Q and A. You know I handled the burglary, I'm sure Haggerty sent you my report when you filed for discovery."

"He did. He also sent me the witness statement you took from Mrs. Mason. Why were you assigned to take her statement?"

"Because I handled the burglary."

"Oh, I see, the burglary had become your specialty, is that it?"

"Matthew, never get sarcastic with a native New Yorker. He can beat you at it in spades."

"Since you're the burglary mavin," Matthew said, ignoring the advice, "then I'm sure you know my client claims the clothes you later found in his backyard were stolen from his house ten days before the murder. Together with the murder weapon. He stated that at the interrogation."

"He did. But Matthew, that's not going to help you, believe me. We've got him cold. Those clothes, that knife . . ."

"They were stolen ten days before the murder, Morrie."

"So your man says. But we found them buried in his backyard the day *after* the murder."

"Any fingerprints on the knife?"

"I'm sure your discovery demand asked for any reports from experts . . ."

"It did."

"Well, didn't you read the report from the lab in Tampa? The knife was wiped clean, blade *and* handle both. But that didn't stop the techs from finding bloodstains—it's almost impossible to get rid of *all* traces of blood on a knife with a wooden handle. Those stains match the stains on the clothes, Matthew, your *client's* clothes, and the stains are Prudence Markham's blood type, Matthew, type B, Matthew. If ever there was a . . ."

"How'd you happen to go digging in the backyard?"

"Matthew, what kind of game are you playing with me here? Didn't you demand documents relating to search and seizure?"

"You know I did, Morrie. My client told me Sears went in there with a search warrant."

"He did."

"On the strength of what a next-door neighbor claimed to have seen?"

"That was enough for the judge who granted the warrant," Bloom said, and sighed heavily. "Matthew, this was a very brutal murder, the M.E. counted fourteen stab and slash wounds, that's *rage*, Matthew, that's pure, unadulterated *rage*. I wish we weren't on different sides of this one, I really do."

"I don't think he did it, Morrie."

"I'm sure he did," Bloom said, and sighed again.

IN THE CIRCUIT COURT
CALUSA COUNTY
STATE OF FLORIDA

AFFIDAVIT FOR SEARCH WARRANT

BEFORE ME, A JUDGE of the entitled **COURT, Personally came:** Det. Ralph Sears , a **POLICE OFFICER** of the **CA-LUSA COUNTY SHERIFF'S DEPARTMENT,** to me well known, and who being by me first duly **SWORN,** made **APPLICATION** for **SEARCH WARRANT,** and in support of this **APPLICATION** on **OATH,** says:

That he has **REASON TO BELIEVE,** and **DOES BELIEVE** that the **LAWS** of the **STATE OF FLORIDA,** particularly:

> **FLORIDA STATUTE(S):** 782.04
> to wit: Murder

have been violated by: Carlton Barnaby Markham,

and it is the **AFFIANT'S BELIEF** that **EVIDENCE** or **FRUITS OF THE CRIME** are presently to be found in the following described **location, to wit:** 1143 Pompano Way in subdivision named Sunrise Shores, located within the city

limits of the City of Calusa, County of Calusa,
State of Florida. 1143 Pompano Way is located
approximately 100 feet east of Flanders Avenue
and 200 feet north of the intersection of
Flanders Avenue and 12th Street. The structure is
a one-story building, beige in color with a
darker brown color trim. Its front door faces west
and is of aluminum construction. The number 1143
is on the wall of the structure to the right of the
door. The structure is on a lot approximately 60
feet wide by 100 feet long. To the right of the lot
is 1141 Pompano Way, owned and occupied by Velma
Judith Mason, a widow. To the left of the lot is
1145 Pompano Way, owned and occupied by Mr. and
Mrs. Oscar Raddison.

Affiant specifically requests warrant to
search a flower bed approximately 4 feet wide and
12 feet long, planted with gloxinias and
gardenias and located approximately 20 feet from
the rear wall of the structure at 1143 Pompano
Way, approximately 6 feet from the easternmost
property line marked by a row of wax myrtles.

THAT THE REASON FOR THE AFFIANT'S BELIEF IS AS FOLLOWS:

1. On 11/20/86 at 2245 hours, affiant responded
    to a radio call from Deputy Sheriff Cpl. Gandy
    and proceeded to 8489 Rancher Road where the
    body of a stabbing victim later identified as
    Prudence Ann Markham was lying in the parking
    lot outside Anvil Studios, a motion picture
    studio.

2. In the company of Det. Supervisor J. Crier,
    affiant proceeded to 1143 Pompano Way,
    arriving at 0020 hours, 11/21/86 After

consultation with occupant, Carlton Barnaby Markham, affiant proceeded with him and Det. Crier to Southern Medical Hospital where positive identification of victim was made.

3. Det. Crier then proceeded to Calusa P.D. Affiant drove Mr. Markham home, arriving at 1143 Pompano Way at 0115 hours on 11/21/86. Affiant then interviewed neighbors on right and left of Markham house.

4. Oscar Raddison, occupant of 1145 Pompano Way did state as follows: (See witness statement attached.)

That on 11/20/86 at 2315 hours, he was awakened by the sound of someone in the backyard of 1143 Pompano Way. He went to his window, looked out, and saw Carlton Barnaby Markham digging in the flower bed behind the house.

That on 11/20/86 at 2320 hours, he saw Carlton Barnaby Markham burying something in the flower bed and then shoveling earth over it.

WHEREAS, AFFIANT PRAYS that a SEARCH WARRANT be issued, according to LAW, commanding all and singular, the SHERIFFS and their DEPUTIES, POLICE OFFICERS acting within their jurisdictions, and STATE ATTORNEY INVESTIGATORS, acting within their judicial circuits of the STATE OF FLORIDA, either in the day time or the night time, or on Sunday, as the CIRCUMSTANCES of the occasion may demand or require, with the proper and necessary assistance, to SEARCH the previously described location, and SEIZE AS EVIDENCE, any of the following:

Any and all evidence that may relate to the murder of Prudence Ann Markham,

in order that such EVIDENCE may be used in the PROSECUTION OF THE CRIMINAL LAWS OF THE STATE OF FLORIDA.

Pet R. Sears

AFFIANT

SWORN AND SUBSCRIBED before me, the <u>21st</u> day of <u>November</u>, A.D., 19<u>86</u>.

Salvatore N. Monello

ACTING AS MAGISTRATE

IN THE CIRCUIT COURT

CALUSA COUNTY

STATE OF FLORIDA

STATE OF FLORIDA, COUNTY OF CALUSA
I hereby certify that the foregoing
is a true and correct copy of the
original filed in this office.
Witness my hand and seal this:
NOV 21 1986

_____

D.N. Terrill, Clerk of Circuit Court

_____

H. Lackler Deputy Clerk

Matthew was just leaving his office that Monday afternoon when the telephone rang. He muttered "Shit," put down his briefcase on the table inside the door, crossed to his desk, lifted the telephone receiver, and said "Hello?"

"Matthew, hi. It's Susan."

His private line. His former wife.

"I hear you've taken on a big one," she said.

"Who told you?"

"Eliot McLaughlin."

The attorney who had handled the settlement agreement for her. The man responsible for siphoning off a goodly amount of Matthew's income each and every month of the year. Matthew bore him no ill will. He merely wished he would get hit by a bus.

"When can I see you?" she said.

Last spring, while Matthew was "sticking his nose into a narcotics case"—as Bloom had so delicately put it—he and Susan, for reasons still not clear to either of them, had begun seeing each other again. "Seeing" was a euphemism. They had, in fact, begun sharing each other's company in a manner a good deal more intimate and passionate than when they'd been man and wife. Go figure it. He hadn't seen her since Thanksgiving Day, when together they'd placed a long distance call to their daughter Joanna at her boarding school in Massachusetts. The Simms Academy. It sounded like a military school for recalcitrant girls. Actually, it was quite good, and Joanna—after more than two months of bitter complaining—seemed genuinely beginning to enjoy it. This may have had something to do with the fact that she'd met a seventeen-year-old quarterback named Thomas Darrow, and they had become what Joanna called "a thing." Joanna was fourteen years old. Matthew could only hope "a thing" wasn't another euphemism.

He and Susan had become "a thing," too.

In provincial, gossipy Calusa, there were not many people who didn't know that Matthew and Susan were seeing each other again. Some people cynically maintained that Matthew's fresh desire had less to do with Susan's obvious charms than with an urgent need to get rid of his onerous alimony burden. Other people genuinely wished that the sound of wedding bells would be heard again in the not too distant future. Still others gave the new (or old, or both) lovers two, three months at the most. But Matthew had been seeing Susan for six months now and when he heard her say, somewhat breathlessly, "When can I see you?" there was an odd little stirring in his groin that he could not attribute to indigestion.

"Tonight?" he said.

"We have a lot to talk about," she said.

"What time?" he asked.

"What time do you get out of there?"

"I was just leaving the office. I'm running out to Sunrise Shores to interview a witness."

"What time do you think you'll be finished?"

Matthew looked at his watch.

"Four o'clock?" he said.

"Come directly here," Susan said. "Do not pass Go, do not collect two hundred dollars."

Oscar Raddison was a man in his late fifties, his blue tank-top shirt bulging with the muscles of a weight lifter, his red running shorts revealing thighs like oaks, his body resplendently tanned, his brown eyes sharp and intelligent. He admitted Matthew to the house, showed no reluctance at all to having their conversation taped or to later giving the same information in a deposition. He even offered Matthew a drink. This was at two-thirty in the afternoon. Matthew declined and Raddison went to the refrigerator to get himself a Heineken beer.

He popped the can, and then said, "I'd like to be finished here before Lou gets home. Louise. My wife. We're going out to an early dinner."

"I won't take much of your time," Matthew said, and started the recorder. "Mr. Raddison, according to the witness statement you gave Detective Sears of the Sheriff's Department . . ."

"Nice feller," Raddison said.

"I haven't met him yet," Matthew said.

"Smart, too," Raddison said. "When I told him about that flower bed, he knew right off he'd find incriminating evidence there."

"You told him this when he came back to the house on the night of the murder, isn't that correct? Well, it would have been morning by then, about a quarter past one in the morning."

"Yes."

"About the same time Detective Bloom was talking to Mrs. Mason."

"I wouldn't know about that."

"Well, her witness statement was taken at twenty after one that morning."

"I still wouldn't know anything about it. Did *she* see him, too? Out there in the garden?"

"What did *you* see?" Matthew asked.

"Carlton. With a spade in his hands. Digging up the garden."

"What time was this?"

"I woke up around a quarter past eleven . . ."

"Was it the sound of the digging that woke you up?"

"No. I had to pee. I wake up two, three times a night to pee. A side effect."

"Of what?"

"I've got a high cholesterol problem, the doctor put me on medication. One of the side effects is excessive urination. I usually go to bed around nine, wake up around eleven, eleven-thirty, then again at two, then again at five, then sleep in till eight, when I get up and go over to Nautilus. Flatulence is another side effect."

"I see," Matthew said.

"I guess I shouldn't be saying all this with that machine going, but it's the truth."

"So you woke up to go to the bathroom at eleven-fifteen . . ."

"Right. And that's when I heard someone digging in the yard next door."

"Someone. Not Mr. Markham."

"Well, I didn't know it was Carlton till I took a look."

"When was that?"

"After I finished peeing."

"Looked from where?"

"The bathroom window."

"Was the light on in the bathroom?"

"No, I never turn it on, it'd wake Lou. I just find my way there in the dark—I've got this little night light in the hall, I never have a problem."

"So the bathroom was dark."

"Yes."

"And you looked from the bathroom window over to the Markham backyard, is that right?"

"That's what I did."

"Where *is* the bathroom, Mr. Raddison?"

"Just down the hall from the bedroom."

"At which end of the house?"

"Right there," Raddison said, and pointed.

"That would be the southern end of your house, wouldn't it? The end farthest from the Markham house."

"The southern end, right. But it's not all that far. And I've got good eyesight, check with my doctor if you like. Never wore glasses in my life, still don't. I saw Carlton plain as day. Digging there in the flower bed."

"With what?"

"Well, with a spade. Or a shovel. Either one, I couldn't tell you which."

"He had a shovel, or a spade, in his hands."

"Yessir."

"And was doing what with it?"

"Digging a hole in the flower bed."

"How large a hole?"

"Big enough to hold them clothes and the knife, I reckon."

"You didn't *see* clothes or a knife, did you?"

"No. I just saw him burying something. But when they came to dig it up . . ."

"But you didn't actually *see* Mr. Markham burying *clothes*, did you? Or a knife?"

"I saw him digging a hole in the flower bed, and putting something in it, and shoveling dirt back over it, and then putting the flowers back in place on top. That's what I saw."

"*Not* bloody clothing or a bloody knife."

"That's what they found in that hole, isn't it? So that's what Carlton had to be burying."

"Did you at any time clearly see what he was burying?"

"Nossir."

"*Whatever* he buried . . . where was it while he was digging the hole?"

"On the ground."

"You saw it on the ground?"

"Nossir, I didn't see it. His back was to me, it must've been at his feet there on the ground. The clothes and the knife. He didn't go back into the house for it, so it had to be on the ground."

"You didn't see him going back into the house?"

"Not specifically, no."

"What do you mean by 'specifically'?"

"I mean I didn't see him actually going back into the house. But he was headed for the front door. Later on. When he was finished out there."

"You said a moment ago that his back was to you while he was digging."

"Yessir."

"Then you didn't see his face."

"Not while he was digging."

"What did he do when he finished digging?"

"Picked up this stuff on the ground and dropped it in the hole."

"Was his back still to you? When he picked up the stuff on the ground?"

"Yes, it was."

"And when he dropped it in the hole, was his back still to you?"

"Yes, it was."

"Then you didn't see what he dropped into the hole . . ."

"I already told you that."

"And you didn't see his face, either."

"Not then."

"Did you see his face when he was shoveling the earth back? Or when he was replacing the flowers?"

"No, not then neither."

"When *did* you see his face, Mr. Raddison?"

"When he was leaving the yard."

"You saw his face as he was leaving."

"Yes. Turned toward me for a minute, and I saw his face."

"For a minute?"

"Yessir."

"Exactly a minute?"

"Well, a minute, more or less."

"Which was it, would you say now? More or less?"

"I didn't time it."

"Could it have been less than a minute?"

"It could've, I really can't say. He turned away from the flower bed and started walking toward the side of the house . . ."

"Going where?"

"Well, I don't *know* where. I guess back to bed."

"Walking toward the side of the house, you say?"

"Yes, the space between our two houses."

"Leading toward the street?"

"Well, he could've got to the street that way. But he could've got to the front door of his house, too."

"Did he have the shovel with him? Or the spade?"

"He did."

"But you don't know, do you, whether this man you saw—let me rephrase that. When this man finished digging, did you see him enter the Markham house?"

"No, I didn't. He passed out of my line of vision. When he started walking between the houses."

"Toward the street."

"Or the front door."

"Well, did you hear a door opening or closing?"

"No, I didn't. I went back to bed."

"Were you in bed when Detective Sears came to talk to you?"

"I was."

"Asleep?"

"Asleep, yes. I pee, then I go right back to sleep."

"Didn't you find it strange, though? Mr. Markham digging in the flower bed at that hour?"

"I thought it was a little peculiar, yes. But they were peculiar people, anyway, you know. Man runs a clock shop, woman makes movies." Raddison raised his eyebrows. "Besides, at the time, I didn't know she'd been killed. I didn't learn that till Detective Sears got here."

"And you felt it important to tell him what you'd seen in the Markham backyard."

"Well, sure. Wouldn't *you* think it was important? Man's wife is stabbed to death, and then you see him burying clothes and a knife? I mean, that's . . ."

"But you *didn't* see what he was burying."

"Well, that's what they dug up."

"A few minutes ago, Mr. Raddison, you said you thought Mr. Markham might have gone back to bed after he finished whatever he was doing there in the backyard. Do you . . . ?"

"He wasn't out there taking a leak, that's for sure. He was burying the clothes and the knife."

"But do you have any reason to believe he'd been in bed *before* he started the digging? He wasn't wearing pajamas, was he?"

"No, he wasn't wearing pajamas."

"What was he wearing?"

"Dark clothes. Pants and some kind of windbreaker, blue or black, but dark anyway."

"Was he wearing a hat?"

"Nossir, no hat."

"Did you see his hair?"

"Yessir."

"What color was it?"

"Yellow as corn," Raddison said, and Matthew's heart sank.

He could not concentrate on what Susan was saying.

They were sitting out by the pool of what used to be the house he shared with her, the house he was in fact sharing with her more and more frequently these days, sipping martinis and watching the tail end of a glorious sunset, and she was telling him that Joanna would be coming home from school on the nineteenth, which was less than two weeks away, and they had to figure out what they were going to tell her about themselves because Joanna was a smart cookie who would realize in an instant that these weren't the same two lively antagonists she'd left back in September when she'd gone off to school.

He was thinking there were too many things missing in this case.

He was wondering how the State Attorney planned to account for all those missing things.

"The trouble, of course," Susan was saying, "is that until *we* know what the hell we're doing, how can we explain it to Joanna? Do *you* know what we're doing, Matthew?"

"I know what I *wish* we were doing," he said.

"That isn't true," she said, and looked him dead in the eye. Full pouting mouth that gave the impression of a sullen, spoiled beauty, brown hair worn sleek and long again after her experiment with a wedge cut, dark eyes somber in a pale oval face, studying him now. "You're a million miles away, aren't you?" she said. She put her hand on his arm. "Tell me."

"No, no," he said. "Let's figure out the Joanna thing first, I know you . . ."

"We've got eleven days before she gets here. What's bothering you, Matthew?"

"Too many things missing," he said, and shook his head.

"Are you talking about the Markham case?"

"Yes."

"What's missing?"

"Do you ever go anyplace without a handbag?"

"Yes."

"Where?"

"Exercise class. I throw my wallet in the glove compartment."

"Anyplace else?"

"Yes. The beach. Same thing."

"But around town . . ."

"I carry a bag. Why?"

"Why isn't the State Attorney concerned about that missing handbag?"

"What missing . . . ?"

"They find a woman dead in the middle of nowhere, fourteen

stab and slash wounds. Her car is parked twelve feet from where she's lying dead on the gravel. The car is locked, the police have to break into it. Her handbag isn't in the car. It isn't in the studio, either. So where is it?"

"Was there a wallet in the car?"

"No. Nothing. No film, either."

"Film?"

"She was editing film out there on Rancher Road. So the film is gone and her handbag's gone, and her keys are gone, so I have to assume the *killer* took all those things, am I right?"

"Well, yes, that sounds reasonable."

"So why doesn't it sound reasonable to Haggerty?"

"Haggerty?"

"The man who's handling the State's case."

"I'm not following you, Matthew."

"I mean, *he's* got to assume the same thing I'm assuming, doesn't he? That the *killer* took those things?"

"Yes?"

"But he thinks my *client* is the goddamn killer! So what happened to all that stuff my client had to have taken if he *is*, in fact, the killer? Where is it? If Haggerty had it, he'd have listed it on his response. So he hasn't got it. So where is it? And where's the shovel or the spade or whatever the hell my client allegedly used to bury his clothes in the backyard? I have to assume he hasn't got that, either."

"So? Can't he make a case without . . . ?"

"Oh, he's sure as hell going to try. But why isn't it *bothering* him?"

"Should it be bothering him?"

"It's bothering *me*. Because it makes me wonder what he's *got*, Susan. Never mind what he *hasn't* got. What has he *got*? What has he got that makes him feel so confident he can send Markham to the electric chair? He hasn't got the missing handbag, the missing keys, the missing film, the missing shovel. The killer's got those, Susan. But Haggerty doesn't seem to give a damn. He's got two witnesses and he's got some bloody clothing and a bloody knife, and he seems content to be going with that alone. Why?"

"Why don't you *ask* him what else he's got?"

"He's already told me what he's got. My demand for discovery specifically listed tangible papers or objects."

"Well . . . is he allowed to hide anything?"

"No, he can't do that."

"He's required to tell you . . ."

"Yes. Required by law. He doesn't have to tell me how he plans to try his case, of course, but . . ."

"But he does have to tell you what evidence he has."

"Yes."

"Well, *has* he told you?"

"I have to assume so."

They were silent for several moments. The sun was all but gone.

She said, very softly, "I wish I could help you, Matthew."

"I'm sorry to bother you with this crap," he said.

They fell silent again.

"What else is bothering you?" she asked.

He sighed deeply.

"Tell me."

"I may be in over my head, Susan. I may be sending an innocent man to the chair because I don't know what the hell I'm doing."

"You *do* know what you're doing," she said.

"Maybe."

"*Is* he innocent?"

"I have to believe that."

"But do you?"

"Yes."

"Then you won't let them kill him, Matthew," she said, and took his hand.

In bed with her, the case was still with him.

The reflected light from the pool outside flickered on the ceiling. In his mind, there was the same elusive wavering of light, slivers of evidence fitfully moving at the whim of the wind. Her long hair fell over his face, her mouth covered his. His eyes were closed, the splintered light danced behind them. She lowered herself onto him.

And for just a little while, he forgot the handbag, forgot the keys and the film, forgot the shovel, forgot all the missing things, and there was only the here and the now, and the remembered heat of this woman he once loved and perhaps now loved anew.

And then he thought again, The *killer* has those things.

The sign on the wooden post read:

ORCHIDACEOUS
Exotic Orchids

There was an address lower on the post: 3755. A dirt road to the left of the post ran off Timucuan Point Road through thick clusters of cabbage palm and palmetto. The place used to be a cattle ranch, and the entire property—a thousand acres of it— was still fenced with barbed wire.

The dirt road ran past a lake shrouded by oaks.

There were alligators in the lake.

The dirt road continued along the side of the lake for half a mile, where it ended at the main house. The greenhouses were set back two hundred yards from the main house, across from what used to be the stables when there were still horses here. Situated catty-wampus to the greenhouses was a windowless, unpainted cinderblock structure that housed the generator. The building was perhaps fifteen feet wide by twenty feet long. It had a dirt floor. It had a louvered ventilating slit high up on one of the walls. A naked light bulb hung in the center of the space, operated from a switch just inside the thick wooden door. There was a padlock on the door.

He unlocked the door and snapped on the light.

She was wearing only high-heeled red leather boots. Soft red leather. The kind of boots that looked rumpled at the ankles. Tall boots that folded over onto her thighs. She had long red hair a shade darker than the boots. A tuft of even darker red hair curled in a wild tangle at the joining of her legs. She sat in the dirt in one corner of the room, behind the generator, her hands tied behind her, her legs bound at the ankles. A three-inch-wide strip of adhesive tape covered her mouth. Her eyes flashed green in the dim glow of the hanging light bulb.

"Evening Puss," he said.

He closed the door behind him, and set down the shopping bag he'd been carrying.

"Miss me?" he asked.

He came toward her, walking around the generator, and she cowered away from him, trying to move deeper into the corner. He looked down at her. He shook his head, clucked his tongue.

"Look at how filthy you've got," he said, "sitting here naked in the dirt. Shame on you. Woman who always took such good care of herself."

He kept looking down at her.

"Maybe I ought to take that tape off your mouth," he said. "You're not gonna scream if I take it off, are you? Not that anybody'd hear you. You promise you won't scream if I take off the tape?"

She nodded.

"You're sure now? You won't scream like you done last time?"

Another nod, green eyes wide.

"Well, then, let's just take off the tape," he said, and crouched beside her. He smiled, twisted her head, found the end of the tape, and with one violent tug ripped it free. She bit her lip, stifling a scream.

"Hurts, don't it, when I pull the tape off that way?" he said.

She was still biting her lip.

"You hear what I said? Hurts, don't it?"

"Yes," she said.

He nodded, got to his feet again, and went back to the door where he'd left the bag.

"You hungry?" he asked.

"Yes," she said.

He carried the bag back to where she sat in the corner.

"Bet you're hoping there's a sandwich in here, ain't you?" he said.

"Yes," she said.

"Bet you'd eat scraps I spit on, wouldn't you?" he said.

She did not answer.

"I asked you a question," he said.

"I'm not *that* hungry," she said.

"Don't get sassy," he said.

"I'm sorry, I . . ."

"Did you hear me ask you a question?"

"Yes, and I'm . . . I'm sorry I was . . . if I sounded sassy."

"Or maybe you don't want me to feed you, is that it?"

"No, I want you to."

"Want me to what?"

"Feed me."

"Even scraps I spit on?"

"No, I . . . I don't want to eat anything like that."

"You getting sassy again?"

"No, I'm not, really. I'm sorry. But . . ."

"'Cause you better not get sassy with me, Puss."

"I won't, I'm sorry."

"I thought you was a woman'd take just about *anything* in her mouth," he said. "Isn't that so? That thou hast transgressed against the Lord thy God, and hast scattered thy ways to the strangers under every green tree?" He scowled and looked at her mouth. "Just about anything in that mouth," he said. "And here you are turning down good, wholesome food."

"You didn't say it was . . ."

"Woman who enjoys *eating* as much as *you* do," he said. He was still scowling. He kept looking at her mouth. And then his gaze suddenly shifted to her breasts. "Oh my, are you cold, Puss?" he asked. "Or just scared?"

"Cold," she said.

"But not scared?"

She did not answer him.

"Is that why you're all puckered up like that?" he asked, and suddenly pinched the nipple of her left breast between his thumb and forefinger. "Because you're cold? Or is it because you're scared?" He squeezed the nipple hard. "Does that hurt?" he asked.

"Yes," she said.

"Oh, excuse me," he said. "So which is it?" he asked. "Cold or scared?"

"Both," she said. "Please let me go."

"You mean let you go *here*?" he said, squeezing harder. "Or let you go *period*?"

"There," she said. "Please."

"Because I *will* let you go, you know. Sooner or later. When I'm finished with you."

"Please," she said.

"Hurts, don't it?" he said.

"Yes! Please oh *please!*"

He released his grip on her.

"There," he said, and smiled. "What do you say?"

"Thank you," she said. She was gasping for breath.

"Bet you wish you had a sweater," he said, "the way this building stays so cool and all. Maybe there's a nice warm sweater in this bag. Wouldn't it be nice if I brought you a sweater?"

"Yes," she said.

"Why?" he asked.

"Because I'm cold."

"Oh. I thought maybe you were modest."

"No, I'm just . . ."

"You mean you're *not* modest?"

"That's not what I meant."

"What did you mean? Are you modest or aren't you?"

"Whatever you say," she said.

"Am I hearing sass again? Answer my question!"

"I meant . . . if *you* think I'm immodest, then . . ."

"Yes, I do."

"Then . . . then I think I'm immodest, too."

"But you don't *really* think so, do you? Not really. Thou hadst a whore's forehead, thou refusedst to be ashamed." He smiled suddenly. "Are you cold, too?" he asked.

"Very."

"And scared?"

"A little."

"Only a little? Aren't you scared I might hurt you again?"

"Yes."

"But only a little. Maybe I didn't hurt you enough. Maybe if you're only scared a teeny-weeny little bit . . ."

"I'm very scared," she said.

"You will be," he said. "You'll be very scared before I'm finished with you." He smiled again. "Poor little Puss," he said, "all naked and shivering and cold in her sexy red boots. Withhold thy foot from being unshod, Puss, and thy throat from thirst. Are you thirsty?"

"Yes."

"Sure wish I had something for you to drink. Sure wish there *was* a sweater in this bag, too, but there isn't. I burned all your clothes last night."

"You didn't."

"Oh, but I did. You won't be needing clothes anymore, will you?"

"What . . . what does that mean?"

"When I let you go."

"When . . . when will that be?" she asked.

"When I'm ready," he said. "Stand up."

She leaned away from the wall, eased herself onto her knees. Struggling, she managed to shove herself into a standing position.

"Move here," he said. "Around the generator. Under the light."

She half-hopped, half-shuffled to the center of the room.

"Shall I untie you?" he asked.

"Yes, please," she said.

"No, I don't think so," he said. "Are you wondering if there's food in the bag?"

"Yes."

"There isn't."

"You said . . ."

"I said I bet you wished there was a sandwich in this bag, that's what I said."

"Yes, that's what you said."

"Something to eat."

"Yes."

"Because poor little Puss is *so-o-o* hungry, isn't she?"

"Yes."

"And thirsty."

"Yes."

"But there's nothing to eat or drink in the bag," he said. "There's only a towel and a pair of scissors."

She looked at him. He was smiling again. And suddenly she began trembling.

"Are you scared?" he asked.

"No," she said.

"The towel doesn't scare you, does it?"

"No."

"Then what? The scissors?"

"Nothing."

"Then why are you shivering like that?"

"I'm . . . cold."

"No. You're scared."

He reached into the shopping bag, took a rolled beach towel from it, and unfurled it like a flag. He draped the towel over her shoulders, arranged it over her breasts.

"Modesty, modesty," he said, "naked, and ye clothed me," and reached into the bag again.

The blades of the scissors caught the feeble light from the overhead lamp.

"We don't want you getting all covered with hair, do we?" he said.

"What . . . ?"

He opened the scissors.

"And he shall pluck away his crop with his feathers," he said, and clutched a tangle of long red hair in his left hand.

Oh my oh my oh my, all the hurly-burly, all the hustle-bustle, all the bullshit of a movie set. Once, when Warren was still walking a beat in St. Louis, he'd pulled duty where they were shooting a movie on location, sergeant must've been paid a C-note to keep order in the streets, maybe more, but none of it filtered down to the grunts.

Man, those movie people!

He never in his life had seen people act so much like walking gods. Strutting around all puffed up with the glory and the wisdom of what they were doing. Citizens standing around goggle-eyed waiting for the star to appear. The "star" was somebody on one of the television series, you blinked your eyes he'd be gone next season. Warren had the feeling that if the director asked some lady to take her baby out of its buggy and smash his head on the sidewalk for the cameras, she'd have wet her pants and said,

"Oh, yes, sir, thank you, sir, in a minute, sir, just let me comb his hair."

Same thing here.

Smalltime shit here, but the same damn thing.

Must've been something about making a movie that gave the people involved the feeling that they were rearranging the universe.

Big truck outside the house on Sabal Key, cars parked all over the street and even the sidewalk. Not a police car in sight, though any zealous cop could have handed out ten thousand summonses. Movie people didn't care. They'd park right on top of a cop's *hat*, you gave them the opportunity. Cables and lights in the truck, all kinds of heavy equipment. Warren walked right past it, up the driveway and into the front door of the house.

Never ask, never explain, that was Warren's motto.

Walk in like you belonged there, Mr. Cool, bit of a strut on, dark glasses helped.

Oh my oh my oh my, here he was back again in downtown St. Louis, except that this was the backyard of a Sabal Key house and all the cameras and lights were set up around a swimming pool, and all the people running around frantically doing their godlike things were shooting a commercial for patio furniture. Didn't matter. They could've been in Rome shooting *Cleopatra*.

"Help you?" somebody asked.

"Nope," Warren said, without even turning to see who was talking to him.

"This is a movie we're shooting here," the voice said, and a body materialized in front of him, hulking, threatening.

Warren lifted his shades onto his forehead and beamed a cold, brown-eyed stare at the man. Big gorilla wearing blue jeans and a blue, sweat-stained T-shirt. A grip, no doubt. They called them grips. Lotsa muscles, no brains, the longshoremen of the movie business. Warren reached into his pocket, took out his wallet, and flipped it open to the police shield they'd given him when he retired from the St. Louis P.D. A fraction of an inch smaller all around than the buzzer he'd worn for five years, but looking like the real McCoy when you flashed it fast.

"Checking," he said, and snapped the wallet shut, and turned away from the man, and over his shoulder said, "Where's Vaughan Turner?"

"Setting up a shot there," the man said. "Is there some problem?"

"No problem," Warren said, and walked away from him, skirting the edge of the pool, which did not look too terribly inviting on a December day with the temperature at fifty-six degrees. Sunny Florida, he thought.

He knew better than to interrupt any of these shakers and movers when they were setting up a shot. Very temperamental, movie people were. You told them a hydrogen bomb had just been dropped over Calusa Bay, they'd say, "Move aside a minute, we have to adjust this flag."

They were adjusting flags now, trying to get the lighting right. He'd picked up a lot of jargon back there on location in St. Louis, you hang around all day scratching your ass, if you had any brain at all in your head you began to understand the language these Martians spoke. They were shooting with an Arriflex on a tripod, what they called "sticks" because the legs were wooden. The man looking through the viewfinder was Vaughan Turner, one of the men Warren was here to see, Prudence Ann Markham's usual cameraman (or cinematographer, if you wanted to get fancy). Turner looked through the viewfinder, and then looked up and said, "Flag it on this side."

He was talking to the lighting director, Lew Smollet, another man on Warren's list. Smollet attached a square of white fabric to the gobo, cutting the light, and turned to look at Turner, who was peering through the viewfinder again. "Take it up to the top,"

Turner said, and Smollet adjusted the flag again, and Turner nodded, and said, "Okay, I want all these cables to go."

A pair of grips began lifting and moving the cables that were snaked on the terrace. A girl in a bikini stood looking bored and chilly near the outdoor lounge chairs that were the *real* stars of the show. Smollet went over to her and held a light meter to her face.

"What've you got?" Turner asked.

"Eleven-sixteen split," Smollet said.

"Okay, I'm ready," Turner said. "Where's Bud?"

"Right here," a man said.

Obviously the director. Chief of all the Indians. Wearing jeans and a white, long-sleeved Ralph Lauren sports shirt with a little blue polo pony and rider on the left pec. Smoking a cigarette, which he ground out on the terrace now. Turner stepped aside as he looked into the viewfinder.

"Looks fine," he said. "I'm ready. Jane?"

"Ready," the girl in the bikini said.

"Danny?"

A man in swim trunks, standing near the diving board, signaled with his hand.

"Okay, let's go for it," Bud said.

"Quiet, please," the assistant director said.

A man sitting behind a sound cart—this had to be Mark Wiley, the third man Warren was here to see—took off his headphones and said, "Are we doing playback?"

"No," Bud said. "Stand by, people."

It was suddenly very quiet. Out beyond the pool, a pelican swooped in low over the gulf.

"Roll camera," Bud said.

"Rolling."

"Roll sound."

"Speed."

"Mark it," the A.D. said.

A man holding a clapstick and standing just in front of the actress in the bikini said, "Thirteen B, take six," and brought the black-and-white clapper down onto the slate on which the same information was chalked.

"Action," Bud said, and the actor in the swim trunks began walking toward the actress in the bikini, who eased into one of the lounge chairs. As the actor approached her, he said, "Hi, honey," and leaned in to kiss her. "Ready to relax on our Tropical . . . ?"

"Hold it, hold it," Wiley said from behind his console, and looked out over the gulf. "Is there a plane out there?" he said. "A motorboat? Something?"

"Cut it, cut," Bud said.

"Yeah, it's a boat," the A.D. said.

Bud sighed. "Okay, let's wait," he said.

Warren sighed, too.

They waited until the boat had gone by, and then they went through the same "Quiet please, standby, roll camera, roll sound, mark it, action" rigmarole another time. Bud cut again to tell his actors that he wanted the dialogue between them *before* Jane sat in the lounge chair. They rolled again, and again Bud cut to tell Smollet he wasn't getting much of a shot, and would he please take another reading? Smollet put the light meter on the actress and gave him a new reading of eleven. They rolled again, and cut again, and rolled again, and cut again, and finally got the shot on the twelfth take.

"Okay, let's move all these toys," Bud said, and the grips started struggling the camera and the lights to the other side of the terrace.

Warren walked over to where Turner was telling one of the grips to "head wrap" something.

"Mr. Turner?" he said.

• • •

The thing Mose and Tick liked most in the whole world was money.

They also liked girls and dope, but they figured if you had money the girls and the dope followed as the night followed the day.

Ever since they'd heard about Prue's murder almost three weeks ago, they'd been following the case with more than casual interest, reading the newspapers, watching all the television coverage. It seemed that her wimpy husband who ran a clock shop had done the lady in. It seemed this very same wimp was being held without bail and being defended by yet another wimp who, from what Mose and Tick could gather, had hardly ever handled a criminal case in his entire career. It seemed that the State Attorney's Office was going for the death penalty, and it further seemed they had a damn good chance of getting it.

None of this interested Mose and Tick.

Money interested them.

Which was why the *omissions* in the news coverage captured their singular attention.

When a good-looking, twenty-eight-year-old blonde gets murdered in staid Calusa, that's headline news, man. Especially if the murder is a stabbing. Knives are scary. Hardly anybody knows what it feels like to get shot, but *everybody* has cut himself accidentally and knows how that can hurt, man, and knows how the sight of all that blood welling up can turn you pale with fright. Stabbings made good headlines. Newspapers loved headlines dripping blood. Television reporters loved talking about stabbings, too. They could show pictures of pools of blood soaking into the ground, and they could show the bloody knife, or a reasonable facsimile of the bloody knife, turning slowly under a harsh light that sent little pinprick reflections of terror darting out into the viewer's living room. Brutal stabbings brought out the very best in news reporters.

Which is why Mose and Tick found it peculiar that none of the newspaper or television reporters had once mentioned that the good-looking twenty-eight-year-old blonde who'd been found floating in her own blood had been directing a skin flick.

It seemed to Mose and Tick that such news was the stuff of excellent headlines, especially in this day and age when the Attorney General's Commission on Pornography had decided there was a definite link between obscenity and violence. Was it possible that no one *knew* she'd been engaged in lighting and framing and shooting delicate footage on the intricate art of tickle and grab? Could that possibly be *possible*? Or were the police and the State Attorney's Office simply playing it smart? Neither Tick nor Mose had ever met anyone in Florida law enforcement who could be considered smart. Still, *were* they withholding the skin-flick bombshell till they could explode it to startling effect and great astonishment at the trial?

Mose and Tick strongly doubted this premise.

Their conclusion was that no one in law enforcement knew about the movie Prudence Ann Markham had been working on since the twenty-ninth day of September.

Which meant that no one in law enforcement was in possession of either the negative or the work print.

Which meant that a very valuable property was kicking around out there someplace in Calusa.

Which was what interested them about the murder of Prudence Ann Markham.

Which was what brought them to Calusa on the afternoon of December ninth.

To find Connie.

Because maybe *she* knew where the film was.

Warren was upset.

He came to Matthew's office at two o'clock that Tuesday after-

97

noon, and began telling him what was bothering him. Together, the two men had a lot of things bothering them.

"To begin with," Warren said, "she didn't use those three guys from Calusa. The crew you gave me. I went out to see them this morning, they're shooting a commercial out on Sabal Key, using some guy's house with a swimming pool there. You ever been on a movie set? It's a madhouse. But I finally managed to talk to all three of them in bits and pieces. None of them worked with her on this film she was shooting. Only one of them—the cameraman, Vaughan Turner—even *knew* she'd been working on a movie. I think he was annoyed that she hadn't hired him. But he didn't know what the project was, thought maybe she wasn't even shooting it here in Calusa. The other two were surprised to learn she'd been working on something without them. *And* annoyed. *More* than annoyed. Outright *pissed*, in fact. I got the feeling this was a pretty close bunch who'd worked together on a lot of stuff, and they didn't like the idea of her hiring other people. Anyway, *they* weren't on the movie, and they didn't know who was."

"Did they have any suggestions?" Matthew asked.

"One of them—the lighting man, Lew Smollet—said there are good people in Tampa, Miami and Jacksonville, but he didn't know whether Prue actually knew any of them since she usually worked out of Calusa."

"Any names?"

"No, but I can get on that if you want me to. Florida's a Right-to-Work state, and none of these guys *have* to belong to unions if they don't want to. But I know there are two different unions for all these technicians, and maybe I can get a list of active members in Florida, if you want me to go that route."

"I think we ought to know who she was working with, don't you?"

"Sure. You don't want me to track down everybody who ever

made a movie in the state of Florida, though, do you?"

"Well . . ."

"Because, Matthew, that would take a long, long time. Has a date been set for the trial yet?"

"Not yet."

"When are you guessing?"

"The calendar's pretty full, we may not get on till February."

"Well, that's not too bad then. I'll get started on it, see what unions these guys might have belonged to, get a list of their people. So that's the first thing. We struck out with her crew."

"What's the second thing?"

"The second thing is crime was up seventeen percent in Calusa County this year, and my cop friends down the old station house tell me it's mostly drug related, which means there're quite a few unsolved junkie burglaries, and if the burglary at the Markham house was a junkie on the prowl who later knifed Prue and stole her pocketbook, we've got a long, tough row to hoe. I'll keep snooping around, but turning up the burglar looks very slim. Are you still listening? I've got more bad news."

Matthew sighed.

"I know just how you feel," Warren said, nodding. "But here it is, anyway. On November tenth, the moon was in the second day of its first quarter. That's a fairly good moon, Matthew. Plus it was a clear night, lots of stars."

"How about the night of the murder?"

"Four days past full moon. Full moon was on the sixteenth. Still pretty big on the twentieth. And another clear night, Matthew. In short . . ."

"Excellent visibility on both nights."

"Yes."

"Wonderful," Matthew said.

"I knew you'd be thrilled. There's more."

"Spare me."

"I went to see Alan Saunders—the friend Markham was planning a fishing trip with? The guy he was supposed to've been with on the night of the burglary? From nine to eleven? Remember?"

"Yes?"

"Saunders now seems sure that Markham left him at around ten, a little after ten. Which would put him back at his own house at ten-thirty or thereabouts, just when Mrs. Mason says she saw him breaking into his own kitchen."

"Terrific," Matthew said.

"You want the worst of it?"

"How much worse can it get?"

"Much," Warren said. "When you talked to Markham, did he mention anything about his first wife?"

"No. *What* first wife?"

"Lady he was married to ten years ago, when he was fresh out of college and living in New Orleans."

"What about her?"

"She was stabbed to death, Matthew."

The State Attorney's Office used to be a motel.

It sat across the street from a ball park that once was used for big-league spring training before the team moved to Sarasota. Now teams sponsored by beer companies played there. The old motel sat behind what used to be the old courthouse. You could still see the twin white towers of the old courthouse—now an office building—from the courtyard surrounded by what used to be motel units but were now offices for the State Attorney's staff. There were palm trees and bougainvillea and hibiscus in the courtyard. It was a sunny afternoon, and you expected to see sleepy-eyed lovers strolling out of the old motel rooms into the courtyard. A brown plastic sign with white lettering was fastened to the wall of one of the old motel units. It read:

OFFICE OF THE STATE ATTORNEY
TWELFTH JUDICIAL CIRCUIT
Skye Bannister
807 Magnolia Boulevard
Office Hours Monday—Friday
8:30 A.M.—5:00 P.M.

It was 3:30 P.M. when Matthew opened the door to the office and told the receptionist he had an appointment with Arthur Haggerty. She asked him to please have a seat. He took a seat on a bench and looked around. You could see where the old motel walls had been knocked down to make a bigger space. There were still marks on the ceilings and walls. An open door at the far end of the room revealed a motel bathroom beyond it: pink sink, toilet and tub. He could see ledgers stacked in the tub.

"Mr. Hope?"

"Yes?"

"Mr. Haggerty will see you now."

"Thank you," he said.

She nodded to a closed door. He went to the door and opened it. No walls knocked down this time. A single motel room disguised as an office. Big desk stacked with legal papers in blue binders, shelves crowded with reference books, a wall covered with diplomas. A law office. But you could still see the telltale tub in the bathroom.

Behind the desk stood a big red-faced man with his hand extended. Unruly brown hair and bright blue eyes. Beer belly hanging over his belt. Wearing tan slacks with brown loafers, a yellow shirt open at the throat, tie pulled down, cuffs rolled up onto his forearms. His grip was firm and dry and strong.

"Arthur Haggerty," he said, "nice to meet you. Have a seat."

Matthew sat in a wooden chair on the other side of the desk.

"What can I do for you?" Haggerty asked.

Matthew got straight to the point.

"Mr. Haggerty," he said, "when I made my demand for discovery, I specifically asked for any police reports made in connection with this case. You . . ."

"You're referring to the Markham case, of course."

"Yes, that's the case I'm handling."

"I'm handling several cases at the moment, you see," Haggerty said, and smiled. "So. How can I help you?"

"I've just come from a visit with my client," Matthew said. "He corroborates information I now have about a murder that took place in New Orleans ten years ago, on which extensive police reports were made, none of which were provided by you in your response."

"Are you referring to the knife murder of Jennifer Bowles Markham, the wife of Carlton Barnaby Markham at the time?"

"I am."

"What's your question?"

"Why wasn't I supplied with those New Orleans police reports?"

"You asked for police reports in connection with the case. By 'the case,' I assumed you meant the murder of Prudence Ann Markham. That's the case you're handling, isn't it?"

"Mr. Haggerty, let's not fence around here, okay?" Matthew said. "We're not in court yet, and you're not playing to a jury. My client tells me he was questioned endlessly about the murder of his former wife. He tells me that for almost a full week he was considered a suspect by the New Orleans police . . ."

"Yes, he was."

". . . but that finally the police decided he'd had nothing to do with the murder."

"Well, the case remains unsolved, if that's what you mean."

"You know exactly what I mean, Mr. Haggerty. He wasn't arrested and he wasn't charged. The murderer was never found."

"Mmm," Haggerty said.

He tented his hands and looked over them.

He waited for what seemed an extraordinarily long time.

Still playing to an absentee jury.

"You know, of course," he said at last, "that Markham never came up with a reasonable alibi for where he was while his wife was being stabbed twenty times on a deserted back street in the French Quarter."

"The New Orleans police . . ."

"Yes, well, the New Orleans police. Markham claimed he was at the *movies*, Mr. Hope. Does that sound familiar to you?"

"He *was* at the movies."

"So he says. And so the police up there apparently accepted. Because they could find no evidence to support a homicide charge. No weapon, no bloody . . ."

"No *anything*. They were newlyweds, they'd only been married for four months, the whole damn experience was shattering to him."

"I'm sure it was. Especially since his wife was playing around with another man."

"Markham didn't know that," Matthew said, "and I don't want to argue an investigation which for good reason never resulted in an arrest. All I want to know . . ."

"Yes," Haggerty said.

Matthew looked at him.

"Yes, I *do* plan to introduce this material at the trial."

"Then why didn't you send me the New Orleans police reports?"

"A communications failure," Haggerty said, and shrugged. "I thought you were interested only in any *Calusa* documents relating to . . ."

"I'd like those reports now," Matthew said.

"Sure," Haggerty said. "I'll have them delivered by hand later this afternoon. Anything else?"

"You know, of course . . ."

"Sure. I'll be waiting for it. And then we'll let a judge decide, okay?"

**IN THE CIRCUIT COURT OF
THE TWELFTH JUDICIAL CIRCUIT
CALUSA COUNTY, STATE OF FLORIDA**

STATE OF FLORIDA,)
     Plaintiff)

          vs,)   CASE NO. 84–2207–CF–A–S9

CARLTON B. MARKHAM,)
     Defendant)

_____

MOTION IN LIMINE

COMES NOW the Defendant, by and through his undersigned attorney, and moves this Honorable Court in limine to instruct the State and all his counsel not to mention or make reference as to the following and for the following grounds:

1. That the Defendant at any time prior to the date of this incident was questioned by the New Orleans Police Department regarding the murder of his former wife, Jennifer Bowles Markham.

2. That the Defendant at any time prior to this incident in the above-styled charge told the New Orleans police that he was at a movie theater on the night of the murder of his former wife, Jennifer Bowles Markham.

3. That the Defendant's former wife, Jennifer Bowles Markham, at any time while married to the Defendant was seeing other men.

4. That the above information is inadmissible at trial, and therefore would be highly prejudicial to the defense if such information was known to the jury, either by the State, voir dire, opening argument or by witnesses listed by the State in the above-styled cause.

5. This motion should be granted because there is no other way this problem can be properly handled before the Court in the above-styled cause and in all probability such an attempt to do such evidence would result in a mistrial.

WHEREFORE, the above-named Defendant respectfully requests this Honorable Court to instruct the State and all his counsel not to mention, refer to, or interrogate concerning, or attempt to convey to the jury in any manner, either directly or indirectly any of the above-mentioned facts relative to the Defendant's background or former wife's background without first obtaining permission from the Court outside the presence of the jury and the hearing of the jury; and to further instruct the State and

all his counsel not to make any reference to the
fact that this motion has been filed and granted;
and further to instruct the State and all his counsel to warn and caution each and every one of his
witnesses to strictly follow these instructions.

MATTHEW HOPE, Attorney
Summerville and Hope
333 Heron Street
Calusa, Florida

BY: _Matthew Hope_

CERTIFICATE OF SERVICE

I HEREBY CERTIFY that a true and correct copy
of the foregoing has been furnished to the Office
of the State Attorney, 807 Magnolia Boulevard,
Calusa, Florida, this the 10th day of December,
1986.

Matthew Hope

Matthew Hope
Attorney for the Defendant

"Denied it, huh?" Frank said.

"Said he saw no reason why Haggerty shouldn't be allowed to
introduce this material."

"What's this about the former wife playing around?"

"The New Orleans cops had evidence that she'd been dating a
musician up there. They were trying to get Markham to admit he
knew about it. That was their attempt at establishing motive."

"*Did* he know about it?"

"Not according to him."

"Is Haggerty going to try showing the *new* wife was playing around, too?"

"I've got his list of witnesses. I don't see anything there to indicate . . ."

"How about this Mason woman who lives next door? You think *she* might testify along those lines?"

"I . . . well, that never occurred to me."

"Then why'd you ask that the material be excluded?"

"Because I didn't want a jury thinking what the New Orleans cops thought. That Markham killed a hot-pantsed wife who was cheating on him."

"Married only four months, huh?"

"Yeah."

"Messing around with a musician."

"A junkie trumpet player."

"I'd have killed her myself," Frank said.

"Which is just why I asked for exclusion."

"How about the guy living on the other side? Raddison, is that his name? You think *he's* got anything on Prue? He was pretty damn interested in everything going on next door. Maybe he spotted a boyfriend going in and out."

"I didn't ask him anything along those lines. I just found out about this New Orleans thing yesterday, Frank."

"Well, if the material's going to be admitted . . ."

"Yeah, I know, I'd better ask some more questions."

The two men were silent for a moment.

"That movie alibi," Frank said.

"I know."

"Always at the movies while his wives are getting stabbed."

"I know."

They were silent again.

"The thing is . . ." Matthew said, and then stopped and shook his head.

"Yeah, what?" Frank said.

"No, nothing."

"Say it."

"The killer up there . . ."

"Yeah?"

"They never found him, Frank."

Another silence, longer this time.

"I know what you're thinking," Frank said.

Matthew shook his head again.

"You're thinking maybe Markham makes a *habit* of stabbing his wives. That's what a jury's going to think, you know. The minute Haggerty brings up the New Orleans murder . . ."

"Well, why the hell do you think I filed the motion?" Matthew said heatedly. "I *know* what a jury's going to think. The son of a bitch got away with *one* murder but he won't get away with *another* one."

"Never mind the jury," Frank said. "What do *you* think?"

Matthew sighed heavily.

"I don't know," he said.

```
            IN THE CIRCUIT COURT OF
          THE TWELFTH JUDICIAL CIRCUIT
        IN AND FOR CALUSA COUNTY, FLORIDA

STATE OF FLORIDA,      )
        Plaintiff      )

                vs,    )   CASE NO. 84-2207-CF-A-S9

CARLTON B. MARKHAM,    )
          Defendant    )
```

DEMAND FOR NOTICE OF ALIBI

COMES NOW THE STATE OF FLORIDA, by and through the undersigned Assistant State Attorney, and pursuant to Florida Rules of Criminal Procedure 3.200, and demands that the Defendant provide notice of any intent to rely on the defense of alibi in the above—styled cause and further states the following:

1. The offense committed, date, time and place of said offense is:
   a. Offense Committed: Murder in the first degree.
   b. Date of Offense: November 20, 1986.
   c. Time of Offense: 2230—2300 hours.
   d. Place of Offense: 8489 Rancher Road, Calusa, FL.

2. The State demands that Defendant provide within said notice of alibi specific information as to the place at which the Defendant claims to have been at the time of the alleged offense and, as particularly as is known to the Defendant or his attorney, the names and addresses of the witnesses by whom he proposes to establish such alibi.

I HEREBY CERTIFY that a true copy of the foregoing Demand for Notice of Alibi has been furnished by <u>hand</u> to: <u>Matthew Hope, Esq.</u>, <u>Summerville and Hope, 333 Heron Street, Calusa</u>, <u>FL</u> on this <u>12th</u> day of <u>December</u>, 1986.

> SKYE BANNISTER
> STATE ATTORNEY
> By: *Arthur Haggerty*
> Assistant State Attorney
> 807 Magnolia Boulevard
> Calusa, Florida

So that's it, Warren thought.

Time to quit lollygagging around and get on the stick. Because this morning's demand for Notice of Alibi meant that he and Matthew had better come up with something damn soon or their man would be sent to the chair on evidence as circumstantial as that supporting Aunt Hattie's phantom lover who she claimed ran off to Kansas City with a high yeller girl named Suella Simms. Aunt Hattie believed that her long-ago lover actually existed, and as evidence of his substantiality had shown the entire family letters presumably written while he was a soldier in Italy during World War II. The letters were from someone named Abner Cross, who Warren later learned had been killed in action in the year 1945 and who couldn't possibly have run off to Kansas City or anyplace else in the year 1949. But try telling that to Aunt Hattie.

And try telling Skye Bannister, via Arthur Haggerty, that Carlton Barnaby Markham, on the night of November twentieth, coincidentally the night of his wife's brutal murder, had first been watching a movie in a theater called Twin Plaza I, in a shopping mall called South Dixie, had later wandered the mall for a bit, and had then dropped into a bar called Harrigan's where he'd watched television while sipping a single drink—*unless* you could come up with someone who could state unequivocally that he or she had actually *seen* Mr. Markham doing one or more of those things.

So that Friday night at eight-thirty P.M., thirteen days before Christmas, Warren pulled his car into the parking lot outside the mall, determined first to find a parking space—which would not be easy with all these Christmas shoppers out doing their thing—and next to find someone who could positively identify Markham's photograph. This was the kind of legwork Warren had detested when he was a detective in St. Louis, the kind he *still* detested, tedious, boring, repetitive and tough on the arches. He found a parking space at last alongside a pickup truck with a shot-gun on a rack across the rear window, locked his car, and went into the mall. He knew this would not be easy, and it wasn't.

He started with the young girl selling tickets at the double the-ater complex, Twin I and Twin II, asking her if she had been working on the night of November twentieth. The girl was chew-ing bubble gum. The rush of people buying tickets for the two movies that had started at eight o'clock was over and she'd been enjoying just sitting there and popping her gum until Warren walked up.

He already knew that on weekdays the movies in these par-ticular theaters ran on a twelve-fifteen, three o'clock, five-thirty, eight o'clock, and ten-thirty schedule. Markham had told Mat-thew he'd caught the eight o'clock show on the night of his wife's murder, a Thursday, so at least the schedule checked out. Got out of the theater at around ten-thirty, he'd said, which also checked out. Wandered the mall a bit, then stopped for a single drink at a bar called Harrigan's, near the mall, got home at about midnight, which was a reasonable time to have made the drive to Pompano Way. But this *didn't* check out with Oscar Raddison having seen him in the backyard burying clothes and a bloody knife at eleven-fifteen. The only way Markham could have been at his house at that time was if he'd been killing his wife at ten-thirty or thereabouts, rather than doing all those other things he said he'd done.

"Who wants to know?" the girl said.

Warren flashed the St. Louis potsie.

"Routine investigation," he said.

"I work every night but Monday and Tuesday," she said. "Was this a Monday or Tuesday?"

"A Thursday," he said.

"Then I was here."

"Recognize this man?" Warren asked, and fished the eight-by-ten blowup out of its manila envelope.

Without even looking at the picture, the girl said, "You gotta be kidding."

"Take a look at it, okay?" he said.

"When did you say?"

"Thursday night, November twentieth."

"How long ago was that?"

"Three weeks ago last night," Warren said.

"And you expect me to remember somebody from *then*?"

She popped her gum.

Warren winced.

"Just take a look, okay?" he said.

The girl looked at the picture of Markham and his wife on a beach, the ocean behind them, the sky wide and blue above them.

"Both of them?" she said.

"No, just the man." And then, at once, "Why? Do you recognize the woman?"

"I don't recognize either one of them," she said. "What'd he do?"

"Nothing. Take another look."

"How many times do I have to look?"

"You didn't sell this man a ticket on Thursday night, November twentieth?"

"You know how many tickets I sell here every night?" she said. "We've got two theaters here, you know how many tickets I sell?"

"How many?" he asked.

"Millions!" she said. "All these people, they're not even *faces* to me, they're voices saying which movie they want to see, and how many tickets, and then they're hands shoving bills across the counter here, that's what all these people are."

"So you don't recognize him, huh?" Warren said.

"How many times do I have to say it?" the girl said.

"Okay to go inside and talk to the people selling popcorn?"

"You want to go inside, you got to buy a ticket," the girl said, "badge or not."

Warren bought a ticket. Never ask, never explain, he thought. Should've walked right in. He was getting old.

Older by the minute, as it turned out.

He knew he would strike out with the concessionaires, and he did.

He knew he would strike out all through the mall as well.

Markham claimed that he'd got to Harrigan's at ten to eleven. It was a five-minute drive from the mall, which meant he'd been wandering around here for fifteen minutes after the movie let out. The chances that anyone had seen him—or would *remember* having seen him even if they *had* seen him—were exceedingly slim. But Warren went through the tiresome routine, anyway, consoling himself with the knowledge that he was killing time until he could cruise Harrigan's; he wanted to get there at the same time Markham claimed to have been there.

And so he checked out the entire mall, moving from store to store and fast-food joint to fast-food joint, rubbing elbows with Christmas shoppers in Bermuda shorts, T-shirts, tube tops, jeans, polyester slacks, floral-patterned short-sleeved shirts, halters, sweat suits, jogging shorts, the *haute couture* of Florida in December, flashing the picture of Markham and his wife, posing questions to people who often became indignant because he was asking them to remember all the way back to November twentieth, when here it was almost Christmas, the busiest time of the year, did he *mind*?

At a quarter to eleven, operating on the theory that regulars of any given bar generally spent the same hours there on any given night, he headed for Harrigan's.

At eleven thirty-two, he got lucky.
Depending upon how you looked at it.

Harrigan's tried to look like a genuine Irish bar on Third Avenue in New York. It succeeded in looking like a fake Irish bar in Calusa. Never mind the brass rails, and the black leather booths, and the polished mahogany, and the cut-glass mirrors, and the waiters wearing green derbies on their heads and green garters on their shirtsleeves. This was ersatz stuff, as phony as the Santa Claus who'd been shaking a bell inside the South Dixie Mall.

Markham had told Matthew he'd sat at the bar watching television and drinking just one martini before heading home at twenty to twelve, a quarter to twelve, so Warren showed his picture to all three barmaids, each of them wearing the same green derby and green-gartered shirtsleeves the waiters wore, but wearing instead of black trousers very short red skirts and red high-heeled shoes, presumably because this was the holiday season. None of the barmaids had noticed Markham in there on the night of November twentieth or on any other night, for that matter. One of them commented that Markham looked kind of cute, but she admitted she was partial to blond men. Undaunted, Warren began canvassing the patrons sitting at the bar. He got lucky, sort of, when a woman looked at the picture and said, "Oh, sure."

Warren's eyes opened wide.

"You recognize him?" he asked, astonished.

"I recognize him is right," the woman said. "Sat right next to me. Ordered a martini with two olives."

Carlton Barnaby Markham had told Matthew he'd ordered a Tanqueray martini, very dry, straight up, with two olives.

Warren closed in on her.

It was very easy to close in on her in that she weighed perhaps two hundred pounds and somewhat overspilled the stool she was sitting on. She was wearing blue slacks and a blue T-shirt with the words FAT IS BEAUTIFUL lettered on the front and back of it. Her sandaled feet were crossed on the rung of the stool. Her hair was the color of straw, falling loose over one ear, pulled back and clipped behind the other ear with a pale blue barrette. A long rhinestone earring dangled from that ear. Warren guessed she was in her mid-forties. It was sometimes difficult to tell with fat people.

"This would've been around the twentieth of November," he said. "A Thursday night."

"The twentieth is right," the woman said. "A Thursday night."

"Around ten to eleven."

"Walked in right about that time is right," the woman said, and nodded, and picked up her drink, and drank heartily from it, and then put it down and belched.

"Did he talk to you?" Warren asked.

"Nope. Just drank his martini, et the two olives, sat here watching television, paid his bill, and walked out."

"Around what time?"

"What time what?"

"Did he walk out?"

"Don't have a watch," the woman said, and showed him her naked wrist.

"Then how do you know what time he walked *in*?"

"*Had* a watch *then*," she said. "Had to hock it to do my Christmas shopping." She reached down for a shopping bag sitting beside the stool, hoisted it as evidence.

"You're sure this was the man?" Warren asked, and showed her the picture again.

"Positive," she said. "But he wasn't with that woman. He was alone as ice cream."

"Ice cream?"

"Alone as ice cream is right," she said.

Uh-oh, Warren thought, and at that same moment, one of the green-derbied, green-gartered, red-skirted barmaids caught his eye and twirled her forefinger against her temple, signaling in universal sign language that the woman was nuts.

"He didn't have any stains on his clothing, did he?" Warren asked.

"Stains?"

"Yes."

"What kind of stains?"

"You tell me."

"No stains is right," she said. "Walked in nice and clean and neat and ordered a Tanqueray martini, very dry, with two olives." She swiveled on the stool, raised her hand to the barmaid who'd signaled she was crazy, and said, "Let me have another one of these, please."

"That's your third one, Hannah," the barmaid said.

"What's wrong with four?" Hannah asked.

The barmaid shrugged and brought her another drink.

"Would *you* remember that?" Warren asked her.

"Remember what?" the barmaid said.

"This man ordering a Tanqueray martini, very dry, with two olives?" Warren said, and showed her the picture again.

"No, I don't remember," she said.

"Ask your friends," Warren said.

"What is this?" the barmaid said. "Are you a cop?"

"Yes," Warren said.

"What'd he do?"

They always wanted to know what a person had done. Even if you were showing a picture of a *victim*, they always asked what the person had done.

"Nothing," Warren said.

"Sure," the barmaid said skeptically. "You come in here asking about a guy supposed to have been here in November, he didn't do nothing."

"He's a friendly witness," Warren said.

"You two remember this guy ordering a Tanqueray martini, very dry, two olives?" she asked, carrying the picture to where the two other barmaids were standing near the cash register, their green-gartered arms folded across their white shirts.

"Straight up or on the rocks?" one of them asked, sarcastically, it seemed to Warren.

"Straight up," Hannah said. And then added, "Yours," and burst out laughing.

The other two barmaids were looking at the picture again.

"You remember that, do you?" Warren asked Hannah. "That he ordered the martini straight up?"

"Yep."

"A Tanqueray martini, very dry, straight up, with two olives."

"Is right," Hannah said, and nodded.

"Madam," he said, "I wonder if you . . ."

"Miss," Hannah corrected.

"Miss, excuse me," Warren said. "I wonder if I might have your full name and your address."

The barmaid was back with the picture. "Why?" she asked. "You gonna ask her out?"

"Either of them remember that martini?" Warren asked her.

"Nope." She handed back the picture. "He wants to take you out, Hannah," she said.

"Fat chance," Hannah said, and then laughed at her own unintentional pun.

"Could I have your name and address, please?" Warren said.

"Fat Hannah," the barmaid said.

"Fat Hannah is right," Hannah said.

"Fat Hannah what?" Warren said.

"Merritt," Hannah said.

Warren was already writing. "And your address?"

"Three-seventy-two Waverly."

"Here in Calusa?"

"Here in Calusa is right," Hannah said. "You want my phone number, too?"

"Please."

She gave Warren the phone number, and then winked at the barmaid. She finished what was left in her glass, belched again, struggled off the stool, said, "I better hurry on home, case my phone starts ringing." She put her hand on Warren's shoulder, gave it a friendly little squeeze, winked at the barmaid again, and walked out of the bar.

"She spent six years at Ice Cream," the barmaid told him. "Up in Tallahassee."

"Ice Cream" may have been a euphemism for "I Scream," which in itself might have been hyperbole. Both nicknames had evolved from the true and proper name with which they slant-rhymed: Iscrin. The Iscrin Institute in Tallahassee was a private mental hospital named after its founder, Dr. Theodore Iscrin. It was sometimes called "The Icepick Institute," in that an alarming number of frontal lobotomies had been performed there in the dim recent past.

A check with the facility revealed that Hannah Isabel Merritt's uncle and sole guardian had committed her to the institution in 1971. She was released in 1977, after a panel of Iscrin psychiatrists suggested to the uncle that her illness could better be controlled by drugs administered in the bosom of the family home. The uncle's name was Roger Merritt, and they found a telephone number for him in Tallahassee. He was ill himself now, scarcely audible on the telephone, but not without a wry sense of humor. He told Matthew (and Warren on the extension) that his niece's release may have been "a matter of expedient economy" on Iscrin's part since he'd fallen behind on the payment of her bills after the automobile accident that had put him in a wheelchair, debilitated his strength, and was now threatening his very life. The last time he'd seen Hannah, "poor soul," was in 1983, when she'd gone down to Calusa to take a job working in a nursery. He hoped she was okay.

"So we've got a witness who spent time in a nut house," Warren said to Matthew the moment they were off the phone. "But she damn well didn't come up with that Tanqueray martini out of a clear blue sky. What do you want to do?"

"Ask her to come in for a deposition," Matthew said. "She's all we've got."

You had to know orchids before you could love them.

Biggest of all the plant families, widest spread geographically. Ranged in height from less than an inch to eighteen feet tall. Some of them had blooms so tiny you almost couldn't see them, others had blooms ten inches across. Came in all colors except black, the good Lord knew what he was doing.

Lots of orchids blooming this time of year.

Christmas was only—well, this was already the twelfth, be Christmas in just a little while.

Lots of orchids blooming.

Most beautiful spot in the whole world was this greenhouse right here.

Beauty everywhere around him.

You walked through the greenhouse here, past the Moth Orchids, what were properly called *Phalaenopsis*, you could be anyplace they grew naturally, Formosa or India, New Guinea or the Philippines—where that *other* bitch had a million pairs of shoes. In all those shoes, had there been any boots? Red boots?

Your Moth Orchid came in reds as bright as her boots, came in oranges, too, yellows, greens, pinks. White ones with lips as red as her boots, as red as her lips. White ones with yellow lips. Spotted, striped or plain, to his mind she was the most beautiful of all the orchids.

Your Moth Orchid was very long-lasting.

He wondered how long *she* would last when he put her out.

Put her out on Christmas Day.

All these orchids should still be blooming then.

Your *Cattleya tenebrosa*. Coppery brown petal with a dusky purple lip.

Your *Cattleya* hybrids with their large white flowers and yellow lips.

Lips.

Opening wide.

Your *Cattleytonia* Rosy Jewel hanging up there in a fern basket high up in the greenhouse, nothing prettier except your Moth. Three-inch fuchsia-colored flowers in clusters of eight, nine blossoms.

The *Paphiopedilum* growing over there near the Kool-Cel unit, where the recycled water was chilly and humid. Her nickname was Lady Slipper, clear green leaves on some of them, mottled on others, big waxy flowers that looked artificial. Lady Slipper.

Your Slipper Orchid, the *Phragmepedium*, was the only one didn't remind him of a woman. Looked like an old Chinese man with a long mustache. Tall spike. Pouch instead of a lip, two long ribbonlike petals on either side of the pouch. Needed the Kool-Cel unit, too. You had to treat delicate things proper or they'd die. Beautiful things. You had to know how to take care of beauty. You couldn't abuse beauty.

He knew how much her beauty meant to her.

Long red hair—well not no more, full pouting mouth, lips as scarlet as blood, eyes as dark green and brooding as the leaves on the *Phalaenopsis schilleriana*, skin as white as the flowers of the *Amabilis*, a beautiful towering woman with pink-tipped breasts and flaring hips and long legs with white thighs and shapely calves and slender ankles, a luminous woman all red and white and pink and green, green eyes, red hair above, red hair below, red lips, pink lips, soft white skin, soft red boots, puss in boots, he didn't think she would much enjoy being ugly.

You sometimes got dazzled by your own beauty, you forgot it was God-given. He would explain that to her. It was like with orchids. You sometimes tended to overlook some of them that were ugly in appearance, you passed them by till you got to know them better, and then they took on their own characteristics and their own personalities and for all their ugliness they became interesting and beautiful in their own right.

Maybe she wouldn't mind being ugly.

7

Calusa was growing and changing, but some things remained ever and always the same.

The average annual temperature, for example, was seventy-three degrees Fahrenheit. That was something like twenty-three degrees Celsius, which only *sounded* much lower.

The average annual rainfall was fifty inches.

There were almost thirty-five miles of white sand beaches in Calusa.

Those were the constants.

Everything else was growing and changing so rapidly that a great many citizens were thinking back to ten years ago as the Good Old Days, kidding themselves into believing Calusa had been just a small fishing village when they'd moved down. Where they'd moved down from, for the most part, was Illinois, Indiana, and Ohio. Now and then you got a former New Yorker like Frank Summerville, but he was a rarity. Calusa, Florida was the American Midwest transported to the Gulf of Mexico.

More and more people kept moving down to Calusa every year.

At the time of the national census six years ago, the city's population was 48,800. Today, it stood at a bit more than 53,000. The county's population back then was 202,000. Today, it was 222,000.

Growth.

Change.

Progress.

Crime was on the increase.

This year, as Warren had reported to Matthew, it had shot up seventeen percent over the year before.

"Drug related," the cops said.

Five years ago, you could maybe buy a dime bag of heroin if you had the right connections.

Today, you could buy crack right on the Whisper Key beach.

Ten years ago, the yellow pages of the Calusa telephone directory had listed no "Escort" services. This year, there were seven of them, one of which offered Senior Discounts.

"Loose women drifting over from Miami," the citizens said.

Five years ago, there was only one topless nightclub in Calusa. It was called Club Alyce. Last year, there were two, the second one calling itself Up Front. A third topless joint had opened this year. It called itself The Naked Truth.

"We will close them all down," said Skye Bannister, the State Attorney.

On Saturday night, December 13, in the growing, changing, progressive city of Calusa, Florida . . .

George Ticknor and Mosley Jones went to The Naked Truth . . .

Matthew and Susan Hope went to the Snowflake Ball . . .

And Henry Gardella broke into the Markham house.

She wouldn't tell any of them her real name.

The name she was using for the picture was Constance Redding. Constance sounded puritanical, like Charity or Felicity, she said, which was amusing for an actress playing a woman who would screw even a squirrel. The last name referred to her flaming red hair. Constance Redding. God only knew what her real name was.

On the set, they called her Connie at first.

And then, later on, Connie Lingus.

She'd toss her red hair and smile.

Then she'd go down on Jake again.

Jake was the black guy playing the miller's son, Tom, who inherited only a cat when his father died. Connie was playing the cat. Puss in Boots. A modern-dress version, but the old fairy tale nonetheless. Jake was his real first name but his last name had been chosen by Prudence Ann Markham, *La Directrice*, as they sometimes called her, when they weren't calling her Otto, after Otto Preminger. She'd plucked the name from the pages of Hemingway's *The Sun Also Rises*. The name was supposed to be an inside joke, since Jake in the book was impotent, and Jake in their movie was insatiable. When you read the credits, you were supposed to get a chuckle out of seeing the name Jake Barnes.

After the first week of shooting, they all came up with comical names to use on the credit cards. The cinematographer wanted to call himself Seymour Hare. The gaffer wanted to call himself Wun Hung Low. The sound man decided he liked I. Kutcha Kokoff. *La Directrice* vetoed all these suggestions. She was going for class and style here, she told them. She herself had decided to use the name Martin N. Prudeaux for her director's credit, on the theory that men didn't want to see a porn flick directed by a woman, and also Prudeaux sounded French, which intimated great sexual knowledge and which also referred back to the source of the fairy tale, the writer Charles Perrault. Not all fairy tales were written by Grimm.

Tick and Mose wished now that they'd gotten Connie's real

name, and also Jake's full name. They figured Prudence Ann Markham, a.k.a. Martin N. Prudeaux, was the only one who knew those names because she was the one who wrote out the weekly pay checks from the Prudent Company's account—but it so happened she was dead. They were pretty sure that Jake was Jake's real first name, but what was the rest of it? And Constance Redding was anybody's guess, flaming Connie Lingus who could engorge organs as large as the one at Radio City Music Hall.

They figured maybe she was a hooker in real life.

Otherwise, where'd she learn how to do all that stuff? Just watching her in action was like spending a month in a Chinese whorehouse. Had to've been a hooker.

So they decided that the best way to get a line on redheaded hookers in the fair city of Calusa was to cruise the topless joints here.

Such was their reasoning.

Which led them to The Naked Truth at ten-thirty P.M. that Saturday night.

At ten-thirty P.M. that Saturday night, Matthew and Susan were dancing to the strains of an orchestra called Oliver Lane and the Goldens. The Goldens were fourteen musicians who specialized in playing tunes of the Forties, sometimes known as Golden Oldies. Matthew and Susan were dancing to the Artie Shaw arrangement of "Stardust," though Oliver Lane's orchestra did not have a violin section.

The people who put together the Snowflake Ball each and every December seemed not to realize that Calusa had during the past ten years attracted a great many young people to whom "Golden Oldies" meant tunes of the Fifties or even the Sixties. When Oliver Lane and the Goldens played "It Seems to Me I've Heard That Song Before," none of these youngsters had ever heard that song before.

Blithely unaware, the gray-haired elders who put the annual event together for the American Cancer Society assumed everyone would be thrilled to dance to "Tuxedo Junction" or "I Cried For You" or "Song of India" or even "Elk's Parade," which, to tell the truth, no one there but Oliver Lane and the Goldens knew had been a Bobby Sherwood hit way back then when you and I were young, Maggie. Oliver Lane and his splendid aggravation had played all of these songs and more tonight. They were now playing "Stardust," and Matthew was holding Susan close and Susan was remarking on how beautiful and handsome everyone looked.

Everyone did indeed look beautiful and handsome.

The main ballroom of the Calusa Hyatt ("overlooking the sparkling Gulf of Mexico," the hotel's advertisements in *The New Yorker* read) had been rented for the occasion, and the Volunteer Women of the Calusa Garden Society had decorated the hall awesomely. A Christmas tree the size of the one that grew to spectacular heights in *The Nutcracker* rose in dazzlingly ornamented splendor against the far wall of the mirrored ballroom, reflecting itself in myriad twinkling images aided and abetted by the several mirrored globes that rotated overhead and sprinkled sparkling reds and yellows and greens and whites across the dance floor and out through the floor-to-ceiling windows that overlooked the sparkling Gulf of Mexico. Actually, the Gulf was rather black and ominous tonight, except for a lone, fearless sailor pushing his forty-one footer under power toward the bridge leading from the mainland to Lucy's Circle. Dark, roiling clouds moved restlessly in the sky overhead, a certain promise of rain, somewhat unusual for December.

But inside the ballroom, all was glitter and gloss.

Smaller floral replicas of the magnificent Christmas tree sat in the middle of each of the tables with their red tablecloths and green napkins, these—the trees, not the linen—to be auctioned off later for the benefit of the American Cancer Society. All the men were in tuxedos, many of them rented, and all the women were in gowns purchased expressly for the gala. The younger women seemed to favor a couture that relied heavily on slits far up the leg and swooping necklines supported only by naked breasts. The elderly ladies—those pouter pigeons who had voted for the Oliver Lane orchestra—were wearing this year an astonishingly varied assortment of sequined and beaded gowns. Frank's wife, Leona—whose firm, youthful bosom rivaled that of any of the young women who'd grown up rocking to the songs of Janis Joplin or Jimi Hendrix—was wearing a silver lamé concoction that seemed still steamingly molten and that caused her to appear more naked than if she'd been in the privacy of her own shower. She was dancing with the very same judge who'd denied Matthew's motion in limine this past Thursday, dancing very close to the old bastard, in fact. Moreover, the old bastard had his hand on her silvery ass.

"Don't touch," the girl sitting in the booth with Tick and Mose said. "Read the sign. You can look, but you can't touch."

She said this because Mose had his hand on her thigh.

"Otherwise we'll get busted," she said.

She was in her mid-twenties, Tick guessed, a not very good-looking blonde wearing a costume that wouldn't have been welcomed at the Snowflake Ball across town because her costume was her underwear.

Tick wondered where the notion had started that a woman in her underwear was sexier than a woman in just her skin. France, he guessed. *La Directrice* had dressed Connie in a startling array of underwear, coming up with variations Tick had never even seen in the pages of *Penthouse*. Connie had looked very sexy in all that underwear, but Connie would have looked sexy in a potato sack. Connie was what was known in the trade as a natural.

The blonde was wearing a black garter belt, black bikini panties, black net nylons and black high-heeled shoes. No bra. Except for her naked breasts, she did not look very natural in her underwear, nor did she look particularly sexy. She looked too heavily made up and too sleazily underdressed, and she stank of cheap perfume, and she seemed much older than her twenty some-odd years, and far more hard-edged, and far more worn. She looked like a hooker.

Which Tick guessed she was.

"How long have you been doing this sort of thing?" Tick asked.

"What are you, a social worker?" the girl asked. "Hey, listen, I mean it," she said to Mose, whose hand was on her thigh again. She plucked the hand off as if it were a piece of lint. "The State Attorney has people coming in and out of here all the time, Skye Bannister, you familiar with that name?"

"No," Tick said.

"The State Attorney," she said. "He'll close us down in a minute if he thinks anything funny's going on in here, which of course it isn't."

"Of course not," Tick said. "What's your name?"

"Kim," she said.

Tick guessed there were eight million girls named Kim in the topless joints across the length and breadth of America.

"Kim, we're looking for a particular person," Mose said.

Straight to the point. Good old fucking dumb Mose.

"What's the matter with me?" Kim said. "*I* happen to think *I'm* pretty particular."

"No, I meant . . ."

"What he meant," Tick said, "is we think a friend of ours may be working in Calusa, and we'd like very much to find her."

"What are you, cops?" Kim said.

"Do I look like a cop?" Tick said.

She looked at him. "No," she said, "but who can tell nowadays? Nowadays you get cops they look more like crooks than crooks do."

"We're not cops," Mose said.

She looked at Mose.

"Then what are you?"

"Friends of this girl we're trying to find," Mose said.

"What girl?"

"A redhead," Tick said.

"What's her name? We got four redheads here, two of them on tonight. One of them's up there dancing right this minute."

They looked toward the small stage around which a dozen or more tables were arranged. A short stout redhead was up there, flailing the air with her pendulous breasts.

"That's not her," Tick said. "The redhead we're looking for is extremely beautiful."

"*I* happen to think *Cindy* is extremely beautiful," Kim said.

Eight million Cindys, too, Tick thought.

"Who's knocking Cindy?" he said, looking toward the stage again, where the girl was now bending over to throw an enormous moon at a baldheaded guy watching her in open-mouthed fascination. "But this particular person we're looking for is really extraordinarily beautiful, you'd agree in a minute if you ever saw her."

"*I* happen to think *I'm* extraordinarily beautiful," Kim said, and tossed her frizzied bleached hair.

"You are, no question about it," Mose said, and put his hand on her thigh again.

"Listen, you understand English?" Kim said, and this time shoved his hand away angrily. "So what is it?" she said to Tick, figuring he was the negotiator here. "You interested in me, or you interested in giving me all this bullshit about this gorgeous redhead you're looking for?"

"We're interested in both," Tick said.

"Never mind both," Kim said, "let's talk about *me*. There's a pickup out back, and the front seat is covered with blowjobs. *If* you're interested."

"What do you get?" Tick asked.

"Twenty-five," she said.

"Here's the twenty-five," he said, reaching for his wallet, opening it, and putting two tens and a five on the table. "Just for sitting here talking to us."

"Thanks," she said, and picked up the bills and tucked them into the waistband of her garter belt. "But that doesn't mean your friend here can get handy. I'm serious about people coming in here all the time looking for something going on. If you're paying for talk, we talk. Period."

"I understand," Tick said.

"But does your *friend* understand?"

Mose was thinking he'd like to go out in the pickup *first*, and then come back in here to talk. He was thinking Tick was throwing twenty-five bucks down the toilet.

"Sure, I understand," he said. "Here's my hands. Right here on the table, okay?" He folded them on the tabletop. "Okay?"

"Just keep them there, okay?" she said.

"Maybe *later* we can go out to the pickup," Mose said.

"Sure, for another twenty-five," Kim said. "Right now, you bought talk." She turned to Tick. "So talk," she said.

"Long red hair," Tick said. "Green eyes. Five-ten, legs that won't quit, tits like melons. Have you seen her around?"

"She sounds like a movie star," Kim said.

Mose was about to say something, but Tick shot him a look.

"What's her name?" Kim asked.

"She was going by Connie," Tick said.

"Yeah, but what's her square handle? Is she a working girl?"

"Maybe."

"Well, don't you *know*?"

"Not for sure."

"Why do you want her?"

"Do you know her? Does she sound familiar?"

"Not really. Why do you want her?"

"Have you been working these clubs long?"

"Two years now. I did a year at Alyce, another six months at Up Front. This is the best of the lot, you ask me. Why do you want her?"

"Ever see her in any of them?"

"From the way you describe her, she doesn't sound like somebody'd be working the topless joints. You're describing a racehorse, somebody'd be working the beach in Miami, have you tried Miami?"

"We're pretty sure she's in Calusa," Tick said.

"Have you called any of the services? That's the kind of girl you're talking about, a hundred a shot. If she really looks like you say she looks. Anyway, why do you want her?"

Tick looked at Mose.

"We're not creeps," he told Kim.

"Nobody said you were. But you're looking for this gorgeous redhead, I got to wonder why? She do something to you? You want to hurt her?"

"No."

"'Cause if that's the story, it's been nice knowing you."

"Okay, I'll be perfectly honest with you," Tick said. "We owe her money."

"For what?"

"She did some work for us."

"What kind of work?"

"She entertained some businessmen for us. Up in Tampa."

"What kind of businessmen?"

"We're in the construction business," Tick said. "We had this

132

land we were interested in, and these two guys owned it, and we wanted to make a deal with them. So Connie helped us."

"Helped you how? I thought you said you weren't sure she's a hooker."

"She entertained them. Went out to dinner with them. Whatever else happened is between her and her priest."

"So how come you owe her money?"

"She checked out the next morning. We've been trying to find her since."

"This is a fairy tale, right?" Kim said. "She checks out without collecting? And you come looking to pay her? Come on, mister."

"I'm telling you the truth."

"Sure. How much money is involved here?"

"Five bills."

"Gets better and better all the time. You know any other businessmen in Tampa? For five bills, I'll go up there and entertain them out of their minds. Boys," she said, standing up and moving out of the booth, "you're full of shit. I don't know any gorgeous redheads going by Connie, and if I did I wouldn't tell you where to find her because you sound like you want to hurt her."

"How about a big black stud named Jake?" Mose asked.

Kim looked at him.

"Hung like an Arabian stallion," Tick said.

Kim turned to him.

"Jake who?" she said.

There was knowledge in her eyes. Tick saw it there.

"Sit down," he said.

She moved into the booth again.

"Jake," Tick said.

"You know this five hundred you were gonna give the redhead?" Kim said. A calculating look on her face now. She was smelling real bread, more than she could earn in a month out in the pickup truck. "You want Jake, I'll take that five up front."

"Make it three," Tick said.

"No, make it five," Kim said.

"What if he isn't the Jake we're looking for?"

"I'll tell you what," Kim said, a thin smile on her face. "Is he six feet tall with shoulders like a wagon yoke and buns like bowling balls? Does he look like Stallone in black face? Has he got a weapon could choke a girl? If that's the Jake you want, then hand over the bills, baby, and we'll talk."

"Four," Tick said.

"Five," Kim said. "And make it fast, 'cause I think I see a live one across the room."

Tick hesitated.

Kim swung her legs out of the booth. "So long, boys," she said.

"What's your hurry?" Tick said, and reached for his wallet again.

Skye Bannister.

Hair the color of wheat, eyes the color of his name. Six-feet-four or -five inches tall, reedy and pale, wearing a tuxedo with black patent leather slippers, a ruffled shirt with enameled Shlumberger studs and cuff links, and a red cummerbund and tie.

Skye Bannister, the State Attorney himself, in person, here at the Snowflake Ball with whiskey on his breath and two or three sheets to the wind.

"Arthur tells me he sent you a demand for alibi," he said to Matthew.

"Got it yesterday morning," Matthew said.

Oliver Lane and the Goldens were playing Harry James's "Sleepy Lagoon." Susan was dancing with Frank. She was wearing a red gown. A green feather was in her dark hair. Matthew watched the feather bobbing out there on the dance floor.

"I hope you come up with something, Matthew, I really do," Bannister said.

Matthew knew he hoped nothing of the sort.

"Because I like you and admire you, I really do," Bannister said.

He poured more wine from the bottle on Matthew's table, lifted the glass to his lips, sipped at it, put it down on the table again.

"A job like mine is a difficult one," Bannister said, and Matthew thought, Oh my God, he's going to make a campaign speech. "It often pits me against men I've worked with in the past, men I like and admire. Like you, Matthew. I like and admire you, Matthew. I can remember the time you and Morrie Bloom worked a number on that black man from Miami, I forget his name now . . ."

"Lloyd Davis," Matthew said.

"Very clever what you did, both of you, getting that confession out of him without making it seem like entrapment. Very clever. Interesting case, that one."

What Bloom still referred to as the "Beauty and the Beast" case, but what Matthew would always think of as the George Harper tragedy. A long time ago. Water under the bridge. Bannister had been an ally then. Now he was an adversary.

"I asked you then—do you remember, Matthew?—I asked you if you were thinking of entering the practice of criminal law, do you remember? And you said, correct me if I'm wrong, you said, 'Not particularly.'"

"I remember."

"And I said, correct me if I'm wrong, I said, 'Don't, I've got enough troubles getting convictions as it is,' or words to that effect, if I recall correctly."

"You do."

"So now you *are* practicing criminal law," Bannister said, and sipped at the wine again. "And you are representing a man charged with a heinous crime, Matthew, a heinous crime, and it is my duty to send that man to the electric chair. As *much* as I like and admire you, Matthew." He shook his head morosely. "That's what's so difficult about my job."

"Don't worry," Matthew said. "You won't have to send him to the chair."

Bannister lookd at him boozily, fuzzily and querulously.

"I plan to see that you don't," Matthew said.

"Ah, Matthew," Bannister said, "good, true Matthew," and recklessly threw his arm around the back of Matthew's chair and onto Matthew's shoulders. "I hope so, I sincerely hope so. Nothing would give me greater satisfaction than to have you prove we've made a grievous error here, Matthew, a grievous error. Your first important case, I know how dedicated you must be to proving your client innocent of the crime as charged, a heinous crime." He picked up his glass again, sloshing a bit of wine onto the black silk lapel of his jacket. "But why are we talking such mordred talk, Matthew, morbid? Have some wine, let's toast the holiday season and peace on earth to men of good will. Okay, Matthew? Some wine, Matthew?" He picked up the bottle with his free hand. "No hard feelings, Matthew?"

"No hard feelings," Matthew said.

Holding his glass in one hand and the bottle in the other, Bannister sloshed wine onto the table from both glass and bottle, and finally found Matthew's glass. "There we go," he said. He put the bottle back on the table. He lifted his glass. "Here's to justice," he said.

Bullshit, Matthew thought.

"Here's to justice," he said, and drank.

• • •

For somebody who was supposed to be such a smart businessman, Henry Gardella had made a lot of mistakes.

"I don't want to be bothered with bills," he'd told her.

That was his first mistake, and his biggest one.

"We've worked out a budget," he'd said. "A hundred and seventy-five grand, including your bonus on delivery. If you bring in the movie for less than that, terrific, buy yourself a new car. I don't want to see bills, I don't want to know what you're paying your actors, or how much it's costing you at whatever lab you use, that's *your* business. *My* business is I want the film made for no more than what I'm paying for it, and I want it delivered on time. You said Christmas, I want it by Christmas. You go over budget, you fail to deliver for one reason or another, then you don't get the twenty-five grand bonus, and I get everything you shot to turn over to somebody else to finish. That's it."

His second mistake was writing a check to the Prudent Company each and every week while she was working. He had figured this was the smartest way and the safest way to do it. He didn't want any of the Miami boys to trace back lab bills or studio bills or *any* kind of bills to Henry Gardella, who if they knew he was financing a porn flick would maybe come around to break his eyeglasses. The Prudent Company could have been anything, it didn't have to be a movie company. In fact, it sounded like an insurance company.

Also, there were laws about making pornography, and he didn't want some bright boy working in a lab someplace in Atlanta or New York looking at all those dirty though stylish moving pictures and saying to himself, Gee, these checks are coming from the Candleside Dinner Theater in Miami, Florida, and they are being signed by a Mr. Henry Gardella, so maybe I ought to drop in on him and hit him up for some change unless he wants everybody in the world to know he's violating Chapter 847 of the Florida Statutes, which is a crime punishable by up to a year in jail and a possible thousand dollar fine. Better the guy should go to Prudence Ann Markham of the Prudent Company and hit on her. Henry wanted his hands to be clean.

So each and every Friday, a check for twenty thousand and some change went out to the Prudent Company at a post office box in Calusa. If she was as honest as he thought she was—for Christ's sake, she looked like a minister's wife!—then she was shooting the film and paying her crew and her actors and her food charges and her immediate lab bills and whatever else from the checks he sent her. Which at the end of five weeks and three days came to a hundred and five thousand bucks. Before she got herself killed, he still expected to pay for all the heavy lab work when she finished her editing and turned in her cut—the mix, the blowup, the answer print, the color composite, all that technical shit. That would have come to another forty-five K, which thank God he hadn't yet given her, but which would have brought the total to a hundred and fifty thousand, which was just what he'd figured in the beginning. Plus the twenty-five bonus on delivery.

The canceled checks had come back to him in Miami:

FOR DEPOSIT ONLY
THE PRUDENT COMPANY

Prudence A. Markham

President

Plus the bank's stamp someplace on the back of each check:

CALUSA FIRST NATIONAL BANK
CALUSA, FLORIDA
PAY ANY BANK

So the checks had been deposited.

And—assuming she'd been honest, which he had to assume—then *his* weekly checks had covered the checks she wrote from the Prudent Company account to the various people she'd been working with. He did not know who these people were, but one or more of them might know what Prudence Ann Markham had done with the goddamn *film*. Was the negative still at a lab someplace? Which lab? Was she storing her workprint in a safety deposit box at Calusa First? Or some other bank? Or at the bottom of a well? Where the hell *was* it?

He didn't think it was in her house.

The police would have found it there, there would have been some mention in the newspapers or on television about a pornographic movie found in the home of the murdered lady film director. No, the film wasn't in her house, and that wasn't why he decided to break into it.

He decided to break into the house because her canceled checks, or her checkbooks, or her bank statements, or any or all of these might be someplace inside there.

He did not think the police would have confiscated anything that had to do with her financial matters. Why would they need such stuff? They already had her dumb husband.

But if the canceled checks, *or* her checkbooks, *or* her bank statements were inside that house . . .

And if he could find them . . .

Why then, baby, he would have *names*.

So at eleven-forty-five that Saturday night, while the floral centerpieces were being auctioned at the Snowflake Ball, he drove out to 1143 Pompano Way.

Velma Mason was watching television when she heard the sound outside.

She was watching an old movie that had come on at midnight.

Velma enjoyed mysteries of all sorts, and this movie was a mystery. Or at least it seemed to be a mystery because there was a lot of thunder and lightning at the beginning of it. There was a lot of thunder and lightning outside, too. It hadn't begun raining yet, but it was certainly fixing to do so. She heard the sound right after the last clap of thunder came from either the television set or outside the house, the thunder rumbling away into the distance, fading—and then the sound.

Velma had very good ears.

She got out of the recliner chair in front of the television set and went to the sliding glass doors at the back of the house. All the trees outside were dancing like savages. She cupped her hands to the side of her face, and peered through the glass. All she saw was blackness. Then she heard the sound again, and this time she identified it.

The sound of breaking glass.

She thought, Oh, no, not again.

She went to the window at the side of the house, and cupped her hands to her face again, and looked out. The Markham house was dark. Not a light showing.

She kept watching.

Oscar Raddison was in the bathroom peeing when he heard the sound.

He had gone to bed at nine, and this was the first of his visits to the bathroom. He would have to go again at two, he knew, and again at five. You could set your watch by the times he went to the bathroom during the night.

He looked out through the bathroom window.

Couldn't see a thing, night as black as a pharaoh's tomb, trees swaying in the wind. There was a flash of lightning. It illuminated the backyards of his house and the Markham house next door. Nothing out there. A boom of thunder. And then the rain came.

Oscar went back to bed.

Henry had cut his hand breaking the window on the south side of the Markham house. Wrapped his handkerchief around it, the handkerchief soaked with blood now, he had to find a towel or something. But he didn't want to turn on his flashlight just yet. Heavy duty torch, he'd used it to break the window, but somehow he'd cut himself anyway.

He stood there in the dark, a short, stout, squat little man wearing blue trousers, a blue T-shirt, a blue windbreaker, and blue socks and sneakers. His eyes blinked behind his eyeglasses. It was pitch black in here, he didn't even know what kind of room he was in.

There seemed to be a whole hell of a lot of ticking everywhere around him. Sounded like he was inside a bomb.

He waited for it to explode or something.

Next door, Velma stood at the window facing the north side of the Markham house, watching, waiting.

Maybe she'd been mistaken.

Night like tonight, there were all kinds of sounds out there. Even on a good night, the raccoons made sounds you thought were witches on broomsticks. Sometimes you heard animals you didn't know *what* they were, roaming around out there, making funny noises. There was another flash of lightning, close to the house. She flinched away from the window just as the clap of thunder came. It was raining to beat the band out there now. She couldn't hear anything but the rain beating on the ground and on the leaves of the palms. Palm rats out there, some nights, they made funny noises, too.

She went back to the window again.

Still couldn't see anything but the blackness outside.

Behind her, on the television set, somebody was saying, "I don't like the looks of this."

She kept watching.

His eyes were adjusting to the darkness. Pupils dilating. Objects taking shape. A chair. A desk. Walls beginning to form around him. On the walls, clocks. A hundred clocks on the walls. All kinds of clocks. All of them ticking. On the wall opposite the window, an opening. Had to be a doorway. He did not turn on the flashlight. He could see pretty well now. Well enough to know that the handkerchief wrapped around his right hand wasn't showing any white at all now. Behind him, wind and rain whipped in through the broken window, causing the curtains to flap like trapped birds. He moved cautiously across the room and went through the doorway.

A living room now. He could make out a sofa and some easy chairs. Sliding doors facing the backyard, illuminated now by another flash of lightning. He hunched his shoulders against the boom of thunder. The lightning flash had also revealed a kitchen beyond the living room. Had to be a towel of some kind in the kitchen, didn't there? Dish towel? Paper towels? Something. He was starting for the kitchen when he tripped over something, goddamn hassock or something, something low, hit his shin on it, almost went flying over it until he caught his balance.

"You dumb fuck," he said to the hassock, and put down the flashlight and rubbed his shin with his left hand.

"How can I be sure you won't cheat on me again?" Susan whispered.

They were in Matthew's bedroom, in bed together, the rain lashing the windows and drumming on the roof. She was snuggled into his shoulder. They had just made love. The bed was warm, his body was warm, she had always loved that about him, the way he felt like an oven in bed. On the coldest nights, in the past, when they were still married, she would roll in against him, her feet freezing, and he would never shy away from her, would always allow her to toast by the fire of his body warmth.

"Because if it ever happened again, Matthew . . ."

She sighed heavily, snuggled closer, comfortable in his arms, this man she had known for so long a time, or thought she had known until that night she discovered there was another woman. Did she really know him now? He had not answered her, she noticed.

"Would you?" she said. Her voice was very small. "Cheat on me again?"

"No," he said. "Never."

The proper answer, of course. He would have been a fool to have answered otherwise. She was silent for several moments, listening to the sound of the rain. Then she said, "Do you think Leona's having an affair?"

"What?" he said.

"Leona. I think she's having an affair."

"No."

"Or looking for one."

"No, I don't think so."

"She dresses like a woman sending out signals."

"She's always dressed like that."

"She does have a good figure, I suppose. But the way she . . .'

"Yes, she does."

"Oh, you noticed."

"I noticed."

Susan was silent again. The rain drummed on the roof. The thunder and lightning were gone now, and the sound of the rain made the bedroom seem cozy and snug and safe.

"Would you go to bed with Leona?" she asked. "If the opportunity . . ."

"Of course not," he said.

"I mean, suppose she came up to you one night and said, 'Matthew, I've always had a yen for you . . .'"

"She doesn't have a yen for me."

"I'm saying suppose. Would you go to bed with her?"

"No."

"Why not? Because Frank is your partner?"

"Yes. And because . . . well, I just wouldn't."

"I think she's looking for somebody to go to bed with."

"Not me," Matthew said.

"Well, somebody."

"I hope not. It would kill Frank."

"It would kill me, too," Susan said. "If you went to bed with her."

She could barely see him in the darkness.

She sat huddled in the corner of the room. The room was cold and damp and stinking of her own waste. Patchy tufts of red hair stuck out all over her head. He had shaved her below as well. She lay cold and naked and shorn, her hands and feet still bound, he would not take off the ropes. He had stuffed a rag in her mouth and wrapped the thick band of adhesive around her mouth and her head again. He had fed her two days ago, but she'd had nothing to eat since. She wondered if he planned to starve her to death.

"You got any answer for that?" he asked. "About how I could ever be sure of you again?"

She nodded.

"You do, huh?"

She nodded again.

"You want to tell me about it? Because I think I've got an

answer of my own, but it might be nice to hear your ideas."

He came across the room toward her, around the generator, stood standing over her. She tried not to seem afraid, but she was. She tried not to cower away from him into the corner, but she did.

"Don't want to hurt you when I rip off the tape," he said. "That hurts, don't it?" He smiled and reached into the back pocket of his jeans. Something in his right hand now, she peered into the darkness, trying to fathom what . . .

A pruning shears.

He slipped one cutting edge of the shears under the tape. She felt the blade cold against the back of her head. He closed the shears. The tape snapped. He peeled it away from her head and her mouth. He held his hand under her mouth.

"Spit," he said.

She spit out the rag.

"Good girl," he said.

Her mouth was dry. It tasted of the rag.

"Want to tell me now?" he said. "How I could be sure about you?"

"You could be sure of me," she said. Saliva was beginning to flow into her mouth again. She licked her lips.

"But how, Puss? I thought I was sure of you before, you know."

"Yes, but it would be different now."

"Because you got no hair anymore, you mean? Because men might not find you too pretty without no hair?"

"Well, my hair . . ."

"Your hair would grow back, wouldn't it?"

"Not if you . . . if you didn't want it to."

"Well, you wouldn't want to go around the rest of your life without any hair, would you?"

"No, but . . ."

"Then how could I trust you if I let your hair grow back?"

"You could trust me."

"How, Puss?"

"Please don't call me that," she said.

"Oh, you don't like that name? I thought you liked that name. You seemed to enjoy it when he called you that name."

"No, I didn't."

"You seemed to."

"But I didn't."

"Oh now, I don't really believe that, Puss."

"Look . . ."

"Yes?"

"If you'd . . . if you'd just let me . . ."

"Yes?"

"Let me out of here . . ."

"Yes?"

"I promise you'd have nothing to worry about ever again."

"I don't believe that either, Puss."

"I promise."

"No, I don't believe you."

"Please believe me. I'd never ever . . ."

"No, I think my idea is better, Puss."

"Wh . . . what idea?"

"How to make sure you won't ever cheat on me again."

"I won't, I promise."

"Oh, I know you won't."

"I won't, really. I've . . ."

"Yes?"

"I've learned my lesson, really."

"You have? You mean you'll be a good girl from now on?"

"Yes."

"Say it. Say you'll be a good girl."

"I'll be a good girl."

"From now on."

"From now on. Forever. I promise."

"I know," he said. "You're going to be a good girl forever, Puss. I'm going to make sure of that."

He smiled again.

He moved closer to her.

"Want me to cut them ropes?" he asked.

"Yes," she said. Her heart was beating wildly. Maybe, maybe . . .

"With these shears here?" he asked.

"Yes. Please cut the ropes."

"Sharp enough to cut through them ropes, that's for sure," he said.

"Then please do it," she said.

"Oh, don't you worry, I'll do it," he said, and opened the shears.

Velma saw light upstairs in the Markham house.

Upstairs where there was the two bedrooms. When Prue was alive, she'd used the smaller one as a little office. Carlton had his own little room downstairs, where he worked on his clocks. Clocks on all the walls. Fiddled with them, took them apart, made sure they kept good time before he carried them over to his shop. Light moving through the upstairs room. Had to be a flashlight, the way the light was moving around up there.

She wondered was it the police in there? Police hadn't been here in a long time now, was it possible they'd come back looking for something? Then why didn't they turn on the regular lights, 'stead of sneaking around up there with a flashlight?

The light stopped moving.

In the room Prue used as an office now.

Moved again.

Stopped again.

Couldn't be Carlton breaking into his own house again 'cause he was in jail, where he belonged. Maybe it *was* the police. Or maybe she'd made a mistake that night when she thought she'd seen Carlton breaking the glass on his kitchen door, maybe it'd been somebody else, somebody coming back now to get whatever he missed last time around, easy pickings, an empty house, the wife dead, the husband in jail . . .

No, she hadn't made any mistake that night, it'd been Carlton, all right.

Then who was it up there now?

She decided to call the police.

She went immediately to the phone and dialed 911.

But by that time, Henry Gardella had found what he was looking for, and was heading down the steps toward the front door.

"Because . . . if I *could* be sure of you," Susan said, "then I'd know what to tell Joanna when we pick her up next week."

"We don't have to tell her anything," Matthew said. "She really doesn't have to know what we're . . ."

"Oh, but she will know," Susan said. "I mean, she *already* knows *something's* different around here, she knew that before she went off to school."

"Yes, she knew that. But we don't need to explain . . ."

"Well, she'll ask. You know Joanna. I love her to death, but she's the nosiest little girl who ever . . ."

"Not so little anymore."

"No, not so little. But the thing is . . . if *I* knew where we were going . . ." She shook her head. "Do *you* know where we're going, Matthew?"

"No," he said.

"Neither do I. I mean . . . are we getting married again or something?"

"I don't know."

"Do you *want* to get married again?"

"I don't know."

"Neither do I."

She was silent for a very long time.

Then she said, "Do you love me, Matthew?"

"Yes," he said. "I love you."

"I love you, too," she said, and almost said, But I'm so frightened.

Because she knew that the cheapest, most expensive words in the English language were "I love you."

Came right out the front door, ran through the rain to the car where he'd parked it up the street, clutching the maroon-colored accordion file to his chest, all her canceled checks in there, all her recent checkbooks and bank statements, the mother lode.

He started the car and began driving back toward the motel.

At the intersection on U.S. 41, he passed a police car going in the opposite direction. The red dome lights on the police car moved into the distance in his rearview mirror.

His hand was bleeding red through the dish towel he'd wrapped around it.

Blood was seeping through the brown paper bag.

He walked through the rain, carrying the bag down to the lake.

Had to be careful walking around the lake. Lost two dogs to the gators in the past year.

Stood on the shore in the rain.

Tossed the bag out as far as he could.

Waited.

Saw one of the gators slither off the bank into the water.
Saw the gator moving toward where the bag had sunk.
Saw the gator disappear under the surface.

He walked back to the house then, to go look at the movie again.

8

On Monday afternoon, December 15, Warren and Matthew had lunch in a Japanese restaurant on Main Street. The name of the place was Cherry Blossoms, and the owner's name was Tadasi Imura. Imura was one of only thirty-four Japanese in all Calusa County. Imura's son was nine years old, and nobody knew his proper name but everyone called him Omen II. That was because everyone believed he had drowned his six-year-old sister in the bathtub. Or allowed her to drown. There had been quite a stink about it. Big police investigation. Skye Bannister desperately searching for a way to pin either a homicide or a manslaughter rap on the kid. A case was never made. Omen II. Nine years old. Slunk around the place in a faded kimono and blue jeans, looking desperate.

Warren and Matthew sat in their socks at a low table, knees under their chins, eating vegetable tempura and drinking sake they hoped Omen II had not poisoned. Warren was telling Matthew about Saturday night's burglary at the Markham house. Omen II lurked around as if trying to pick up tips on future criminal activities.

"According to my pals down at the station house," Warren said, "there was blood all over the place. They figure the burglar cut himself going in, trailed blood all through the house."

"How'd he go in?" Matthew asked.

"Through a window in a spare room on the ground floor. Markham used it for repairing clocks."

"Is that what the burglar was after?"

"The clocks, you mean? Who knows? Markham's in jail, and nobody's asking him anything. They're playing this very cozy, Matthew, 'cause they don't want this *new* burglary casting a shadow on the *old* burglary, which they claim Markham himself did. From what I can gather, they don't think the clocks were the target. Too many expensive ones still hanging on the walls there. Of course, nobody says a junkie has to know an expensive clock from his own asshole."

"Do they think it was a junkie?"

"That's the party line, but the guy I talked to says it doesn't read like your typical junkie smash-and-grab. Prue's jewelry was still upstairs in the master bedroom, for example, and there were lots of little doodads around a junkie could hock in a minute."

"Then what *was* he after?"

"The blood trail led upstairs to a second bedroom Prue used as an office. Drawers pulled out of all the desks and filing cabinets, papers strewn all over the floor."

"Any safe up there?"

"Nope. Not according to my source. Why? What are you thinking?"

"Maybe he was after that film she was working on."

"Only ones who'd know if there was film in that office would be Prue and maybe Markham."

"I'd better go talk to Markham again, ask him what she kept in there."

"You might also ask him what the hell she was working on. And who with."

"I already did. The first time I met him."

"And?"

"He didn't know. A *film* is all he said."

"That's sort of peculiar, isn't it?"

"Not according to the guy at Anvil. He told me the same thing. Very secretive, very guarded about her work."

"Maybe she was a spy," Warren said, and grinned.

"Maybe," Matthew said. "If you need me, I'll be at the jailhouse. And later I'll be stopping by Haggerty's office. I want to see his face when I deliver a demand for discovery on the police report."

"Oh yes, oh yes," Warren said. "'Cause even if the guy only stole a roll of toilet paper, we've got a *second* break-in now, and for all we know it was the same guy pulled the *first* one."

"I'd love to know what he was after," Matthew said.

Checkbooks.

And bank statements.

And canceled checks.

Spread all over the desk in Henry's motel room.

A joint checking account for the Markhams, nothing of any use to him there, checks made out to Florida Power & Light, and General Telephone, and Calusa Sanitation, and Visa and MasterCard, and shops and markets all over town, the usual paper trail of a busy, active couple.

It was the Prudent Company account that interested him.

The statements for that account showed that the checks he'd sent her had been deposited every week like clockwork, but he'd already known that from the canceled checks returned to him by his own bank. He wanted to know what checks *she'd* written, and he was specifically interested in any check that might provide a clue to where the goddamn *film* was.

He found a great many checks written to a company called Techno/Industrial Labs in New York City. It seemed reasonable to believe that this was the lab Prue had been using. He did not for a moment believe she'd chosen a lab so far away because she was being cautious. He suspected her choice had been prompted by the expectation of quality work, somewhat lacking down here in the boonies. She knew, of course, just as he knew, that making porn flicks in the state of Florida—or *any* state in the Union— was against the law. The lab handling her film in New York was breaking the law of that state in the same way that she was breaking Florida's law.

But—

The specific Florida statute applying to obscenity—and Henry had studied this very carefully before embarking on his maiden movie-making venture—was Chapter 847. It stated that a person was guilty of a misdemeanor of the first degree if he had "in his possession, custody or control with intent to sell, lend, give away, distribute, transmit, show, transmute or advertise in any manner, any obscene, lewd, lascivious, filthy, indecent, sadistic or masochistic book, magazine, periodical, pamphlet, newspaper, comic book, story paper, written or printed story or article, writing, paper, card, picture, drawing, photograph, *motion picture film*"—and so on.

A misdemeanor of the first degree was punishable by a term of imprisonment not exceeding one year, and a possible thousand-dollar fine. Small potatoes when one considered the possible rewards to be reaped. Smaller potatoes when one considered the Catch-22 of most obscenity laws: the burden upon the State to *prove* that the material under consideration was indeed obscene within the meaning of the law. Section 847.07 of the Florida Statutes offered a guideline:

Considered as a whole and applying community standards, material is obscene if:

a) Its predominant appeal is to prurient interest; that is, a shameful or morbid interest in nudity, sex or excretion;

b) It is utterly without redeeming social value; and

c) In addition, it goes substantially beyond customary limits of candor in describing or representing such matters.

Such a definition might apply to two-thirds of the R-rated films showing in any American motion picture theater. That was why Henry had decided to embark on a splinter career in the producing of pornographic but classy motion pictures. First let them catch him—which would have been difficult because he'd covered his tracks so carefully. Then let them charge him, if ever it came to that. And *then*, fat chance, let them prove that the product was pornographic.

He dialed 1-212-555-1212 and got a number for Techno/Industrial in New York. He rehearsed his pitch for perhaps two minutes, and then dialed the number the operator had given him.

"Techno," a woman's voice said.

"Yes, this is Harold Gordon, accountant for the Prudent Company here in Calusa, Florida?"

"Yes, sir?"

"May I speak to one of your officers, please?"

"One moment."

Henry waited.

"Hello?" a man's voice said.

"This is Harold Gordon," Henry said, "accountant for the Prudent Company here in Calusa, Florida? Who am I speaking to, please?"

"Rudy," the man said.

"And your last name, sir?"

"Holman. Who did you say this was?"

"Harold Gordon, accountant for the Prudent Company."

"Yes, Mr. Gordon?"

"I'm closing out our books for the year, going through the checks Prudence Ann Markham wrote to your company . . ."

"Yes?"

"And I was wondering if you could help me regarding some of them."

"Help you in what way?"

"Well, I'm trying to sort this out . . . have you got a minute?"

"Sure. I guess."

"Mrs. Markham was somewhat vague as to just what specific services her checks covered . . ."

"Uh-huh," Holman said.

"For example, I'm assuming most of these checks were written for the processing and the dailies."

"Yes, including our shipping charges."

"Yes, those would have been the checks she wrote in October and early November . . ."

"Uh-huh."

"Can you tell me, Mr. Holman, were any answer prints ever sent to her?"

"I don't think she's that far along, is she?" Holman said. "I don't think the picture's locked yet, is it? I know she was still working on it when she pulled the neg. What'd she do? Decide to go with another lab?"

"I'm sorry, what do you mean?"

"For any further work she needed."

"I still don't . . . did she seem unsatisfied with the work you'd . . . ?"

"Well, when she pulled the neg . . ."

"Pulled the neg?"

"Asked us to send the negative down."

"The negative?"

"Yes, sir."

"Send it down?"

"Down to Florida "

"The *negative?*" Henry said.

"Yes, sir. I was surprised, too, I thought we'd been doing a pretty good job for her. I mean, I was hoping we'd go the full route with this picture. I mean, once she had her workprint and sound tracks cut, we planned to do the mix for her sound people, and conform the neg, and do the sixteen answer print and the thirty-five blowup . . . I mean the whole damn shebang right through to the composite. So she pulls it all away. So I've got to ask myself what for? A negative's a delicate thing, even a speck of dust can scratch it, I don't know why she wanted it down there instead of safe in our vault up here. We've got a climate-controlled vault up here. Only thing I could figure is she wanted to move to another lab. Anyway, we sent it down to her. I mean, she's the customer, right?"

"By Federal Express?"

"No, sir, by personal messenger. We don't treat negatives lightly. I wanted to make damn sure it got to her."

"And did it?"

"Yes, sir."

"When was it delivered?"

"I can check if you like," Holman said.

"Yes, would you please?"

"Hold on."

Henry waited.

He could hear papers rustling on the other end of the line. Finally, Holman's voice came back on.

"It went down by personal messenger on the seventeenth of November. We billed her for it, air fare and all, you must have her canceled check there."

"Yes, I'm . . . uh . . . sure I have," Henry said. "Where did you send it, can you tell me? The negative."

"1143 Pompano Way," Holman said. "Calusa, Florida."

Her house, Henry thought.

"Mr. Holman," he said, "when you say she might have been considering a move to another lab . . ."

"Well, that's the only thing I could think of. People usually store the neg here even after they've got their release print. But all at once, she wants it back. So I have to figure another lab, am I right? The quarter-inch tapes, too. She pulled those, too."

"What do you mean?"

"The sound recordings. She wanted us to send those back, too."

"Did you?"

"Sure did."

"By messenger?"

"Yep, in the same package."

"To the same address?"

"Yes, sir."

"Then you . . . you mean you don't have anything there at all?"

"Zilch," Holman said. "It's all in her hot little hands."

"Do you have any idea who that other lab might be? The one she was considering?"

"Nope."

"I see, I see," Henry said. "I see." He was silent for several seconds. He didn't know what else to say. He felt as if someone had kicked him in the balls. "Well . . ." he said at last, "then these . . . uh . . . checks I have . . . they're for payment in full, is that correct? There's no further balance due?"

"All squared away," Holman said.

"Well, thank you very much, sir," Henry said.

"When you see her, tell her I think she made a big mistake," Holman said, and hung up.

"Shit!" Henry said, and slammed the receiver back on the cradle, and began sorting through the checks again.

That Monday, Tick and Mose got their first genuine lead to Jake Barnes.

On Saturday night, Kim—the lady in the black lingerie at The Naked Truth—had told them his real name was Jake Delaney—which they'd immediately doubted because Delaney was Irish, wasn't it, and Jake was as black as midnight. Furthermore, he was living not in Newtown which was where most of the *black* people in Calusa lived, but instead in a house on Fatback Key, which was where a lot of the *white* people in Calusa lived.

Tick was beginning to think he'd pissed five hundred bucks into the gutter.

Kim went on to explain that Jake's aunt had been married to a white man named Fred Delaney, and that she had brought up Jake when his mother ran off to New York on the trail of a man who'd knocked her up a second time. Not the same man who'd knocked her up with Jake. A different man. In fact, Jake was ten years old at the time, handsome as rain in a dry summer, and he never saw his mother again, nor whoever his mother was carrying in the oven when she ran off. His aunt and her white husband took the kid in and gave him the name Delaney. Kim couldn't remember what his *real* name used to be, or at least the name he was born with, since people usually thought of the name you were born with as your *real* name even if you'd changed it legally when you were twelve and were now going on eighty. That was a funny thing about changing your name in America, Kim said in a sidebar, seemingly pissed off because she'd legally changed her own name to Kim Arden two years ago, and people still called her Mary Androssini, which was the name she'd been born with, but which wasn't her *real* name anymore since she had a court order to prove it. Oh well, what the fuck, she said.

Tick was beginning to believe more strenuously that his five hundred bucks would buy nothing but a long pointless monologue.

Anyway . . .

The thing was . . .

Jake was living in a house on Fatback Key because he was a chauffeur for a swinging couple that came down here from Chicago only from January to May, and the rest of the time he took care of the house for them, and took care of a lot of willing white chicks in addition to the wife when she was there, spreading them wide on the king-sized bed in the upstairs bedroom with a distant view of the Gulf and doing them the way they only before had dreamt of being done, because he was *one* sexy, handsome dude, this Jake Delaney, who could have had any girl on the beach, white, black, purple, he was that gorgeous and that talented. Kim shyly admitted that she herself had succumbed to Jake's charms, which was how she happened to know so much about him, Jake being not only gorgeous but also gregarious and garrulous.

It was during one of their sessions out at the beach that Jake mentioned he was going to star in a movie they'd be shooting right there at the Chicago couple's house on Fatback Key. Tick and Mose both knew that house well; they had lugged more damn shit in and around it for more than a month. They hadn't known, however, that Jake was caretaking the house. They thought Prue had rented it from somebody she knew. Lots of people liked to see their houses in movies, even porn flicks. It made them feel as if they were in *Architectural Digest*. This particular house was set far back from the beach and far from the main road as well. You could drive in there with a film crew for *Gone with the Wind* and nobody would notice you. Perfect for what they were doing. They were using every room in the house, shooting daytime interiors mostly, except for a few scenes where Connie blew Jake in the ocean in broad daylight. So it now looked as if Jake might have been the one who arranged through the Chicago couple for Prue to use the house while they were away in the Windy City. Which was maybe a good sign. If he'd been that close to Prue, getting the house for her and all, then maybe she'd told him where the film was before her dumb husband knocked her off.

Anyway . . .

The thing was . . .

Jake wasn't living in the Fatback Key house just now.

Tick wanted his five hundred bucks back.

"Where the fuck *is* he living?" he asked.

"Well, I don't know exactly," Kim said.

"Give me my five bills," Tick said. "Right this fucking minute."

"Hold on, will you?" Kim said. "The thing is . . ."

The thing was . . .

Back in November sometime, Jake dropped by the club and told Kim they'd finished shooting this movie they were working on, and he was going to be a millionaire. Kim figured at first that he meant he was going to be a big movie star, which wasn't too far out a possibility because he had Eddie Murphy and Billy Dee Williams beat in spades, no pun intended, and there wasn't a woman who could come within a hundred yards of him without going damp. He told her he had to go down to Mexico—

"Mexico!" Tick said.

—Mexico, Kim said, to scout out a situation for the director of the movie, and that after he got back they'd be going down there with something more precious than gold, those were his exact words, more precious than gold. She thought he was talking cocaine, but she didn't ask. The point was—

"What *is* the fucking point?" Tick said, somewhat heatedly.

—the point was he was taking the Lincoln Continental the Chicago couple left in the garage down here, and driving up through the corners of Alabama and Mississippi and then across Louisiana and through Texas, and then on across the border to he didn't say where. And because it was such a long drive, he was taking a chick with him to while away the time (please let it be me, Kim thought) and they'd be gone two, three weeks, and he'd stop in again when he came back, say hello, which meant it wasn't going to be Kim after all.

"Who *was* it?" Tick asked impatiently.

"A hooker named Amber Wilson."

"When did they get back?" Mose asked.

"Jake's still down there," Kim said. "But I heard he kicked Amber out. I think maybe he got tired of her. There's lots of Mexican girls down there in Mexico."

"Where do we find this Amber Wilson?" Tick asked.

"Well, that's the thing of it," Kim said.

"*What's* the thing of it?"

"I heard she got busted for bringing some pot back with her."

"Busted? Where?"

"Texas."

"Texas!"

"But maybe she didn't. This is all stuff I heard around."

"If she didn't get busted . . ."

"Maybe she didn't . . ."

"Then where does she live here in Calusa?"

"Newtown," Kim said.

Carlton Barnaby Markham did not seem to appreciate jail-house life. He looked much paler than he had before, and he was also considerably more irritated.

"I think you should be agitating for bail," he said.

"I can't get you out on bail," Matthew said.

"Have you tried?"

"I've talked quietly to Judge Mancuso. He's the man who denied bail in the first place, and who also denied my motion in limine. He thinks you're a maniac."

"Terrific."

"He thinks you'll run if he gives you the slightest opportunity."

"I would," Markham said.

"Don't say that. Not even in jest."

Markham scowled.

"So I just sit here until February, whenever the hell, whenever we go to trial."

"I'm afraid so."

"This is Russia, right?"

"No, this is America. Mr. Markham, there are some questions . . ."

"For Christ's sake, call me Carlton. You're always so goddamn formal."

"I'm sorry."

"Don't be so goddamn *sorry*, either. Your job is to get me out of here so . . ."

"I already told you . . ."

"I'm not talking about getting me out on bail, I'm talking

about getting me out *period* so I can get on with my goddamn *life!*"

"That's exactly what I'm trying to do. I already told you we've found a witness . . ."

"Sure, a fat old broad with bats in her belfry."

"But all we've got for the moment."

"A jury'll take one look at her . . ."

"Well, let me worry about the jury, okay?"

"Sure, you worry about the jury. I'll worry about the electric chair."

"I'm worried about that, too, Carlton, believe me."

Markham nodded, but he did not look convinced. "So what are these questions you have?" he said.

"Your house was broken into again last night," Matthew said.

"What?"

"Yes. Along around midnight. I don't know what was taken yet, if anything. I'll be making a demand for discovery when I leave you. But I'd like to know what Prue kept in that upstairs office of hers."

"Files, records, correspondence, that's all."

"Is there a safe up there?"

"No. Why? If he was after money . . ."

"I thought she . . ."

". . . then he was barking up the wrong tree. Prue and I weren't exactly wallowing in the stuff."

"I thought she might have kept film up there."

"Film? No."

"She was working on a film when she was murdered, so I thought maybe . . ."

"I don't see what *film* has to do with her murder."

"Well, there isn't any, you see."

"Any what?"

164

"Film."

"A goddamn junkie killed my wife for the few dollars in her handbag, and I'm charged with her murder, and you're talking about film. What the hell does film . . . ?"

"She was working on a *film*," Matthew said. "And now there *isn't* any film. And I have to ask myself why."

"What are you suggesting? That Prue was killed because of some dumb commercial she was . . . ?"

"Is that what she was working on? A commercial?"

"I don't know what she was working on. A commercial, a documentary, who *cares*?"

"These documentaries she made in the past? Were any of them controversial?"

"No. What do you mean? Controversial? How?"

"Could they be considered exposés of any kind? Were they investigative journalism?"

"No, no, nothing like that. She did the one on child abuse that got the prize, and another one on manatees, they're an endangered species, you know, and one on . . ."

"Did the child-abuse film ruffle any feathers?"

"It was shown in every school in the state. I told you, it won a prize."

"This new film she was working on . . ."

"I don't know what it was."

"Never mentioned it to you?"

"Never. She sometimes got like that. I didn't know about the manatee film until she'd finished it."

"*Could* it have been controversial?"

"The manatee film?"

"No, the one she was working on. She wasn't doing a film about fixing horse races, for example, or selling dope to little . . . ?"

"I told you, I don't know *what* she was working on."

"Began work in September, is that right?"

"The end of September, yes."

"When did she work? Daytime? Nighttime?"

"Mostly at night."

"Where?"

"I don't know."

"Who was financing the film?"

"What?"

"Who was financing it? You said a few minutes ago that you and Prue weren't exactly wallowing in money. Doesn't it cost . . . ?"

"I don't know who was financing it. I told you I don't know anything *about* the damn film!"

Matthew looked at him.

"Then you don't think there's the remotest possibility that your wife may have been working on something that someone, *anyone*, might have found threatening to his or her . . ."

"I told you," Markham said. "I do not know what she was working on. Shall I say it again? I do not know what she was working on. Nor do I see how pursuing this line of approach is going to help me one damn bit!"

Matthew kept looking at him.

"Sorry," he said at last. "Just an idea."

It was not until two days later that Tick and Mose found Amber Wilson.

She was the color of her given name, amber to be sure, a girl who—or so her neighbors had reported—referred to herself with great dignity as "black" although she could have passed for white anywhere in the world. What you'd call a mulatto, Mose guessed, or a quadroon, or an octaroon, or a nectarine, or whatever the hell. What his grandfather back in Georgia would have called a "high yeller gal."

She was sitting on a blanket on the Sabal Key beach, wearing a green maillot slit high up on the leg and slashed low between her abundant breasts. Two white boys wearing swim trunks and Duke University sweatshirts were tossing a Frisbee some ten feet from where she sat. Tick and Mose, dressed for the street, came slogging through the sand toward where she sat studiously ignoring the boys trying to get her attention.

"Miss Wilson?" Tick asked.

She looked up. Her eyes were the color of the sky, a pale, bluish-gray. Somewhat slanted. Set in an oval face with high cheekbones. Mose wished he'd have been the one who took her to Mexico. He also wondered why Jake Delaney had sent her back home. Jake had seemed very intelligent otherwise.

"The lifeguard over there says you're Amber Wilson," Tick said. "Mind if we sit down and talk to you a minute?"

Tick knew she was thinking Cops.

"Okay?" he said.

Amber shrugged.

Both men sat on the blanket. The Duke Frisbee-players, probably Boggers, were wondering what she saw in these two jerks that she didn't see in them. They picked up their toy and wandered farther up the beach.

"We've been trying to find you since Monday," Tick said, figuring he'd let her go on thinking they were cops for just a little while.

"Oh?" Amber said. "How'd you find me now?"

"Lady who lives next door to you said you went to the beach."

"Well, I guess I did," Amber said, "since here I am at the beach."

"We hear you just got back from Mexico," Mose said, getting straight to the point as usual. There were times when Tick wondered why he bothered with Mose at all.

"If you heard I was busted at the border, that's bullshit," Amber said. "Are you cops or what?"

"We're looking for Jake Delaney," Tick said, ignoring the question.

"He's in Mexico, and *he* didn't do anything, either."

"We know he didn't do anything," Tick said. "But we're real anxious to talk to him."

"What about?"

He wondered if she knew Prue was dead.

"When did you go down to Mexico?" he asked.

"We left on the fifteenth," Amber said.

"Last month?"

"Well, since today's the seventeenth, and the fifteenth of *this* month would've been two *days* ago, then it couldn't have been *this* month, could it, since I'm sitting on the beach here, don't you think?"

Wise-ass nigger, Mose thought.

"You're saying it was last month," he said.

"Bright," Amber said.

Like to punch you right in your fuckin' nigger mouth, Mose thought.

Tick was thinking if she left five days before Prue got killed then maybe she didn't know about the murder. He was also trying to think whether or not this was good or bad for them. He figured he'd play it by ear a bit longer.

"Why'd Jake go down to Mexico?" he asked.

"Business," she said.

"Dope?" Mose asked.

Good old Mose.

Amber merely looked at him. Her look could have killed a cockroach.

"We're friends of his," Tick said, figuring he'd quit playing games.

"I'll bet you are," Amber said.

"We worked with him on that movie out on Fatback Key."

She studied him.

"Really," he said.

She kept studying him.

"That's what we want to talk to him about."

"I don't know anything about that movie," she said.

"'Cause we understand he went down there to scout out a situation for the director of the movie," Tick said, and watched her eyes.

She didn't even blink.

"What we want to ask him . . ."

"You're cops, ain't you?" Amber said.

"No, no," Tick said.

"Who you think you're kidding here?" Amber said. "The lady got herself juked, and now you're giving me all this jive about Jake scouting a situation for her, you're cops."

So she knows about Prue, Tick thought.

"We're not cops," he said.

She studied him again.

"Really," he said.

"We worked with him," Mose said.

"You I wouldn't believe if you told me you're wearing a red shirt," Amber said, which he was wearing.

"We're not cops, I mean it," Tick said. "All we want to know is what kind of situation he was scouting for her. We'd ask him ourselves, only he's in Mexico. He'd tell us in a minute if he was here. We're *friends* of his, for Christ's sake."

"It wasn't nothing illegal," Amber said.

"Then what was it?"

"Whyn't you go to Mexico and ask *him*?"

"Where in Mexico?" Tick asked.

"Mexico City."

"Scouting for what?"

"How much is this worth to you?" Amber asked.

It always got down to money. You talked with a hooker, it was always cash on the line. There were no hookers with hearts of gold left in the entire world. But he had learned his lesson with Kim Arden née Mary Androssini.

"All I can spare is a hundred dollars," he said.

"Make it two hundred," Mose said.

Tick's mouth fell open.

"I mean, make it fifty," Mose said, and grinned apologetically.

"No, two hundred sounds about right," Amber said.

"What am I buying for two hundred?" Tick asked.

"You want to know what he was scouting in Mexico, don't you?"

"Something else I want to know, too."

"What's that?"

"The square handle of the girl who was in the movie with him."

Amber looked at him.

"Do you know her name?"

"I know her name," Amber said.

"Her address, too?"

"No."

"Then all it's worth is a hundred."

"Make it a bill and a half."

"You've got it," Tick said, and reached for his wallet. He counted out six twenties and three tens.

"Thanks," Amber said, and slipped the money into her beach bag.

"So?" he said.

"How do you want it?"

"First the girl's name."

"Margaret."

"What's her last name?"

"Dill."

Easy to remember, Tick thought. Like a dill pickle.

"Does she live here in Calusa?" he asked.

"Yeah, but I don't know where. I already told you I don't know her address."

Punch her right in her nigger mouth, Mose thought.

"Jake never dropped anything that would . . ."

"No. He just kept talking about her all the time. Meg this, Meg that . . ."

"He called her Meg?"

"Yeah."

"You said Margaret."

"Meg's her nickname. They were real tight, huh? I think he was making it with her even when they weren't in front of the camera. Well, you know Jake."

"So it's Margaret Dill," Tick said.

"Meg," Mose said.

"Either one," Amber said, and shrugged.

"All right, what about Jake? What's he doing down there in Mexico?"

"Like you said. Scouting for the lady directed the movie."

"Where? Mexico City?"

"Mexico City."

"What kind of scouting?"

"For bread," Amber said. "And a place to work."

"A place to work? In Mexico?"

"Yeah. She was gonna finish the movie Jake was in."

"*Puss in Boots*?"

"What's that?"

"That's the name of the movie we were shooting. Did Jake say she was going to finish *Puss in Boots*?"

"He didn't tell me the name of the movie. He said it was the

171

movie he'd starred in, and she needed a place and the bread to finish it."

Tick looked at Mose and then turned back to Amber.

"Jake didn't have the movie with him, did he?" he asked. "He wasn't carrying reels of film, was he? Or sound tape? Anything like that?"

"No, no."

Then it's still here in Calusa, Tick thought.

"While you were down there," he said, "did you hear she'd been killed?"

"No, I only found out about that when I got back."

"Do you think Jake knows?"

"I doubt it. You ever been to Mexico? It takes a hundred years to make a call back to the States."

"Did he *try* calling her back here in the States?"

"No, 'cause he didn't yet find what he was looking for. He was still looking when he showed me the door. I had to turn four tricks to get airfare back." She smiled radiantly. "He can be a pain in the ass sometimes, Jake."

"So what was the plan?" Tick asked.

"The plan?"

"I mean, once Jake got the money and a place where she could work . . ."

"She was gonna join him down there."

"When?"

"Soon as he scored."

"How much money was he looking for?"

"Who knows? However much it takes to finish a movie."

"Does he plan to come back here?" Tick asked.

"No, I think he's gonna ship the car back to these people he works for, and then stay down there. They were gonna go in business together."

"Who? Jake and the people he works for?"

"No. Jake and the lady got killed. They were gonna make movies down there. Least, that's what he told me. He's full of shit sometimes, Jake."

"He was starting a business with Prue?"

"And her husband," Amber said.

9

Joanna Hope came running into the baggage area, long blonde hair trailing, blue eyes flashing, arms spread wide. "Mom! Dad!" she shouted, and rushed to where Susan and Matthew were standing, waiting for her, and threw her arms first around Susan, and then broke away from her and embraced Matthew, and then hugged and kissed Susan again, and then said, "Wow, it's great to see you guys, you both look terrific, what a lousy flight it was, the lady sitting next to me spilled Coke all over my blouse, does Coke stain, Mom?"

She looked marvelous.

Fourteen years old, she seemed to have added two inches to her height since she'd left in September. Blue jeans and a white shirt with an amoeba-like blot over the pocket, leather fleece-lined jacket like World War II fighter pilots used to wear—"I'd better take this off before I die from the heat"—brown leather tote bag slung over her shoulder, brown boots. She looked seventeen. She looked like a young lady. Matthew had forgotten how beautiful she was. He hugged her again.

"You look gorgeous, honey," he said.

"Oh, sure, sweet talker," she said, "I've got a zit right on the end of my nose."

"You've lost weight," Susan said.

"Soccer," she said, and flexed her muscles like Wonder Woman. "Also I've been eating that crappy food up there, can we go someplace good for dinner tonight? There's one of them, Dad," she said, "wow, that was *fast*! I'm dying to take a swim, is the pool warm enough? God, what a gorgeous day, it's been snowing for the past week up there, no, the blue one, Dad."

He yanked the bag off the luggage belt and set it down on the floor. Susan immediately pulled it back and away from the crowd of people craning and jostling. Just like old times, he thought. A team. Hope to Hope.

"The other one's a duffel, Dad," Joanna said, "it's full of dirty laundry."

"When are you due back?" Susan asked.

"Here's your hat, what's your hurry?" Joanna said, and laughed. "Not till the fifth, ain't that great? God, I was freezing to death all last week, do you think I can buy an electric blanket to take back up with me? There it is, Dad, the one with all the bulges and the Simms sticker. Could we go for steak tonight? At the Innside Out? I've been dying for a good, thick steak. Tommy said the first thing he was going to eat when he got home was a whole roast pig, he *loves* pork. That's Tommy I told you about, Thomas Darrow," she said, and rolled her eyes, "he lives in North Carolina, let me carry the duffel, Dad . . ."

"No, no . . ."

"Lotsa muscles, no brains," she said, and hefted the bag onto her shoulder, and began walking toward the exit door, long-legged strides, tall and beautiful and rattling on a mile a minute.

"I hope the washing machine's working, I've got *tons* of stuff to do. Also, Mom, if we get a chance, can we go shopping at the Circle one day, because Tommy asked me to the Glooms, and the only formal I've got up there is the one I wore to Daisy's mother's wedding when she got married again, do you remember the one? I wore it to the Sugarcane Hop when I was flat-chested, the horrible green thing that used to have the big red flower on it that we took off and you tried to fix the bustline? And I have to do all my Christmas shopping, too, there's no place at *all* near Simms where you can buy anything decent even if you *could* rent snowshoes to get to town, we had four feet of *snow*, can you believe it, Tommy built a fort and we had a terrific snowball fight, you guys don't know what you're missing down here."

"Yes, darling," Susan said, and glanced at Matthew.

He knew they were both thinking the same thing.

How come our darling daughter hasn't yet mentioned the somewhat startling and amazing fact that we are here *together* to pick her up?

In the car, Susan's car, the new Mercedes she'd bought this year, trading in the Mercedes she'd got in the settlement agreement, together with the house and half the state of Florida— it still rankled when he thought of the way Eliot McLaughlin, her mealy-mouthed attorney, had taken him to the cleaners because he was the "guilty" party—Matthew asked, "What's the Glooms?"

"The Glooms? Oh, the Glooms. It's a big formal thing Prescott has in February, to dispel the February Glooms, you know? You see, what it is, Simms is an all-girls school in name only, bet you didn't know that when you shipped me up there, did you, Mom? Actually, the Prescott campus is right next door, and we share classes with the boys from Prescott, and it's really like we're one school, the Simms Academy-Prescott School, which is terrific, otherwise I'd never have met Tommy. The Glooms isn't really the Glooms, either, I mean that's not what it's really called, it's really the Winter Moon Ball, but Tommy nicknamed it the Glooms, and it caught on, and now everybody calls it the Glooms, which flies in the face of tradition because it's been the Winter Moon Ball since Harriet Beecher Stowe went to school there, which she didn't, you know, but we're studying *Uncle Tom's Cabin*, which Tommy thinks is a hoot! This is new, Mom, isn't it, what'd you do with the old one? Have you still got the Ghia, Dad?"

"Yes, I . . ."

"It *smells* new, Mom. I love the smell of new leather. Boy, am I glad to be *home!*"

Matthew suddenly hugged her to him.

"Hi, Daddy," she said.

Checks made out to Jake Delaney, Techno/Industrial Labs, George Ticknor, Tortini Pizza, Ron Sterling, Federal Express, Mosley Jones, Jr., Terrence Blair, Alison Lewis, Repro Sound Systems, Franklin Moving & Storage, Betsy Knowles, Alfred Basilio, Palm Deli, Mark Davidson, Philippa Donnelly, Anvil Studios, Klaven Film Supplies, 7-Eleven, Florida Power & Light, General Telephone, Margaret Diehl, and Prudence Ann Markham herself.

All of them marked "For Services."

Henry had to figure a cameraman, a lighting director, a sound technician and two grips. Had to figure the rest were actors and actresses, four women and two men. Had to figure all the other checks were for buying and renting and moving and feeding and generally keeping even this small-time operation on the tracks, it staggered him to think of the headaches involved with a Hollywood production.

But the check that interested him most was a check written to a firm called Calusa Travel. Of all the checks written on the Prudent Company account, this was the only one not marked "For Services." This one was marked "Mexico."

Henry opened the Calusa telephone directory. There it was, Calusa Travel. This was a Saturday, he hoped.they were open. Tuning up his Harold Gordon accountant's voice, he dialed the number.

"Calusa Travel, good morning," a woman's voice said.

"Good morning," he said, "this is Harold Gordon, accountant for the Prudent Company here in Calusa?"

"Yes, Mr. Gordon, good morning."

"Good morning," Henry said. "Who am I talking to, please?"

"Ginny Holmes," the woman said.

Henry wondered if it was Ginny or Jenny. In the Deep South, Ginny and Jenny sounded exactly the same. If somebody asked you could she borrow a pin, she didn't want something to fix her bra strap, she wanted something to write with.

"Miss Holmes," he said. "I'm closing . . ."

"Mrs. Holmes," she said.

"Mrs. Holmes, excuse me. I'm closing out the company's books, and I have a check here written by Prudence Ann Markham to your firm. I was wondering if you could fill me in on what the check was for."

"A shame what happened to her," Ginny said.

"A terrible pity," Henry said. "Which makes it all the more important that I put her books in order. For the attorneys handling the estate, you know."

"Yes, I see," Ginny said. "Just one moment while I pull the file."

Henry waited.

When she came back on the line, she said, "Yes, I have it now. What was it you wanted to know?"

"The check was a sizable one, I was wondering if you could let me know what services . . ."

"Well, we're a travel agency, you know."

"Yes, I know."

"Mrs. Markham called us for airline tickets and a hotel reservation."

"Yes," Henry said. "Airline tickets to where?"

"Mexico City," Ginny said.

"Let me just jot that down," Henry said. "Airline tickets to Mexico City."

"Yes, and a hotel reservation."

"At which hotel, please?"

"The Camino Real."

"And this was for when?"

"They planned to leave on the first."

"Of?"

"Pardon?"

"The first of?"

"Oh. December. A Monday."

"You said *they*. Who did you mean by *they*?"

"Mrs. Markham and her husband."

"Were leaving for Mexico together on the first of December?"

"Yes. But, of course, there was the trouble."

"Yes. He killed her."

"Yes."

"Yes," Henry said. "And the room you booked at the hotel . . ."

"Was a double."

"I see. For Mr. and Mrs. Markham."

"Yes."

"I see. And they were returning when?"

"They were one-way tickets."

"No return?"

179

"No return."

"An open return, perhaps?"

"No, just one-way tickets."

"To Mexico City. On the first of December."

"Yes."

"I see," Henry said.

"Yes. Actually, I'm happy you called, Mr. Gordon. I was wondering whether I should ask for a refund on the tickets. After the trouble . . ."

"Yes, the murder."

"Yes. *Mrs.* Markham can't make the trip, you'll forgive me, and *Mr.* Markham is in jail. So what should I do? I've been wondering."

"Send a refund, yes," Henry said.

"That's what I thought," Ginny said. "I'll notify the airline, and send my own check in refund for the full amount. Shall I make it payable to the Prudent Company?"

"Yes, please do that."

"Where shall I send the check?" Ginny asked.

"To her bank, if you will. For deposit to the Prudent Company account."

"I'll get that off on Monday," Ginny said. "I'd send it out today, but I'm all alone here."

"Monday will be fine," Henry said. "Thank you very much, Mrs. Holmes."

"A terrible shame," she said, and hung up.

A terrible shame is right, Henry thought. A terrible shame that Prudence Ann Markham was planning to skip, most likely with the film he himself had paid for, and taking her dumb husband with her besides. Why the hell had he killed her? Was he planning a cross of his own? Knock off the lady, grab the film, run down to Mexico with it, and sell it to one of the *banditos* down there? Life is very complicated, Henry thought, and truth is stranger than fiction. Meanwhile, Markham was in jail, and the film was only God knew—Christ, was it in the *house*? Had he missed the forest for the trees? Did he have to break into the house all over again, cut his hand all over again, there had to be an easier way to make a living.

Sunlight streamed through the open Venetian blinds onto the checks spread on the desk top. Damn Venetian blinds were filthy, he should have looked for a better motel, but he'd been intent on keeping a low profile.

He leafed through the checks again.

He felt fairly certain that Tortini Pizza, Federal Express, Repro Sound Systems, Franklin Moving & Storage, Palm Deli, Klaven Film Supplies, 7-Eleven, Florida Power & Light, and General Telephone would not know what Prue or her dumb husband had done with the film.

That left Jake Delaney, George Ticknor, Ron Sterling, Mosley Jones, Jr., Terrence Blair, Alison Lewis, Betsy Knowles, Alfred Basilio, Mark Davidson, Philippa Donnelly, Margaret Diehl, and Anvil Studios.

Anvil Studios seemed like the most likely bet.

He pulled the telephone to him yet another time.

On Sunday morning, four days before Christmas, the Hope family had brunch together on the terrace of a hotel/tennis complex called Island Dream, out on Stone Crab Key. The day was sunny and bright, the waters of the Gulf calm. The buffet table was dressed with sprigs of holly and ropes of pine, but this was Florida and even the huge Christmas tree just inside the sliding glass doors leading to the terrace could not generate for Matthew any sense of holiday spirit.

This was Florida.

And in Florida, at about this time last month, a young woman had been brutally slain while leaving a film studio on Rancher

Road. It was difficult to think of bloody murder on a day like today. Far simpler to concentrate on the cornucopia of culinary delights offered on the festively dressed table, far easier to listen to the chatter of smartly dressed men and women who'd come directly from church to wine and dine on the sunlit terrace where not fifty feet away the sparkling waters of the Gulf lapped gently at the white sand beach and a girl in a black bikini strolled idly by, her head ducked in thought.

Better to heap your platter high with poached eggs and sausages, roast beef and turkey, buttered green beans and home fried potatoes. Better to sip at your Bloody Mary and forget for the languid moment that Prudence Ann Markham had been killed, and that her husband had been charged with the murder, and that her husband was your client, and that he had seemed to bridle unnaturally when asked again about the film Prudence had been working on. Forget all that for now. This was Sunday. This was the twenty-first day of December, four days before Christmas, and you were here in the sunshine with your family (of sorts, in that it was no longer a family in the legal sense) and your daughter was talking again (as she had done incessantly since Friday afernoon) about Thomas Darrow, Jr., her Tommy, the love of her young life.

". . . even bigger than he is, and *he's* six-two. I mean, when I saw him coming out of the blue at Tommy, my heart jumped into my mouth. Tommy was on the thirty-yard line, I guess it was, with the ball tucked under his arm and racing for the touchdown that would've given Prescott the game, I mean there was only half a minute left before it would be over with Choate at seven and us at six. And it looked like he had a clear field, do you know? Nobody in sight until this absolute *goon* suddenly pops up out of the woodwork and goes straight for Tommy, and I thought, Oh my God he's a steamroller, he'll squash Tommy flat, they'll pick him up in pieces. But Tommy caught him out of the corner of his eye, and he did this little sort of twist, he looked like a bullfighter, I swear to God, he's so graceful, and the goon took a flying leap at him and landed flat on his face while Tommy ran through the goal posts and jumped in the air and threw the ball down, and bang went the gun, and Prescott had it twelve to seven, God, he's so terrific!"

"Can you two excuse me a minute?" Susan said.

"Am I talking too much?" Joanna asked.

"No, no, darling, I have to visit the ladies'."

She folded her napkin near her plate, kissed Joanna on top of her head, slipped Matthew a sidelong wink, and moved off, pink pleated skirt swaying about her legs, long strides like Joanna's, pink disappearing into a sea of white and pastel blues as she passed the crowd around the buffet table.

Matthew was alone with his daughter.

"You say he lives in North Carolina?" he asked.

"Chapel Hill," Joanna said. "Dad, does this taste all right to you?"

She extended her fork. Matthew tasted the potato pancake on it.

"Uh-huh," he said. "Why? What's wrong with it?"

"I don't know, it tastes kind of funny. Maybe I've gotten so used to the crap at Simms that now anything *good* tastes weird. Tommy says the school cook must've worked in a prison, he's so good at institutional food."

"How old is he?" Matthew asked.

"Tommy or the school cook?" Joanna said, grinning.

"The school cook, of course," Matthew said.

"Tommy's seventeen, but he's already a senior. He's very bright, Dad, head of the debating team, writes a column for the school newspaper, I mean in *addition* to being Prescott's star quarterback."

"What does his father do?"

"He teaches philosophy at U.N.C. Tommy's not sure what he wants to do yet, he thinks he may want to be a doctor like his mother. She's a psychiatrist. Tommy says he grew up with a copy of Plato in one hand and a copy of Freud in the other."

"What does he look like?"

"Tommy or Freud?"

"Plato," Matthew said.

"Well, let me see," Joanna said. "He's got high cheekbones and a beautiful mouth, and black hair, and *gorgeous* brown eyes, and I guess I told you he's six-two, and he weighs about a hundred and ninety, and he moves like a dancer, and he's absolutely wonderful, that's what he looks like."

"I'm dying to meet him," Matthew said.

"I was hoping you and Mom would . . . listen, I don't know what's going on with you guys, and I really don't *want* to know, in fact I'm afraid to ask. But I thought it might be nice if you both came up for Parents' Day in March, get to meet Tommy and his parents, that'd be nice."

"I'll ask your mother," Matthew said.

"Do you think it might be possible?"

"I think so."

"'Cause that'd be terrific. U.N.C. has its spring break around then, so Tommy's father can get away for sure. It's a matter of his mother arranging her schedule so none of her patients'll think she's abandoning them. She's really got a heavy caseload, lots of blacks of course, but plenty of white patients, too."

Matthew looked at her.

"Tommy's black," she said. "Didn't I tell you?"

Susan was back.

"Did I miss anything?" she asked, and sat, and put her napkin on her lap.

"My turn," Joanna said, and shoved back her chair. "Did you check out the desserts, Mom? I think I'll really pig out today."

She moved off swiftly, through the open sliding doors, past the buffet table, disappearing into the crowd.

"You okay?" Susan asked.

"Guess who's coming to dinner?" Matthew said.

By five o'clock that Sunday afternoon, Henry had talked to only four of the people on his list. He had struck out at Anvil Studios yesterday, where he'd talked to a conceited little shit who thought he was running MGM and who told him he didn't know where Prue's precious film was, but it certainly wasn't there at Anvil, and he was tired of people coming around *asking* him about it. Henry wondered who these people asking about it might have been, but Michael Andrews had not amplified.

There had been no listings in the Calusa directory for George Ticknor, Mosley Jones, Jr., Terrence Blair, Alison Lewis, Alfred Basilio, or Mark Davidson.

That left Jake Delaney, Ron Sterling, Betsy Knowles, Philippa Donnelly, and Margaret Diehl.

He called the number listed for Jake Delaney and got no answer. He jotted down the address of the house on Fatback Key.

He called the number listed for Ron Sterling, and got an answering machine. He told the machine he would call back, and jotted down the address on Twelfth Street.

He called Betsy Knowles, told her he was the man producing the film Prudence Ann Markham had been working on, and made an appointment to see her at noon.

He called Philippa Donnelly and made an appointment to see her at two.

There were seven Diehls listed in the Calusa directory, none of them Margarets. He spoke to six of them. None of them had ever heard of Margaret Diehl. The only one of the Diehls he could not reach by telephone was a man named Burgess Diehl. Every time he called the number, he got a busy signal. He jotted down the address on the Timucuan Point Road, and then tried Ron Sterling again. This time Sterling himself picked up, and Henry made an appointment to see him at four.

Betsy Knowles turned out to be a creamy-complexioned, freckle-faced twenty-three-year-old with a body that could stop a charging rhinoceros. She was very happy to meet the producer of *Puss in Boots*, and told him she was available for any other films he might be thinking of making in the future. She crossed her legs recklessly, toyed with her cleavage incessantly, offered Henry a mint julep with mint fresh from her own garden, and said she'd had a marvelous time working with Jake and Ron and the other three women, Philippa, Alison and Connie. She said that doing group sex with people you didn't know could be a very trying and arduous experience, but Prue had been very patient and gentle with all of them, and she couldn't understand why the crew sarcastically called her *La Directrice* or even Otto, who was Otto Preminger, who was supposed to be a first-class prick on the set.

The crew, she told Henry, consisted of:

Mark Davidson, the cameraman, who lived in Tampa.

Terrence Blair, the gaffer, also Tampa.

Alfred Basilio, the sound technician, Tampa again.

And George Ticknor and Mose Jones, both grips, both from Tampa.

"She was using a lot of Tampa people," Betsy said. "Alison lives in Tampa, too."

Which was why Henry hadn't been able to find any of them in the Calusa directory.

"But who's Connie?" he asked. "I don't seem to have her name."

"Connie Redding," Betsy said. "Well, Constance."

"Does she live here in Calusa?"

"I think so."

"But you're not sure."

"No. What a nice girl, I mean it. She was the star, you know, but so sweet. And so beautiful. When I say 'star,' I mean she had most of the big scenes, we were in there just for variety, you know. She was the one did all the heavy stuff with Jake."

"Jake Delaney," Henry said.

"No, Jake Barnes," Betsy said. "Not that I envied her. I had one scene with him, where he put that enormous fucking thing in my mouth, I almost choked to death. Phew," she said, and smiled angelically.

"I've been trying to reach him," Henry said. "Would you know if he's still at this address on Fatback Key?"

"I think he's in Mexico," Betsy said.

Mexico, Henry thought.

"How about Margaret Diehl?" he said. "Do you know where I can reach her?"

"Who?"

"Margaret Diehl."

"I don't know anybody named Margaret Diehl. Did she say she was on the picture?"

"Well, I haven't talked to her. I just thought . . ."

"'Cause if she did, she's lying. Lots of girls like to say they're in the movie business when they aren't."

"Yes," Henry said, and nodded. "Actually, the reason I called, I was wondering . . ."

"Well, I'm glad you did," Betsy said, and smiled and uncrossed her legs, and then crossed them again.

"I was wondering . . . you know what happened to Prue, of course."

"Oh, of course, my God I thought I'd be next."

"What do you mean?"

"Well, I thought it was some maniac had a thing about porn flicks or something. I relaxed when it turned out to be only her husband."

"Yes," Henry said. "But I was wondering . . . you worked so closely with her . . ."

"Well, it *is* a pretty close relationship," Betsy said, "you know, the camera practically inside you and all."

"Yes," Henry said.

"And Prue right in there calling the shots and making sure the lighting's right, and the exposure, and everything's in focus and all. It *is* a very close relationship."

"I'm sure," Henry said. "Which is why I thought she may have told you where she was keeping the film."

"The film?"

"Yes. The negative. Or the work print. The film."

"Gee, no, I'm sorry," Betsy said. "Would you like another julep?"

Philippa Donnelly served him martinis.

She, too, was delighted to be meeting the producer of the film she'd been acting in. She was a tall, willowy, twenty-seven-year-old blonde with Dolly Parton breasts and a Carol Channing mouth. She was wearing a kimono and high-heeled slippers when she opened the door for Henry, and the first thing she offered him was a martini. He had the feeling, as their meeting progressed, that she would have offered him the sun and the moon and the stars as well, had he been of a mind to accept such lavish gifts in promise of future work, but Henry had business on his mind.

She, too, listed everyone who'd worked on the movie, all those goddamn people he'd have to track down in Tampa if he struck out here.

She, too, told him that Connie Redding had been a dream to work with.

"There were scenes, you know, where I had to go down on her, which can be embarrassing or even disgusting if you're not a dyke, which I'm not, by the way. But she was so *sweet* . . . I mean *literally* . . . that everything was just a wonderful pleasure."

Henry wondered if she knew what the word "literally" meant. He guessed maybe she did.

He asked her if she knew anyone named Margaret Diehl.

She said she did not.

After his second martini, he asked her if Prue might have mentioned where she was keeping the film she'd shot. Philippa was sitting on the couch, one leg casually draped over the arm of it, high-heeled slipper dangling, the kimono somewhat accidentally open to reveal a glimpse of pubic hair several shades darker than the hair on her head.

"I think she was working on it at Anvil," Philippa said. "That's where she was killed, you know."

"Yes," Henry said. "But the film isn't there."

"Well, where is it then?" Philippa asked.

"I don't know. I was hoping you might know."

"Well, no, I don't," Philippa said. "I hope it isn't lost, do you think it might be lost? 'Cause we got some really wonderful stuff. There's this one scene where Jake is ramming it into me from behind, and I'm going down on Ron . . ."

Ron Sterling was twenty years old.

He wanted to be a movie star.

He told Henry he could be the next Tom Cruise. Or Sean Penn. Or Judd Nelson. Or Emilio Estevez.

Henry had never heard of any of these people.

He told Henry that working on *Puss in Boots* had been an enjoyable and educational experience, especially the scenes he did with Connie Redding, though most of her *big* scenes were with Jake, of course. He wondered if maybe when Henry was doing the producer's cut, he could slant the movie a bit more in his direction, show some of the really terrific *love* scenes he'd played with Connie, as opposed to the *sex* scenes, because what he was looking for was a career as a romantic lead, somebody like Rob Lowe, whom Henry had never heard of, either. Who *were* all these people?

Sterling did not know where the film was.

He thought Prue might have been keeping it at Anvil, where she'd been editing it.

"She was a total bitch, you know," he said. "How long did she expect a person to keep a hard-on?"

So at five o'clock that evening, after having talked to one person yesterday and three more today, Henry climbed back into the rented Ford he was driving, found a pay phone in a shopping mall—he wondered why there was a dearth of pay phones in the city of Calusa, Florida, didn't people make public telephone calls here?—dialed the number for Burgess Diehl again, and again got a busy signal.

As he drove across U.S. 41 and onto Timucuan Point Road, he was thinking that Constance Redding had to be Margaret Diehl. Otherwise there'd have been checks made out to Conance Redding. That had probably been the name she was using on the picture, Constance Redding. Be difficult to cash checks under a phony name, though, so she'd had them made out to her real name. Margaret Diehl. Who maybe was related to the Burgess Diehl in the phone book, whose address was 3755 Timucuan Point Road.

Or maybe not.

Either way, Henry figured a nice drive in the country couldn't hurt on a beautiful day like today.

"Cat got your tongue?" he asked.

No answer from her. Lay there in the corner, naked except for the boots.

"Just as well," he said, "the things you did with that tongue of yours."

Eyes wide in her head.

"Never realized you were so talented, Puss."

Silence in the cold, damp cinderblock room.

"Of course, that's all behind you now, ain't it? Never going to do nothing like that ever again, are you?"

Silence.

"Thought I'd drive you up to Ananberg early Christmas morning, set you out on the sidewalk there. Think you'd like that, Puss? Set you out like a common streetwalker, maybe put a little sign around your neck, I have sinned in the Lord's eyes, think you'd like that? Tell the world what you are?"

Silence.

"Be fitting, don't you think? Get there around midnight, set you out early on the morning our Lord was born, who died for your sins, Puss, died for them. Set you out on the sidewalk for all to see, a reminder that you broke the Lord's commandments in the vilest possible way, set you out, Puss. Set you out naked and ashamed in the Lord's eyes, set you out on the sidewalk there near the manger there in the middle of town. Behold, therefore I will gather all thy lovers, with whom thou hast taken pleasure, and all them that thou hast loved, with all them that thou hast hated; I will even gather them round about against thee, and will discover thy nakedness unto them, that they may see all thy nakedness. Set you out, Puss."

He stared down at her.

"See what I brung back with me?" he said, and showed her the cleaver.

Silence.

"Wherefore, O harlot," he said, "hear the word of the Lord. Thus saith the Lord God; Because thy filthiness was poured out, and thy nakedness discovered through thy whoredoms with thy lovers, and with all the idols of thy abominations . . ."

He ran his thumb along the cutting edge of the cleaver.

"I will judge thee," he said, "as women that break wedlock and shed blood are judged, and I will give thee blood in fury and jealousy."

He nodded.

"So will I make my fury toward thee to rest," he said, "and my jealousy shall depart from thee, and I will be quiet, and will no more be angry."

He nodded again.

The sign outside read:

ORCHIDACEOUS
Exotic Orchids

No name. No Burgess Diehl, like in the phone book. But this was the right address, there on the post below the sign, 3755 Timucuan Point Road. Dirt road leading in off the main road. Henry made the turn.

It was a beautiful day, and the mint juleps and the martinis were still working their magic, and he felt very happy, felt almost like bursting into song as he drove past foliage that looked like a jungle in here. The road ran past a big lake. Kept on twisting and turning, full of potholes, bumpety-bumpety-bump. Henry drove along it for half a mile or so, he guessed, came at last to a house. Well now, he thought. Hothouses back there behind the house, exotic orchids, right? Little cinderblock building near them, looked like a chicken house or something. He pulled up the brake, turned off the ignition key, and got out of the car.

He was walking toward the house when a door in the cinderblock building opened. A man came out. Looked like a farmer. Big tall man with wide shoulders and muscular arms, Henry figured him to be in his early forties, craggy face, blond hair, bib overalls with no shirt under them, muddy workboots. He was carrying a bloodstained cleaver in his right hand, and a bloodstained brown paper bag in his left hand. Chicken farmer, Henry thought. Out back getting his Sunday night dinner. Whap! The idea was comical somehow. Henry almost laughed.

"Mr. Diehl?" he said.

The man stared at him.

Blue eyes. Shaggy eyebrows above them. Tanned, leathery face.

"I'm Henry Gardella," Henry said.

The man said nothing. Kept staring at him.

"I'm trying to locate a woman named Margaret Diehl. I've been calling all day, thought I'd come out in person." He smiled. "Would you happen to know her?" he asked.

He still thought this was pretty funny. Big dumb chicken farmer standing there with a cleaver in one hand and his chicken dinner in a bag in the other hand.

"What do you want with her?" the man said.

"Are you the Mr. Diehl who's listed in the phone book?"

"What do you want with her?" the man said again.

"If she's the woman I'm looking for, I produced a movie she . . ."

The words scarcely left his mouth. The man's eyes flared. A sound like a mixture of pain, anger and torment burst from his mouth. He dropped the bloodstained brown paper bag. He raised the cleaver.

Holy shit, he's *coming* at me! Henry thought.

All at once, it didn't seem so funny anymore.

"Hey," he said, "listen . . ."

But the man was closing the distance between them, cleaver raised above his head, eyes blazing.

"Whoremaster!" he shouted, and Henry turned and started running.

He ran toward the lake.

He was suddenly very sober.

He could hear the man's heavy breathing behind him.

Kept running toward the lake.

Saw something lying there on the bank, long and gray and . . .

He stopped dead.

Holy . . .

A hand closed on his shoulder. He felt himself being spun around.

"No, don't," he said.

10

At ten o'clock on Tuesday morning, December 23, Cynthia Huellen came in to tell Matthew she hoped the office Christmas party this year wouldn't be as rowdy as the one last year. Cynthia was a native Floridian with long blonde hair and a glorious tan that she worked at fanatically; never a weekend went by that did not find Cynthia on a beach or a boat. Twenty-five years old, employed by the firm as a receptionist, she was easily the most beautiful person in the law offices of Summerville and Hope. Matthew and Frank kept telling her to quit the job and go to law school instead. She already had a B.A. from the University of South Florida, and they would take her into the firm the minute she passed her bar exams. Cynthia just grinned and said, "No, I don't want the hassle of school again."

Apparently she did not want the hassle of another rowdy party again, either. Matthew had left the party early last year. He did not know whether it had become rowdy or not. But here was

Cynthia telling him that the otherwise staid and proper attorneys who worked here (four of them in addition to Matthew and Frank) had drunk a bit too much and had conveniently forgotten during a long afternoon of wassail that some of them (two) were married and some of them (the other two) were going steady with girls Cynthia actually *knew*. And whereas she didn't mind a little camaraderie and brotherly love, she, and the other three girls working here, didn't like being chased around desks, either.

"So maybe you can sort of drop a few hints here and there, because it can get a little embarrassing, okay?"

The party was scheduled to begin at four that afternoon.

Matthew promised he would drop a few hints.

At ten minutes to eleven, Cynthia buzzed him to say that a Mrs. Holmes from Calusa Travel was on five. "Are you planning a trip?" she asked.

"Did she say what it's about?" Matthew asked.

"Nope."

"I'll take it," he said, and punched a button in the base of his phone, and lifted the receiver.

"Hello?" he said.

"Mr. Hope?"

"Yes?"

"Ginny Holmes, Calusa Travel."

"Yes, Miss Holmes," he said.

"Mrs. Holmes," she said. "I'm sorry to be bothering you this way, but I don't know where to send this check."

"What check?" he said.

"It would have gone out yesterday afternoon, as I promised Mr. Gordon . . ."

"Mr. Gordon?"

"Yes, the accountant for the Prudent Company."

"The Prudent Company?"

"Yes. Mrs. Markham's company. The refund check was ready

to go out yesterday afternoon, but Mr. Gordon never told me which bank to send it to."

"I'm sorry, Mrs. Holmes," Matthew said, "but I'm not following you."

"He told me to make it payable to the Prudent Company, and send it to her bank for deposit to the account. But he never said which bank it was. And I deposited *her* check back in November, so I don't have it anymore to look at."

"Her check?"

"Yes, for the airfare to Mexico City. And the hotel deposit. I'm afraid I can't get the deposit back from the Camino Real. They were supposed to be there on the first, you know, so it's a little late to be canceling now. I suppose I should have telexed them the moment I read about her getting killed and Mr. Markham being in jail. But as I explained to Mr. Gordon, I really didn't know what to do. Anyway, I have the check for the airfare, so if you'll just tell me which bank to . . ."

"Mrs. Holmes," Matthew said, "I'm still not . . ."

"This *is* Matthew Hope, isn't it?" Ginny said.

"Yes?"

"I assumed . . . I read in the paper that you're representing Mr. Markham, so I automatically assumed you were also handling Mrs. Markham's estate."

"No, I'm not," Matthew said.

"Then who is, would you know? When Mr. Gordon called, he said he was getting things in order for the attorneys handling the estate. Do you know where I can reach them? Or Mr. Gordon, either one? I'd really like to get this check off my mind."

"I'm sorry I can't help you," Matthew said.

"Harold Gordon?" she said. "An accountant?"

"No, the name isn't familiar to me."

"Could you ask Mr. Markham when you see him? Which bank her account is with?"

"I certainly will," Matthew said, and picked up a pencil. "You say this was for a trip the Markhams planned to take on January first?"

"No, December first," Ginny said.

"Tell me about this trip you'd planned," Matthew said.

They were in Markham's cell. On the wall just inside the barred door, there was a white porcelain sink with two push-button faucets. Just beyond that was the toilet bowl, no seat on it, just the white porcelain bowl and a roll of toilet paper sitting on the neck of the bowl where it was fastened to the wall. A former prisoner had inked a calendar onto the wall, and had crossed out the days he'd spent in this cell, a big x through each day. Markham had been here for almost a month now. He sat on a dirty foam rubber mattress on the wall-fastened cot opposite the sink and the toilet, his hands folded and dangling between his knees.

He sighed, looked up at Matthew, and said, "Who told you we were planning to skip?"

Matthew blinked.

Skip?

Nobody had told him that Markham and his wife had been planning to *skip*. This was news to him. He decided to run with it.

"Tell me about it," he said. "You were leaving for Mexico City on the first of December, is that it?"

"If you already know . . ."

"Do you want to go to the electric chair?" Matthew said.

Silence.

"Then tell me."

The silence lengthened.

"Okay, the hell with it," Matthew said, and went to the cell door. "Can you let me out of here?" he called to the corridor.

"Take it easy," Markham said.

"No, I won't take it easy," Matthew said. "Either you tell me what this is all about or I walk."

"All right, all right, calm down," Markham said.

"I'm listening," Matthew said.

"It was her idea," Markham said.

"Prue's?"

"Yes. To take the film and run. Finish it in Mexico, if she could find facilities down there and get a . . ."

"Why Mexico?"

"She figured Gardella wouldn't bother chasing us all the way down there."

"Gardella? Who's Gardella?"

"Henry Gardella. The man financing the movie."

"I thought you told me . . ."

"Yeah, well."

"No, never mind 'Yeah well.' You told me you didn't know who was financing the movie. You told me you didn't know anything *about* the movie. Now you . . ."

"Yeah, well . . ."

"You say that one more time . . ."

"I'm sorry," Markham said.

"If I'm hearing you correctly, she planned to run to Mexico with the film this Gardella person had financed . . ."

"That's right."

"Why?"

"So she'd have a *hundred* percent of it, instead of *ten* percent."

"Was that supposed to be her end? Ten percent?"

"Of the gross," Markham said. "She figured the picture might do eight, nine million theatrically. Plus God knew what on the cassette. Prue'd done all the work, she didn't see why Gardella should get the biggest piece of the pie."

"Except that he'd put up the money to . . ."

"A measly hundred and seventy-five thousand," Markham said.

On Matthew's block, a hundred and seventy-five thousand wasn't very measly.

"And he hadn't paid *all* of that yet. He'd only paid out a hundred and five by the time she was killed."

Only a hundred and five, Matthew thought.

"She figured she'd use the film as collateral," Markham said. "When we got down to Mexico. Show what she had to get the loan she needed to finish it. Find a distributor later on, cut him in for a piece of it, but nowhere near as much as Gardella would be getting if she . . ."

"Where do I find this Gardella? Is he here in Calusa?"

"Miami. Why do you want him?"

"Because I'm *still* trying to keep you out of the electric chair. If Gardella found out your wife was planning to disappear with that film . . ."

"There's no way he could have known that. Nobody knew about Mexico but the three of us."

"*What* three of us? What the hell *else* haven't you told me?"

"Me, and Prue, and Jake."

"Who's Jake?"

"Delaney. He was in the movie. But he's got connections. He went down to Mexico to see about getting the loan."

"Why didn't she go herself? Why didn't you go?"

"I told you. Jake has connections."

"What kind of connections does a person need to . . . ?"

"Well, you know."

"No, I don't know."

"He knows people who . . . you know . . . people who don't always operate within the law."

"Crooks, are you saying?"

"Well, yes, I suppose you could put it that way."

"Why did the loan have to come from people outside the law?"

"Well, it might've been difficult otherwise."

"Why?"

"Because of the nature of the film."

Matthew looked at him.

And suddenly, came the dawn.

"Was your wife making a pornographic movie?" he asked.

Markham nodded.

"Who's this Gardella?" Matthew said at once. "Mafia?"

"No, no."

"But someone outside the law?"

"No, he runs a dinner theater in Miami. He's a legitimate businessman."

"Who was financing a pornographic movie," Matthew said.

"Well, there's lots of money to be made in porn," Markham said.

"Why didn't you tell me all this from the beginning?"

"I thought . . ."

"Your wife was breaking the law. It's entirely possible that her murder . . ."

"I don't think so."

"Where's this Jake Delaney person? Is he back in Calusa?"

"I haven't heard from him. I think he's still down there."

"Does he know your wife's dead?"

"I don't know."

"Could *he* have killed her? And *then* gone to Mexico?"

"No. He went down there on the fifteenth."

Matthew looked him square in the eye.

"Did *you* kill her?" he asked.

The same question he'd asked at their first meeting.

"No," Markham said.

The same answer.

"How do I know that? You're telling me this film can earn

eight, nine million dollars, more when you throw in the cassette. How do I . . . ?"

"I loved her. Why would I have killed her? This was our way out. That damn clock shop . . ." He shook his head. "Prue doing movies that brought in peanuts. Even the one that got the prize, what do you think she realized from that one, after all was said and done? Ten thousand? Fifteen? We figured . . . if we could pull this off . . . this would be only a beginning, do you see? She could go on doing the same kind of movies, we'd make a fortune. So why would I have killed her?"

"Maybe because you wanted it all."

"No," Markham said. "No. I loved her."

"Then why didn't you tell me all this? If you loved her so damn much, and you *didn't* kill her . . ."

"I didn't think you needed to know about the movie."

"You didn't see how that could have any possible bearing on the case, huh?"

"I didn't want it to come out."

"Why not?"

"Well, the film . . . well, it's valuable, you see."

"Yes, so you told me. It's worth eight or nine million dollars."

"Well, more."

"So you decided not to tell your attorney about it."

"Well, it had nothing to do with her murder."

"You don't know that for a fact! Why'd you withhold such important . . . ?"

"Because I . . . I thought . . . I thought if Jake could come up with the money we need down there . . . well then . . . then after the trial . . . after you got me off . . . I'd go join him. And we'd go ahead just the way we planned. Finish the movie, find a distributor . . ."

"Without Prue."

"Well, yes, without her. We could find people to finish it. Edit it, do whatever else needed to be done. We had the negative, that wasn't a problem, Prue made sure she got that back from the lab. So if they found me innocent . . ."

"Did Delaney take the film with him to Mexico?"

"Well . . . no."

"You said you planned to use it as collateral . . ."

"Once he found the right people, yes. We planned to show them the film later. When we got down there."

"You planned to take the film down with you?"

"Well . . . yes. That was the plan."

"Then you know where it is," Matthew said.

Markham said nothing.

"Do you know where the film is?" Matthew said.

Still no answer.

"*Do* you?"

Markham nodded.

"Where?" Matthew said.

He parked the Karmann Ghia in the gravel lot outside a low, white stucco building, its pristine facade broken by a row of a dozen or more red doors. There were six yellow-and-green moving vans in the lot, each decorated with the company's name—Franklin Moving & Storage—and a logo depicting a little man in knee breeches, flying a kite. Under the little man's buckled shoes was the motto FRANKLIN! FAST AS LIGHTNING! Rock music blared from inside a windowed office at the far end of the building. Matthew walked over the gravel to the red door set between the windows, opened it, and stepped into a Christmas party in full swing.

There were at least two dozen girls in the place, all of them dressed somewhat less elegantly than the women at the Snowflake Ball had been, but resplendent nonetheless in party dresses and high-heeled shoes. The men in the room, outnumbered by at least two to one, were wearing a motley assortment of clothes, some of them in suits or sports jackets, others in blue jeans and short-sleeved shirts and looking as if they'd just come off the road after a long haul from Maine. A decorated Christmas tree blinked first yellow and then green, the only lights on it, an obvious homage to the company's colors. Red and green streamers were hanging from the ceiling, stretching from corner to corner. Santa Claus cut-outs were on all the walls. On one wall was the same little man who was on the side of the trucks, wearing his little knee breeches and his little buckled shoes and flying his little kite. A bar had been set up in one corner of the office, and most of the revelers were gathered around it, pouring liberally from what appeared to be a fine selection of booze.

A bell had sounded over the door when Matthew came in. How anyone had heard it over the din was a miracle, but a woman wearing a tight green skirt and a red tube top broke away from the bar, turned to look at him, and then said, "Well, well, reinforcements."

She came to him as fast as lightning, click, click, click, click, high-heeled shoes zapping the floor, wide grin on her generous mouth, red hibiscus tucked behind one ear, blonde hair brushed back from it. Pale skin, cheeks flushed. Slender, and tall, and moving as gracefully as a dancer. Long, shapely legs, firm breasts in the shirred red tube top. He guessed she was in her early thirties. He also guessed she'd been drinking a bit.

"Whoever you are, come in," she said, "we're short of gorgeous men." She extended her hand. "Marcie Franklin," she said, "I'm the boss."

"Matthew Hope," he said, taking her hand.

"Any relation to Harry?" she said at once.

"Yes. I played Larry Slade in a college production."

"Hey," she said, "somebody literate! Tell me what you think about Bergman."

"Ingrid or Ingmar?"

"Oh, my God, I think I'm falling in love," she said. "I've been in Calusa only six months, came down from New York to take over the business when my father died, and I'm so starved for conversation, I'm ready to call Dial-a-Prayer. Are you married?"

"Divorced," he said.

"Good," she said. "Oh, wow, Santa must've brought you."

Matthew smiled.

"I'm serious," she said. "Every guy I date in this town wants to talk about football. I say, 'How'd you like *Ginger and Fred*,' they say they don't watch old musicals. I say 'Fellini, *Fellini*,' they say they don't like Italian food unless it's the Pizza Hut. I say, 'What'd you think of *Kiss of the Spider Woman*,' they say I don't know the lady. I say, 'Okay, how about *The* goddamn *Color Purple*?,' they say I prefer red. I mean, wow! Do you like movies?"

"Yes."

"Want to go to the movies with me tonight? Think it over, don't leap to a hasty conclusion you may later regret. I'll be thirty-three next month, I like tall men with dark hair and brown eyes, I'm sensitive and intelligent, and some people think I'm gorgeous. I like expensive restaurants and fancy motorcars, Beethoven and . . ."

"You sound like a personals ad in the *Village Voice*," Matthew said.

"Oh, my God, I *am* falling in love," she said. "He knows the *Village Voice*! Are you from New York, too?"

"My partner is. He talks about it all the time."

"Where are you from?"

"Chicago."

"Pity," she said, and grinned.

She had not let go of his hand. Her green eyes danced all over his face, checking out his mouth, checking out his eyes, checking out his mouth again. Yellow and green from the Christmas tree bounced off her eyes.

His own eyes roamed her face—

Blink, yellow, blink, green—

Oval and pale. Orange lipstick on her mouth. High model's cheekbones—

Blink yellow—

Checking her out.

White even teeth behind the wide grin—

Blink green.

Hey, he thought.

Watch it.

"Come have a drink," she said, and—still holding his hand— led him to the bar. "Jimmy," she said to a man in shirtsleeves, "please fix a drink for Matthew Hope. What are you drinking, Matthew?"

"Well . . . uh . . . just a little gin, please, on the rocks," Matthew said.

What's happening? he thought.

"Gin on the rocks for Matthew," she said, and released his hand. She tugged at her tube top again, pulling it higher on her breasts. "I am *very* happy to meet you, Matthew," she said, and grinned again. Wide grin. Luscious mouth. "Merry Christmas."

"Merry Christmas," Matthew said, and accepted the drink Jimmy handed over the bar. "Thank you," he said. "Cheers," he said to Marcie.

"Finish your drink," she said, "and then come dance with me. Lucille!" she called across the room. "Put on something romantic! Matthew wants to dance with me!"

The music stopped abruptly. The roar of the crowd sounded louder now that it was gone. There was a delay of perhaps a

206

minute or so—voices, laughter, ice tinkling in glasses—and then another tape started, soft and slow. Watch it, he thought.

"There you go," Marcie said, and walked into his arms.

He still had the drink in his right hand.

She moved in tight against him.

He almost spilled the drink.

He steered her toward one of the desks. His right hand behind her, the drink still in it, he put it down blindly on the desktop. She pulled him close again. More people were moving out onto the floor now; it seemed suddenly very crowded and steamy. Watch it, he thought, watch it.

"I was wondering . . ." he said.

"Me, too," she said. "Oh, Matthew, you have set me wondering."

"Is there someplace we can go to talk? It's a little loud in here."

"What did you want to talk about, Matthew?"

"Storage," he said.

"Oh my, storage," she said. "This is Christmas, Matthew, let's not talk about storage. Bah-humbug on storage. Let's talk about kissing. Dance me over to the mistletoe, Matthew."

"Seriously, could we . . . ?"

"Let's not get too serious, Matthew, we've only just met."

"Isn't there someplace . . . ?"

"Yes, there is definitely someplace," she said, and broke out of his arms, and reached for his right hand, tugging at the tube top again with her left, and led him to a door near the bar. She opened the door with her left hand, and pulled him into a smaller office. She closed the door behind them. And kissed him at once.

"God," she said, and melted into him again, and kissed him again.

He remembered what he had told Susan.

About never cheating on her again.

Marcie's tongue was in his mouth.

"Listen," he said, breaking away from her, trying to hold her away from him, "there's . . . really, there's something we have to talk about."

"What can we possibly find to talk about at this particular moment in time?" she said.

Her arms still around his neck.

"I'm a lawyer," he said.

"So?" she said. "Sue me."

And thrust her crotch against him.

"I'm . . . I'm here on behalf of a client," he said.

"I'll bet," she said.

"Who stored something here."

"Stored?"

"Film."

"I wouldn't be surprised," she said, and cupped his face between her hands, and lifted her mouth toward his again.

He pulled away.

"Can we talk first?" he asked.

He was trembling.

"Please," he said.

"Three minutes," she said, and took his hand and led him to a couch on the far side of the room. She sat. She folded her hands primly in her lap. The tube top was slipping again. She made no move to tug it up over her breasts. He sat beside her. "So talk," she said.

"Prudence Ann Markham," he said. "The Prudent Company."

"What about her?"

"Her husband told me she was renting a storage bin here."

"So?" Marcie said.

"Was she?"

"This is the girl who got killed, isn't it?"

"Yes."

"Yes, she was renting a bin here."

"Air-conditioned, her husband said."

"They're *all* air-conditioned," Marcie said.

"One key, her husband said."

"That's all I give is one key. I don't know what people store here, and I don't ask. For all I know, half the cocaine in the state of Florida is behind those little red doors out there. One key is all I give. You give two keys, you've got two people. If you've got two people, you've also got trouble." She grinned. "As with us, Matthew. Big trouble, Matthew. From minute one. Has this ever happened to you before? This kind of heat lightning? I'm trying very hard to keep my hands off you, Matthew. Has this ever happened to you before?"

He tried to remember.

Had it been this way in the beginning with Aggie, long, long ago, the first time he'd ever cheated on a contract in his life? This kind of immediate reaction? Eyes meeting, hands touching? He had made a new contract with Susan, a contract of sorts, but a contract nonetheless. Yet sitting here with a woman he'd met not ten minutes ago, he was thinking he wanted to rip that damn tube top off her breasts. He suddenly wondered what had happened to all those fine new promises he'd made to Susan.

"*Would you? Cheat on me again?*"

"*No. Never.*"

He wondered if he was merely a no-good philandering bastard.

Hey, hold it, he thought, I'm not *married*!

Then why was he sitting here feeling guilty?

I'm in trouble, he thought. Big trouble.

She was right.

"Let's finish talking," he said.

And when we finish talking? he wondered.

"Is there a master key?" he asked.

"There is."

"Can you let me into the bin she was renting?"

"Nope."

"Why not?"

"'Cause you're not the key holder. I only let key holders . . ."

"I can ask for a warrant," Matthew said.

"So ask for it."

"This is a murder case I'm defending."

"This is the right to privacy *I'm* defending."

"Oh, are *you* a lawyer, too?"

"Don't go smart-ass on me, Matthew. You've got two minutes left."

"But who's counting?"

"I am."

"Marcie, there's something in that bin that may . . ."

"No, there's nothing in it," she said.

"What do you mean?"

"Somebody cleaned it out."

"How do you know that?"

"I saw the van."

"What van? When?"

"The night she was murdered."

Matthew looked at her.

"A van was here on the night she was murdered?"

"Yes. A man unlocked the bin, took everything out of it, and put it in a van."

"What kind of van?"

"One of these little delivery vans."

"You saw him doing this?"

"I did."

"Where were you?"

"Working right here in the office."

"What time was this?"

"Around midnight, somewhere in there. I work hard, Matthew."

"So do I."

Eyes meeting again.

She clenched her hands in her lap.

That mouth.

"What did the man look like?" he asked.

"Big blond guy wearing overalls."

"Blond?"

"Blond."

"Would you recognize him if you saw him again?"

"Sure. You've got one minute, Matthew."

"Opened the door with a key?"

"With a key."

"Had to be Prue's key," Matthew said, thinking out loud.

"Whoever's," Marcie said, and shrugged, threatening the tube top's tenuous hold.

"You said you only give one key . . ."

"That's not all I give, Matthew. Forty seconds."

"So it had to be hers. Why didn't you call the police?"

"About what? Somebody taking something from one of the bins? Is that a crime?"

"It is if the somebody just killed . . ."

"I didn't see a murder, Matthew. I saw somebody emptying a bin. Thirty seconds."

"Emptying it into a van."

"A van."

"What kind of van?"

"A white one."

"What make?"

"I don't know. He was probably a musician or something."

"A musician? You said he was wearing overalls."

"Maybe he plays at barn dances. Twenty seconds."

"What makes you think he was a musician?"

"Because of what was lettered on the side of the van. In pink."

"What was lettered on the van?"

"Ten seconds."

"What was lettered there?"

"Orchestrations. Nine . . ."

"Orches . . . ?"

"Eight. Orchestrations, right."

"You saw that on the side of the van?"

"Orchestrations. Seven."

"Anything else?"

"Just that."

"That doesn't make sense."

"Six."

"No name or anything? Just . . ."

"Orchestrations. Five . . ."

"Marcie . . ."

"Four . . ."

"You've had a little bit too much to drink . . ."

"No, I haven't. Three . . ."

"And I have to get back to my . . ."

"Two . . ."

". . . office."

"One," she said. "Now kiss me again before I die."

"Marcie . . ."

"You said you weren't married . . ."

"I'm not."

"Are you gay?"

"No."

"Then kiss me. I know you want to."

"I do."

"Then do it."

Green eyes wide.

"Please," she said.

God, that mouth.

"Kiss me," she said.

"I'm sorry," he said.

He rose, moved swiftly toward the door.

"I'm sorry," he said again.

"So am I," she said. "You're breaking my heart, do you know that? I've known you for fifteen goddamn minutes, and you're already breaking my heart."

He looked at her.

Long and hard and wonderingly.

"Marcie . . ." he said.

"Oh, go the hell back to your office," she said, and buried her face in her hands.

He looked at her a moment longer, and then opened the door and sidled out, and closed it immediately behind him.

11

It was Christmas Eve.

Ever since Monday, Tick and Mose had been running down every damn Dill in the Calusa telephone directory—eight of them in all—with no luck whatsoever. They were both exhausted. Mose wanted to go out and get drunk. This was at eleven o'clock in the morning. Tick wanted to find Margaret Dill. He said they had to go see Amber Wilson again. Mose said maybe Amber Wilson would like to go out and get drunk with them, and the hell with Margaret Dill. Mose had no head at all for business. Mose didn't realize, as Tick did, how much money they could make on that movie, if they could find it.

But first they had to find Amber Wilson again.

They went back to the crumby little apartment she was living in down there in Newtown, and her talkative next door neighbor—a big fat black woman who looked like Aunt Jemima, complete with a red bandanna on her head—told them she hadn't seen Amber since early yesterday morning, heard she was out on a boat with some people. Tick took this to mean that she was out on a boat entertaining fishermen. He asked the neighbor if she knew which boat Amber was on, and the neighbor said when Amber usually went out on a boat it was through Opus Charters, operating out from behind the Hyatt. Tick and Mose thanked her and then drove south on 41 to the Hyatt.

Opus Charters rented everything from fishing boats to yachts. The owner of the operation, a man named Charlie Oppenheimer, told Tick and Mose that Amber and two other girls had gone out yesterday on a thirty-six-foot Grand Banks with some men down from Clearwater. The captain of the boat had told Charlie they were heading down for Venice, planned to spend the night out on the water—the boat slept six comfortably in air-conditioned cabins. Charlie expected they'd be back sometime this afternoon. He told them all this when he thought Tick and Mose were interested in a similar excursion. Only later did he think they might have been cops. The thought would keep him awake all night while he was waiting for Santa to come down the chimney.

At two o'clock that afternoon, Tick and Mose were sitting in the Hyatt bar, overlooking the dock and the Gulf of Mexico. Mose was drinking mimosas. Tick kept kidding him about a mimosa being a fag drink. He himself was drinking something called a Banana Dynamite, which had seven different kinds of rum in it and a little bit of banana cordial. On the Gulf, the sailors were out in earnest. It was a fine bright day, and there was a good wind and no chop at all.

"We don't find Connie today," Mose said, "I want to go back to Tampa. I don't want to spend Christmas in this shitty town."

"I was thinking," Tick said, "we don't find her today, we go back up and give those two girls a ring we met last month."

"Yeah, Revlon," Mose said.

"I still got her number, the blonde's," Tick said.

"What was her name again?" Mose said.

"Rachel," Tick said.

"No, the redhead's. Revlon's."

"Gwen," Tick said.

"Yeah, Gwen," Mose said, and licked his lips. "That's a good idea, we give them a call."

"Christmas Eve, they'll probably be busy."

"Worth a shot," Mose said. "Maybe we oughta call from here, set it up."

"Well, let's see we can't find Connie first."

"I was Connie, the money she got for that movie, I'd be up in New York right this minute, spending it."

"She didn't get all that much," Tick said.

"How do you know what she got?"

"I'm just guessing. Two bills a day maybe?"

"New York's great around Christmas," Mose said. "Florida sucks around Christmas."

"That must be it now," Tick said, and nudged Mose.

A boat was pulling into the dock. Two men in Hawaiian-print sports shirts jumped ashore and began doing things with ropes. A third man in the same kind of shirt kept waving directions to them.

"There's Amber," Tick said.

She was standing on the bow, wearing a yellow wraparound skirt that flapped open to reveal the long line of her leg. With one hand, she was clutching a straw hat to her head. In the other hand, she was carrying a beach bag, the same one she had slipped Tick's hundred and fifty bucks into for giving him information about a woman who didn't exist.

"Let's go," Tick said.

He looked at the check, put several bills on the bartop, and shoved back his stool.

Out on the dock, the men in the Hawaiian-print shirts were

giving the girls last-minute holiday hugs and farewell kisses. Three girls. Two of them white, the other one Amber, who could've passed for white. The girls waved ta-ta to each other and went off in opposite directions, the two white girls heading for the bar where maybe they hoped to drum up a bit more trade, giving Tick and Mose the once-over as they passed them, Amber heading for the angled wooden walkway that led toward the roundabout in front of the hotel. Tick and Mose fell into step beside her.

"Hello, Amber," Tick said.

"Well, well," Amber said.

"Ain't no Margaret Dill in Calusa," Mose said, straight to the point.

"Gotta be," Amber said, unruffled. "Jake told me she lives here."

"*Where* here?" Tick said. "We checked every damn Dill in the phone book."

"Maybe she's unlisted."

"Jake must've given you a clue," Tick said.

"No clue a'tall. Just her name. Margaret Dill. Or Meg. You pays your money and you takes your choice."

They were at the roundabout now, under the hotel marquee. She looked up toward 41. Mose figured he'd break her nigger arm if she tried to get in a taxi before telling them what they needed to know.

"You sure he said Dill?" Tick asked.

"Dill, Dill," Amber said. "Margaret Dill." She turned to a uniformed bellhop who came out of the hotel. "Think I'll be able to get a taxi here?" she asked. "Or should I call for one?"

"They come by every five minutes," the bellhop said.

"I've been here five minutes already," she said.

The bellhop shrugged. Amber looked up toward 41 again.

"Think," Tick said. "Something he might've said. Like the

217

mainland, or one of the keys, or out toward . . ."

"He didn't say nothing but her name."

"Margaret Dill," Tick said.

"How many times you have to hear it?" Amber said. "Margaret Dill, that's right. Dill, *Dill.*"

It was dumb Mose who finally tipped, not for nothing had he come along in the fair state of Georgia.

"Are you saying *Deal?*" he said.

"Dill is what I'm saying," she said. "Right."

"Like when somebody says it's a good deal?"

"A good dill, right."

"Like deal the cards?" Mose said.

"Dill the cards, right," she said. "Margaret Dill."

They can't even talk straight, Mose thought.

There were thirteen names listed under ORCHESTRAS & BANDS in the Calusa directory's yellow pages:

Ambrose Herb Orchestra

BALLARD JOE ORCHESTRA
ALL OCCASION MUSIC
* CLUB DATES *
* WEDDINGS * PARTIES *
Experienced and Professional

Calusa Symphony Society

Condon Richard & The Commissioner's
Jazz Band

ESTIES MARTY ORCHESTRA
Wedding Receptions – Country Club Dances –

House Parties – Cocktail Trio – Keyboard
Soloist – Strolling Musicians – Guitarist

FRANCO BOBBY – ENTERTAINMENT
Performed at the Governor's
Inaugural Ball
A Specialist on All Styles & Sounds
MUSIC "DESIGNED" FOR "YOUR" SOCIAL EVENTS
Weddings * Cocktail Parties * Club Dances
3-20 Men from Maine to Florida

KING RONNIE BIG BAND
Florida's Leading Big Swing Band

MELLOW MUSIC BY ROXANNE
"ONE GAL" BAND
PRIVATE PARTIES
MELLOW SOUNDS
While You Chit & Chat
Grand Openings * Recep
Office Retirement Parties
ROXANNE DAVIES

MUSIC MAKERS THE

PRODUCTION STYLES UNLIMITED, INC.
Entertainment Agency
SPECIALIZING IN CORPORATE FUNCTIONS
Kurt Meyers – Entertainment Consultant

SEARS JOHNNY MUSIC STUDIO

Tampa Symphony Society

BILL WADDELL & HIS RECORD MACHINE
Jazz – Rock – Contemporary

Warren Chambers took a deep breath.

Christmas Eve, he thought.

Try to find a musician on Christmas Eve.

They were alone together for the first time since Joanna came home last Friday.

It was three o'clock in the afternoon on the day before Christmas, and they were decorating the tree in the house Matthew used to share with Susan and his daughter, who was out delivering Christmas gifts to friends up the street. The radio was tuned to WUSF. They were listening to Christmas carols. Everything felt right. Just like old times. But everything felt wrong.

He had not yet mentioned his close encounter yesterday.

Nor had either of them mentioned the fact that fourteen-year-old Joanna seemed to be head over heels in love with a black boy named Thomas Darrow, Jr.

Matthew wasn't sure he wished to broach either subject.

He remembered a frantic telephone conversation he'd had with his daughter when she'd learned that Susan was planning to send her off to the Simms Academy:

"She says it'll be good for me. She says St. Mark's is getting run-down. She says . . . you won't like this, Daddy."

"Tell me."

"She says too many black kids are infiltrating the school. That was the word she used."

And not ten minutes later, in a somewhat more frantic telephone conversation:

"Daddy? What Mom said, actually—about the infiltration—what she said was 'niggers.' Two black kids've been admitted to the school."

"Terrific," Matthew had said. His former wife from Chicago, Illinois, was turning into a Florida redneck.

A Christmas ornament fell from his hand. It bounced on the carpet, miraculously intact. He picked it up and looked at his watch.

"Got a taxi waiting?" Susan asked.

"I was hoping to hear from Warren by now. I gave him the number here, just in case."

"Warren?" she said.

"Chambers," he said. "A private eye I've got working for me." He hesitated.

The moment seemed ripe.

"He's black," he said.

"Is he good?" Susan asked.

"Very," Matthew said.

He wondered if he should tell her he had enjoyed kissing Marcie Franklin yesterday. He wondered if he should tell her he'd debated calling Marcie Franklin today. He wondered if she'd really used the word "niggers" to describe those two black kids who'd been admitted to St. Mark's. He wondered if he was spoiling for a fight. He wondered if he wanted out.

"Susan," he said, and took a deep breath.

"I don't know how I feel about it," she said.

My wife, the mind reader, he thought. Excuse me, *former* wife.

"We're talking about Tommy, right?"

"Who else?" Susan said. "How do *you* feel about it?"

"She's fourteen," he said. "This, too, shall pass."

"Suppose it doesn't?"

"So?"

"I'm asking *you*, Matthew. Don't put *me* on the spot."

"A long time ago," he said, "before I met you, I dated a black girl named Ophelia Blair. I was in high school. She was in my English class. Ophelia Blair."

"Is this confession time?" Susan asked.

An edge to her voice. Maybe *she* was the one spoiling for a fight.

"A bright beautiful girl. I dated her only once. Kissed her a lot, tried to get in her pants, told her I loved her . . ."

"Matthew, I really . . ."

"Begged her to go all the way because I'd never done it with a black girl."

"If you're suggesting that Joanna . . ."

"Let me finish this, may I?"

"Not if you think Joanna and that boy . . ."

"This has nothing to *do* with Joanna!"

"Then why are you telling it? And please spare me any more quaint adolescent expressions, okay? Get in her pants, go all the way . . ."

"Damn it, I *was* an adolescent! I'd never done it with a *white* girl, either, I'd never done it with *anyone!* The point is . . ."

"Yes, Matthew, please get to the point."

"The point is I robbed her of her uniqueness, Susan. To me, she was only a black girl. To her, she was Ophelia Blair. She never dated me again."

"Is that the end of the story?"

"That's the end of it."

"Thank God. Would you mix me a martini, please?"

He went to the bar, took out a bottle of Beefeater gin and a bottle of vermouth, and mixed a pitcher of very dry, very cold martinis. He carried hers back to where she was sitting on the sofa, head tilted, examining the tree for spots bare of ornaments, places they had missed.

"Thanks," she said, and raised the glass. "Merry Christmas."

"Merry Christmas," he said. "Are we about to have a fight?"

"I thought we just had one," she said, and drank.

"What I think I'm saying, Susan . . ."

"I know what you're saying. You're saying Thomas Darrow, Jr., may be a very special individual in his own right . . ."

"*Is* a very special individual, according to Joanna."

"*Is*, fine. A very special individual who *also* happens to be black."

"Which upsets you."

"Yes. It upsets me."

"Why?"

"Matthew, don't ask stupid questions. Joanna's fourteen years old. She doesn't need the kind of trouble even *adults* can't handle."

"Some adults handle it just fine."

"I'm sure."

"Susan, I have to ask you something. When you decided to pull Joanna out of St. Mark's . . . did you use the word 'niggers' in reference to . . ."

"I've never used that word in my *life!*" Susan said.

"Not even when you were referring to the two black kids who . . . ?"

"Never! What the hell's wrong with you?"

"Joanna said you did."

"Joanna was lying."

"She told me . . ."

"She would have told you *anything* to keep from being sent away! How can you even *think* . . . ?"

"On the phone later, you said you were pulling her out because the school was being overrun by inferior students."

"It was. Look at it now. Would you be happy if Joanna was still . . . ?"

"Did you mean *black* students, Susan?"

"I did not."

"Back then, when I asked you that same question, you said, 'We're in Florida.' What did you mean, Susan?"

"Is this a court of law?" she said. "If so, I'd like an attorney, please."

"Did you mean that black students in Florida are somehow inferior to . . . ?"

"I don't remember the conversation, and I don't know *what* I meant. If it was one of our *usual* conversations, we were probably yelling at each other . . ."

"The way we are now," Matthew said.

"You started it," she said.

There was a deep and ominous silence.

"I'm going to ask her to stop seeing him," Susan said.

"I wish you wouldn't."

"I don't think she knows the kind of trouble . . ."

"She's happier than I've ever . . ."

"I'm *not*!" Susan shouted. "The very thought of . . ."

She stopped the sentence.

"Of what?" Matthew asked.

Susan shook her head.

"I'm sure they kiss," he said, "if that's . . ."

"Don't!" she said.

Another silence. Longer this time.

"I'm sorry," she said. "But you were talking about my daughter."

"My daughter, too," he said.

"Well, if you know this bothers me, you shouldn't . . ."

"I think you'd be making a big mistake if you . . ."

"Can you please *stop* this?" she said. "Can't you see . . . ? Can't you . . . ? How can you *possibly* suggest that Joanna and this boy . . . ?"

"They're kids, Susan! What the hell do you think kids do? They neck, they pet, they even . . ."

"Damn you, shut *up*!" she said, and hurled her drink into his face.

On the radio, a choral group began singing "Silent Night."

He took out his handkerchief and dabbed at his face. His shirt was wet down the front. He looked at his shirt as if wondering how it had got all wet. He kept staring at his shirt. He was about to tell her he had kissed someone yesterday. And enjoyed it.

The telephone rang.

On the radio, the singers were telling the world that all was calm, all was bright.

The telephone kept ringing.

Susan got up and walked into the kitchen. She snatched the receiver from the wall phone. "Hello," she said icily. She listened. "Just a moment, please," she said, and came back into the living room.

"For you," she said. "Warren Chambers. And then you can go, please."

Bad enough when she was only kissing him.

That was in the beginning.

Early on in the movie.

The *real* fairy tale, the one he'd read when he was a kid, was about a miller who when he died left his mill to his oldest son, and his donkey to the middle son, and his cat to the youngest son, whose name was Tom. Tom figured all he could do with the cat was make a pie of him and then sell his skin. But the cat started talking, told him all he needed was a pair of high boots, and a fine hat with a feather, and a small sack, and he'd make young Tom rich. So Tom got him all these things, and through a lot of lying and finagling the cat pretended first that Tom was a marquis or something—a baron, maybe a count, this was a long time ago when he'd read the story—and tricked the king into thinking Tom was rich and finally Tom married the king's daughter and lived happily ever after.

That was the fairy tale.

In the movie . . .

But thou hast played the harlot with many lovers . . .

In the movie, this nigger just out of jail meets a girl is a harlot, and he dresses her up in high red boots and fine clothes and she lies and connives with two other girls and a young white boy, and in the end the nigger is rich and the harlot is a movie star.

Meg.

A movie star.

Bad enough at the beginning of the movie.

Only kissing him then. Kissing the nigger. Mouth open wide to receive his mouth, promising him diamonds and gold, only buy me the boots, baby, lips meeting, and a fine hat with a feather on it, and silky underwear, opening her mouth to him, her blouse to him, showing him her breasts. Yet I had planted thee a noble vine, wholly a right seed; how then art thou turned into the degenerate vine of a strange plant before me?

Later on in the movie . . .

The things she did with the nigger and the three other women, the boy, the things she did.

Was the nigger bothered him most.

For though thou wash thee with nitre, and take thee much soap, yet thine iniquity is marked before me.

Sitting in the living room of the main house, he watched the flickering images on the screen, watched them over and over again, over and over.

And I brought you into a plentiful country, he thought, to eat the fruit thereof and the goodness thereof; but when ye entered ye defiled my land, and made mine heritage an abomination.

"I think you got it wrong," Tick said. "I think maybe she meant Dill, after all."

"No, she was saying Deal," Mose said. "I know how niggers talk, she was saying *Deal*."

226

"Then how come we called every fucking Deal in the phone book, eleven Deals altogether and none of them ever heard of a Margaret Deal? You got it wrong, Mose."

"I got it right," Mose insisted.

"I want to go back over the Dills again," Tick said. "Maybe we missed one."

"I'm telling you it's *Deal*!"

"Where's that phone book?" Tick said.

"You'll be wasting your time looking at all those Dills again."

"I wasted my time looking at all the *Deals*, too."

"Wasn't no Margaret *Dill*, either. All those numbers we called, nobody knew of any Margaret Dill."

"'Cause maybe we missed one. Where's that book?"

He opened the directory again to the page starting with Dieck-mann at the top and ending with Diners Club/Carte Blanche at the bottom.

"Check these off on your list," he said.

"I'm telling you we got them all."

"Check them off *anyway*," Tick said, and began reading. "Dill, Abner."

"Got it."

"Dill, Bernard."

"Right."

"Dill, Evan."

"Right."

"Dill, Roger."

"Yeah."

"Dill, Rosalie."

"Uh-huh."

"Dill, Samuel."

"Yes."

"Dill, Thomas."

Mose sighed.

"You got a Dill, Thomas?"

"I got a Dill, Thomas."

"Dill, Victor."

"Yes. That's all of them," Mose said.

"That's all of them, yeah," Tick said.

He was starting to turn back to the page the Deals were on, thinking maybe they might've missed one or more of the Deals, had his hand ready to turn back the page, when his eye fell on the first listing at the top of the page, *Dieckmann Frank*, and his eye and his hand hesitated, his eye drifted several names down the page to where first one name, and then six other names popped out of the page at him:

> Diehl Andrew
> Diehl Bertram
> Diehl Burgess
> Diehl Candace
> Diehl Carl
> Diehl Joseph
> Diehl Randolph

"Well, well, well," he said to Mose.

It was almost six o'clock.

Some four blocks away from Warren's office on the corner of Ross and Cameron, the First Congregational Church chimed the hour three minutes too early. Matthew looked at his watch. Warren looked at his watch.

"There are thirteen people listed under Orchestras and Bands," he said. "I managed to reach only eight of them."

"In person or on the phone?"

"Three in person, the rest on the phone. I had to do a bit of tightrope dancing, Matthew, 'cause I couldn't come right out and say, Hey, you didn't happen to clean out a storage bin rented by a lady was killed back in November, did you? What I said was I was looking to rent a van to transport some instruments in, and I heard you had such a van, and if you do I sure could use it on New Year's Eve for this gig in Sarasota. None of them had a van, none of them I spoke to anyway."

"So where do we go from here?" Matthew asked.

"Let it go till tomorrow, I guess, though I doubt we'll have any better luck on Christmas Day."

"Which ones did you cover?"

"Well, take a look," Warren said, and opened the telephone book to the yellow pages, and leafed past NURSES and OFFICE and OILS and OPTOMETRISTS, until he came to the page listing ORCHESTRAS & BANDS. "The ones with the check marks after them are the ones I got to."

"Did you look under Music?"

"No," Warren said. "Shit, why didn't I think of that?"

He was starting to turn the pages back, when Matthew said, "Wait a minute."

The last listing under ORCHESTRAS & BANDS was:

BILL WADDELL & HIS RECORD MACHINE
Jazz - Rock - Contemporary

Under that, there was a new heading:

► **ORCHID GROWERS**
Elite Orchids, Inc.
Franco's Orchid Farm
Graham Orchids
Green Orchid The
Michael's Orchids
Orchidaceous

"There it is," Matthew said.

• • •

Tick was driving.

Mose was complaining.

"We should've used the phone," he said.

"Sure. A lot of luck we had already with the phone," Tick said.

"Those last two guys didn't think too kindly of us stopping by on Christmas Eve."

"Fuck 'em," Tick said. "What's that address again?"

"Thirty-seven fifty-five."

"Take a look at the next mailbox, tell me what it says."

He slowed the car as they approached a mailbox on the right side of the road.

"Thirty-six forty-three," Mose said.

"Almost there," Tick said. "Let me do all the talking this time, okay?"

"You did all the talking last time," Mose said.

"No, you were the one who said we were looking for a girl worked on a movie with us."

"So? What was wrong with that?"

"They thought we were lying is what was wrong."

The sky behind them was turning red.

"Pretty sunset coming," Tick said.

"I wish we were back in Tampa," Mose said.

"Let's find Connie first," Tick said. "Or Margaret. Or whoever the hell she is."

The car kept moving along Timucuan Point Road, heading east.

This scene now . . .

The nigger unzipping his fly.

Meg on her knees.

Looking up at him, angelic smile on her face.

Oooo, she says.

No sound on the film. He had to read their lips. Knew it by heart now, anyway.

Take it, he says.

All that? she says.

For starters, he says, and grins.

He sat in the darkness of the living room, shotgun on the floor beside the easy chair, anybody else came around looking for her, sniffing after her, they'd find the wrath of God. Wanted to pick up the shotgun right this minute, blow the nigger off the screen, blow him to hell and gone, *Wherefore* will ye plead with me . . .

Looks up at him.

Tastes like milk chocolate, she says.

Takes him in her mouth again.

Lifts her head.

And honey, she says.

In her mouth again.

Mmmm, she says.

Lifts her head.

Do you come white? she asks.

Smiles.

Takes it again.

Mmmm.

Moves her mouth off it. Looks at it. Admires it. Rolls her eyes again. Licks it. Closes her eyes. Says, Mmmmmm. Takes it in her mouth again, the mouth of the just bringeth forth wisdom, but the froward tongue shall be cut out. Her hand moving on it. Her lips moving on it.

Don't let up, he says.

She murmurs something around it.

That's it, Puss.

She moans around it.

Don't stop, Puss.

Mmm, she says.

Now, he says.

He giveth snow like wool, he scattereth the hoarfrost like ashes.

Oh, baby, baby, he says, black hands in her red hair.

Mmm, she says.

Rolls her eyes again.

You like that, Puss?

Mmmmm.

"There it is," Tick said.

"There it is, for sure," Mose said.

They were crouched outside the window of the house, peering in under the bottom three inches of the drawn shade. They were looking at Jake Delaney milking himself on Connie's lips.

A man sat watching the movie.

Big blond guy in overalls.

Eyes fixed on the screen.

Like he was in a trance.

On the screen . . .

Think you can make me hard again?

Well, why don't we just try, honey?

They knew those words by heart.

Slow steamy smile.

Well, why don't we just try, honey?

They'd shot this scene the next day, but it looked like it followed immediately after the cum shot, made Jake look like a superman who could get another erection in the wink of an eye. Connie teasing him with her tongue and her lips, rolling him over her cheeks and her closed eyes, taking him between her breasts, stroking him against the cleft of her ass, closing both hands on him, tugging him gently, yanking him hard, letting up, rolling those green eyes, smiling that slow steamy smile again, hand stroking him gently again, head bending swiftly to him, tongue darting, and then straddling him, spreading herself wide to him, camera in for the close shot, rolling off him, going at him with her mouth again, playing, teasing, camera on her tongue, tight close shot, teasing, playing, driving Jake wild till he turned into a human battering ram again, sixty seconds flat, and only a day late.

"What do we do?" Mose asked.

"Why, we ask the man for our movie," Tick said.

He reached for the shotgun the moment the knock sounded at the door.

He snapped off the projector.

"Who's there?" he said.

"Mr. Diehl?"

A man's voice.

Ye all have transgressed against me.

"What do you want?" he asked.

"Mr. Diehl, we'd like to talk to you about that movie."

He raised the gun, turned it toward the door.

"Come in," he said. "It's open."

They made the right turn at the Orchidaceous sign, drove up the potholed road in Matthew's Ghia, Matthew at the wheel, Warren sitting beside him, his knees crowding him in the small car. The sky to the west was purple now, darker here over the land surrounding the lake, a bluish-black, night falling rapidly, silent night, holy night.

It was five hours before Christmas.

There was a house up ahead.

Dark.

Behind the house, two looming buildings with rounded tops.

"Must be the greenhouses there," Warren said.

Matthew nodded.

Angled toward the greenhouses, over to one side, a cinderblock structure.

They could hear noises out on the lake.

Thrashing.

Up ahead, in the car's headlights, a door opened in the cinderblock building.

A man appeared in the doorframe, his back to them.

He was dragging something.

"Hey now," Warren said.

Matthew stopped the car.

The man in the doorframe turned. Just his head. Arms still extended in front of him, bent over, holding something. Blond hair caught in the beams of the headlights. Warren was already getting out of the car. The man dropped whatever it was he was dragging. Matthew got out of the car on his side. The man reached inside the door. When he turned again, his whole body this time, a shotgun was in his hands.

"Down!" Warren shouted, and Matthew threw himself flat on the ground as a blast from the shotgun ripped yellow on the blue-black night. Warren was running toward the man. Warren had a pistol in his hand.

"Drop it!" Warren shouted, and the man fired again.

Warren took a quick step to the right, miraculously dodging the blast, twisted to face the man again, pistol in both hands now, a policeman's crouch. "Freeze!" he shouted, but the man came at him, holding the shotgun by the barrel, swinging the stock as if it were a club, the stock flailing the air, striking nothing but the night.

Warren fired.

His first shot took the man in the shoulder.

The man kept coming.

Warren fired lower this time, taking the man in the right leg, knocking him off his feet.

The man twisted and groaned in the dirt.

Warren came over to him.

"Okay?" he said, breathing hard. "Enough?"

The man tried to get to his feet.

"Mister, you're gonna be dead," Warren said.

And the man fell forward onto his face.

"Bingo," Warren said.

Matthew was walking toward the cinderblock building. Warren knelt beside the unconscious man, nodded, and then slipped the pistol back into his shoulder holster. Matthew was still walking toward the cinderblock building.

The Ghia's headlights illuminated the open doorway.

Matthew looked down at what was just inside the door.

"Oh, Jesus," he said, and turned away.

Warren ran to him.

"What . . . ?"

"Oh, Jesus," Matthew said again.

Warren looked down at the torn and mutilated body in the red leather boots, a garland of bloodred orchids around her neck. An instant of pain knifed his eyes, but that was all. It came, and it was gone, and he was once again a cop who had seen this before, had seen worse before.

Matthew had never seen anything like it in his life.

Matthew was bent over double, vomiting into the dirt road.

12

The Q and A took place in Burgess Diehl's room at Good Samaritan Hospital. Present with the stenographer and Diehl were State Attorney Skye Bannister, Assistant State Attorney Arthur Haggerty, Detective Morris Bloom of the Calusa P.D., Detective Ralph Sears of the Calusa Sheriff's Department, and Attorney Matthew Hope.

"Roll it," Haggerty said to the stenographer.

Date, time, place, people present, Haggerty read the routine information into the microphone. When he read Diehl the Miranda warnings, Diehl said, "I don't need no lawyer."

"And do you understand that even if you don't have a lawyer present, you still have the right to stop answering questions at any time?"

"I do."

"And you also have the right to stop answering at any time until you talk to a lawyer, if you decide later on you want to talk to one. Do you understand that?"

"Yes, I understand."

"Because this is America," Skye Bannister said.

"Very well then," Haggerty said. "Mr. Diehl, before I begin the questioning, is there anything you'd like to tell us about what happened? If you'd like to tell us in your own words . . ."

And he told them.

I knew about the movie, of course, knew she was working on a movie. I just didn't know what *kind* of movie.

A year and a half ago, must've been, she worked with this woman before. The woman was doing some kind of school movie about child abuse, and Meg was working at a day-care center at the time, she's very good with children, Meg. The good Lord never saw fit for us to have our own children, but she gave her heart to these other children day in and day out. That's where she met this woman for the first time. When they were doing scenes at the day-care center.

So she told me, Meg did, that this woman was doing another educational movie, and she wanted her to help out with the costumes on it, Meg's good with a needle and thread, too. Said it would only be from the end of September till early in November sometime, be a good opportunity to earn a few extra pennies.

So I said yes.

I mean, she'd never lied to me ever, she'd never withheld things from me ever.

But then I found the checks.

Four checks. Each for fifteen hundred dollars. The first one dated October third, the last one dated October twenty-fourth. She hadn't deposited them yet, I guess she was still trying to figure out where she could deposit them, how she could keep all this money from me. They were in the top drawer of her bureau, in back, under her panties. I forget what I was looking for in her drawer where she kept her panties.

Where are you getting this kind of money, I asked her, what are you doing to earn this kind of money? For Services, the checks read, what *kind* of services I asked her, where'd you get these, I asked her, what're these checks for? What does For Services mean?

And she said I shouldn't be going through her drawers, anyway, she said her drawers were private. So I said why is this Prudent Company paying you fifteen hundred dollars a week for services? She said I *knew* she was working for this woman who was making an educational movie, I've been doing costumes for her, I told you all about it. I'm doing wardrobe for her. That's why I'm gone five days a week, I've been doing wardrobe on this movie, you never listen when I tell you anything, you're so busy with your orchids all the time.

I said that seems like a lot of money for stitching and sewing.

She said well, movies pay a lot of money, movies are a big business.

I said I wanted to see them making this movie she was working on, and she said no, you can't do that, it's a closed set. I didn't know what that meant, a closed set. She told me the director of the movie, the woman who was paying her to make the costumes, was a very temperamental lady who didn't like anyone hanging around while she was working, that was what a closed set meant. She kissed me then and told me not to worry, they'd be finished shooting on the fifth of November, which was only a bit more than a week away, and then she'd be home every day, and we'd have all this extra spending money.

The night she kissed me, I didn't know where her mouth had been.

On Halloween night— this was four days later, four days after we'd talked about her doing costumes—she told me that they had to shoot this scene at night, it was a big costume party scene, she had to be there at night. I said sure, fine. But I followed her. She drove the VW out to Fatback Key, me behind in the van, keeping a safe distance behind her, I wanted to see what she was doing to earn fifteen hundred dollars a week.

I could have killed them all that very minute, the things I spied that night. For all nations have drunk of the wine of the wrath of her fornication, and the kings of the earth have committed fornication with her, and the merchants of the earth are waxed rich through the abundance of her delicacies. And I heard another voice from heaven saying, "Come out of her, my people, that ye not be partakers of her sins, and that ye receive not of her plagues. For her sins have reached unto heaven, and God hath remembered her iniquities." And I beheld another beast coming out of the earth, and he had two horns like a lamb, and he spake as a dragon. And I saw three unclean spirits like frogs come out of the mouth of the dragon, and out of the mouth of the beast, and out of the mouth of the false prophet. I could have killed them all. Standing outside there in the dark, looking in at them, spying what they were doing, I could have killed them all, God forgive me.

And yet . . .

Forgive them, for they know not what they do.

But . . .

The false prophet knew.

The woman, you see. The blonde woman telling them what to do. And they worshipped the dragon which gave power unto the beast. She knew.

I followed her home that night.

Didn't even know her name at the time.

Prudence Ann Markham.

Didn't even know her name.

That was the first time I followed her.

They finished the movie on the fifth day of November, same as Meg had told me they would. Nothing to worry about anymore, she said. She'd be home every day now, no more going out to stitch and sew her *costumes*, oh no, little Puss in Boots safe at home now.

I was still following Prudence Ann Markham.

Because I figured . . .

This is a *movie*.

This is something people will *see*, Meg naked and unashamed, doing vile things with the beast and the others, the three other women and the young boy. I didn't know yet what I was going to do about Meg, had no plans for her yet, but I knew I had to get that movie, had to keep people from seeing that movie, had to make sure nobody saw what I didn't want them to see, what it was wrong for them to see, what the good Lord had never intended anyone to see, had to get that movie, destroy that movie, burn that movie.

She was working on it at a studio out on Rancher Road. Drove to the storage bin each night, took cans of film out of it, carried them with her to the studio, drove back to the bin again when she was finished there each night. Had a key to the storage bin.

I figured I had to get that key.

Had to get that key to get the movie.

Destroy the movie.

Followed her each night from the storage place to her house on Pompano Way. Followed her. And they worshipped the dragon which gave power to the beast. Had to destroy the movie. Had to destroy the dragon responsible for the movie, responsible for what Meg had become.

Still didn't know what I was going to do about Meg.

That only came to me later.

I'm not dumb, I'm not a stupid person. I knew I had to destroy this woman so I could get the film she carried with her each night to the studio, get the key to the storage bin where maybe there was more film, destroy the movie. But how would it serve the Lord if I destroyed myself at the same time? No, no, I'm not stupid.

She was married, I knew that by then, I'd seen her husband at the house there on Pompano Way, knew she was married, what kind of a man allowed his wife to do such things? To spew such filth upon the earth? So the idea came to me, it occurred to me that I could kill two birds with one stone, three birds if you counted the movie, destroy the woman and her husband both and then destroy the movie.

I broke into the house on the tenth of November, watched the house till they were both gone, knew the house would be empty. Stole his clothes and the knife. Some other things, too, so they wouldn't know what I was after. Stole some of *her* clothes, too, I still have them, they're in Meg's bureau where she used to keep her things before I burned them. I still look at the woman's clothes sometimes, I look at them. Wonder what kind of a woman could do such things. Look at her clothes and wonder. Still wonder.

Gave myself a little time after I broke into the house. Figured I'd wait a week so nobody'd make any connection. Then decided ten days'd be better. Followed her to the studio. Waited outside for her. She come out, it must've been twenty to eleven, around then. It didn't take more'n a minute to do it to her. Got my clothes—*his* clothes—all covered with the filth of her blood while I was doing it. Took the cans of film and tape in this aluminum carrying case and her pocketbook and her keys. It wasn't no more'n ten minutes from Rancher Road to my house, another ten minutes to shower and change my clothes—I'd already locked Meg in the generator room by then, though I still didn't know what I was going to do with her. I wrapped the bloody clothes and the knife in a plastic garbage bag, left the house around eleven it must've been, took me fifteen minutes or so to get to Pompano Way, I must've got there around a quarter past eleven, thereabouts. I buried the bloody clothes and the knife in the backyard, behind the house, in the flower bed. Then I went to the storage bin and opened it with her key, and took what was inside there. Got there around midnight, I guess. Took everything was inside the bin.

I watched that movie a lot.

Still do.

Never saw anything in my life like what's in that movie.

People shouldn't be allowed to see movies like that.

I'll burn it one day.

For wickedness burneth as the fire.

"Mr. Diehl," Haggerty said, "I show you this Polaroid photo taken by the Sheriff's Department at 3755 Timucuan Point Road earlier tonight. Is this your wife, Margaret Diehl?"

"But the wicked shall be cut off from the earth," Diehl said, "and the transgressor shall be rooted out of it."

"Sir? Is this photograph I show you, this picture of a woman in red boots . . . is this your wife Margaret Diehl, sir?"

"For the husband is the head of the wife, even as Christ is the head of the church," Diehl said.

"Is this your wife, sir?"

"Therefore, as the church is subject unto Christ, so let the wives be to their own husbands in every thing."

"Mr. Diehl, can you tell us what happened to your wife? To this woman in the photograph. *Is* this your wife, sir?"

"What?"

"Your wife. Is this woman your wife?"

"*Was* my wife."

"*Was* your wife? Do you mean she's no longer your wife because she's dead, sir?"

"Dead? No, no."

"Sir . . . this woman in the photograph. Sir, her arms have been amputated . . ."

"Yes, I know."

"Do you know who amputated her arms, sir? And mutilated her breasts?"

"I did."

"Then, Mr. Diehl . . . did you kill your wife, Margaret?"

"No. Kill her? No, no. I was gonna put her out tonight. On the street. Near the manger."

"Put her body out on the street?"

"Put *her* out on the street. For all to see her shame. For it is a shame even to speak of those things which are done of them in secret."

"But your wife is dead, sir. The Medical Examiner . . ."

"No, sir."

"Mr. Diehl, the Medical Examiner estimates that she's been dead for quite some . . ."

"Then who've I been talking to? Speak not in the ears of a fool, for he will despise the wisdom of thy words."

"Did you cut off her arms, Mr. Diehl?"

"The fingers."

"Sir?"

"I started with the fingers. To punish her for what she'd done with her hands. For what evil is in mine hand? And when ye spread forth your hands, I will hide mine eyes from you . . ."

"Mr. Diehl . . ."

"Yea, when ye make many prayers, I will not hear. Your hands are full of blood."

"When you say you started with the fingers . . ."

"That's a lie."

"Sir?"

"I cut off her hair first. Everywhere. All over her body. Her head, down there . . . everywhere."

Silence.

Haggerty turned to Bannister.

"Skye? You want to take this?" he said.

"Mr. Diehl," Bannister said, "I'm Skye Bannister, the State Attorney. I wonder if I might be able to help you make yourself a bit more clear. As I understand this, you cut off your wife's fingers, and then her arms . . ."

"First her hair."

"Then her fingers . . ."

"No, then her tongue. I cut out her tongue. But the tongue can no man tame. It is an unruly evil, full of deadly poison. And the tongue is a fire, a world of iniquity. So is the tongue among our members, that it defileth the whole body and setteth on fire the course of nature, and it is set on fire of hell."

"You cut out her tongue . . ."

"Let the woman learn in silence with all subjugation."

"And then her fingers, and her hands . . . her arms . . ."

"His own hands shall bring the offerings of the Lord made by fire, the fat with the breast, it shall he bring, that the breast may be waved for a wave offering before the Lord. They'll see her tonight, when I put her out beside the manger. See her naked, the whore, except for the boots. I stitched her mouth shut, too, with nylon sail thread, so she'd never be able to use it again for the things she done. Stitched her shut down there, too, for a whore is a deep ditch and a strange woman is a narrow pit."

Skye Bannister sighed.

It was eleven-thirty on Christmas Eve, and outside in the hospital parking lot a Christmas tree blinked red and green to a starry night.

"Mr. Diehl," he said, "is there anything you'd like to add to what you've already told us?"

"You'll find something in the water," Diehl said.

"Sir?"

"How much more abominable and filthy is man, which drinketh iniquity like water?"

"Mr. Diehl, is there anything you'd like to change or correct in what you've . . . ?"

"Nothing," Diehl said. "I don't want to change nothing I done."

Bannister looked at his watch.

"Time completed, twenty-three hundred hours, thirty-one minutes," he said into the microphone, and then, to the stenographer, "It's a wrap."

They left Diehl's room.

In the corridor outside, Bannister said, "Meese's people were right."

"What?" Matthew said.

"The Attorney General's Commission on Pornography. They were right. Pornography leads to violence."

Matthew said nothing.

On Christmas morning, he wondered what he was supposed to do.

He had already informed Markham that the charge against him was being dropped. He was a free man. Free to get on with his goddamn life, as he'd once called it.

"What about the film?" Markham asked.

"What about it?" Matthew said.

"When do I get the film back?"

"I'm sure they'll need it for Diehl's trial," Matthew said. "To establish motive."

"What about after the trial? I was counting on that film for . . ."

"You'll have to ask Bannister about that."

"Bannister? What the hell does . . . ?"

"He may want to burn it," Matthew said.

And now, at a little before ten o'clock on Christmas morning, he wondered what he was supposed to do. He had not heard from Susan since she'd asked him to leave her house last night. He had planned to spend Christmas with her and Joanna. Open presents together. Just like old times. Maybe the man was right, he thought. Maybe you can't go home again. He lifted the phone and dialed her number.

Joanna answered the phone.

"Hi, Dad," she said. "Merry Christmas."

"Merry Christmas, honey," he said.

"Mom tells me you won't be coming over today."

"Oh?"

"What happened?"

"Well . . . I'm not sure," he said.

"You guys are very confusing," Joanna said.

"That's for sure," Matthew said, and then hesitated. "Joanna . . . if anyone tells you to stop seeing Thomas . . ."

"Who would tell me that?"

"Well, if anyone should . . ."

"I can't imagine anyone . . ."

"Honey . . . no one has the right to censor your mind or your heart."

"Huh?" she said.

"Just remember that."

"Well, sure," she said. "Shall I get Mom?"

"Please," he said, and hoped he'd made himself clear.

When Susan picked up the phone, it was indeed like old times. He used to wonder which Susan he'd be talking to on any given day, the Witch or the Waif. On Christmas, he was sort of expecting the Waif. Instead, he got . . .

"Matthew, I don't think you ought to come over today, do you? I've been doing a lot of thinking about last night, and it seems to me we've been rushing into something perhaps neither of us is quite ready for. The argument last night was too reminiscent of painful times in the past, and quite frankly I'm not eager to cover the same ground all over again. I know you're eager to see Joanna, this *is* after all Christmas, but perhaps you can spend tomorrow with her, exchange your gifts then, if that's all right with you. I think it might be worse for her if all three of us spent the day together, considering the uncertain climate between us just now. Don't you agree?"

"Sure," he said.

"So," she said.

"So," he said.

There was a long silence.

Then she said, "Matthew, don't you . . . ?"

And paused.

And said plaintively, "Matthew, don't you think I'm right? I mean, what's the use of . . . oh, shit, I just don't know."

"Neither do I," he said.

"Can we give it a little time?"

"Sure."

Another silence.

"And I won't say anything to Joanna," she said.

"About?"

"Her boyfriend."

"Oh."

"I'll give *that* a little time, too."

"Good," Matthew said.

"So," she said again.

"So," he said.

"Merry Christmas," she said.

"Merry Christmas," he said.

There was a click on the line.

He put the receiver back on the cradle.

He went out into the living room.

He mixed himself a martini. Ten o'clock in the morning.

The telephone rang.

Susan, he thought. A change of heart.

Or Joanna. In tears.

He walked to the kitchen counter, picked up the phone.

"Hello?" he said.

"Matthew?"

A woman's voice.

"Yes?"

"This is Marcie Franklin."

"Oh, hi," he said.

"Merry Christmas," she said.

"Merry Christmas."

"I wanted to apologize for the other day. I guess I *did* have one too many, I'm not normally that brazen."

Silence.

"I'm glad this is the right number," she said. "I got it from last year's phone book."

More silence.

"Well," she said, "I know you must be busy, this is Christmas Day, I just wanted to . . ."

"Are you free for lunch?" he said.

"I thought you'd never ask," she said.